Crane ==== French-
clan   Canadian
girl   *voyageur*

MashKiigiKwe
=(2)(Swampy Woman)
====(3)Fishbone
    (4)Quill
Mary Kashpaw
{m. AwunMauser}

Polish ===(2) Pauline (1)=== MiKwomengwane
aristocrat   Puyat{I}   (BirdShaKing
                               Ice Off
                               Its Feathers)

                    Shesheeb

Pauline   Napoleon   Bernadette
Puyat{II}   Morrissey   Morrissey
(Sister
Leopolda)

Eli   Nector =·=·=·= Marie   Sophie   {Other
Kashpaw   Kashpaw   Lazarre Morrissey   children}

The
LAST REPORT
on the
MIRACLES
at
LITTLE NO HORSE

The
LAST REPORT
on the
MIRACLES
at
LITTLE NO HORSE

Louise Erdrich

HarperCollins*Publishers*

HarperCollins books may be purchased for educational, business, or sales promotional use. For information, please write: Special Markets Department, HarperCollins Publishers Inc., 10 East 53rd Street, New York, NY 10022.

The author would like to thank the editors of *The New Yorker*, where "Naked Woman Playing Chopin" and "Le Mooz, or The Last Year of Nanapush" first appeared, in slightly different form.

FIRST EDITION

Family tree hand-lettered by Martie Holmer

Designed and composed by Elliott Beard

Printed on acid free paper

Library of Congress Cataloging-in-Publication Data
    Erdrich, Louise
    The last report on the miracles at Little No Horse : a novel / Louise Erdrich
      p. cm.
    ISBN 0-06-018727-1
    I. Title.
    PS3555.R42 L37 2001
    813'.54—dc21   00-047198

01 02 03 04 05 ❖/RRD 10 9 8 7 6 5 4 3 2 1

Nindinawemaganidok

There are four layers above the earth and four layers below. Sometimes in our dreams and creations we pass through the layers, which are also space and time. In saying the word nindinawemaganidok, or my relatives, we speak of everything that has existed in time, the known and the unknown, the unseen, the obvious, all that lived before or is living now in the worlds above and below.

—Nanapush

THE OLD PRIEST

1996

The grass was white with frost on the shadowed sides of the reservation hills and ditches, but the morning air was almost warm, sweetened by a southern wind. Father Damien's best hours were late at night and just after rising, when all he'd had to break his fast was a cup of hot water. He was old, very old, but alert until he had to eat. Dressed in his antique cassock, he sat in his favorite chair, contemplating the graveyard that spread just past the ragged yard behind his retirement house and up a low hill. His thoughts seemed to penetrate sheer air, the maze of tree branches waving above the stones, clouds, sky, even time itself, and they surged from his brain, tense, quickly, one on the next until he'd eaten his tiny meal of toast and coffee. Just after, Father Damien's mind relaxed. His habit was then to doze again, often straight into his afternoon nap.

A period of waking confusion plagued him, usually before the supper hour, sometimes and most embarrassingly while he said late afternoon Saturday Mass. When lucid again, Father Damien repaired for the evening to his desk, a place from which he refused to be disturbed. There, he wrote fierce political attacks, reproachful ecclesiastical letters, memoirs of reservation life for history journals, and poetry. He also composed lengthy documents, which he called reports, to send to the Pope—he had in fact addressed every pontiff since he had come to the reservation in 1912. During his writing, Father Damien drank a few drops of wine, and usually, by the time he was ready for bed, he was what he called "pacified." This night, however, the wine had the opposite effect—it sharpened instead of dulled his fervor, sped instead of slowed the point of his cracked plastic pen, focused his mind.

> *To His Holiness, the Pope*
> *The Vatican, Rome, Italy*
> *The Last Report on the Miracles at Little No Horse*
> *From the pen of*
> *Father Damien Modeste*

> *Your Holiness, I speak to you from a terrible distance. I have so much to tell you, and so little time. A desperate gravity has hold of me these days. I am sure that my death must at last be near. That is why I address you with such familiarity and in such haste. Please forgive my awkwardness. I don't have time to revise!*
>
> *My hand is distressingly shaky, but legible enough, I hope?*
>
> *I have no idea whether any of my previous letters have reached you—the body of my correspondence stretches back over the course of this century, but those most recent are, naturally, addressed to you. My letters contain documented evidence from a variety of sources, including actual confessions. I kept the identity of one murderer, in fact, a secret, an anguish I taste even now. Aternus Pater, you have in your possession enough material to fill at least several vaults of file cabinets. Dare I hope, since this will be the last of my reports, that at long last you will see fit to answer?*

Here Father Damien broke off and crankily adjusted his wooden office chair. His brain throbbed with light. He threw his pen down with a clatter and glared with unfocused intensity at the neat arrangements of envelopes, index cards, parish stationery, postage stamps, and research files that filled the niches of the keyhole desk. He often found instinctive comfort in organizing the small things around him, and now, dissatisfied with what he had written, he reached out to tidy the edges of papers, nudge and tap desk objects into place. He fussed for several moments before he understood the source of his darkness. Apparently, one couldn't hope for a reply, oh no, that would be all too human, wouldn't it! An actual response from the Pope after a lifetime of devoted correspondence. Or could he call it that, implying as the word did some reciprocity, at least the semblance of an exchange? In all of this time, Father Damien had not received so much as a form reply. Even an autographed photo postcard would have been something. But no, not even that. His was a one-sided conversation, then, a monologue, a faithful and dogged adherence to truth and, of course, concern for what he'd seen developing across the acorn-studded grass, behind the wall of scrub oaks, over there, within the whitewashed convent. . . .

A great swallow of red wine—this fierce clarity, perhaps it was the vintage? A potent year, no doubt. Father Damien took the bottle in his hand and examined the label. An obscure beaujolais, pungent and grapey, left by some extremely thoughtful parishioner on his very doorstep. It was the wine, yes, French wine blue-red on his tongue and clear, causing him to assign blame where blame was useless. His mood softened. After all, Father Damien leaned back, lips to his glass, and took a smaller sip, the Pope was a busy man! Did he have time for these wretched backwaters, and a persistent and pathetic cleric who couldn't even write in a straight line anymore without employing a child's ruler? *No time, no time for either the nonsense or the vast spiritual transactions that I have witnessed. No time.*

Not receiving the honor of a reply from your great office, I have nevertheless continued, over the years and from the earliest days of my assignment to this remote reservation, to document the series of unusual events that has given rise to

*speculation regarding the Blessedness of one Sister Leopolda
Puyat, recently (though perhaps not entirely) deceased.
Although not formally released from my vow of secrecy
regarding what is revealed to me under the seal of Confession,
I have taken it upon myself after years of nights of soul-
wrenching argument to furnish certain segments of these
proofs from long soliloquies delivered to me in the privacy of
the confessional box.*

*I hope, in these instances, that my revelation of confessed
sins has been warranted by the serious nature of my quest. I
did not lightly undertake to break the trust bestowed upon
me, as I have said. Without placing blame specifically on any
of your predecessors, I must say that it would have helped
enormously if one or another pope had seen fit to guide me in
respect to this question long ago! But no doubt, Fountain of
Faith, there were reasons past my vision, substance beyond
my power to digest. Perhaps the silence from beyond these
poor boundaries has been a test, a shrewd marker of my
endurance, my belief.*

If so, let this last report confirm my lack of doubt.

Again, the burning hands, arthritis, and a writer's cramp. Father
Damien put down the pen with care this time and wrung his left hand
with his right as though squeezing water from a cloth. He had not
written for so long or with such single-mindedness—it had been
many weeks, months perhaps. Even two glasses into the bottle of
wine, his thoughts continued to flow with such rapidity that he
decided not to quit. After all, how many such nights did he have left
on earth? His hand, long and crooked, beautifully worn and supple,
oval nails of opaque tortoise, surprised him on the stem of the glass.
For a long time he had been old, then he was past old. A living
mummy. Of all people to have become so ancient! Himself! He put
his hand to his hair, just wisps of thin and brittle stuff parted by the
white scrawl of the scar that unwrote so many of his early memories.
And the heart in his chest, so touchy, so tremulous. Easy things had
become difficult. For instance, children. He had always loved to be
around them, but now their exuberance was rattling. Their voices and

quick movements dizzied him. He had to sit, allow his heart to settle, and restore his strength. And his hearing had become quite tricky—sometimes he heard everything, the undertones in Chopin's preludes, which he still played, though with a fumbling energy, the rustle of his own bedsheets, and at other times all sounds were cloaked by the roar of an unseen ocean.

Even so, he still excelled at listening to confessions. With his hearing aid at full power, he bent to the screen of secrets. More than any other blessed sacrament, Father Damien enjoyed hearing sins, chewing over people's stories, and then with a flourish absolving and erasing their wrongs, sending sinners out of the church clean and new. He forgave with an exacting kindness, but completely, and prided himself in dispensing unusual penances that fit the sin. People appreciated his interest in their weaknesses as well as his sense of compassionate justice. Also, he knew when they lied to him. He read their hearts. He was a popular confessor. There were those, he knew, who waited to unlock their secrets until they witnessed him personally entering the box, and others who even backed out of the church when one or the other of his younger colleagues, Father Dennis or Gothilde, slipped through the narrow door. Hearing sins was work that required all of the tactful knowledge he had developed during the years spent among these people. *His people.* He was proud to say he had been adopted into a certain family, the Nanapush family, whose long dead elder had been his first friend on the reservation. Whose daughter, Lulu, was as his own daughter now. But did she, did any of his trusting friends, family, parishioners, suspect? Could they imagine? Of course, one could say that in his letters Father Damien had burst the seal Christ had set on words spoken in that box—but only to a higher confessor. The gravity of his confidences was such that he could not risk revealing all to even so local an officer of the Church as a bishop. To address the Pope was, he had to think, next door to confiding in God. Still, it made Father Damien uncomfortable that he should have taken on such a lonely responsibility.

If you would *deign* to answer, he thought now, but stifled that twinge of irritation with another sip of the remarkable wine.

The night was mild, and Father Damien rose to let in that spectral air. He hoisted a small-paned window and the sigh of night-singing grasshoppers and crickets entered his small study. A pure sound, welcome, promising a light refreshing rain. Clearing everything away, washing the world innocent. If only he, too, could be washed to perfect goodness, forgiven! Father Damien drank deeply of the old, secret pain, and once more took up the pen.

> And if you would kindly take the trouble to look back into your files, you'll find that I've been faithful in every respect, conscientious to the letter of my vow, except in regard to the problem of the confessional.
>
> As long as the subject of Penance has been raised, however, I must also begin this final report by admitting that I address you abjectly, as a sinner and also as an impostor, hoping for an absolution. But lest your judgment of what I have to say be prejudiced by what I have decided to tell before death robs me of the chance to make a dignified revelation, I will save my explanations for later. For now, let me begin by humbly calling to your attention the various reports that I have mailed carefully to Rome. Because of the utmost secrecy of my undertaking, I have, of course, kept no copy of these epistles, relying instead upon the vast array of conscientious scribes with whom I picture Your Holiness surrounded, and whom I am quite sure will have studied and remarked upon the lengthy documents that I have sent to Popes Pius X, Benedict XV, Pius XI, Pius XII, John XXIII, Paul VI, and yourself, my gracious and eternal father.

The wine changed suddenly to water. In a reverse miracle, Father Damien's heart faltered, and he could almost feel the vagueness flooding upward into his mind like a ground fog. He capped his pen. Slowly and with regret, he turned off his desk lamp. In the sheer moonlight, he allowed his eyes to adjust and then he tapped his fingers on the letter to the Pope and pushed it underneath a set of files. He smoothed his cassock carefully as he rose and walked across the room to the only other piece of furniture within it—the dark and gleaming rectangular box of strings and keys that he loved with a human love. He stroked the glossy finish of the piano gently, as though touching the hair of a sleeping child, then turned away, walked across the narrow hall.

He used the bathroom, brushed his teeth, and washed vigorously, then tottered in exhaustion to his bedroom, a neat cubicle with just space enough for a single bedstead of new-painted white iron, a small rectangular wooden bedside table, a rough bureau of varnished pine, and a hanging closet, cedar scented but shallow. Father Damien tugged the chain on the lamp and then made sure the door was firmly shut. He first removed his starched white collar, laid it with care on the top of the bureau. Next he unbuttoned his cassock, stepped out of it, and arranged it on a slender hanger that he set upon a brass hook. The black gown was outmoded, but he refused to jettison the garb in which he had originally understood his calling. With a clothes brush, he sleepily swiped at a few bits of lint, then struck away a bit of dust from the black cloth and turned back to sit on the edge of the bed. Bending with an incremental tediousness, he removed one moosehide moccasin, waited for a moment or two, and then took off the other. He set them lightly on the floor on either side of his feet.

By the time he finished that task, he was breathing hard. He continued to sit, clad only in a thin cotton undershift, rubbing one foot with the other. His feet were clean, delicately arched, tough soled, white, and young looking. His thoughts were mightily drifting, but then, suddenly, there was yet one more burst of reason. A second wind! A delayed reaction. That last gulp of wine had powered him. With hungry movements, Father Damien reached into the bedside table drawer and drew out his emergency pencil and pad of notepaper.

If memory serves me right, and I am over one hundred years old, the first of my reports dealt with an occurrence that forever set me on my course, and caused me to assume the mantle under which I have since served with joyous devotion. With no offense to your prodigious memory, let me begin at last by telling the truth.

Father Damien continued to write on the notepad, ripping each page off and piling it beside him as soon as he finished. Bare feet dangling, he scrawled what he could remember. "3 A.M.," his report began, "In the Thrall of the Grape." He wrote with increasing swift-ness and passion, against his waning energy, for an hour and a half. When he had finished, he sank forward, set his feet down, and slowly balanced. Standing, he pulled the thin undergarment over his head and shook it out once before hanging it on an iron hook nailed to the back of the door. He was so tired that the room tipped. But he man-aged to stick to his routine. He lifted a neatly folded nightshirt from the top dresser drawer and laid it on the bed. Then, with slow care, he turned off the bedside lamp and in moonlighted dark unwound from his chest a wide Ace bandage. His woman's breasts were small, with-ered, modest as folded flowers. He slipped the nightshirt over his head and took a deep breath of relief before crawling between the covers. At once, he fell deeply into slumber. During the night, assailed by dreams, he turned over once, unconscious, and knocked across the floorboards the sheaf of papers he had written.

PART ONE

The
TRANSFIGURATION
of
AGNES

1

Naked Woman
Playing Chopin

1910–1912

Eighty-some years previous, through a town that was to flourish and past a farm that would disappear, the river slid—all that happened began with that flow of water. The town on its banks was very new and its main street was a long curved road that followed the will of a muddy river full of brush, silt, and oxbows that threw the whole town off the strict clean grid laid out by railroad plat. The river flooded each spring and dragged local backyards into its roil, even though the banks were strengthened with riprap and piled high with rocks torn from reconstructed walls and foundations. It was a hopelessly complicated river, one that froze deceptively, broke rough, drowned one or two every year in its icy run. It was a dead river in some places, one that harbored only carp and bullheads. Wild in others, it lured moose down from Canada into the town limits. When the land along its banks was newly broken, paddleboats and barges of grain moved grandly from its source to Winnipeg, for the river flowed inscrutably north. Across from what would become church land and the town park, over on the Minnesota side, a farm spread generously up and down the river and back into wide hot fields.

The bonanza farm belonged to easterners who had sold a foundry in Vermont and with their money bought the flat vastness that lay along the river. They raised astounding crops when the land was young—rutabagas that weighed sixty pounds, wheat unbearably lush, corn on cobs like truncheons. Then six grasshopper years occurred during which even the handles on the hoes and rakes were eaten and a U.S. cavalry soldier, too, partially devoured while he lay drunk in the insects' path. The enterprise suffered losses on a grand scale. The farm was split among four brothers, eventually, who then sold off half each so that by the time Berndt Vogel escaped the latest war of Europe, during which he'd been chopped mightily but inconclusively in six places by a lieutenant's saber and then kicked by a horse so ever after his jaw didn't shut right, there was just one beautiful and peaceful swatch of land about to go for grabs. In the time it would take for him to gather the money—by forswearing women, drinking cheap beers only, and working twenty-hour days—to retrieve it from the local bank, the price of that farm would drop further, further, and the earth rise up in a great ship of destruction. Sails of dust carried half of Berndt's lush dirt over the horizon, but enough remained for him to plant and reap six fields.

So Berndt survived. On his land there stood a hangarlike barn that once had housed teams of great blue Percherons and Belgian draft horses. Only one horse was left, old and made of brutal velvet, but the others still moved in the powerful synchronicity of his dreams. Berndt liked to work in the heat of this horse's breath. The vast building echoed and only one small part was still in use—housing a cow, chickens, one depressed pig. Berndt kept the rest in decent repair not only because as a good German he must waste nothing that had come his way but because he saw in those grand dust-filled shafts of light something he could worship.

The spirit of the farm was there in the lost breath of horses. He fussed over the one remaining mammoth and imagined one day his farm entire, vast and teeming, crews of men under his command, a cookhouse, bunkhouse, equipment, a woman and children sturdily determined to their toil. A garden in which seeds bearing the scented pinks and sharp red geraniums of his childhood were planted and thrived.

How surprised he was to find, one morning, as though sown by the wind and summoned by his dreams, a woman standing barefoot, starved, and frowzy in the doorway of his barn. She was pale but sturdy, angular, a strong flower, very young, nearly bald and dressed in a rough shift. He blinked stupidly at the vision. Light poured around her like smoke and swirled at her gesture of need. She spoke with a low, gravelly abruptness: *"Ich habe Hunger."*

By the way she said it, he knew she was a Swabian and therefore— he tried to thrust the thought from his mind—possessing certain unruly habits in bed. She continued to speak, her voice husky and bossy. He passed his hand across his eyes. Through the gown of nearly transparent muslin he could see that her breasts were, excitingly, bound tight to her chest with strips of cloth. He blinked hard. Looking directly into her eyes, he experienced the vertigo of confronting a female who did not blush or look away but held him with an honest human calm. He thought at first she must be a loose woman, fleeing a brothel—had Fargo got so big? Or escaping an evil marriage, perhaps. He didn't know she was from God.

SISTER CECILIA

In the center of the town on the other side of the river there stood a convent made of yellow bricks. Hauled halfway across Minnesota from Little Falls brickworks by pious drivers, they still held the peculiar sulfurous moth gold of the clay outside that town. The word Fleisch was etched in shallow letters on each one. Fleisch Company Brickworks. Donated to the nuns at cost. The word, of course, was covered by mortar each time a brick was laid. Because she had organized a few discarded bricks behind the convent into the base for a small birdbath, the youngest nun knew, as she gazed at the mute order of the convent's wall, that she lived within the secret repetition of that one word.

Just six months ago, she was Agnes DeWitt. Now she was Sister Cecilia—shorn, houseled, clothed in black wool and bound in starched linen of heatless white. She not only taught but lived music, existed for those hours when she could be concentrated in her being—which was half music, half divine light, only flesh to the degree she could not admit otherwise. At the piano keyboard, absorbed into the notes that rose beneath her hands, she existed in her essence, a manifestation of compelling sound. Her hands were long and blue veined, very white, startling against her habit. To keep them supple, she rubbed them nightly with lard, sheep's fat, butter, whatever she could steal from the kitchen. During the day, when she graded papers or used the blackboard, her hands twitched and drummed, patterned and repatterned difficult fingerings. She was no trouble to live with and her obedience was absolute. Only, and with increasing concentration, she played Brahms, Beethoven, Debussy, Schubert, and Chopin.

It wasn't that she neglected her other duties, rather it was the playing itself—distilled of longing—that disturbed her sisters. In her music Sister Cecilia explored profound emotions. Her phrasing described her faith and doubt, her passion as the bride of Christ, her loneliness, shame, ultimate redemption. The Brahms she played was thoughtful, the Schubert confounding. The Debussy she sneaked in between the covers of a Bach Mass was all contrived nature and yet gorgeous as a meadowlark. Beethoven contained all messages, but her crescendos lacked conviction. However, when it came to the Chopin, she did not use the flowery ornamentation or the endless trills and insipid floribunda of so many of her day. Her playing was of the utmost sincerity. And Chopin, played simply, devastates the heart. Sometimes a pause between the piercing sorrows of minor notes made a sister scrubbing the floor weep into the bucket where she dipped her rag so that the convent's boards, washed in tears, seemed to creak now in a human tongue. The air of the house thickened with sighs.

Sister Cecilia, however, was emptied. Thinned. It was as though her soul were neatly removed by a drinking straw and siphoned into the green pool of quiet that lay beneath the rippling cascade of notes. One day, exquisite agony built and released, built higher, released more forcefully until slow heat spread between her fingers, up her arms, stung at the points of her bound breasts and then shot straight down.

Her hands flew off the keyboard—she crouched as though she had been shot, saw yellow spots and then experienced a peaceful wave of oneness in which she entered pure communion. She was locked into the music, held there safely, entirely understood. Such was her innocence that she didn't know she was experiencing a sexual climax, but believed rather that what she felt was the natural outcome of this particular nocturne played to the utmost of her skills—and so it came to be. Chopin's spirit became her lover. His flats caressed her. His whole notes sank through her body like clear pebbles. His atmospheric trills were the flicker of a tongue. His pauses before the downward sweep of notes nearly drove her insane.

The Mother Superior knew something had to be done when she herself woke, face bathed with sweat and tears, to the insinuating soft largo of the Prelude in E Minor. In those notes she remembered the death of her mother and sank into the endless afternoon of her loss. The Mother Superior then grew, in her heart, a weed of rage all day against the God who took a mother from a seven-year-old child whose world she was, entirely, without question—heart, arms, guidance, soul—until by evening she felt fury steaming from the hot marrow of her bones and stopped herself.

Oh God, forgive me, the Superior prayed. She considered humunculation, but then rushed down to the piano room, and with all of the strength in her wide old arms gathered and hid from Cecilia every piece of music but the Bach.

After that, for some weeks, there was relief. Sister Cecilia turned to the Two Part Inventions. Her fingers moved on the keys with an insect precision. She played each as though she were constructing an airtight box. Stealthily, once Cecilia went on to Bach's other works, the Mother Superior removed from the music cabinet and destroyed the Goldberg Variations—clearly capable of lifting into the mind subterranean complexities. Life in the convent returned to normal. The cook, to everyone's gratitude, stopped preparing the heavy rancid goose-fat-laced beet soup of her youth and stuck to overcooked string beans, boiled cabbage, potatoes. The floors stopped groaning and absorbed fresh wax. The doors ceased to fly open for no reason and closed discreetly. The water stopped rushing continually through the pipes as the sisters no longer took advantage of the new plumbing to drown out the sounds of their emotions.

And then, one day, Sister Cecilia woke with a tightness in her chest. Pains shot across her heart and the red lump in her chest beat like a wild thing caught in a snare of bones. Her throat shut. Her hands, drawn to the keyboard, floated into a long appoggiatura. Then, crash, she was inside a thrusting mazurka. The music came back to her. There was the scent of faint gardenias—his hothouse boutonniere. The silk of his heavy, brown hair. A man's sharp, sensuous drawing-room sweat. His voice, she heard it, avid and light. It was as though the composer himself had entered the room. Who knows? Surely there was no more desperate, earthly, exacting heart than Cecilia's. Surely something, however paltry, lies beyond the grave.

At any rate, she played Chopin. Played in utter naturalness until the Mother Superior was forced to shut the cover to the keyboard gently and pull the stool away. Cecilia lifted the lid and played upon her knees. The poor scandalized dame dragged her from the keys. Cecilia crawled back. The Mother, at her wit's end, sank down and urged the girl to pray. She herself spoke first in apprehension and then in certainty, saying that it was the very devil who had managed to find a way to Cecilia's soul through the flashing doors of sixteenth notes. Her fears were confirmed when not moments later the gentle sister raised her arms and fists, struck the keys as though the instrument were stone and from the rock her thirst would be quenched. But only discord emerged.

"My child, my dear child," comforted the Mother, "come away and rest yourself."

The young nun, breathing deeply, refused. Her severe gray eyes were rimmed in a smoky red. Her lips bled purple. She was in torment. "There is no rest," she declared, and she then unpinned her veil and studiously dismantled her habit. She folded each piece with reverence and set it upon the piano bench. With each movement the Superior remonstrated with Cecilia in the most tender and compassionate tones. However, just as in the depth of her playing the virgin had become the woman, so the woman in the habit became a woman to the bone. She stripped down to her shift, but no further.

"He wouldn't want me to go out unprotected," she told her Mother Superior.

"God?" the older woman asked, bewildered.

"Chopin," Cecilia answered.

Kissing her dear Mother's trembling fingers, Cecilia knelt. She made a true genuflection, murmured an act of contrition, and then walked from the convent made of bricks with the secret word pressed between yellow mortar, and the music, her music, which the Mother Superior would keep from then on under lock and key as capable of mayhem.

MISS AGNES DEWITT

So it was Sister Cecilia, or Agnes DeWitt of rural Wisconsin, who appeared before Berndt Vogel in the cavern of the barn and said in her mother's dialect, for she knew a German when she met one, that she was hungry. She wanted to ask whether he had a piano, but it was clear to her he wouldn't and at any rate she was exhausted.

"*Jetzt muss ich schlafen,*" she said after eating half a plate of scalded oatmeal with new milk.

So he took her to his bed, the only bed there was, in the corner of the otherwise empty room. He went out to the barn he loved, covered himself with hay, and lay awake all night listening to the rustling of mice and sensing the soundless predatory glide of the barn owls and the stiff erratic flutter of bats. By morning, he had determined to marry her if she would have him, just so he could unpin and then from her breasts unwind the long strip of cloth that bound her torso. She refused his offer, but she did speak to him of who she was and where from. In that first summary she gave of her life she concluded that she must never marry again, for not only had she wed herself soul to soul to Christ, but she had already been unfaithful—her phantom lover the Polish composer—thus already living out too grievous a destiny to become a bride. In explaining this to Berndt, she merely moved her first pawn in a long game of words and gestures that the two would play over the course of many months. She didn't know, either, that she had opened to an opponent dogged and ruthless.

Berndt Vogel's passion engaged him, mind and heart. He now prepared himself. Having dragged army caissons through hip-deep mud
after the horses died in torment, having seen his best friend suddenly
uncreated into a mass of shrieking pulp, having lived intimately with
pouring tumults of eager lice and rats plump with a horrifying food,
he was rudimentarily prepared for the suffering he would experience
in love. She had also learned her share of discipline and in addition—
for the heart of her gender is stretched, pounded, molded, and tempered for its hot task from the age of two—she was a woman.

The two struck up a temporary bargain and set up housekeeping.
She still slept in the indoor bed. He stayed in the barn. A month
passed. Two. Each morning she lighted the stove and cooked, then
heated water in a big tank for laundry and swept the cool wooden
floors. Monday she sewed. She baked all day Tuesday. On Wednesdays
she churned and scrubbed. She sold the butter and the eggs Thurs-
days. Killed a chicken every Friday. Saturdays she walked across the
bridge into town and practiced the piano in the grade school base-
ment. Sunday she played the organ for Mass and at the close of the
day started the next week's work. Berndt overpaid her. At first she
spent her salary on clothing. After she had acquired shoes, stockings,
a full set of cotton underclothing and then woolen, too, and material
for two housedresses—one patterned with twisted leaves and tiny
blue berries and the other of an ivy lattice material—and a sweater
and at last a winter coat, after she had earned a blanket, a pillow, a
pair of boots, she decided on a piano.

This is where Berndt thought he could maneuver her into marriage, but she proved too cunning for him. It was early in the evening
and the yard was pleasant with the sound of grasshoppers. They sat on
the porch drinking a glass of sugared lemon water. Every so often, in
the ancient six-foot grasses that survived at the margin of the yard, a
firefly signaled or a dove cried out its five hollow notes.

"Why do so many birds' songs consist of five?" she asked idly.

"Five what?" said Berndt.

They drank slowly, she in the sprigged berry dress that skimmed
her waist. He noted with disappointment that she wore a normal
woman's underclothing now, had stopped binding her breasts. Perhaps, he thought, he could persuade her to resume her old ways, at

least occasionally, just for him. It was a wan hope. She looked so comfortable, so free. She'd taken on a hardiness. Though still thin she had lost her anemic pallor. She had a square boy's chin and a sturdy, graceful neck. Her arms were brown, muscular. In the sun, her fine hair, growing out in curls, glinted with green-gold sparks of light and her eyes were deceptively clear.

"I can teach music," she told him. "Piano." She had decided that her suggestion must sound merely practical, a moneymaking ploy. She did not say how well she could actually play nor did she express any pleasure or zeal, though at the very thought each separate tiny muscle in her hands ached.

"It would be a way of bringing in some money."

He was left to absorb this. He might have believed her casual proposition, except that Miss DeWitt's restless fingers gave her away and he noted their insistent motions. She was playing the Adagio of the Pathetique on the arms of her chair, the childhood piece that nervously possessed her from time to time.

"You would need a piano," he told her. She nodded and held his gaze in that aloof and unbearably sexual way that had first skewered him.

"It's the sort of thing a husband gives his wife," he dared.

Her fingers stopped moving. She cast down her eyes in contempt.

"I can walk to town and use the school instrument. I've spoken to the school principal already."

Berndt looked at the three-quarters-moon bone of her ankle, at her foot in the brown, thick-heeled shoe she'd bought. He ached to hold her foot in his lap, untie her oxford shoe with his teeth, move his hands up her leg covering her calf with kisses, breathe against the delicate folds of leafy cloth.

He offered marriage once again. His heart. His troth. His farm. She spurned the lot. The piano. She would simply walk into town. He let her know that he would like to buy the piano, it wasn't that, but there was not a store for many miles where it could be purchased. She knew better and with exasperated heat described the way that she would, if assisted with his money, go about locating and then acquiring the best piano for the best price. She vowed that she would not purchase the instrument in Fargo, but in Minneapolis. From there, she could get it hauled cheaper than the freight markup. She would take the train to Minneapolis and make her arrangements in one day and return by night in order not to spend one extra dime on either food she couldn't carry or on a hotel room. When he resisted to the last, she told him that she was leaving. She would find a small room in town and there she would acquire students, give lessons.

She betrayed her desperation. Some clench of her fingers gave her away. It was as much Berndt's unconfused love of her and wish that she might be happy as any worry she might leave him that finally caused him to agree. In the months he'd known Agnes DeWitt, she had become someone to reckon with. Even he, who understood desperation and self-denial, was finding her proximity most difficult. He worked himself into exhaustion, and his farm prospered. Sleeping in the barn was difficult, but he had set into one wall a bunk room for himself and his hired man. He installed a stove that burned low on unseasonably chilly nights. Only, sometimes, as he looked sleepily into the glowering flanks of iron, he could not help his own fingers moving along the rough mattress in faint imitation of the way he would, if he could ever, touch her hips. He, too, was practicing.

THE CARAMACCHIONE

The last grand piano made by Caramacchione had been shipped to Minneapolis, and remained unsold until Agnes entered the store with her bean-sock of money. She made friends with a hauler out of Morris and he gave her a slow-wagon price. The two accompanied the instrument back to the farm during the dog days. Humid, hot weather was beloved by this particular piano. It tuned itself on muggy days. As the piano moved across the table fields of drought-sucked wheat like a shield, an upended black thing, an ebony locust, Miss Agnes DeWitt mounted the back of the wagon and played to the clouds.

They had to remove one side of the house to get the piano into the front room, and it took four strong men the next day to do the job. By the time the instrument was settled into place by the window, Berndt was persuaded of its necessary presence, and proud. He sent the men away, although the side of the house was still open to the swirling light of stars. Dark breezes moved the curtains; he asked her to play for him. She did. The music gripped her and she did not, could not, stop.

Late that night she turned from the last chord of the simple Nocturne in C Minor into the silence of Berndt's listening presence. Three slow claps from his large hands died into the waiting quiet. His eyes rested upon her and she returned his gaze with a long and mysterious stare of gentle regard. The side of the house admitted a great swatch of moonlight. Spiders built their webs of phosphorescence across black space. Berndt ticked through what he knew—she would not marry him because she had been married and unfaithful, in her mind at least. He was desperate not to throw her off, repel her, damage the mood set by the boom of nighthawks flying in, swooping out, by the rustle of black oak and willow, by the scent of the blasted petals of summer's last wild roses. His courage was at its lowest ebb. Fraught with sheer need and emotion he stood before Agnes, finally, and he asked in a low voice, "*Schlaf mit mir. Bitte. Schlaf mit mir.*"

Agnes looked into his face, openly at last, showing him the great weight of feeling she carried, though not for him. As she had for her Mother Superior, she removed her clothing carefully and folded it, only she did not stop undressing at her shift but continued until she slipped off her large tissue-thin bloomers and seated herself naked at the piano. Her body was a pale blush of silver, and her hands, when they began to move, rose and fell with the simplicity of water.

It became clear to Berndt Vogel, as the music slowly wrapped around him, that he was engaged in something for which he would have had to pay a whore in Fargo, if there really were any whores in Fargo, a great sum to perform. A snake of dark motion flexed down her spine. Her pale buttocks seemed to float off the invisible bench. Her legs moved like a swimmer's, and he thought he heard her moan. He watched her fingers spin like white shadows across the keys, and found that his body was responding as though he lay fully twined with her underneath a quilt of music and stars. His breath came short, shorter, rasping and ragged. Beyond control, he gasped painfully and gave himself into some furtive cleft of halftones and anger that opened beneath the ice of high keys.

Shocked, weak and wet, Berndt rose and slipped through the open side wall. He trod aimless crop lines until he could allow himself to collapse in the low fervor of night wheat. Sinking back, he bit off a tickle of kernels, chewed the sweet must. It was true, wasn't it, that the heart was a lying cheat? And as the songs Chopin invented were as much him as his body, so it followed Berndt had just watched the woman he loved make love to a dead man. Furthermore, in watching, he'd sunk into a strange excitement beyond his will and let his seed onto the floor Agnes had just that afternoon scrubbed and waxed. Now, as he listened at some distance to the music, he thought of returning. Imagined the meal of her white shoulders. Shut his eyes and entered the confounding depth between her legs.

BLESSING

Then followed their best times. Together, they constructed a good life in which the erotic merged into the daily so that every task and small kindness was charged with a sexual humor. Agnes DeWitt was perhaps too emotionally arrogant to understand what a precious gift she shared with Berndt. She possessed, and so easily, a love most humans never know, yet are quite willing to die or go mad for. And Agnes had done nothing but find her way into the barn of a good man who had a singular gift for everyday affection as well as the deepest tones of human love.

Through fall and winter, Agnes DeWitt gave music lessons, and although the two weren't married and Miss DeWitt, existing in a state of mortal sin, took no communion, even the Catholics and their children subscribed. This was because it was well-known that Miss DeWitt's first commitment had been to Christ. It was understandable that she would have no other marriage, and also, although she did not take the Holy Eucharist upon her tongue she was there at church each morning, faithful and extremely devout. And, so, when the priest spoke from the pulpit, his reference was quite clear.

"Jesus insisted that Mary Magdelene be incorporated into the holy body of his church and it is said by some that in her hands there was celestial music. Her heart clearly contained the divine flame—and she was loved and forgiven."

Therefore, every morning Miss DeWitt played the church organ. She of course played Bach with a purity of intent purged of any subterranean feeling, but strictly and for God.

ARNOLD "THE ACTOR" ANDERSON

Only a short time into their happiness, the countryside and the small towns were preyed upon by a ring of bank robbers with a fast Overland automobile. This was before small towns even had sheriffs, some of them, let alone a car held in common to chase the precursors of such criminals as Basil "the Owl" Banghart, Ma Barker's Boys, Alvin Karpus, Henry LaFay. The first, and most insidious, of these men was Arnold "the Actor" Anderson.

The Actor and his troupe of thugs plundered the countryside at will, appearing as though from nowhere and descending into the towns with pitiless ease. The car—the color of which was always reported differently: white one time, gray the next, even blue—always pulled idling into the street before the doors of the bank. The passenger who emerged was sometimes an old man, other times a pregnant woman, a crippled youth, someone who inspired others to acts of polite assistance. A Good Samaritan would open doors and even escort the Actor to the teller, at which point the object of good works would straighten, throw off his disguise, shout to his gang in a ringing voice, and proceed to rob the bank. It would all be over in a trice. Sometimes, of course, there was resistance from a bank official or an intrepid do-gooder, in which case a death or two might result—for the Actor, who took on the disguises and masterminded the activities of the gang, was entirely ruthless and cared nothing for human life. It was said that he could be quite charming as he shot people, even funny. Eight people in the past two years had perished laughing.

One clear but muddy spring day Miss DeWitt removed her egg and butter money from the crevice between two stones in the root cellar. She told Berndt that she was walking to town to deposit the money against the mortgage payment. He agreed, absently. Touched her arm. They'd had a breathless week of sex. Some mornings the two staggered from the bedroom disoriented, still half drunk on the perfume and animal eagerness of the other's body. These frenzied periods occurred to them, every so often, like spells in the weather. They would be drawn, sink, disappear into their greed until the cow groaned for milking or the hired man banged and swore on the outside gate. If nothing else intervened they'd stop only out of sheer exhaustion. Then they would look at each other oddly, questingly, as though the other person were a complete stranger, and gradually resume their normal treatment of one another, which was offhand and distracted, but with the assurance of people who thought alike. Even when they fought, it was with impatient dispatch. They were eager to get to the exciting part of the fight where they lost their tempers and approached each other with a frisson of rage that turned sexual, so that they could be slightly cruel and then surrender themselves to tenderness.

He arranged her against the wall, held her chin in one cupped hand and drew his other hand slowly up beneath her skirt until she gasped, pretended to open herself to him. Just as he unbuckled his pants to enter her, though, she shoved him off balance, ducked from under his arm, and ran out the door laughing at his awkward hops and shouts. She slowed and picked her way along the ruts of the muddy road, breathing in anticipation of their night. Their night in which she would not refuse him. The huge canopy sky threatened gray-blue in the northwest, but the weather was far away and the wind desultory, the air watery, clear, the buds split in a faint green haze. The first of her tulips were pink at the green lips, ready to bloom. Under the tough grama and side oats, the new shoots of grass were strengthening and gathering their power. She thought of Berndt's head tossed back, the cords running taut from the corner of his jaw. The way he nearly wept as he threw his famished weight into her again and again, and the way he glanced sideways, hungrily, after, until they began once again. Her need to touch him moved through her like a wave and she stopped, distractedly, passed a hand over her face, almost put her errand off, but then moved on.

The bank was a solid square of Nebraska limestone, great windowed with deep blond sills and brass handles on the doors. The high ceiling was of ornate, white, pressed tin set off by thick crown moldings and a center medallion of sheaves of wheat. In the summer great fans turned the sluggish air, and the velvet-roped lanes and spittoons, the pink and gray mica-flecked granite countertops, and the teller's cages seemed caught in a dim hush of order while outside the noise of the town continued, erratic. The relationship between the getting of money, a scrabbling and disorderly business, contrasted with the storing of money, an enterprise based on the satisfactory premise that human effort, struggle, even time itself, could be quantified, counted, stacked neatly away in a safe.

Outside, on the day Miss DeWitt walked swiftly into town, the streets seemed unusually quiet and orderly. Even the bum sleeping against the side of the young elm had his arms neatly folded, and the one automobile parked, idling, was an elegant car of the sort—well, yes—she thought, oddly, that a bishop would use. Sure enough who but a priest should remove himself from the back seat kicking to the side his black soutane. With a meek and tentative squint at the bank, through tiny rimless eyeglasses, he made his way up the walk and steps. On the way, he bowed to Miss DeWitt, who followed him respectfully. As they walked together up the roped path in the lobby she said to him, loudly and clearly, in an amused tone of voice, "Sir, why this pretense? You are not a priest!"

Whereupon the stooped old man straightened, magically broadened, and waved a hand across his face very much as she herself had, in the road, to erase her thoughts. Only he erased his character. He removed his glasses and from beneath his robe drew a snub-nosed pistol, which he pointed straight at Miss DeWitt's forehead.

"Righto," he said.

There was no other perceptible signal, but all of a sudden another male customer held a gun out as well, first at the chin of a florid redheaded woman teller and then at the broad chest of the other teller, a young dark-haired bristling man. This young former baseball star's heart filled immediately, then swelled. He wanted to be a hero, but was struggling with the how of it. Foolish! Foolish! Miss DeWitt wanted to tell him. But it was clear from the beginning that he had just the right amount of stubborn stuff in him to be killed. Which he was. When he fell down dead behind his cage of iron, mouth open to catch the punch line of a joke, the money was harder to get. The redhaired woman was handed a canvas bag, called upon to open his drawer, and instructed not to trip the alarm. When she did anyway,

the eighteen customers, including Agnes, were all instructed to gather
in one corner behind the velvet rope. Exactly, Miss DeWitt thought,
like a flock of blank-eyed sheep. There was a shout outside. It was the
sheriff, Slow Johnny Mercier, who really was slow and clumsy, and
his deputy with him, pistols drawn. They stood just outside the door
yelling for the robbers to come out.

It was clear, then, to Miss DeWitt and probably to the others that
their sheriff was an amateur and that the professional involved was
inside the bank. For the Actor continued gesturing to the red-haired
teller to add to the bills, add more and add more. Then, in his dull
black robe with its give-away wrinkles, creases that no self-respecting
Catholic lay or nun housekeeper would have allowed him to don, and
his ridiculous brown Episcopalian shoes, he sprang to the bunched
people swift and graceful as a wolf, chose from just behind the rope
Miss DeWitt.

He chose her as though choosing a dancing partner. He did everything but bow—walked up to her and took her hand with a polite but
peremptory firmness, so that it would not have been out of character
with his manner for the two of them to step out onto the dance floor
and begin a slow waltz. And it was as though they were engaged in
some sort of dance as they walked out the door. Only she was held the
wrong way. When she stumbled, perhaps purposely, not following his
lead, he wrenched her closer. As he pulled her against the door of the
car he'd entered, as she balanced on the running board, he called out,
"Come after me and I will blow her head off, Mister Sheriff."

Then the ragged bum who had sat with arms neatly crossed at
the side of the street accelerated the car with a roar. Slow Johnny the
sheriff, solid in his tracks, raised his pistol, sighted carefully along the
barrel, pulled the trigger, and shot Miss DeWitt. She took the bullet in
the hip. So much was happening all at once—more shots fired, mad
swerving to avoid an ice truck, two children diving into the roots of a
lilac bush, sheer speed—that she felt the impact as a blow that rang
her bones, but did not pain her, until the car hit a great freak of earth
that nearly threw Miss DeWitt halfway into the open window on the
driver's side. Immediately, she was cast into an almost mystical state
of agony. The heavens seemed to open. Black stars rang down. She
heard the motor and then, later, more gunshots as from a great, muted
distance. Thick strains of music looped through her mental hearing,

all jumbled and spectacular. Held on the running board by an arm that seemed strung of pitiless wire, proceeding at a dreamlike pace down the smoothly tamped and rolled roadbeds that led out of town, in a state of clarity and focused keenness she told herself, I am being kidnapped. I have been shot.

As the auto jounced her along she began to lose certainty. In her pain she imagined herself back at the convent in her tiny closet of a room. She closed the door, crawled doglike into the wet bush of unconsciousness, lay huddled small and unknowing. From time to time, she experienced a moment of reprieve. She was capable of standing upright. Gravely, she surveyed the country she passed through and found in the faint spring clouds of green a raw sweetness. The robber's arm gripped her waist. She gripped the luggage rack. Her hair, unpinned and flying backward, made a short banner in the wet, fresh wind.

The Actor took the old Patterson road, by which she knew he understood the lay of the land, and by which, too, she knew if he took the turnoff he would pass by one of Berndt's fields, their fields, where Berndt was likely to be working. Her heart pounded in hope. But the driver dressed in rags did not turn and she then thought instantly in great relief that Berndt wouldn't be put in danger now. Just as she did so, the car sped first past the hired man and then farther on, Berndt, on his big slow horse, plodding. He was dragging along a harrow to be repaired. She tried to hide herself when he came by, but she was still balanced on the running board. So it was, he saw her approach from down the road like a figurehead on the prow of a ship. She stood at grand attention, her one leg a flare of blood. He stopped. His face went slack with uncomprehending shock. She rushed by close enough for their hands to meet and then she was gone, swallowed into the distance.

BERNDT VOGEL

Berndt followed the car not because he saw fear in her eyes—there was none, only a dreamy concentration—but because he grasped the whole scenario. Unhitching the harrow, then turning on his horse, he had no precise notion of her danger or any thought of how to rescue her but acted on instinct and absurdity. He was not afraid for her. Having met her in the first place nearly naked within the smoky radiance of his own barn, he knew she would survive the ordeal. There was always a side to her he could not touch. He felt indeed that she was a woman created of impossibility.

Although he sent his horse along at a smart pace, the car was soon out of sight. He had to keep an eye on the road to know from the tire marks at each turnoff that they had, in fact, stayed on the main road. And they did, moving farther from him at every moment. He moved, following them, wondering in useless desperation the location of Slow Johnny. On the chase?

No, not quite. The sheriff and the deputy, in trying to commandeer a car, met resistance not so much from the owner's lack of agreement about the need for it, but because Slow Johnny was a notoriously poor driver. Beyond that, the two or three citizens whom he approached thought he would do more harm than good chasing down the Actor and probably get Miss DeWitt completely killed, if not himself, the deputy, and any bystander in a stone's throw radius.

Berndt was far ahead, then, of any other form of help. As he traveled along behind the Actor's car, he put his mind to the subject. By the process of recalling certain news items about local robberies, he had pretty well figured out what was happening. His equilibrium failed, and he experienced a wave of terror for Agnes so intense that he whipped the poor horse to a momentary froth. As soon as the Percheron rocked into a huge gallop, Berndt realized that he would kill his horse if he continued. Speed now was useless, and besides, with each mile covered he gained a distinct advantage. The car would eventually run out of gas. The horse, if Berndt was careful to conserve its energy, would last. And then, too, Berndt had the advantage of terrible road conditions. Since it was spring, it would be surprising if any car could get through the big washout Berndt knew of six miles up the road.

THE BLUE HORSE

The Actor's car ripped through the silent country until, just as Berndt anticipated, they hit the washout. The car shimmied to a perplexed stall. The Actor pulled Agnes roughly into the back seat and the driver revved twice without result. With a fabulous jolt the powerful engine caught and they lurched free, only then to slip off the other side of the road into a more serious predicament. There was no moving, not at all, no matter how the men pushed, roared, swore, kicked. Turning in a circle of frustrated fury, the Actor spied at some distance the horse, the rider.

"Look sharp," he spoke. The men and he changed suddenly to meeker, commoner sorts and began to work with assiduous uselessness on the car's engaged tires. Pulling up beside them, Berndt casually offered his assistance. The words did not strangle his throat. He was calm. He tapped his farmer's brim as he glanced into the back seat. The Actor had spread a blanket over Miss DeWitt's legs, and she looked all right, though pale and dazzled.

Berndt did not know that the Actor, with an eye to concealing the stolen money, had taken wads of it from the canvas bag. During the ride he had thrust as many bills as he could into his shirt. He had shoved the bag itself under the blanket, next to Miss DeWitt, whom he instructed to not bother getting out of the car. He smiled a genial greeting to Berndt, who nodded at Miss DeWitt, and set to work.

As did she. Quickly, surreptitiously, with a busy intelligence, Agnes pulled sheaves of bills between her fingers and thrust these bills into the ripped lining of her jacket—and was able to feel, in spite of the swooning pain in her hip, that she was very glad to have been a careless seamstress. As for Berndt, by eagerly hooking the good beast to the car's bumper and making an ostentatious show of straining its powers, Berndt made every appearance of helping the gang. Yet by degrees, through prods and signs, he actually caused the horse to mire them ever deeper. Soon they were in a more helpless state than before. The Actor didn't see it at first, but then, trained to supersensory human clues, he caught a glance between the farmer and the hostage that betrayed their connection. Just as he moved to grab the reins and question this, there appeared at last Slow Johnny and the deputy, riding in the dead teller's car.

The men of the law stopped close upon the robbers and gingerly stepped toward them, guns drawn.

"You're done for," shouted Slow Johnny.

"Halt, you jackass!"

Crouching so that his body was shielded by the car door and his gun level with the head of Miss DeWitt, the Actor warned off the sheriff.

"Back! Back!" Berndt signaled to Johnny.

"I'll shoot her, yes by damn I will," called the Actor.

At a great distance from herself, Agnes felt her mouth open and words emerge. She spoke to the Actor, who cried out, warningly, again. Slow Johnny, though, was hard of hearing as well as slow and he kept walking forward. Berndt saw the thumb of the Actor lift off the hammer of the gun. He struck him just as the gun went off, so that the last Agnes DeWitt saw of the Actor was his unflinching look at her. The last thought she had about him was amazement that he did not regard her words or her life as important or even useful at all, or have a moment's hesitation about ending all of the thousands of hours of tedious intensity of musical practice, ending the rippling music that her hands could bring into being, ending the episodes of greed and wonder in the arms of Berndt, and the several acts she'd learned to do that men paid whores great sums to perform and that she enjoyed, and further back, ending her time of devotion in the convent where her sisters had already unsewn, pressed, and restitched her habit for another hopeful. None of which was of any consequence. Not even the mountains of prayers for the souls so like his or the vivid attempts beseeching Mary to intercede. Nothing mattered. None of that. And beyond that, to her childhood and the tar roofs of the homestead and the alien bread of her mother's cruel visions and her father's terrifying gestures of love and all the precious jumble of her littleness, her thoughts, her creamy baby skin, her howls and burbles, all of this was as nothing to his casual wish to kill her.

This fact smote her as a marvel and a sorrow, and she knew it was because of what she saw, straight on, in the Actor that she so fervently loved Chopin. And God. Now, she had to give herself entirely to God's will, whatever that might be. And it was just as she wondered, indeed, if for her to die was that will, that the gun went off at her temple and blackness stormed behind her eyes.

While Berndt jumped to her side, the Actor neatly grabbed the reins and somehow pulled himself onto the table-broad back of the horse. He dug in his heels, gave a desperate kick to the horse's belly, and they were off, though the horse slowed at once just as soon as they entered the vast horizon-bound treeless wet field of thick gumbo. Berndt, kissing Agnes in a strange roar of grief, then followed the Actor, leaving the other two bank robbers and Slow Johnny and the deputy shouting back and forth and leveling their guns but not knowing whom to shoot. Berndt walked straight on. Just as he had when the car sped past, he understood his advantage lay in the increase of distance. He knew how exhausted his horse was, and he knew, too, that he, Berndt, could bend over from time to time to clean off his feet, but his horse could not. Either the Actor would have to dismount, or the horse would eventually slow to a stop, repossessed by the dirt.

And so it was—a low-speed chase.

There in that empty landscape they were a cipher of strained pursuit—one man plodding forward on the horse, the other plodding after. They seemed on that plain and under that spun sky eternal—bound to trudge on to hell no matter what. The clods on the hooves of the horse were soon great rich cakes. Still, on and on, slower, they pressed. Then slower yet so that the Actor kicked in savage indignation until the horse's flanks bled. Slower yet. Berndt kept coming. The Actor screamed straight into the ear of the horse. With a frantic ripple of muscles it attempted to undo itself from the earth. Only sank itself farther, deeper. Raging, futile, the Actor saw the horse was stuck, leaped off, and put the pistol to its eye.

The shot echoed out, a crack. Another thinner crack echoed, against the mirage horizon. By the time the echo was lost, the horse was dead. Berndt saw his horse kneel in the wet cement dirt the way the animals worshiped the Christ. Then, to Berndt's grief and rage, there was added a contemptuous bewilderment, which made him capable of what he did next.

The next bullet that the Actor fired struck Berndt in the chest but went through without touching a vital organ. Berndt merely felt a stunning rip of fire. He staggered one step back and then kept moving. When the bullet after that struck him mortally, he seemed to absorb it and strengthen. Rising to the next steps, he skipped from the mud. The Actor's face stiffened in green shock and he fired point-blank.

The empty chamber clicked over just as Berndt clasped the Actor by the shoulders and spoke into his face.

"If you hadn't shot my horse, you wouldn't have to die now," said Berndt, abstractly stating a fact by which he perhaps meant that he would have preferred to deliver the Actor to the terrors of justice, or perhaps that Berndt would have preferred to die in the place of the horse, or yet, that the last bullet would have been his own *coup de grâce*. As there was life left in him, Berndt set his hands with a dogged weariness upon the Actor's face, put his thumbs to the gangster's eyeballs, and pressed, pressed with an inexorable parental dispassion, pressed until it was clear the gangster's aim would be forever spoiled. Then Berndt toppled forward onto the ground, into the nearly liquid gumbo, pinning the Actor full length.

It was hours before anyone got to the scene and in that time Arnold "the Actor" Anderson could not budge the dead man. Inch by inch, with incremental slowness and tiny sucking noises the earth crept over the Actor and into him, first swallowing his heels, back, elbows, and then stopping up his ears, so his body slowly filled with soupy, rich topsoil. At the last, he could not hear his own scream. Dirt filled his nose and then his tipped up straining mouth. No matter how he spat, the earth kept coming and the mud trickled down his throat. Slowly, infinitely slowly, bronchia by bronchia the earth stopped up each passage of his lungs and packed them tight. The ground absorbed him. When at last the first member of the reluctantly formed posse arrived, he thought at first the robber had escaped, but then saw how only the hands of the Actor, clutching Berndt's arms and back like a raft, still extended above the level of the horizon.

FRÉDÉRIC CHOPIN

After she came to, nursed by her own former sisters in the hospital, a bullet crease shadowing her mind, did Agnes DeWitt sorrow in her bones that she had teasingly pushed Berndt away that morning? Did she dream all that month, while she hovered in and out of death, of his entering and her receiving him? Recall looking into his eyes pillowed close to hers? Long for the rough cup of his hand on her breast?

No, not for a moment. Rather, she thought again of music. Chopin. The kind bullet that split and roped her scalp had remarkably fused her musical joys with all memories of Berndt.

She didn't even recall, donning her jacket, how it came to be fitted behind the satin lining with an astonishing amount of money. Though she'd lost portions of her memory, she had not lost her wits, and she said nothing. Counted it in secret. Kept it safe in a Fargo bank. So she was well off. Berndt had written a will in which he declared her his common-law wife and left to her the farm and all upon it. There, she continued to raise rose-comb bantams, dominickers, reds. She played piano, too, for hours, and practiced more intensely than ever. She began to read. In the convent, she had not been permitted to read beyond her daily prayers and the lives of the saints. Now, with a town library full of volumes she'd never touched, she became a reader. A wolfish, selfish, maddened, hungry reader who let the chickens scream and peck one another to death, who ignored the intelligent loneliness of the pig and forgot to milk the groaning cow. She read or she played piano, did little else except that she did keep teaching. Only her toughest chickens survived.

Perhaps a season or so after Berndt's death, her students noticed she would stop in the middle of a lesson and either pick up a book to gulp a page in with her eyes, or smile out the window as though welcoming a long expected visitor. One day the neighbor children went to pick up the usual order of eggs and were most struck to see the white-and-black-flecked dominickers flapping up in alarm around Miss DeWitt as she stood bare upon the green grass.

Tough, nonchalant, legs slightly bowed, breasts jutting a bit to either side and the dark flare of hair flicking up the center of her. Naked. She looked at the students with remote kindness. Asked, "How many dozen?" Walked off to gather the eggs.

That episode with the chickens made the gossip table rounds. People put it off to Berndt's death and an unstringing of her nerves. Still, she lost only a Lutheran student or two. She continued playing the organ for Mass, the celestial Bach, and at home, in the black, black nights, Chopin. As she had formerly when a Christ-dedicated virgin, she played with unbearable simplicity. Her music was so finely told it hurt to listen to the notes that struck the high sweet breeze. If she was asked, once, by an innocent student too young to understand the meaning of discretion but having overheard some story about Miss Agnes DeWitt—some very alert student longing perhaps to see the dimple where the bullet was dug from her hip or push aside the lively darts and strands of her hair to find the curved clef of a scar—if that student were to ask Miss Agnes DeWitt why she did not wear her clothes, sometimes, Miss Agnes DeWitt would answer that she removed her clothing when she played the music of a particular composer, when she played at her finest, and when the mood would strike her. No other display of appreciation could express her pure intent. Miss DeWitt would meditatively nod and say in the firmest manner that when one enters into the presence of such music, one should be naked. And then she would touch the keys.

FATHER DAMIEN MODESTE
(THE FIRST)

When she didn't show up for several days on end to play the organ, it was known that Miss DeWitt was suffering from nerves again. Incrementally, tortuously, unnecessarily, she was unblessed by tiny fragments of memory. Berndt materialized, cruelly, touch by touch, until he was all there but not there. A word and a look, a moment they had spent together, had apparently entered the heart of Agnes to be kept sealed and safe until, for no particular reason, she was to be tormented by an elusive recovery. She shut herself away. Some people grieve by holding fast to the love of others, some by rejecting all companionship. Some grieve with tears and some with dry howls. Some grieve like water, some burn. Some are fuel for the fire of sorrow and some are stone. Agnes was pure slate, dark and impenetrable.

Even books didn't help—she began and discarded them until they threatened her couch in tottering stacks.

A priest en route to his Indian mission and taking wayfarer's advantage of the local rectory's hospitality was dispatched to the suffering widow with communion—of which she now partook as she lived no longer in a state of mortal sin. She heard his knock, but did not rise to meet him, only called out from her place on the couch that he should enter, and so he did. Father Damien Modeste was a small, prunish, inquisitive man of middle age who had been called by his God, from a comfortable parish near Chicago, to missionize Indians. Momentarily intrigued, she sat up, but then almost immediately she lost interest. He gave her communion. Took what food she'd set out. And then, as she was silent in her blanket, brooding, he remained a bit longer and attempted to raise her spirits by telling her of his zeal.

"I am going north," he insisted, and went into detail regarding the harrowing details of his trip to the reservation. "Letters addressed to me by my fellow priest, Father Hugo, confirm the deep need for my service. Oh, there had been inroads. We are not the first generation of priests, but the devil . . ."

Here Father Damien paused, gauging Miss DeWitt's despairing reserve, licked his thin lips, and went on, "The devil works with a shrewd persistence, Miss DeWitt, and is never known to give up a soul merely because it is a thing willed in heaven. Our labor is required here on earth, in the ordinary world. Evil, oh yes, evil—"

"What do you know of evil?" Miss DeWitt's attention shifted suddenly from the acorn pattern of the wallpaper to the prematurely withered face of the missionary. He opened his mouth to go eagerly forward. But before he could speak, Miss DeWitt did.

"I've seen evil," she told her confessor, firmly. "It has blue eyes and brown shoes. About size ten. The feet are narrow. The hands are square. The build is slight and I'd say the face, though not handsome, has an intriguing changeability about it. Though I am only now repossessing my memory of all the specifics, Father Modeste, I've seen the devil himself and he was disguised in a rumpled cassock."

Father Modeste, already in possession of the story, nodded with barely hidden avidity.

"God dispensed great justice that day."

"Selectively."

Now Miss DeWitt glared tiredly at her piano.

"I couldn't play this afternoon. Something haunts me, as though another terrible memory is ready to pour into my mind and only a sheer finger's breadth of earth is holding it in place."

"I suppose you are referring"—here Father Damien coughed delicately—"to your . . . ah . . . companion."

"Yes," Agnes admitted, unwillingly. She hated being pegged and didn't much like this priest with the avid eyes. She touched the frail mend of the bullet's crease. "Only a short time ago, I was a sister in the local convent, having taken my temporary vows at a very young age. I remember every word, every Mass, every confession I made, every note I played. But only at times do I remember Berndt's features. And yet I recall with unwished clarity the face of the man who killed him! Fortunately, I often see another man, one I've never met, hair parted far over to the left, a deep-eyed brow, a broad, beaky nose, a small and rather full mouth and low cheekbones, lumpy and sad."

"Is it him?" The priest was curious.

"Him who?"

"Your companion, may he rest—"

"No, not him," said Agnes DeWitt, her fingers moving suddenly, flying on the tea plate, tapping, possessed by the thought of the photograph reproduced in the frontispiece of her favorite musical text. *Chopin! Chopin!* Father Modeste changed the subject in some bemusement. What was there to say? He tried to round the horn and cleave to his original subject all in one sentence.

"Miss DeWitt, it is said that God often enters the dark mind of the savage via musical pathways. For that reason, I've studied translations of the hymns laid down in Ojibwe by our studious Father Hugo. Ah, poor unfortunate Father Hugo! His death of the sweating fever was compared by witnesses, I have it in a letter, to Christ's agony in the garden. Blood, yes, beads of it all over him. He sweated blood from every pore of his body."

Diverted, Agnes imagined the scene. It seemed to her that almost any pain was sympathetic to her loss and she inserted herself immediately into the concept of fantastic suffering.

"Aren't you afraid?" she asked, but her voice was mocking, for truly, there was more to fear for her in a simple bank visit.

Father Damien raked his strands of hair back. His hand was a yellow claw. Something about the distracted way he mumbled out an answer in the negative told Agnes that he was, indeed, nervously disposed. The urge to tease him came upon her.

"I would be afraid," she said. "Not so much of the Indians themselves, but of the many plagues and vermin that assail them—most pathetic of all God's doomed creatures! Lice are very catching, for instance, and the devil trains them to descend in droves on the unwary priest who forgets to bless himself before he enters one of their homes."

Father Damien was silent in surprise.

"Oh, I'll bless myself all right," he said at last. "With a lye bath every week. And constitutionals. I will look after my health."

Agnes DeWitt could not help but tease more sharply. "Will you really bathe in lye? How brutal! And what grave difficulties such a pious man as yourself will face when confronted with their shamans and hocus-pocus! I am sure they indulge in séances."

"Most likely."

"Trance states, those are probably common. And potions, elixirs, that sort of anodyne."

"No doubt."

"There are so many shapes to the evil you will have to contend with. They have, some of them, a tradition of devouring strangers!"

Father Damien could not help glancing down at his lean thighs, pressed together under his cassock. They didn't look all that tempting even to him. He really had to go. He dispensed a quick blessing and left with the cookies pressed on him by Agnes DeWitt, whom he had managed, though not by the avenues he'd attempted, to cheer so thoroughly that she rose from her couch, folded her blanket, and sitting down at her piano laughed so hard her fingers dropped off the keys.

THE MISSION

Into her brooding there intruded an absurd fantasy, the possibility of escape, though it was to a place few would consider so—the mission and the missionary life. She thought of doing good. Alleviating the pain that others felt might help to assuage her own. She began to pray, asked to regain the clarity of her original religious impulse, her early vocation. Chopin had stolen her from Christ to give to Berndt. Christ had stolen Berndt from her to take for himself. Now she had only her Chopin, his music, for Christ was preoccupied with introducing

Berndt to all of the other farmers in heaven and for Agnes he seemed to have no time. She prayed. He did not answer. Chopin was more reliable. She could not stand the farm—not without Berndt. Now that she remembered him, the place was treacherous with the raw ache of memory that returned in unexpected bits, then vanished before she could get the whole of it firmly laid out in her mind.

In her thoughts, she spoke to the priest again, questioned him strenuously, found her own answers. The Ojibwe, she had heard, the Indians up north, were an agreeable people not known for their ferocious instincts, even in the past. She was, of course, not afraid. She was curious, and her curious nature led her down tangled pathways. What was it like up there—wild? She could understand wild. Though her world was tame, the peace she sought was lost within the wilderness of her own heart. Sometimes she howled and savagely tore the wallpaper of her bedroom and then lay on the floor. Spent, she thought that there was no place as unknown as grief.

THE FLOOD

The river pushed over the banks that spring and ripped from the ground the dead horse, the mired car, and the money that had lain unseen underneath the gangster, fallen out of the waistband of the trousers he'd worn under the cassock. The horse swirled to pieces, the car tipped slowly downward, the money floated in thin wads straight north and was in a month or two plowed into the earth of a Pembina potato field. Meanwhile, Agnes kept hers locked in the Fargo bank. Tracing her elusive memories, she had gone where life was deepest many times, and she did not fear the rain. Of course, she did not know the history of the stream—at times deceptively sluggish or narrow as a whip, then all of a sudden pooling in a great, wide, dangerous lake with powerful currents that moved earth in tons. What began as a sheer mist became an even sprinkle and then developed into a slow, pounding shower that lasted three days, then four, then on the fifth day when it should have tapered off, increased.

The river boiled along swiftly, a pour of gray soup still contained, just barely, within its high banks. On day six the rain stopped, or seemed to. The storm had moved upstream. All day while the sun shone pleasantly the river heaved itself up, tore into its flow new trees and boulders, created tip-ups, washouts, areas of singing turbulence.

Agnes rushed about uneasily, pitching hay into the high loft, throwing chickens up after the hay, wishing she could toss the house up as well, and of course the fabulous piano. But the piano was earth anchored and well tuned by the rainy air, so instead of fruitless worry, Agnes lost herself in practice. She had an inner conviction that, no matter how wide the river spread, it would stop at her front doorstep.

She didn't know.

Once this river started to move, it was a thing that gained assurance. It had no problem with fences or gates, wispy windbreaks, ditches. It simply leveled or attained the level of whatever stood in its path. And moved on, closer. Water jumped up the grass lawn and collected in the flower beds. The river tugged itself up the porch and into the house from one side. From the other side it undermined an already weak foundation that had temporarily shored up the same wall once removed to make way for the piano. The river tore against the house from all around. And then, like a child tipping out a piece of candy from a box, the water surged underneath, rocked the floor, and the piano crashed through the weakened wall.

It landed in the swift current of the yard, Agnes with it. The white treble clef of her flannel nightdress billowed as she spun away, clutching the curved lid. The thing was pushed along, bobbing off the bottom of the flower beds first and then, as muscular new eddies caught it, touching down on the shifting lanes of Berndt's wheat fields, and farther, until the revolving instrument and the woman on it reached the original river, that powerful vein, and plunged in. They were carried not more than a hundred feet before the piano lost momentum and sank. As it went down Agnes thought at first of crawling into its box, nestling as though for safety among the cold, dead keys. So attached was she to the instrument that she could not imagine parting from it but, as she actually struggled with the hinged cover, Agnes lost her grip and was swept straight north.

2

3 A.M., March 20, 1996

IN THE THRALL
OF THE GRAPE

REPORT THE FIRST
THE MIRACLE OF MY DISGUISE

Your Holiness, I was the woman on the lid of the piano.

*Agnes. Beloved of Chopin and Berndt Vogel, raiser of
chickens, groomer of blue horse, girl shot by the Actor. Student
of memory. I remember some things and have forgotten others.
I do know that I was tumbled into the flood of the cold Red
River, which is not red but a punishing gray. Whirling once,
twice. Even now, the ride stands clear. I sank toward the sludge
bottom, struggling in my gown, my shoes like clods on my feet.
I had the sense to tear them off and tried to get the nightdress,
too, but I had sewn it with too many buttons. This proved my
salvation, as it filled with air and ballooned around my
shoulders like a life buoy. So I whirled off. I opened my mouth
to wail. There was darkness, and I sank into its murmur.*

I met the undertow, a quick dark funnel not visible from shore. It must have pulled me farther down the stream, for when I came up, I was floating swiftly, moving in a grand swell. The current crested at the surface and all I had to do was paddle lightly. Even in my swirling gown, it took almost no effort. My dress caught air and floated behind me like a wedding train. It could have dragged me under, but instead I was pushed along. Buoyant, I dropped fear, dropped worry, went beyond cold into a state beyond numb. The rush was so swift and strong.

Blessed One, I now believe in that river I drowned in spirit, but revived. I lost an old life and gained a new. Memories resurfaced. Berndt's square hand in mine. The careful baritone of his warm voice. Perhaps, soon, I would join him. Then again perhaps I would live. The latter prospect suddenly intrigued me. I looked at the banks as I swept by and I wondered why Agnes was sad in such a strange world. Things look different from the middle of a flooded river. In the flow, time is erased. I had new eyes. Branches of toppled trees and upended roots. Houses split. The banks undercut and caving. Cows. Horses. Cows.

I took the groaning roar that widened before me to be the mouth of a great white drop, and yet I stayed calm. I moved on faster, faster. But it was not tangled white foam rapids that met me. Instead, it was a drowning herd of cows, hundreds of cows. Wedged in trees, they had made a floating bridge so compact that I stepped, half frozen, onto it like a raft, stumbled across to the bank, fell off there to firm ground.

Once my feet touched solid earth fear came over me. I went utterly weak; my strength drained. I sank upon the ground and knew nothing more.

MIRACLE THE SECOND
DIVINE RESCUE OF MISS DEWITT

1912

Knocked out by exhausted fear, Agnes slept. That cessation of awareness proved a bridge between her old life and her new life. Before she woke, she was one who believed without seeing, felt spiritual emotion without experience of its source, kept an orderly faith and haphazard observance without the deepest marks of conviction. Creation had spoken to her in ways she could encompass—in the splendor of sexual love, the grand Dakota sky, the arcane language of cramped, black musical notes. Yet her God had never sent a spirit, never spoken to her directly, never employed a visible shape or touched Agnes with a divine hand, unless you believe that God's hand was Berndt's and nudged the wrist of the Actor, causing the bullet to plow a shallow groove instead of to burrow deep. She had believed in her music. Now she was to lose that. But that loss would be replaced.

She woke later, who knows how much later.

It was night. Lamplight, a glowing glass, a roof over her, four walls. Agnes found that she was lying on a bed, covered with a quilt and a sheepskin. The air was heavy and warm with the smell of cooking venison and she was hungry. Beyond all measure, starving! She was young, barely a woman, and never full. A spoon was held to her lips. She moved toward it, lured like an animal, and she tasted a broth of meat that brought tears to her eyes. Then she saw a man's hands held the spoon and the bowl. She slid her gaze up his strong arms, his shoulders, to his broad and open face.

Kindness was there, sheer kindness, a radiance from within him fell upon her and it was like a pool of warm sunlight.

Instantly, she remembered the river.

"Who are you?" she asked, but without waiting for an answer she grabbed the bowl and drank its contents with such a steady greed that it was only when she'd reached the very bottom that she realized several things all at once: they were alone in the tiny hut, no woman had prepared the soup, and she was naked in the bed.

The sheepskin dropped away from her body, and she felt the slight breeze of his breath along her throat. He stroked her hair, smiled at her. She felt warmth along her thighs, hovering elation. Bands of rippling lightness engulfed her when he moved closer. And then his hand, brutalized and heavy from work, fell gently as he held her arm and took away the empty bowl, the horn spoon, and wiped her lips. She felt his rough hair as he leaned closer, as he moved his length alongside her on the creaking boards, as he slowly turned her toward him. His breathing deepened, he relaxed. She lay there, too, spent and comfortable, curled against a sweetly sleeping man, a very tired man who smelled of resin from the wood he'd chopped, of metal from the tools he'd used, of hay, of sweat, of great and nameless things that she'd known, as in a dream, in her human husband's arms.

She lay her head beside him, and although she remained awake for many hours in that beautiful stillness, listening to his even breath, eventually she, too, fell asleep.

Morning dawned with rain on the wind, the sky a sheet of gray light. Agnes remembered where she was, turned, and found that he was gone. Not only that, but she was lying in no comfortable settler's shack, but in an empty shell of a long abandoned hovel with the wind whipping through, swallows' nests in the eaves, no sign of the man, no bowl, no track, no spoon, no sheepskin covering or blanket. Only her nightclothes fit back onto her, dry, still smelling of the river. She stood in the doorway for a long while. As she stood there, she gradually came to understand what had happened.

Through You, in You, with You. Aren't those beautiful words? For of course she knew her husband long before she met Him, long before He rescued her, long before He fed her broth and held Agnes close to Him all through that quiet night.

Dear Pontiff,

Since then, through the years, my love and wonder have steadily increased. Having met Him just that once, having known Him in a man's body, how could I not love Him until death? How could I not follow Him? Be thou like as me, were His words, and I took them literally to mean that I should attend Him as a loving woman follows her soldier into the

battle of life, dressed as He is dressed, suffering the same
hardships.

Modeste

THE EXCHANGE

Disoriented, Agnes walked farther north instead of south, for the
river's flow was mixed up in swirls and futile commotions now and
there was no clear sign of the current's force. The sky, too, was a low
ceiling of thick gray through which the sunlight diffused evenly over
the flooded landscape—no direction to be gathered. So Agnes walked
and in walking she saw too much. A tangle of rats. Skeletal twisted
machinery from tattered farms. A baby carriage with no baby in it.
Pieces of houses. A basket of eggs afloat. A priest hanging on a branch.

Not far up the river Agnes DeWitt came upon poor Father Damien
Modeste, whom she freely admitted she disliked even as she pitied
him now. The drowned man was snagged in a tree, gaping down at her
with a wide-eyed and upside-down quizzicality. The wreckage of the
rectory auto was already sucked upstream, if he had taken the auto.
She didn't know. Perhaps he was on foot. For a long while, she sat
near the tree with the body, considering. She prayed for a sign—what
to do? But she already knew. Once she was ready, she acted. She dis-
lodged the priest with a branch that she used like a hook, pulling him
down. His body, weighted like a sand-filled sack, shook the loose
roots of the tree as it struck the ground. The man was green-white,
and in his death more powerful than in life, more severe. Agnes had
no way of digging him a grave but to use her two hands. The ground
beneath was so soft, so saturated, that she was able to scrape out a
rough hole to fit him, though it took her the day. All the time that she
worked, the certainty grew.

It was nearly twilight before she rolled him in. Her heavy night-
gown was his shroud. His clothing, his cassock, and the small bundle
tangled about him, a traveler's pouch tied underneath all else, Agnes
put on in the exact order he had worn them. A small sharp knife in
that traveler's pocket was her barber's scissors—she trimmed off her
hair and then she buried it with him as though, even this pitiable, he
was the keeper of her old life.

She could think of nothing to which she was required to return. In fact, as though the cold water had flooded her brain, her memory, again, was a distressing patchwork of eroding islands. Berndt was gone, she knew that, and she remembered that she had loved him, she thought. Also gone: the blue horse, her lovely lattice dress, her leather boots, and even her chickens were probably drowned, too. She could at least recall the chickens in reassuring detail, each of them particular and opinionated. The hens made such a proud fuss over each new egg. Even in the muck, covering the dead priest, she nearly laughed, thinking of her chickens. Then she breathed out, troubled.

There was something, something . . . it was huge and it belonged to her, and it was vast. . . . When she tried to grasp at it the form faded like a dream. A grand dream, prophetic and important. Lines, black dots. She shook her head. Whatever it was, gleaming for a moment, shiny black, had it to do with her hands? She flexed her fingers doubtfully. Sound? She hummed a few bars of Die Lorelei, German *Lied*. Was she a singer? She cleared her throat, tried her voice. No, that definitely wasn't it. Well, whatever it was, it was gone. She had no way of knowing that she had lost the vast gift of her music, but she did have the sense that the stark, searching motions of her hands were part of some larger complex of actions. Well, she shrugged, let them tingle away on the ends of her arms. Let them drum, and step-march and ripple. There was nothing to hold her back, now, from living the way she had dreamed of in the hot dark of her loss.

When Father Damien's grave was tamped over, she stood hungrily in the wreckage as the dusk winds blew the clouds aside. The clear sky revealed its map, star after star, until the world was again marked out for her. In the priest's hidden pouch there was money, some papers, a crust of cheese. A biscuit spongy with river water. She squeezed out the biscuit and ate the handful of crushed wet crumbs. The priest's clothes were wool. Though damp, she was warm enough. In time, the moon bobbed up in a cool blur to show her way, and then, under its light, Agnes began to walk north, into the land of the Ojibwe, to the place on the reservation where he had told her he was bound.

3

LITTLE NO HORSE

1996

A gentle morning. Lucid, calm, the sky a sweet wash of virgin's cloak blue and a sparkling freshness of temperature. A visitor knocked loud and hard on Father Damien's door, but there was no answer because wild floods raged in Father Damien's sleeping head. Trees cracked over in his dreams. Walls crumbled into the river. Stones. The visitor, a priest, grew discouraged and left, but returned in the early afternoon to find Damien sitting just outside the door on his tiny patio, snoring mildly in the unusually warm slant rays of sun. Although the visiting priest drew a chair up noisily and sat, creaking and shifting his weight, although he coughed and even muttered aloud, Father Damien did not stir. The visitor was forced either to disturb the ancient one or to wait with uncharacteristic patience for the old priest to awaken naturally.

The man's vibrant red-gray hair was plastered down in stubborn tufts. Though polite, he looked from his sharp eye to have a temper and a fluent tongue. He was Jude Miller, a thickly built, shrewd and impatient priest. An athletic concentration in his stance suggested a man anticipating a tennis serve . . . that never came. At last, he folded his arms, the forearms lightly downed in coppery hair, and put one hand to his squared-off jaw. His fingers were blunt and he looked to have a powerful grip. He wore a clerical collar, a casual short-sleeved shirt, blue jeans, and soft-soled court shoes. After sitting in obvious frustration, he came to a decision to use his time, somehow, if only to observe. He leaned forward in scrutiny of the old priest, who still slept in warm sunlight next to the remains of a late breakfast.

In his age, Father Damien had developed the odd and almost alien appearance of a wrinkled but innocent child. His head still grew bits of fluff and it was large in proportion to the rest of him. His body was hunched and leathery, his lean arms and legs bent wood. Because of his tender feet, he wore soft moccasins at all times. On his off days, he shuffled to keep his balance and used two canes, one in each hand, like ski poles to anchor and guide him. Other days, he was fervently young and walked in surprisingly limber strides. When asked, he said the source of his longevity was not God but the devil, who constantly tempted him with healthy idleness. He took long walks around and around the yard, the grounds of the church, the cemetery where he greeted and sometimes reminisced with the dead—for Father Damien was more connected with them than with the living, and even sensed their changing moods.

Father Jude Miller took in the venerable, elfin appearance of the man who slept, head thrown back in the chair, sensitive mouth slightly gaping in a frown. Other than his mouth, the old priest rested neatly, feet close together, hands clasped, head cradled by the fold of the battered easy chair.

A great leaf-shaped pattern of clouds passed over the sun, and a breeze lifted, but the day was still unseasonably warm. Now, as though summoned from within, the still sleeping Damien leaned forward and propped his hands on his knees. His eyes drifted calmly open. They were vast and staring, and had returned to the murky blue of newborn's eyes, so his look had a fixed, blind, amphibious clarity. He gazed straight at Father Jude. "Are you there, my Lord?" said Father Damien. "Where is the soup?" Father Jude Miller had heard of the old man's waking confusion. Instead of pursuing any possible answer he sat in polite suspense until Father Damien's thoughts focused. It took some time. At first, Father Damien called the younger priest closer and whispered in some anxiety that there were no stamps. He needed stamps. Foreign postage. Airmail.

"Commemoratives, please," said Father Damien, looking significantly at the visitor. He fumbled two letter-folded pages from his gown and thrust them at Father Miller, who read in some bewilderment.

Most Estimable Pontiff,

Having revealed to you the specifics of my story, it is my profound hope that you will take into consideration my motives in assuming the identity of your drowned and wretched servant Modeste. I can only think how heavily my unusual act must weigh upon your sense of the right and proper order of your servants' vocations. However, should you be indisposed to mercy, may I request that you take into consideration the seven principal goods I have accomplished on this most lonely of God's outposts?

Number one: I have vanquished the devil, who has come to me in the form of a black dog.

I have also contained, discharged, influenced, and negated the dangerous pieties of a nun of questionable allegiance (this requires a separate letter).

Two: I have caused there to be cleanly disposal of wastes that threatened the health of our parish. I have made improvements in the style, location, and comfort of the venerable institution known as the outhouse.

Three: I have introduced the wholesome peanut to the diet of the indigenes.

Four: I have willingly exchanged my prospects for eternal joy in return for the salvation of the soul of one of the more troublesome of my charges (who loves me but who doesn't in the least appreciate my sacrifice).

Five: In resolving a specific injustice levied by the ignorance of government officials, I have assisted in attempting to add twelve townships to the tribal land base.

Six: Although my mind is a tissue of holes, I have learned something of the formidable language of my people, and translated catechism as well as specific teachings. I have also rendered into English certain points of their own philosophy that illuminate the precious being of the Holy Ghost.

Seven: I have discovered an unlikely truth that may interest Your Holiness. The ordinary as well as esoteric forms of worship engaged in by the Ojibwe are sound, even compatible with the teachings of Christ.

Lastly, this. May I ask if you would be so specifically kind as to answer this letter!

I remain, a hopeful penitent,

> *Yours in the Lamb.*
> *Father Damien Modeste*

As though suddenly realizing he had broken some taboo, the old priest snatched the letter from Jude Miller's hands.

"Who are you?"

Trying to regain his balance, Father Jude introduced himself.

"Believe it or not," he said, with self-deprecating amusement, "I am sent here by the Vatican."

There was an eerie sweep of wind through the trees. Then silence. The old priest took this news like an electric blow and went rigid in his chair. The current of the statement so held him that Father Jude became concerned, at last, that the old priest's heart had seized. Just as he was reaching forward to take his pulse, Father Damien sagged forward onto his knees. Arms outstretched, he tried to speak but could not, although an odd sound caught in his throat, *eft, eft*. His head nodded back and forth, slowly, unbelievingly. An expression of wordless wonder gradually fixed itself onto his features and then joy welled in Father Damien's eyes, spilled over, sank down his cheeks.

A good long while passed before Father Jude Miller dared address the old priest again, for the palpitations of the old man's frail heart caused a dizzy sweat and then his lungs, brittle with age, shuddered in his chest like rawhide sacks and refused to inflate properly. But, although when he tried to speak, Father Damien's skin mottled and his lips went cyotic blue, he managed to welcome the visitor he believed had come straight from the Pope. He even managed to address him in Italian phrases he had memorized for the occasion. All of this alarmed Jude, but just as he was about to rush for the phone to summon an ambulance from the reservation hospital, Father Damien emitted a huge dragging cough. Loud as a death rattle, it had the effect of clearing his chest and restoring his oxygen so that he suddenly snapped back to consciousness.

"Ah, *bene, bene,*" he declared, gazing happily at Father Jude. "And when does the inquiry into the life of Leopolda begin?"

Father Jude, whose mission it was to impart the news of the inquiry, a most highly secret undertaking entrusted to him by eminent Catholic authorities, was taken aback. The route to sainthood was exhaustive and the proceedings highly confidential. Not only was he having trouble adjusting to Father Damien's instant recovery, but the old priest behaved as though he knew in advance his visitor's commission. In a way, this was irritating. Never before had Father Jude's assistance been required by Church authority at such exalted levels, never before had he imagined, even, the type of trust that was abruptly bestowed on him by reason of his lifelong proximity to the people and places now in question. What was for him an awesome and unexpected undertaking, however, seemed for Father Damien entirely expected.

"A lay Catholic, a professor of sorts, has introduced the subject. She has written a great deal on Sister Leopolda but from, you understand, an academic standpoint. We are looking now for firsthand and thoroughly witnessed fact."

Father Damien took this information to himself with prideful glee. Father Jude was nonplussed at such enthusiasm.

"And who will form the council, do you think?" Father Damien now inquired in the bright tones of a younger man. As though he was still involved in the machinery of the Church, he began to speculate aloud. Some of those whom the old priest named were dead or married. Still, he was not so entirely out of touch as his feeble appearance would excuse. The old one named several eminent scholars, Jesuits who were known as investigators, and he inquired shrewdly after the opinions of Bishops Retzlaff and Kelly, Archbishop Day, and the status of any petitions or people's acclamations. In addition, he asked whether proofs had yet been furnished of Leopolda's intercessions and gave his opinion that the most delicate points would rest upon the singular question of her mode of existence.

"By which you mean . . ." Father Jude gazed into the fairy-pale face, the white hair spread in a flossy halo, the great uncanny eyes.

"Her daily example." Father Damien raised one finger in the air. "Did she lead an exemplary existence? Was she fair, was she honest? Did she give up her foodstuffs, her blankets, her comforts to the poor? Did she have any bad habits, tipple unblessed communion wine? Smoke?" Here Father Damien gave a dry cruel laugh that surprised Jude. "Had Sister Leopolda indulged herself in some area she might have sinned less forcefully in others . . . ? Yes, yes! If only she had smoked!"

Father Damien held up two fingers in a V.

"I don't smoke," said Father Jude.

"Well then, look, neshke . . . I only have one on special occasions."

Early on, Ojibwe words and phrases had crept into Damien's waking speech and now sometimes he lapsed into the tongue, especially in his frequent confusion over whom he was addressing.

"Neshke! Daga naazh opwaagaansz!" He gestured again at a small tin box set on the tilting plastic lawn table. Father Jude opened the box, removed a cigarette from a package, lighted it for the old priest, and then sat down patiently to wait as Father Damien breathed in the rank, dry heat. As he intermittently drew quiet puffs and gazed into the fractured halos of moving branches, he spoke.

"Now tell me"—Father Damien's lips pursed in a calculating bud—"what would be the most, let us say, *effective* time to reveal what I know of this departed nun's character?"

Father Jude attempted a reply, but the side-to-side jolts of Father Damien's mental processes were wearing. Father Damien disregarded the other priest, smoothed his cassock thoughtfully around his knees, adjusted his eyeglass lenses along his nose, and continued in tones of firm analysis.

"I would like to establish myself as the crucial witness in the archive. I want to tread the quicksand of the bureaucratic process. I want to walk on hidden trails of solid ground! I have lived, I believe"—here Father Damien raised a finger to his lips, inhaled absently from the now dead cigarette—"a quiet life. I have sought no following, engaged in no behaviors, holy or otherwise, that would bring me notoriety. I have done only as I was directed by Jesus, with whom I have a personal understanding. In no way have I attempted to invoke or incite spiritual response from others based solely on features of my own personality. I have tried, in other words, to serve God invisibly."

Father Jude Miller held his peace with an air of vacant gravity. He believed he knew where the old priest was heading, and he did agree: the nun in question's life had been a contrast. No retiring servant was she, Leopolda, but a fiercely masterful woman whose resounding bitterness of spirit had nonetheless resulted in acts of troubling goodness, inspirations, even miraculous involvements. Which raised the question: Were saints only saints by virtue of their influence, their following, their reputation for the marvelous, or was there room for personal failure—especially when, as evidenced by the miracles and eighteen letters so far, the results of that difficult life were so dramatically good?

"I have here," said Father Jude, "a copy of a crudely written letter that I will read to you in order to inform you more thoroughly on the important uncertainties we face in regard to Leopolda."

"By all means."

"'Dear Bishop,'" read Father Jude, "'I run my farming operation just west of town nearby which the place is where the nun Leopolda was hit by lightning and her ashes blown into the convent beehives produced in one $2.99 jar (large) of honey I bought from there concern the following cure of livelong piles. . . .'"

Father Damien remained impassive as Jude finished out the missive.

"And this one," Father Jude went on, choosing from a file folder he had with him. "'I am a strict atheist engaged in the practice of medicine. My specialty is cardiac surgery. My private practice, based in Fargo, North Dakota, encompasses unusual cases from the surrounding region. In February of this year I saw a young girl who suffered a severe case of an unusual virus that destroyed the membrane surrounding the heart and had begun to attack the muscle itself . . .'"

"That last," said Father Damien, lips pressed in a worried line, "fully documented?"

"Complete."

"Ah then . . ." Father Damien shook his head. Consternation soured his features. "What to make of it. Medical cures!"

"Well, the one, the first . . ." Father Jude shook his head, raised his brows.

"I would never make light of piles," said Father Damien, "but is there incontrovertible proof that this man suffered from hemorrhoids through the course of his life and then was cured by the honey sold by the bee-keeping nuns? The proof is marginal, at best.

"And this ash and bee connection, what of that?" Father Damien went on. "Can you shed some light on that?"

"What light I can." Father Jude took a long sip of water. "According to the most lucid witness—the person who saw Leopolda in the hour before her death—Leopolda was left in the garden to pray, and of course, as we regret, struck by a bolt of lightning. Next morning, we remarked on the mysterious cross made of ash that was found in the place she'd been left—of course no one knew she was missing yet. The ash blew into the flowers. The flowers, visited by bees, were the source of the wonder-working honey, and then of course . . . the witness—"

"Who was this witness?"

"Sister Adelphine. She cared for most of Leopolda's earthly needs. The night she died, Adelphine left her sitting piously in her ground-floor cell, which opened into the garden. The old nun often ventured outside, to contemplate the image of Christ as she saw it in the growing plants."

Jude stopped, eyeing a wan cinnamon bun left on Father Damien's plate. He couldn't help it. His appetite was constant, vexing.

"Have it," said Father Damien, wishing it were an adequate bribe.

Father Jude reached over and delicately, with his soft, blunt fingers pinched up the bun and ate it in two bites.

"The question, or task before us right now," he said, chewing, "is establishing your knowledge of Sister Leopolda, your history, your"—here he sought the word—"claim. No, I don't mean that exactly. Your authority. Your expertise. Frankly"—and here Father Jude smiled—"I don't anticipate a problem. Everybody else . . . her contemporaries are dead."

"Oh really," said Father Damien, and though he cast down his eyes in seeming respect there was a gloating satisfaction in his frail voice that made Father Jude glance sharply at the profile of the older priest. As soon as he felt his composure slip, Father Damien recovered and assumed a righteous, blank, carefully focused clerical air. Still, Father Jude's pale eyes remained upon him, and the gaze he maintained revealed a sharp speculative intelligence.

"Just for the hell of it," he said, smiling a tight smile, "or the heaven of it. I'm going to ask, I mean, in general. Was she?"

"Was she what? What are you saying?" said Father Damien, although he knew full well.

"Was she a saint?" asked Father Jude simply.

There was silence after his question, in which a hush of wind trembled in the leaves. Suddenly, through that corridor of extreme quiet, there sounded a harsh cacophony. Crows with human thrill had mobbed a great owl. The bird floated eerily, like a gray thrust of wind, in and out of Father Jude's eyeshot, chased by a wheeling tumble of black feathers. Dark laughter. Their shrieks seemed to Jude's ears both hilarious and foul. Father Damien's voice barely cut through the din.

"There is your answer," he said.

Creamed corn and ground-beef casserole, macaroni, a dish of hot, vinegary string beans, squares of rhubarb crumble. Lunch came wrapped in foil with twin place settings. At a small table of chipped enamel, set outside beneath the wild grapevine arbor, the two sat and made appreciative sounds as a brooding and massively built woman removed the aluminum sheets, folded them for future reuse, and loomed silently over Damien.

"Father Jude, I would like to introduce you to Mary Kashpaw. She is my housekeeper, keeper of the church grounds, master general of all you see."

A slight smile tweaked the corner of Mary Kashpaw's line of a mouth, cut like a seam in stone. Her eyes gentled as they rested on the old man, then narrowed as she turned her attention to Father Jude. As she slowly assessed the visitor, she stiffened into a mountain and became so monumentally rooted that it was almost a surprise when she walked away. Slightly shaken by her presence, though without any reason he could discern, Jude busied himself, poured thin coffee into white ceramic mugs. Father Damien frowned.

"Have you," he peered behind Father Miller, "brought a bit of wine, perhaps, to complement the meal?"

"If I'd known." Father Miller hooked his shoulders.

"No matter." Father Damien waved his hands. "Best, anyway, that I abstain. At least for this particular afternoon."

"You'll need your wits about you." Father Miller was teasing, but even so his demeanor was challenging enough to quicken Damien's pulse, causing, in turn, an increase of circulation that often led to heartburn. Damien picked slowly at his food, raised a string bean to his lips, bit the end off, chewed, put it down again. In the meantime, Jude Miller ate two-handed, busily sopping up extra juice with a piece of soft white bread while rhythmically forking the hot dish into his mouth. He was a powerful and appreciative eater, and he gave his whole attention to the mediocre meal, took another portion of the string beans, polished his plate with more bread, ate his dessert with gusto, settled back to the coffee while Damien nibbled another bean.

"They're good," said Jude Miller, unconvincingly.

"Mary Kashpaw. I know her beans, only too well. A little white vinegar, pinch of sugar, salt."

"Pepper, too," Jude said, coughing. He put down his fork. "Your housekeeper . . ." He asked how long she'd been with Father Damien, and was surprised when he answered that the great woman had worked on the grounds, cared for the church and graveyard, lived with the nuns since she was a child, and then cared for his household since she was grown.

"The story of her existence is also my story here," said Father Damien. "Her story and mine are twined up from the roots of the place. There is no telling my story without hers! It began immediately after my arrival here in 1912, with a visit to the notorious Nanapush, who tricked me into obtaining for him a wife. Mary Kashpaw was the victim of my earliest mistake, an innocent, though she has seen all of life one way or another since. It all goes back to conversion, Father, a most ticklish concept and a most loving form of destruction. I've not come to terms with the notion even now, in my age, when I should be peacefully moldering up there on the hillside with the bones of my friends."

Father Jude followed the other priest's gaze, saw the gentle brown granite markers, the sheltering oak trees, the pale lichen-eaten crosses, the neat and faded plastic flowers on wire legs, the whole array of memoria spread out up and over the quiet hill.

PART TWO

The
DEADLY
CONVERSIONS

4

THE ROAD TO
LITTLE NO HORSE

1996

The old priest tottered exhaustedly into his little house and closed himself into the bathroom. Washed his face, his hands, dried them carefully and slowly with a soft hand towel. Combed his white fluff. He felt a burning sensation along the corners of his eyes and he realized that he needed to weep. That afternoon with Father Miller, he'd drowsed and awakened to hear himself talking, talking too eagerly, though of course he kept back his deepest secrets. He'd known then what memories he was headed for, what scenes, what sorrows beyond imagining that had forever changed him. No! He lunged toward his desk, for the task of letter writing would, he hoped, throw him off course and allow the memory of his first years to pass him much as storms passed over bearing within their clouds whirlwinds that did not touch the earth.

On the Eve of St. Dismas, once again. At some late hour.

Dear Holy Father,

It is with a sense of gratitude and excitement that I address you tonight, largely in order to praise and give thanks for the notice denied me by your predecessors, but also, if I may be so unworthy, to lodge a small complaint. Although you've no doubt dispatched a priest deemed competent by his superiors here in the Middle West of the United States, I feel it my compelling duty to sadly inform you that not only is Father Jude Miller an obvious amateur at interviews, but he seems to have in coming here some agenda ulterior to that which he is dispatched to learn. In short, master of my vocation, I think he's something of a dud. With false intentions to boot. I cast no aspersions upon those who chose him for this task. Your cardinals did, of course, check his credentials, but with the explosion of technology these days it is so easy to present an impressive paper face to the authorities when in actuality the subject lacks . . .

Useless ploy. He smelled the ashes of fever, the scent of wormwood and roses, tinctures of blessed oil. Here it came. Father Damien's vision sank inward, into the past.

THE ARRIVAL

1912

Just as in a dream or under extreme duress, we make plans and decisions that panic us with their force and strangeness by the light of day, so Agnes shocked herself. The first morning that she woke on the train heading north, in disguise, she reeled with her own foolhardiness and thought of leaping out of the caboose. The train was slow enough, but was traveling through a waste of open land in which only rarely could she pick out the slightest human feature. Surely she'd die of exposure out there. And then the train stopped at a small board shack hardly bigger than an outhouse.

She spent the night there, curled around the lukewarm flanks of a rusted stove. Tomorrow, she thought, I'll get rid of this cassock and be Agnes DeWitt again, formerly Sister Cecilia, who has lived enough for two women and two nuns already, let alone a mission priest. She imagined that she'd find some way of trading clothing or if all else failed come clean with the nearest sane person in North Dakota. But she was alone. And considering what she'd just done, probably no judge of sanity. The next morning, she waited miserably for the driver who, it said in a tattered note nailed to the wall, would transport the priest to Little No Horse. By the time the wagon arrived, Agnes was so famished with hunger that she had dipped into a sack waiting next to her and chewed some raw, dusty oats. Though in a daze of passivity, when she found herself climbing into the seat of a rough wagon drawn by winter-shagged horses and driven by a man still rougher than the whole lot, her heart clenched and the urge again took her to bolt back into the skin of Miss DeWitt. But how could she? Perhaps once the wagon stopped, once they'd arrived, she'd seize a chance.

They started out for the reservation in the wake of a killing sickness, on the eve of St. Dismas in the gain of the year. March, Onaabani-giizis, it is called. Crust-on-the-snow moon, for the angle of the sun strikes just so, enough to melt and refreeze the surface while the snow lies beneath. Ever after that day, Agnes was to mark St. Dismas upon her calendar because it was the first day of her existence as Father Damien, the first day of the great lie that was her life—the true lie, she considered it, the most sincere lie a person could ever tell.

Agnes was a person of deep curiosity, and so even in extremity she couldn't help observing all around her that was new. She rode along with interest, even though her brain was half frozen and she suffered stabs of intense cold. On the way to the reservation, she found intriguing correspondences with her old life. The river was flooding three hundred miles to the south because to the north its mouth was still frozen. So in a way, she thought, the region had conspired with itself to bring her north, to dump her from her house into the current where she was rescued and where she changed clothing with the priest—ah, the priest's clothes! That was another thing. Even now, the driver treated her with much more respect as a priest than she'd ever known as a nun. He was deferential, though not uncomfortable. Agnes was surprised to find that this treatment entirely gratified her, and yet seemed familiar as though it was her due. Robes or not, I am human, she said to herself. So this is what a priest gets, heads bowing and curious respectful attention! Back on the train, people also had given Father Damien more privacy. It was as though in priest's garments she walked within a clear bell of charged air.

Priest or not, the rain fell, wetting and then filming the road with a dangerous slick, coating her face and icing the goods crowded into the loaded wagon. She hunched underneath a powerfully dusty old buffalo robe, shook miserably, and then warmed as the ride bumped her forward, into her strange new life.

Kashpaw was the driver's name. He was the first Indian she'd ever met and he would be one of the first she'd bury, come that summer and the feast of saints. He was dark and in the cold his skin took on a purplish cast. Dressed as he was in a French red wool capote with a swirl of hot yellow turban cloth and weighted by moosehide leggings, great mitts made of wolves' fur, velvet shawls, and another curly buffalo robe thrown on besides, he was a mountain of texture and sharp color. He spoke, of course, no German, only some English, and his French was of a vintage extremely valuable were it only wine. In addition, that eighteenth-century trapper's French was knocked aside or disarranged by words only to be guessed at—probably the language spoken by Ojibwe. And yet in spite of their language problems, Agnes couldn't help questioning Kashpaw eagerly. Something new was at work, she could feel it, an ease with her own mind she'd never felt before, a pleasure in her own wit she'd half hidden or demurred. As Agnes, she'd always felt too inhibited to closely question men. Questions from women to men always raised questions of a different nature. As a man, she found that Father Damien was free to pursue all questions with frankness and ease.

On the long drive north, she learned all of the polite Ojibwe she could cram into her brain—how to ask after children and spouses, how to comment on the weather, how to accept and appreciate food. These last phrases, unfortunately, would be useless until there actually was food on the reservation.

The road was slick, frozen muck under the hooves of the wild, tough horses, so Kashpaw halted the wagon. From under the seat he took eight snugly made straps that fitted neatly around the horses' pasterns. He fixed onto the bottom of their hooves sharply studded contraptions that enabled them to grip the ice. Along they went, then, more secure. As they traveled, Kashpaw laboriously made known further details of the situation Father Damien would face. There was starvation, but with luck the thaw would end its grip. In addition to the priest, Kashpaw had picked up eighteen sacks of horse-grade oats. This rough slurry was to be distributed among twice as many families and would make up their diets until the false winter entirely broke— the snow and ice still looked to have a strong hold on the land.

"What can be done?"

Kashpaw looked shrewdly at Father Damien. He took in the open, girlish earnestness, the curiosity, the restless hands tapping patterns on the robes, the intelligent regard. At last, he decided the priest was both harmless and worth challenging.

"Some say, go back to the old ways."

"And what do you say?"

Kashpaw narrowed his eyes at the ice road, snapped the reins lightly on his horses' rumps. When he smiled to himself, his huge soft face rounded in gentle humorous curves that Agnes found compelling. The only Indians she'd known were pictures in a book—in her part of Wisconsin, they were hated and cleared out. Once she had escaped her family, entered the convent, and taken up music, of course, there was very little to see or know of the outside world. So this new sort of human next to her, his self-possessed knowledge, upset her with an intense wish to understand everything about him.

"Here's what I say," he answered at last. "Leave us full-bloods alone, let us be with our Nanabozho, our sweats and shake tents, our grand medicines and bundles. We don't hurt nobody. Your wiisaakodewinini- wag, half-burnt wood, they can use your God as backup to these things. Our world is already whipped apart by the white man. Why do you black gowns care if we pray to your God?"

All that he said was strange to Agnes, and again she had to question him on each point. The half-burnt wood referred to half-breed people. Nanabozho was someone she would hear of often—a god, a story figure. The sweats and the shake tents were houses where

Ojibwe ceremonies took place. All of this, he took his time to patiently explain. Agnes watched him closely, memorizing him, feeling in her heart he was so certain of himself that he would be impossible to convert. The great firm slabs of Kashpaw's cheeks were pitted with dark pocks. As she found out later, he had survived that particular killing scourge only to lose many of his family. The abyss of loss had led him to his present complex marital situation—a problem with which Father Damien would presently become involved. For the time, as they endured the miles, Kashpaw's openhearted ease was reassuring. Between the two, there grew a pleasant, thoughtful, silence. The space around the wagon, boundless and gray, serene and cold, changed only subtly as they passed through on the nearly invisible road. Suspended in the whiteness, they could have been traveling in place. The wheels moved, the wagon jounced and rocked, but nothing changed. The land rolled on in bitter white monotony.

The cold bit down, harder. Kashpaw maintained a politely fixed expression while his thoughts turned. He was a shrewd man, and he sensed something unusual about the priest from the first. Something wrong. The priest was clearly not right, too womanly. Perhaps, he thought, here was a man like the famous Wishkob, the Sweet, who had seduced many other men and finally joined the family of a great war chief as a wife, where he had lived until old, well loved, as one of the women. Kashpaw himself had addressed Wishkob as grandmother. Kashpaw thought, *This priest is unusual, but then, who among the zhaaganaashiwug is not strange?*

The two fell deeper into private thoughts, and let the screeching and knocking of the wheels take over until at last the horizon grew, upon its distant edge, a deeper set to the filmy pearl, then a definite gray patch that slowly gained detail. There were hills now, covered in bare-leafed oak, and soon there were houses among those hills, small and modest little cabins neatly plumed with smoke, for a windless, icy seizure gripped the settlement and woods beyond. The wind of the great plains dropped off in this complex shelter, diminished by windbreaks of earth and mixed forest. They passed into the hills, through a town that centered around a modest trader's store, seeing only one or two Indians at a distance. The people were dressed in farmers' clothes, some in thin swaths of cloth and some heavily jacketed in wools.

The road to the settlement at Little No Horse led up, gently at first, but there was in those days a fierce, ungraded climb near the end. At last, the ice became too smooth for even the strong horses—their heavily feathered fetlocks and thick necks showing draft blood along with Sioux war-pony fleetness and nerve. One nearly slipped to its knees. Kashpaw stopped the wagon and wished Father Damien *bonne chance* in climbing the rest of the way on foot.

All alone, then, bearing on her back the thinly strapped bag, Agnes slipped and toiled, smashing continually through the snow's glassy crust. The sharp ice pierced the crude leggings she'd made of a rough stole found in the priest's bag and bloodied her shaking calves. By the time she clawed and scrambled to the hilltop, she was exhausted to the point of nausea and lay down to gasp for breath.

There was stillness, the whisper of snow grains driven along the surface of the world. It was the silence of before creation, the comfort of pure nothing, and she let herself go into it until, in that quiet, she was caught hold of by a dazzling sweetness. In the grip of this sudden, sumptuous bloom of feeling, Agnes rose and walked toward a poor cabin just behind the log church. Entering this new life, she felt a largeness move through her, a sense that she was essential to a great, calm design of horizonless meaning. There was the crooked-built church, the cabin silent as a shut mouth, the convent painted a blistering white—the scenery of Father Damien's future.

Silence held.

In that period of regard, the unsettled intentions, the fears she felt, the exposure she already dreaded, faded to a fierce nothing, a white ring of mineral ash left after the water has boiled away. There would be times that she missed the ease of moving in her old skin, times that Father Damien was pierced by womanness and suffered. Still, Agnes was certain now that she had done the right thing. Father Damien Modeste had arrived here. The true Modeste who was supposed to arrive—none other. No one else.

DEATH ROBES

All great visions must suffer the test of the ordinary, and Agnes's was immediate. She unlatched the door of the small tight-built cabin, her first rectory, and stood in the dim entry adjusting her eyes to the sadness. Just here, Damien's predecessor, Father Hugo LaCombe, tough and well trained, one of the first, had died of a sweating fever. Upon the cabin's floor a scatter of stiff photographs. Agnes picked up the card of a woman, perhaps a sister of Hugo's, wearing a floral hat. His brother, cradling a gun. These people stared out, frozen in a bad dream. She stacked the pictures on the table. Touched an extra folded cassock, underclothing, a silver holy medal on a nail driven into the frosted gray wood next to the window. The bed made of sagging willow poles was covered with heavy quilts and buffalo robes, stripped beneath. Had someone at least taken out the linen? No, there it was, balled in a corner, rusted with the blood of poor Father Hugo and, even in the cold, smelling of shit and gall.

Father Damien didn't want to pray. Nevertheless Agnes went down on her knees and spoke earnestly aloud. There was no answer but the howl of wind rattling shingles, the mice drifting in the eaves. There was no wood for a fire. No water but ice. Enough, she thought. Wearily, she climbed into Father Hugo's deathbed. She wrapped herself tightly into the death robes, slept.

She dreamed first of black nails driven through the tender bloody sac of her heart. Dreamed second of Berndt's trusting gaze. In a third dream, which lasted the rest of the night, Agnes ate and drank at an endless table. Boiled carrots. Foaming milk. Fresh, buttered potatoes in their jackets, thick stews of meat and onions. She woke more desperate with hunger than ever in her life, her stomach gnawing, pinching, her mouth still working on the rich imaginary meal. Some Catholic on the train had given her a bit of jerky, which she chewed still huddled in the quilts. There was no need to dress, as she'd slept in Father Damien's clothes for warmth. There was no washbasin. She reached out, rubbed her teeth and face with a handful of snow sifted onto the sill of the ill-fitting window. She combed the tatters of her hair back with stiff fingers, swatted strings of dust from her arms and chest. She then bundled on the dead priest's heavy black wool cloak and walked out.

MIRACLE OF THE MEAT

The nuns lived in a small white frame building of two rooms, one for eating and one for sleeping, pitilessly cold within. There were no sisters in sight, but on the rough board table Agnes spied a pot of tea steeping lukewarm on a towel. She drained it from the spout, then opened a cupboard and found a poor rock-hard bit of bread beside a thimble's worth of raisins. The meal, however paltry, gave her the strength to walk over to the church, where the six nuns had dragged themselves to say their morning prayers.

Snow as fine as smoke blew in as she entered the church, but the nuns did not move. They knelt, hunched in cold, swathed in layers of patched wool, quiet as stones. There was only one parishioner in attendance, and in spite of the extremity of the cold and the tension of her first test in saying Mass, Agnes noticed her. The girl seemed, in her stiffness, to creak as she turned to watch. She stared as Father Damien walked to the nave of the church.

The girl's nose jutted, her face was white and beak-thin, and her mouth was shaped by birth into a pale and twisted line. She stared at the priest with great, starved, black, disturbing eyes. Stared unblinking and with fixed aggressiveness. Young and scrawny as a new bird, she opened her mouth as though to shout, then shut it as Father Damien put out his hands to the women, the sisters, and held their hands and greeted them—the sight of their resigned and exhausted faces washed over him with a familiar tenderness.

"My dear sisters in Christ, my dear, dear sisters . . ."

They rose in surprise. Apparently, Father Damien wasn't expected to arrive—thus the terrible disorder of the cabin. Their faces, gazing dull, were the maws of starved animals and their fingers were limp as wilted stalks. By the shape of their skulls, the wrinkled hands of privation, it was easy to see death was poking through their very skins. For the first time, now, Agnes was afraid, for she knew that the food she had eaten back in the convent was absolutely all they had.

"Let us pray," Father Damien's voice squeaked. Agnes tried to control the shaking and keep her voice low, but her tongue was thick with cold despair. She remembered to venerate the relic in the altar— what was it: splinters from the true cross? a filing from St. Peter's manacles? perhaps a bit of bone, a slice of skin, a toe, an ear? What saint? How would she find out or ever know? It was the priest's job to know. There was no altar boy, no vestments, and the chalice was humble pewter, but when Father Damien opened the sacristy and found fourteen holy wafers and a thread of wine, he turned in elation to the sisters.

"We have no choir"—he was already half delirious again with hunger—"but we will raise our best hymn! Body of Christ, blood of Christ, same here as in the richest cathedral. This is our cloth-of-gold." He touched the burlap weave of the mantle, laid out on the altar stone. "This is our pearl-studded gospel." He lovingly stroked the rag-bound book. "Our incense is God's own breath—the wind through these rough walls!"

The women sighed together, all except for the one parishioner, the seething girl in a black scarf. She laughed out loud, screeched really, then coughed to contain her mirth. The nuns seemed numb to her. They prayed together and a cloud of breath stirred from their lips. Their hands were blistered with cold, their cheeks frostbitten and raw. The priest's words were brave, but the sisters were at the razor edge of their endurance. They slumped against the wood of the pews, barely managed to hold themselves upright.

At least, now, the fire in the little tin stove had begun to warm the cabin of the church.

The Mass came to Agnes like memorized music. She had only to say the first words and all followed, ordered, instinctive. The phrases were in her and part of her. Once she began, the flow was like the river that had carried her to Little No Horse. In the silences between the parts of the ritual, Father Damien prayed for those women in his charge.

"*Quam oblationem, tu Deus, in omnibus quaesumus, benedictam . . .*" He crossed his breast five times, within those words, and the next: "*Qui pridie quam pateretur, accepit panem in sanctas ac venerabiles manus suas . . .*" And lifted his eyes and said the words "*Hoc est enim corpus meum,*" and the bread was flesh.

Of course it was, as it always was.

"*Hic est enim calix sanguinis mei novi et aeterni testamenti: mysterium fedei . . .*" The wine was blood.

And again, as she had before, the strange girl in the front pew emitted a sudden croak of laughter.

On her lips, in her mouth. Real and rich, heavy, good. Agnes choked with startled shock. She hesitated, put the food to her mouth again. Real! Real! Hunger roared in her as she broke the bread. Ate the flesh. Delivering the communion meal to her starving sisters, Agnes was caught in a panic of emotion. She heard nothing, saw nothing, went through the rest of Mass on reeling instinct. Was it really true and had they, as well, experienced what she'd felt? Was this something that happened, always, to priests? Did their part of the sacrament transubstantiate in real as well as metaphorical terms? Had the dry thin consecrated Host turned into a thick mouthful of raw, tender, bloody, sweet-tasting meat in the mouths of the sisters? And the wine to vital blood? And were they all full, as Agnes felt, satisfied and calm? They finished the Mass and stumbled back, holding one another by turns, all except for the black-eyed child, who abruptly left, quite alone, prompting Agnes to ask the nun nearest for the name of this striking person.

"She's a Puyat," said the sister. "Her name is Pauline. She is here every morning, most devout, but . . ." She paused as if to say something more, but only shrugged as though, after all, she was too weak to explain.

Once alone, Agnes went dizzy with questions.

Had Christ's real presence entered them? Certainly, now, they were saved from the place of skulls, from the bones of death. Were they fed with the fat of the wheat and honey out of the rock? Was this just part of the ritual or was it miraculous?

That night, she composed Father Damien's first letter.

March 1912

Gracious Leader of the Faith,

I write in humble fearfulness and wonder. To whom else might I turn? I beg you to indulge me, Your Holiness. Please forgive my attempt to explain, though it be insufficient. It is just that to reconstruct, to go back, to establish the scene requires at present a spiritual energy I cannot summon. I am reeling. I have such questions.

To wit: Have you or your holy minions knowledge of a case

*in which the transubstantiated body and blood of Christ has
in actuality (and I mean physically, not only in a spiritual
sense) nourished the flock?*

*In other words, did the wafer turn into visible meat, the
wine to actual blood?*

*And also, to your understanding, would it be wrong for a
cleric to request a visit by the devil, just to make certain of
his physical shape?*

I await your reply.

SISTER HILDEGARDE'S VIEWS

The Superior, Sister Hildegarde Anne, was a woman of German
resourcefulness. Short, boxy, impenetrable, she had saved her sisters,
as well as many others, early on that winter by ordering the church
horse butchered while it still had flesh, and distributing its store of
oats and grain. She had a toughness of expression unusual in a nun,
and spoke bluntly. Also, she was effortlessly cheerful in a way that
often outraged or frightened other people. Now, for instance, as she
spoke to Father Damien in the intimacy of the kitchen, she shaved
the last of that poor beast's hooves into a pot of boiling soup water. As
she worked, she hummed and then sang out, trimming the great
rocky chunk of chitin with a sharp filet knife. Beside the soup pot,
half a precious potato soaked in salted water. The sparsity didn't seem
to bother her. Someone had left six other potatoes and a rind of bacon,
held now under lock and key. All of this would keep the religious
band alive today, and today, she said, was as far as she ever went in
her prayers.

Although Agnes felt what she felt, believed what she believed,
about what had happened during the Eucharist, the two exchanged no
more than a significant sentence. Agnes was to find that Sister Hildegarde was of such deeply skeptical stock that she did not entirely
accept her own experience as true. Hildegarde's concerns were down-
to-earth. Since she was on the reservation to be useful, she lost no
time in telling Father Damien how he could make himself useful too.

"Father," said Hildegarde, "you must go visiting with the sacrament. The poor Indians are dying out. Now is a good time to convert them! They live like wretches anyway, and then the sweating fever takes them. Some are gone in only hours once the illness sets in, so you must be quick. Some wait for death to walk down the road. They just sit patiently, singing, drumming, and prepare to get sick. You could easily baptize them while they're tranced."

"What cures this fever? Who is our doctor?" Agnes ignored the nun's avidity regarding souls. Yes, she thought, Father Damien was bound to baptize. But she must read up because she couldn't remember much of anything about the ritual or the words. She pursued the subject of the illness itself.

"We have no regular doctor, but the cure is plain. Food, warmth."

"Simply that?"

"It is possible, with skillful care, to nurse even a weak subject through this fever. We could have saved Father Hugo, had he only come to us!"

"Why didn't he?"

"Father Hugo wouldn't endanger us, and so hid his condition. Barred himself inside of his cabin. He was sick to death by the time we broke in. And then, of course," she said with hurt pride, "you found the place in sad repair. We hadn't any notion you would stay there but had a place for you with a pious family. You see, we have not entered to clean for fear of the fever . . . only the Puyat doesn't fear most illness. She was supposed to have cleaned."

"The one at the Mass this morning?"

"That one."

"No need," Agnes said, anxious even then to avoid contact with the girl. "I'm trained to keep my surroundings in good order."

"Oh," Hildegarde was a bit surprised. "Very unlike poor Father Hugo!"

Poor Hugo. With a powerful thrust, a scene stabbed into Agnes's mind. She saw the priest laboriously sinking, taking leave of the world alone, speaking his good-bye prayers. She struggled to gain control of her exhaustion. The walk from the river had been endless, the train smoky and jolting, the miserable wait in the foul railroad hut a foretaste of hell. The drive with Kashpaw was encouraging, but Agnes had hardly slept the previous night and now could not battle the pressure of tears and more tears. She tried to lean on last night's certainty, tried to keep her faith with the Christ who had fed her broth and taken on a human shape to give her comfort. She must follow through with the original plan, the vision. But to find herself here, in the midst of another's vocation, was shockingly difficult. What had she supposed? Father Damien was in charge of these souls!

"I am nowhere near as strong as the confidence Christ has placed in me," she said to Hildegarde Anne, who sighed.

"None of us is."

Agnes was tempted, next, to confess the specifics of her identity, the nature of her calling, to this good nun. After all, she looks much more capable than I, she thought with a certain faint hope. But Sister Hildegarde, perhaps sensing the despair of her tormented self-sympathy, squeezed Agnes's hand in hers so hard she cracked the knuckles.

"I prayed for a priest just like you," she said, "young, with a tough, fresh faith!"

So Agnes shut Father Damien's mouth on that revelation.

"Show me all you know of this place," she demanded instead, steadying Father Damien's voice and stilling the quaver in her heart.

Sister Hildegarde drew out a path with the stub of a pencil. "This bisects the land they call 'their' reservation," she said. "The place is shaped roughly like a house with a square beneath and one slanted roof, a jutting outpost like a chimney. They'll lose all the land, of course, being unused to the owning of land. Incredibly, it makes no sense to them. They avow, in their own peculiar way, that the earth is only on loan. Yet, it's going constantly into private ownership and already they are selling out to lumber interests. Father, your poor charges cannot read the documents they sign."

Here, Hildegarde was obviously distressed—she hated a bad business deal. "The government is not so much our problem," she blurted out. "It is the thieves that surround us!"

She showed every path and road, labeled cabins on the reservation, pointed out where certain of the most faithful parishioners lived.

"Here, here, and here"—she pointed at nearly every spot—"the sickness has taken someone. Here, it took them all." She stabbed out several places upon her map. Seeing the nun's finger smash down, Agnes's heart was touched with horror. The still cabin. The huddled forms. The unspeakable loneliness. Tears flashed again and Hildegarde, seeing this, slapped a dish towel on Father Damien's arm.

"No use for that," the nun grumped. "Now here, here, here, and here all died but two, I've heard—a stubborn girl, an old man. They live out there yet."

"I must go to them."

Sister Hildegarde agreed, but looked a bit worried. "Father Damien, they live way out in the bush, if they're living at all yet. The older man is a stubborn, crafty, talkative sort, much resistant to conversion. The vile things he says, the reprobate! He had a big old toot with my communion wine two years ago. Sneaked it from my cellar cask. He's too tricky to die, him. And the other, that Fleur. Truly the daughter of Satan, so they say. The two of them, almost the only ones to survive from their respective families, are rumored to have special powers."

As the nun spoke, Agnes breathed in deep drafts to gather control of her sorrow, and when she had, she took on the studied authority she'd mustered in private.

"I'm always intrigued with special powers," she said mildly. "What sort of skills do you mean?"

Hildegarde shrugged, dismissive. "The usual. Drumming their drums. Singing until it breaks your ears. Shaking stuffed skins, rattles, and bones, so I've heard. All ineffective against the slightest of colds."

"I see." Though Agnes did not see. "What else?"

"They are the last of their families, as I've said. I think that gives them some sort of conjuring skill. There are magicians among them, of course, cheap tricksters. They throw their voices and levitate. They scare the gullible to death and are said to wing balls of fire toward their enemies at night. We've seen a few, you know, whiz by us up here! Unimpressive!"

"So you believe in their skills."

Hildegarde looked sharply at the priest.

"Believe, why yes, just as I believe it is possible to hide coins and pebbles behind the ears of small children and draw these objects forth to delight them. It is easy to mystify children. Their conjurers employ just such means to prey upon the gullible. That is all."

I am sent here, thought Agnes, to accept and to absorb. I shall be a thick cloth. Therefore, she nodded and said nothing in answer, but only thanked the nun for speaking frankly.

Some Rules to Assist in My Transformation
1. *Make requests in the form of orders.*
2. *Give compliments in the form of concessions.*
3. *Ask questions in the form of statements.*
4. *Exercises to enhance the muscles of the neck?*
5. *Admire women's handiwork with copious amazement.*
6. *Stride, swing arms, stop abruptly, stroke chin.*
7. *Sharpen razor daily.*
8. *Advance no explanations.*
9. *Accept no explanations.*
10. *Hum an occasional resolute march.*

A parishioner had left a Sears catalog near the door of the church, and Agnes rifled through it secretly, as much to revisit the clothing, the china, the unfamiliar feast of powders and perfumes, as to scheme a way to purchase Dr. Feem's Scientific Programme of Muscular Expansion, a kit that involved a set of dumbbells, a book of directions, and one muscle tonic that promised to improve the tone of the entire upper body and another bottle that worked on the half below.

5

SPIRIT TALK

1912

The reservation at the time was a place still fluid of definition, appearing solid only on a map, taking in and cutting out whole farms sometimes on the say-so of the commissioner, or the former agent Tatro, and other times attempting to right itself according to law. It was a place of shifting allegiances, new feuds and old animosities, a place of clan teasing, jealousy, comfort, and love. As with most other reservations, the government policy of attempting to excite pride in private ownership by doling parcels of land to individual Ojibwe flopped miserably and provided a feast of acquisition for hopeful farmers and surrounding entrepreneurs. So the boundaries came and went, drawn to accommodate local ventures—sawmills, farms, feed stores, the traplines of various families.

Many did sell for one simple reason. Hunger. As the government scrambled for the correct legal definition of the land, any fluctuation meant loss, any loophole was to the advantage of the thieves, boosters, businessmen, swindlers, sneaks, Christians, cranks, lumber and farm dealers, con artists, and reprobates of all types who had drifted to the edges of reservations hoping to profit from the confusion.

Into this complex situation walked Father Damien, with only the vaguest notion of how the ownership of land related to the soul.

THE LOSS

She transformed herself each morning with a feeling of loss that she finally defined as the loss of Agnes. Ah, Agnes! She lived at night in the shelter of bedclothes. Disappeared in daylight, bandages wrapped as when she had been a nun. As she left the cabin, her thoughts became Damien's thoughts. Her voice his voice, which deepened as his stride lengthened and grew bold. Agnes's speech had always been husky and low for a woman. Father Damien's voice was musical, for a man. There were gestures left over from the convent, and also from her life as a woman in love. In the convent, she'd been taught to walk with eyes downcast. Now, Father Damien tipped his chin out and narrowed his gaze, focused straight ahead. As a farm wife, Agnes had leaned out with a hand on her hip, carried things on her hip, nudged doors open and shut with her hip. Men didn't use their hips as shelves and braces. Father Damien walked with soldierly directness and never swayed. Nor did he touch a finger to his tongue and smooth his eyebrows, or glance at himself in mirror surfaces. Sternly, he nodded up and down when he listened instead of tipping his head to the side.

Between these two, where was the real self? It came to her that both Sister Cecilia and then Agnes were as heavily manufactured of gesture and pose as was Father Damien. And within this, what sifting of identity was she? What mote? What nothing?

Now and then Agnes recalled a tiny portion of her encounter with the Actor, and she came to understand it as a sure prefigurement and sign of what was to come. The Actor had influenced the quality of Father Damien's disguise, for when Agnes was held by that rope-tough arm against the car door she'd felt remote enough, from blood loss, to marvel at and assess the Actor's change in personality from priest to robber.

Father Damien was both a robber and a priest. For what is it to entertain a daily deception? Wasn't he robbing all who looked upon him? Stealing their trust? Shameful, perhaps, but Agnes was surprised to find that the thought only gave her satisfaction. She felt no guilt, and so concluded that if God sent none she would not invent any. She decided to miss Agnes as she would a beloved sister, to make of Father Damien her creation. He would be loving, protective, remote, and immensely disciplined. He would be Agnes's twin, her masterwork, her brother.

NANAPUSH

Agnes said Father Damien's office early and long one morning, with extra fervor because she was still in bed. She needed the strength. She had decided to visit the reprobate Nanapush, who survived marginally in the bush somewhere with the young woman named Fleur. The air deeply chilled her and cold stabbed up through the icy boards. She put on every stitch of clothing, even Father Hugo's. Still, she trembled walking out into the bitter air. Longing for the sad warmth of her predecessor's willow-pole bed, imagining the comfort of burrowing under the leaden quilts and buffalo robes, she ate a sorry breakfast of cooked potato skins and tea. Such food, now, only worsened the stab in her stomach. She was comforted by the news that the roads were open and there would soon be supplies, enough for everyone. Six wagons would be arriving with relief.

She wrapped her blistered and frost-burned feet in several layers of the nun's dish towels, pulled on her boots, then she took from Sister Hildegarde the scratchings of a map. Before she could think about what she might encounter, or change her mind, she started off, walking into the bush.

Her trek began on a road of packed ice that turned to snow that turned to unpacked snow that turned to nothing, so that she would have sunk to her knees at every step, were it not that Sister Hildegarde had insisted that she sling Father Hugo's snowshoes across her back. She tied them onto her feet and then, in shelter of the trees where the crust on the snow was tough, she was able to maneuver with an almost galloping swiftness. Physical elation filled her. She made her way through wild throngs of birch, skirted the cracked, sere slough grass, pushed through thickets of red willow. The sun was high and bright, but the air was cold and bubbled in her blood like sleep. Several times, sitting down to rest, she imagined curling up in the snowy bays underneath the trees, but she always forced herself to her feet, kept moving.

At the time, she still possessed an untested belief that, having survived the robbery, the chase, the bullets, and the flood, then transformed herself to Father Damien, she could not be harmed. That inner assurance would make her seem fearless, which would in turn increase the respect she won among the Anishinaabeg. So complete was her faith that on the journey to visit Nanapush she ignored the hardship and even danger she might encounter if she lost her way.

What occupied Agnes was the misery of concealing the exasperating monthly flow that belonged to her past but persisted into the present. As she sprang along on the clever winglike snowshoes, she occasionally asked the Almighty, in some irritation, to stop the useless affliction of menstrual blood, so she could more confidently pursue the work cut out for an active priest. Her requests were heeded, for she definitely felt a lessening and then a near cessation. The heavy cramping faded until, stopping to change the cloth that she buried deep in snow, she found it barely spotted with darkness. No sooner had the evidence vanished than she felt a pang, a loss, an eerie rocking between genders.

The sun was sweet, the air liquid. Kneeling in the momentary warmth, she washed lightly with a handful of fresh, wet snow. She shivered with shock and a lost sensation gathered, swept through her, and was gone with a shimmer of musical notes. She closed her eyes, tried to make the physical climax into a prayer, but her mouth dropped and she cried out in a quiet voice, feeling the ghost touches of her lost lover.

When at last she returned to the present, stood again to make her way, Agnes consulted the angle of the sun, the trees, the careful map Sister Hildegarde had drawn, anxious not to lose the new priest. It did not take her long to arrive at the place. It looked ordinary enough—a low cabin made of silvery logs with a split-plank door, the spaces between the logs tamped with a fine cracked yellow-gray gumbo.

There was nothing about the cabin to suggest it was the home of a serious miscreant, a guzzler of communion wine, an unregenerate and eager pagan who gave Sister Hildegarde such trials. The place was quiet. There was among Father Hugo's papers a crude calendar, which sometimes included notes on the Indians he'd baptized—the day and hour. One day there were the words "Baptize Nanapush." Under that self-command the exclamation *"Folly!"* Agnes took a step forward. It was said that Mr. Nanapush had excellent command of English as a result of several years with Jesuit teachers. It was also said that the old man had stubbornly retained and deepened his Ojibwemowin and that he wrote and thought in his language and conducted the very rites and mysteries that Kashpaw had mentioned.

"Boozhoo! Aaniin!" Agnes called out the various greetings she'd learned from Kashpaw. She stood shifting uneasily from foot to numb foot. No sound came in answer, no stirring from inside. Up and down the side of a nearby tree, a tiny gray-capped bird zipped, uttering a sharp complaint. Some curled brown leaves, still attached to the nodes of an oak tree, ticked together. And then the wind stopped. Everything stopped. The stillness was profound.

In that cessation, Agnes DeWitt was flooded with uneasy agitation. A prickle touched on the back of her neck, and she gave her head a shake. A low unease struck her. A voice cried out. She whirled. No one. Now a piping child's voice, laughing, but again no source. She felt a mutter of presences, rustling and arguing on all sides, and she froze in place as their voices, speaking incomprehensible words—only a few of which she knew from Kashpaw's talk—crushed toward her.

The voices merged with her senses, filling her head. She tried to regulate her breathing, not to panic, but a vast weakness swallowed her and she thought she heard, maybe knew, could not be sure—were there spirits beyond the experience entrusted to her so far?

"Who are you?" she whispered. "What are you?"

She waited, increasingly disturbed, for long moments, until finally there was nowhere to go but in. Making the sign of the cross, she burst through the door of the lonely cabin into the stink of ghosts.

Two beings, hollow and strange, stared quizzically out of the shadows at the priest, who gaped at them in return. One frowned in dignified hauteur at the crack of light within which the priest was caught, there in the doorway, hand on his throat and eyes wide in snow-blind shock. Another blinked and passed its hands across its bone features. Agnes stepped closer, pity flooding her as well as a curious horror at their condition. At first, she could not tell the old man from the young girl. Their faces were pale smears, porous and frail as birch-bark masks. Their hair burst out, ferocious, alive with sticks, mud, lice, tangled in intricate bushes on their heads. Their eyes glittered from deep in gray pits. They moved as though they'd break apart. As though their bones were brittle reeds. They were shells made of loss, made of transparent flint, made of the whispers in the oak leaves, voices of the dead.

THE LIVING

When the new priest burst into the cabin door, causing that great crack of light to interfere with death, the girl and old man were annoyed. That they were abandoned by their families who took the four-day journey into the sun-going-down world was bad enough. That some of the dead came back and waited outside the door, urging them to follow although their bodies clung to life, that was hard. And now, just as they had weakened and slid into a state somewhere between death and life, a drifting torpor from which they saw far ahead down the road and also marvelously lived vivid scenes from the past, here came this priest.

The light dazzled, the dark spun. The priest's pleasant interest was both irritating and surprisingly powerful. Fleur felt a faint impulse stirring in her to melt snow, or fetch water, then make tea, which meant a fire must be kindled, which seemed impossible and then imperative. She was sure that she was mostly dead. She hadn't moved from her corner for days, maybe weeks. But somehow on stick legs she lurched out the door into blinding radiance. Light stabbed into her brain, subsided gradually to show the world in whirling shapes. A crust had formed across her mouth. She put a handful of snow on her lips, to unseal her tongue, and allowed a trickle of water to pass down her throat. Then the painful knowledge that now she would rejoin this life, which was only loss after loss, caused her heart to catch in a sob that became a snarl, and she struck out wildly at the air, behind the house, in the deep, warm snow.

As for Nanapush, he still blinked inside the cabin like an owl and whispered bewildered answers to the priest's awkward questions in his language. Finally, in English, Nanapush said, "That is enough from you, my friend, quite sufficient. Now for a moment you must be silent. The master calls and I must go out and have a shit." Then, holding his pants up with both hands, the old man toddled from the cabin and did not return for quite some time.

Fleur brought in wood, sticks, some rolls of flammable bark, and quickly brought up a blaze in the rusty can used as an indoor stove. Outside, as the sun was at its height, they could hear the dripping of snow water from the trees. They could hear the clumps of snow sliding down the mud-pole sides of the house. Water dripped from the soaked sod roof down the inside walls. The ice was retreating, but not inside of Fleur. She hated priests. The priests had brought the sickness long ago in the hems of their black gowns, in their sleeves, in the water they flung on people to make them holy but which might as well have burned holes in their skin. All these things, and more. She'd like to stab the priest's heart, pull it out of his body. She'd look into his face as he died and take satisfaction from his anguish for all her loved ones, her little brother and sisters, her beloved father, her mother who had died last of all.

Who should see such things?

"What can I do to make you feel better?" asked the priest. "Gigaa minwendam i'in?" he tried in Ojibwe.

In spite of herself, she almost laughed. What he actually said was, Can I make you feel good? Which was easy to take as sexual. Mistakenly, the priest took the smile for encouragement and earnestly tried out a little more Ojibwe, which now made her hold her hand up to her mouth to stifle the laugh that almost emerged. What was it that made the black robes desperate to gather up the spirits of the Anishinaabeg for their god? Fleur decided that the chimookoman god was greedy, which made sense as all the people she had seen of their kind certainly were, grabbing up Anishinaabeg land, hunting down every last animal and wasting half the meat, swiping all they could. She banged a can of water on the stove and went out. She could not be around the

priest. He stank. Or she stank. She would fire up a blaze to heat
stones for a sweat and purify herself. She would smoke her clothes
with sage. Burn sweet grass to clean the cabin's air, sweep the sad lit-
ter out, the chewed twigs, the nests of hungry mice. Then she would
know it was not she, but the priest, who stank. And the old man. He
could use a sweat and a good wash, too. For sure, she hated priests. As
she left the cabin, voices surrounded her, airy hands plucked at her
sleeves, but she shook them off. She pushed snow away from the
stones, the grandfathers, gathered last summer when no one knew
what killing sorrows this winter would bring.

As for Nanapush, he entered the door and pleasantly announced to
the priest, "I have accomplished my end." When the priest looked
amused, instead of chastising Nanapush, the old man was sufficiently
interested to want to live just a little longer in order to shock the
priest. He rubbed his numb hands, his feet, and thought perhaps he
would tell this priest the story of the inquisitive mouse rained on by
the big vaginas, and how the mouse reported to and described these
beings to his friends down in the holes that had filled with piss and
nearly drowned them out. Or maybe the story of how Nanabozho got
his penis changed from smooth to knobbed on the end when a clam
he tried to fuck closed tight. Or maybe he would just proceed in his
best English to tell the priest the many and specific ways he had made
love to his wives, all of whom he'd outlived, but then the thought laid
his heart down. He couldn't breathe for the sorrow. He sat in the blankets, speechless. For a long time, he tried to gather himself out of his
despair and perhaps the priest sensed this, which was good, for Father
Damien maintained a neutral, kind, meditative watchfulness that had
in it no hint of impatience.

The water boiled. Fleur came in, made spruce-needle tea, went out
again. The priest and the old man sipped the stuff from cans. Maybe,
thought Nanapush, as with all things there was a reason for this
intrusion and something in it for himself. He set his mind to it. There
must be some way that Nanapush could use this priest, if he couldn't
get rid of him. And the priest looked set to stay. The priest would
probably not do much about Nanapush's lack of zhooniyaa—priests
never gave out money, that he knew. And food, from the starved look
of the black robe, was probably not forthcoming. He didn't seem to

have so much as a piece of bannock with him. No, there was not much good that this priest could do in an immediate way. Nanapush thought harder. Grief over his last wife still pressed him, and it was perhaps that grief and longing, coupled with the Nanapush-like need to take advantage when advantage could be taken, that led him to decide—since the priest had yanked him from the calm world of the dead to thrust him into the strife of the living, where he did not want to go—he at least would not sleep in a cold bed. No, if he had to stay alive, Nanapush would get a wife—a big, warm one. She would make a little nest for him every night, blankets spread over cedar boughs. He'd curl beside her and he'd get warm and then he'd make them both happy with what he'd been given, his gift, unless that, too, had starved so skinny it was useless.

So while he sat quietly, Nanapush's mind was really hard at work, and when it found a direction, his tongue was triggered and wouldn't stop. Somehow, and Nanapush did not know how it would occur, the talking itself, if he did it long enough, always brought him by round-about and unexpected ways to the place he intended. And so although he started somewhere altogether far from any discussion of wives or beds, he had no doubt that he would end up where he was going. He spoke what came to mind then, and told a story that he suddenly recalled hearing from a zhaaganaash-akiing Cree.

NANABOZHO CONVERTS THE WOLVES

Nanapush

Our Nanabozho was like me, said the old man, launching it, very poor once—in fact, so poor he didn't even own a rotten old rag such as I have to dress in, no, he had to go naked and his family, too. So it interested Nanabozho very much when he heard the Frenchmen were traveling around his home ground buying up furs and wolf pelts and buffalo robes. Yes, he thought, that sounded very interesting. He even saw people who had many furs and had bought warm new clothes. But yet, sadly enough, Nanabozho had no furs to sell.

So he went to a Frenchman anyway and tried to persuade him to give some credit, telling him that soon he would have a great many furs to put down on his debt.

Then the Frenchman, who believed Nanabozho, gave him blankets and coats and even a gun. Also, a great deal of clothing. Nanabozho brought these things home and gave them all to his wife. But she was angry and called him crazy.

"How are we going to pay?" she yelled.

"Oh," said Nanabozho, "I will go back to this Frenchman. You'll see."

So Nanabozho went back to the Frenchman and this time he asked for some medicine, poison. He took that poison home and then told his old woman to give him some fat, which she did. She gave him fat. Then he turned around and put that poison into the fat. He patted out many little flat lumps of poison fat and cooled them until they were hard. Then he took them all and went to look for the wolves.

Nanabozho walked along until he came to a place where there was a wolf.

"Brother," said Nanabozho, "come here!"

But the wolf would not, saying, "You only want to kill me!"

"No, my little brother," said Nanabozho, "I want to hire you."

Well, that sounded interesting to the wolf, so he came around.

"I want to give you the job of going everywhere to summon all the wolves and the foxes, oh yes, all the best-looking of the wolves and foxes, to come and see me, on this little hill. I have taken the Jesus road, my friends, and I wish to preach to you all!"

Then once the wolves and foxes arrived, he spoke some more.

"My brothers," he said, "these things I am going to tell you are good, and you should accept them indeed! If you take on this religion, no one can kill you. It's true. But if you do not believe along with me, you will surely die. Now look what I have for you!"

Nanabozho displayed the poisoned lumps of fat.

"If anyone eats of this, long will he live!" declared Nanabozho.

Then the wolves all threw themselves forward, hoping to live long, and Nanabozho dispensed the fat.

A wolf would come forward, eat the fat, then go. One by one, Nanabozho placed the fat in their mouths, and the foxes, too, until the fat was all gone. And then Nanabozho held up his hand and blessed all the wolves, saying, "Long may you live!" And as he said this and blessed them, the wolves leaped in the air and howled, turned twice in agony, and fell back to earth dead.

That's the way Nanabozho gave religious instruction to the wolves. After he saved their souls, he skinned them all and the foxes, too, and as he walked to the French traders carrying their skins, he laughed and laughed. Truly, he said, I have converted them—to money.

That's all. Mi'sago'i!

*   *   *

Fleur had entered the cabin to hear the end of the story, and with a cold sarcasm laughed at the unmanly priest and asked what he thought of that?

Father Damien, for a fact, looked extremely thoughtful. He said nothing as he sipped the tea, and at last he answered that he thought the story was extremely clever but that, if he read the meaning right, the Anishinaabeg were not as stupid as wolves nor did Father Damien need to skin them in order to pay his debts. Nanapush looked happily at the priest now, and started feeling glad he was alive, if only to be presented with the challenge of rattling a promising opponent. At the same time, just to speak of those lumps of fat made him so hungry that his stomach stabbed and groaned. He tried to kill the hunger with another swallow of tea.

GAAG

After they had finished the last drop of tea, the three looked gloomily at the walls of the little cabin, as though the tamped poles would somehow leak porridge. As they gazed with a sad, fixed blankness into their private fantasies of food, they heard a sound. At the very first scrape of this sound, Nanapush held up his hand. "Bizindan," he whispered. He looked at Fleur, and then upon his face there appeared the happy wonder of a child discovering a stash of sweets. The priest listened, mystified. The sound occurred again, right at the southeast corner of the cabin. It was, there was absolutely no mistake about it, a definitive chomp. A munch. A distinct chewing sound.

"Gaag," said Fleur, and she and Nanapush dropped down to their knees, crept across the dirt floor wearing such gleeful looks that Father Damien, caught up in their madness, crawled behind them out of intense curiosity. Their stealthy whispers inhibited him from asking any questions. Anyway, they'd forgotten about him. They went outside, stood, slowly sneaked around the side of the cabin and found there an enormous porcupine. Startled, it removed its teeth from the log side of the house and backed away, eyeing the humans with a grave and glistening black stare, apprehensive and somehow, thought Father Damien, pleading.

Fleur gently crept near the animal, brushed her hands over the porcupine's quills so they all lay one way. Suddenly she grasped it and raised it by its ferocious tail, at which point it gave a very human gasp, a surprised *eeee!* With a giant's swing, she brained the creature on the side of the house, and then knelt with her knife and gutted it in the yard.

In the past few weeks, in the extremities of hunger, Father Damien was surprised to find how many things he'd eaten that he'd formerly considered inedible. Even covered with quills, the porcupine was making his mouth water. So he gladly helped Nanapush split wood and build up a fire, stoking it so furiously that the flimsy tin stove turned red hot. Fleur brought in the animal and quickly removed its best quills, dipping her hands in a shovelful of wood ash from time to time in order to increase their grip. When she had the quills she wanted off, she spitted the porcupine and roasted it slowly, singeing the remaining quills into the flesh. That, said Nanapush, gave the gaag a better taste.

Nanapush talked quickly and happily, now, waiting for their meal. He spoke of oddities and miscellany until the meat was roasted. Then they ate. They ate every little scrap. They ate the toes, they ate the brains. Sucked every bone completely clean. Only the teeth and nails were left when, in a genial well-fed mood, Father Damien asked Nanapush if he knew the man named Kashpaw who had given him a ride to the reservation.

Nanapush did not answer the simple question at once. He stared at the priest in what seemed a sudden fit of idiocy. His mouth dropped. His eyes dulled. That was a smoke screen. He was thinking. For to his great delight, there it was, it all spread from that one question. Nanapush had at last found a way through the thicket of words to the end he sought. And it was easy, so easy, it all lay ripe before him now.

Changing his expression suddenly to a look of intelligent interest, Nanapush said that of course, Kashpaw was as close as a brother. He told Father Damien that he and Kashpaw had been through much together in their youth, had hunted near and far, through the northern plains, and even lived for a short time in the same lodge. He went on to say that Kashpaw and he were half brothers and that a more distant relative of Nanapush's was married to him.

"Of course," said Nanapush casually, "he has so many wives that this one relative, a niece of my uncle, her name is Fishbone, is hardly noticed in that woman-wealthy lodge."

"Wives?" said Father Damien.

"Oh yes," said Nanapush.

"How many?"

"Let me see . . ." Nanapush proceeded ostentatiously to try to remember exactly, to count on his fingers.

"Four left now. That's all."

Father Damien was still not shocked, but he was at least intrigued, and as he was clearly stumped for what to say, Nanapush was satisfied. Besides, he was just beginning the slow work of influencing the priest, and he didn't want to frighten him off. Therefore, he chose other subjects for a short time until the priest himself returned to the question of the wives.

"My . . . colleague"—Father Damien coughed; he was referring to the actual Father Damien, now long buried in the shadow of a tree—"was concerned about the problem of irregular unions. This must be what he meant. How are such things dealt with here? Who has the authority?"

Nanapush, though thrilled to be asked the very question he had sought, still did not reel in the priest, but let him drag the line. Again, pretending not to have heard, he spoke of his empty trapline and the lack of good weather until Father Damien grew impatient and tried once more.

"The authority on such matters," he reminded.

"Ah!" Nanapush pretended to collect himself. "Pardon an old man. Here is the truth. Father Hugo was forced to break many an illegal liaison, and his zeal was well-known. But since he died, well, my friend Kashpaw moved down here and got bold. Even some of us old traditionals," he said, in a fit of outrageous betrayal, "think that he should get rid of some of his wives!"

"Eyah! So you can have one!"

Fleur was outraged by the old man's cunning attempt at sanctimony, and in spite of her hatred of black robes she tried to warn the priest. If Father Damien had only listened, she gave away the transparent strategy right there. "Don't you see, he just wants a wife all for himself? He's willing to break up his friend's life just to do it."

But Father Damien was dazed with the unaccustomed feeling of a full stomach. Nanapush pulled a long face, though, and answered he only wished that he could handle a wife, but that was impossible in his present weakness.

It wasn't that Nanapush ever wanted to hurt his friend, or that family, or to lay blame for all that would happen on Father Damien. Nanapush was incapable of imagining such things as would occur. He knew very well that Kashpaw's situation had to give, somehow or another. Though the arrangement was based on complicated practicalities and all were seemingly content in Kashpaw's lodge, a change was coming. Drawing near. No, it wasn't that Nanapush wanted to destroy his friend's family and peace of mind, or even that he had to have one of those wives (although if given his choice, Nanapush knew which one he'd pick). It was only that he saw what he saw, and the time was coming. It was like when they were boys and they dammed up a stream to collect the fish. Below the dam, they set out a net, ready for when they let the water go. That was all Nanapush wanted to do. When the dam burst, he wanted to be there, downstream, to catch the fish that swam into his hands.

Now came Father Damien's first lesson in Ojibwe social planning. When he rose to take his leave, Nanapush gathered his blanket and snowshoes, ready to leave with him. Fleur had crawled into her small, domed sweat lodge, removing herself in disgust. It was a surprise to

Father Damien that by listening to Nanapush's description of Kash-paw's whereabouts and nodding politely, he had in actuality agreed to visit, but as they walked Nanapush persuaded him that, though it was growing dark, Kashpaw's place was not far off, right on the way back to the church, in fact, and even better, there was a good possibility that Kashpaw's family might have food in the kettle, for not only Kashpaw but a couple of his wives and sons were good hunters. Even though his stomach had felt bursting tight an hour before, Father Damien's starving body had magically emptied it. Food sounded good. So it was that Father Damien was introduced to the endless Ojibwe visit, in which a get-together produces a perfectly convincing reason to seek another, and then that visit another, and so on. Father Damien tramped earnestly along and looked forward to meeting the household of Kashpaws.

6

THE KASHPAW WIVES

1912

Their arrival at Kashpaw's camp was greeted with a loud blast from Mashkiigikwe's powerful rifle. She stood in the clearing, round and strong as an autumn bear, the barrel held upright in one hand. With a fascinated contempt, she observed the priest's clumsy approach. Obviously, the black robe was still not adept at walking through the bush. Thorns grabbed his cassock. Vines bound his ankles. His steps gave way in pockets of watery snow. Exhaustion gripped him. His weak knees trembled as he slogged behind Nanapush, from whom the wife of Kashpaw had already turned with a groan of disgust.

Kashpaw lived with his wives in two houses, one a cabin very similar to Nanapush's, the other an old-style lodge constructed of limber saplings bent over, sunk in the earth, tied, and covered with slabs of bark. There was also a rough pole shed, which housed the horses that Kashpaw loved and bartered. Several milled in a corral; others were picketed by the edge of the woods, where they could paw up old grass through the snow.

Mashkiigikwe returned, bloody to the elbows. In her hand, she held a dripping piece of the deer she'd just shot. When Kashpaw appeared, she tossed the meat to him and delicately, wielding his razor-sharp hunting knife, he sliced it into strips and offered each of the men a portion in greeting.

Even without the vast red capote, the yellow turban, the buffalo robe, wool shawls and velvet, Kashpaw was impressive. He was a powerful, hunched, comic-looking man, rather ugly Father Damien supposed, looking at him closely, and yet attractive for his keen eye and a sense of barely withheld mirth. The priest and Nanapush entered the smaller bark lodge behind Kashpaw. He began singing a soft tune in a mournful and teasing tone. Inside the shadowy large birch-bark lodge, well behind him and seemingly unaffected by the cold, two women worked at some task with a concentrated air.

"Boozhoo!"

At his word, one of the wives poked her head at the men. She wore a red knitted hat that flopped over her brow like a crest, her nose was sharp, and Father Damien could not help thinking of her as an angry woodpecker. Of the two, she was much older, and she seemed to have been disturbed in the midst of a satisfying tirade, for she jumped up and laughed harshly at her sister wife, who suddenly rushed from the hut, stifling a racking sob.

Nanapush and Father Damien settled themselves on a pile of skins and blankets, and Kashpaw made all of the gestures of a generous host while Father Damien appreciated all he saw and ate like an affable guest. Nanapush sat back. He made an effort to stop his tongue, to contain himself. It was important to proceed with delicacy. Not to give away his plan, but to let it unfold as if it were natural, in the course of things. He told himself that all he had to do was put the priest into the situation, and wait. Priests and extra wives were mutually opposed, he had seen it before. This priest was of course much younger, oddly feminine, and a good deal subtler than Father Hugo, but that his intentions were fundamentally those of a priest, Nanapush had no doubt.

While he sat at Kashpaw's fire and waited, Nanapush appreciated the wife of his friend, the hunter who'd just shot the deer, the one whom he intended to take for his own when the dust settled. Mashkiigikwe's legs were oak fence posts and her neck, solid, was packed with a power that surged up through her body and flashed from her eyes. He drifted in admiration as she tore wolfishly at a piece of deer liver with strong little teeth, and chewed each piece with a thoughtful frown, as though she was masticating some inner meaning from her food. Yet, when well fed, she could be very jolly, too. Her singing voice was of a surprising lilt and softness, and her songs were often children's games. It charmed Nanapush to watch her and spurred him to help matters along.

Children popped out, hair sticking straight up. They were deliciously round, seemingly healthy, and completely naked. Two ran out just as they were into the frigid air and, chased by the oldest wife, dove back into the lodge, bearing in their fists some tiny tidbit from the carcass. And then two men showed up, young men, older sons of the sharp-tongued Margaret. A boy named Nector glanced inside, took in the configuration, nodded, and left. A quiet woman emerged, fully pregnant, from a pile of robes and arranged the children carefully before her. She was softer, plainer than the others, and moved with extreme grace, even pregnant and huge. She rubbed the faces of the children, patted their hands, and when she was given a piece of the venison she spitted morsels of it on green sticks, elegantly roasted the meat, and cooled each bit with her breath before offering it to each child. They obeyed her with huge gravity. As they chewed, she ate, too, and told them a teasing story in her language.

Her name was Fishbone, and Father Damien later baptized her Marie. Margaret, of course, already had a chimookoman name and was a good Catholic, except in respect to her married life. The woman she had caused to cry, Quill, was later christened Marie as well. As for Mashkiigikwe, Father Damien never got a chance to name her, for she cleft to her own religion, and would have knocked the dipper of blessed water from his hand.

The priest sat silently and simply watched the goings-on around him, while the other men talked over old times. It certainly was not Father Damien's intention to walk into the family and make a declaration of any sort, but Nanapush kept giving him encouraging sideways glances, then somewhat sterner nods, even little gestures. Finally, Nanapush purposely let a lull develop in the conversation, which he'd artfully maneuvered toward his topic of interest by inquiring about the health of each wife, and in that small silence he motioned toward the priest.

"Let the priest speak," he encouraged.

"If you'd ever shut up," said Margaret, "the priest would have spoken before."

"My friend Nanapush has such a kind heart," said Kashpaw, "that he had to ask after each one of the women." Kashpaw glanced shrewdly at Margaret, and she gave a sour little suspicious frown.

"Funny that he is so interested in our health." She turned away. She was unripe gooseberry, pure vinegar. Margaret's presence puckered up the room like a basket of chokecherries. Her glance dried laughter, her hard snakelike impenetrable glare shook men to the core but also, in Kashpaw's case anyway, caused a certain shiver of interest. There was something both frightful and seductive about her cold temperament. As for Kashpaw, he allowed as it was odd that Nanapush was suddenly so very solicitous, but he sat back with amusement and said nothing else, for he knew very well the reason for his old friend's attentive inquiries. They were nearly brothers, after all, and had sat with their foreheads touching, smoked their pipes in grief over many deaths. Kashpaw knew the lay of his friend's mind and understood that he was lonely, that his bed was cold, his arms empty, his wiinag bored, his days given to sad memory. Kashpaw knew his own wives were now more than a source of envy, they were a possible selection pool for Nanapush himself if this priest, who sat with them now trying not to look bewildered, prevailed upon him to give them up. Oh yes, Kashpaw had no illusions. Yet he didn't hold these things against Nanapush but accepted the scheming as an inevitable part of his friend's nature. The fact was, Kashpaw enjoyed anticipating Nanapush and thwarting his plans, so when the priest failed to respond to the pointed hints he dropped, Kashpaw was happy to further distract the priest. He asked questions, as if he was considering conversion. Can Jesus kill a windigo? Why did their god kill Father Hugo? He enjoyed the slow attention that Father Damien gave the questions, and even more, the steaming frustration of his friend beside him. He would have a good laugh later on with Margaret over the way Nanapush prodded and tried to steer the priest toward his purpose.

Father Damien, for his part, finally tired of receiving obscure signals from Nanapush. He made motions, as though to leave, which panicked Nanapush into blurting a reproach.

"You are the one who is supposed to hold forth!" Losing all sense of reserve, and infuriated by Father Damien's blank stare, he cried out the louder. "It's your job to set this married man right! You are the priest!"

Father Damien's expression did not change. He merely regarded Nanapush with bemused speculation, seeing the shape of the subterfuge at last—and he was the last one to see it, he was sure. How naïve of him, how willingly he'd been put to the use of this rascal. Visit, indeed! The priest had merely been the tool of this old man's lust.

"Nanapush," said Father Damien, sternly, at last. "I see why you have taken me to visit Kashpaw. It is your hope that I will forbid him to have his wives!"

"Ii'iih," said Nanapush, trying to slow himself down now that his game was discovered, "isn't it the rule of the church? One husband? One wife?"

"Well, yes," said Damien unwillingly.

"See there!"

"You are putting words into my mouth," said Father Damien, angry at the entire situation, exasperated with Nanapush. "Of course it is Church doctrine, but Kashpaw does not belong to the Church."

Nanapush was suddenly crushed. He had not foreseen this.

"Do you mean to say it is a question of belonging to the church?" he shrieked. "Then if Kashpaw stays a pagan he can keep his wives?"

"I have no say in it." Father Damien was now at the exploding point. He could feel Nanapush trying to herd him through a small gate and stubbornly decided to dump doctrine, sound principle, everything that he should rightly have defended as a priest, in order not to let this man's woman-hunger steer him too.

"But he will go to hell!" Nanapush was desperate. "I only fear for my friend, as the hell of the chimookomanag sounds extremely painful." He then proceeded to paint a picture of the flames and pincers that made Kashpaw and Margaret, and then the entire lodge, roll with laughter.

"To be quite specific about it, no," said Father Damien when the hilarity was spent. Even he had been tempted to laugh at the old man's transparent pretense at saving his friend. "Kashpaw will go to a place called Purgatory where there isn't much to do, and where he won't ever see God."

"I've seen enough chimookomanag anyway," said Kashpaw, "without having to meet the one responsible for creating the white race."

"I'd like to see him," said Mashkiigikwe. "I'd tell him what I thought of his work." She spat. Father Damien ignored her, focused on the seething Nanapush, and couldn't help an unpriestlike thought from coming to him. Earlier, the old man had told him something of his life, and now he decided to use his revelation against him.

"Nanapush," said Father Damien, in a voice that got everyone's attention, "you have told me that you, like Kashpaw, were at one time the husband of several wives. What was your reason?"

Nanapush reluctantly told his story.

PATAKIZOOG!

Nanapush

Father Damien, said Nanapush, struggling with resentment but soon, as always, caught up in the pleasure of talking, if you must know these things, only listen to my story, for it is the way things happened until only just these last few seasons. Here's how it goes:

Our band of people in the north were struck at one time with the spirit of disease. The spirit killed so many of us that when the dead were counted it was found that we survivors numbered less than a quarter of our camp. At the time, I wasn't born, yet I am told how the mourners sat grieving together, willing themselves to be struck down, too. But the destroying spirit had passed. It was then suggested that they kill themselves, all together for courage, and journey as a band to meet their beloved dead in the land of the aadizokaanag. But then one older, wiser woman, a large woman, strong and powerful, stood upright and spoke.

"Mii'e etaa i'iwe gay onji shabwii'ing," she said, "gakina awiyaa ninaandawenimaa chi mazhiweyt. Neshke idash tahnee pahtahney-nahwug gey ani bimautiziwaad."

There were some who looked shocked, who protested, who were

surprised that she would exhort the women to make babies in their sorrow, to order the men to stand up their wiinagag, to endeavor valiantly to procreate until they dropped! But, as she had always been a faithful and virtuous woman, they listened to her. She calmed them down and explained her idea. She pointed out how the Bwaanag, or Dakota, to the south had fought against the whites to try conquering them, but that hadn't worked out as well as the Ojibwe method of making Michifs and wiisaakodewininiwag. She said what everyone knew, that the Creator gave his people the Ojibwe a special love skill that they could always use in times of crisis.

"Gakinago giigaa kitchi manitiminin. Ininiwag, dagasaa patakizoog! Ikweywug, pagetinamahgehg! Ahau, anishinabedok, patakizoog! Ahua! Manitadaa!"

With that, she left them to think. As the evening went on, they all came to see it her way. They saw that if they followed her advice there would be new Anishinaabeg by the turn of three seasons. She had even closed by saying that although her hair was gray, she intended to have more children.

In fact, that very night, she picked the strongest and handsomest young man left among the people. That young man, Mirage was his name, did a lot of work all that night, and the next and next—but the women kept him fed and warm and they all got pregnant. The old woman was my mother, and the young man, who still lives, was made chief for the great duties he continued to perform with his uncounted wives. He re-created our tribe. So you see, that which you Catholics abhor—our gift, which is to mazhiwe at any time of the day or night—is why we do remain strong and why we have not died out.

And as you see, Father Damien, your friend Nanapush has only followed his mother's orders. I am an obedient son.

That is it! Mi'sago'i!

*　　　*　　　*

Kashpaw's powerful shoulders hunched around his ears as he listened to Nanapush, and his tiny eyes, dark with shrewd hilarity, took in the configuration before him.

"My reasons are no better or worse than those of Nanapush," he said. "I, too, am the son of that generous young stud who saved us all, and one of the woman who gladly slept with him. We survived. I am proud of it. Why should I change?"

Nanapush looked resentfully at Kashpaw, who simply shrugged, and let his eye wander appreciatively over the tight barrel of Mashkiigikwe's rear.

"What would the white god want with you, anyway?" he said to Kashpaw. "You're ugly and full of mischief!"

Kashpaw made a mocking face.

"Maybe Jesus wants to know my love medicine."

"Howah! More likely you can sell your knowledge to Matchimanito, the bad spirit. Eyah." Nanapush stroked his chin. "I always wondered how it was you got these women to live with you. Now my question is answered. You worked your love snares."

"This is the only love snare I need." Kashpaw gestured down at his sex. Father Damien kept his gaze steady, though his breathing faltered. Nanapush was not in the least embarrassed, but craned to look critically into Kashpaw's lap. "Yes, it is shaped like a snare, all right, limp and skinny!"

"Saaa!" Mashkiigikwe walked up behind Nanapush and swiped at his head with her brush, an ingenious thing, not store-bought but created of clipped porcupine quills fastened into a strip of rawhide.

"I don't hunt with snares, sweetheart," Nanapush crooned to Mashkiigikwe. "I use a nice, long, heavy stick."

Mashkiigikwe sneered down on him with amused contempt, stuck her little finger out, and wiggled it at him.

"All you're good for is bait," she declared.

"Let's go fish together, then," said Nanapush.

"I only fish with my old man."

"What do you do," Nanapush inquired, "those lonely nights when he satisfies your sisters?"

Mashkiigikwe's mouth opened. She glared at him with false outrage.

"Me," said Nanapush confidingly, "when I had six wives—"

"Six!" Mashkiigikwe interrupted, laughing sarcastically. "He was drunk and seeing double!"

Nanapush ignored her. "I was able to put them all to sleep!"

"By talking!" said Kashpaw, not in the least embarrassed or offended at Nanapush's suggestive behavior with his wife. He only snickered to himself and looked significantly at Father Damien, who felt that it was his responsibility to take charge and return the conversation to some semblance of a priestly visit; therefore, he accidentally asked a question that would have repercussions, "Mr. Kashpaw, have you solemnized your vows with any one of your wives?"

Kashpaw shrugged. What did it matter, his frown said, but one of the wives did step up.

"Niin sa!"

It was Margaret, her red hat bobbing. Beneath it her tough face was carefully cut as though with fine tools. Her thinning hair still rose fiercely off her brow and was collected in braids. Her mouth, both sweet and treacherous, now twisted sarcastically. Perhaps, thought Father Damien, she would have been beautiful—if there was any softness to her. Her voice was sharp as thorns. "I forced him to take the Eucharist and then we were joined by Father Hugo." She looked furiously from side to side, as though someone would challenge her.

"Kashpaw says they scrap like badgers," said Nanapush. "The other wives send them from the house when they fight. She bit him once."

Kashpaw displayed his arm, a short, thick white scar.

"Right to the bone," said Margaret in satisfaction.

"Have you confessed your sin?" Father Damien asked, irritated by this woman's smug ferocity.

"What sin?" she answered. "He deserved it."

"Dispensing punishment is God's task and right," Damien went on. "In all ways a good spouse is gentle."

"And slow," said Nanapush solemnly to Mashkiigikwe, "and takes his time where it counts, and . . ."

She turned away and hummed, as though suppressing a yawn.

"If the priest won't say it," Nanapush lost patience at last, "I will say it. Kashpaw! You have too many wives. You'll have to get rid of at least three!"

Kashpaw probably expected this outburst, for now, with a dramatic pause, he concentrated on his pipe, drew it from its case of red cloth and fitted its bowl to the carved stem. Once he had done this, everyone around him fell silent and in the vacant quiet the coals of the fire hissed and flared. He loaded the rose-red bowl with pinches of tobacco, then proceeded to light the pipe and to draw meditatively on the stem, emitting two thin streams from the corners of his mouth.

At last, he set down his pipe and looked reproachfully at his visitors. His expression slowly registered convincing bewilderment. "Wives?" he said. "Who is calling these fine ladies my wives?" Craftily, he feigned insult, knowing that he could be considered in violation of certain laws, not of his tribe's making, but of the government's. "I offer shelter to these women beneath my roof."

"And I," said Nanapush, unable to contain himself around Mashkiigikwe, turning to her, "I offer shelter to you in my bed. And since my cabin has a leaky roof, I'll offer to lie down over you to keep the rain off."

He looked directly at Mashkiigikwe, who pressed her lips together in pretend fury and then covered herself with indifference.

Kashpaw ignored this absurd sweet talk and addressed the priest. "I am still interested in this god who kills off his favorites, wipes them from the earth. I would like to know"—here he eyed Damien with frank curiosity—"what makes you walk behind this Jesus?"

This question of great simplicity caused the priest's thoughts to wheel together like a flock of startled birds. What indeed? What cause? All Father Damien could do at first was contemplate the pattern of the flock out of which the great logos of his passion was written.

"It is love," he said. "That is the sole reason. Love."

The others looked uncertian. In the Ojibwe language the word does not exist in the same sense—there is love out of pity, love out of kindness, love that is specific to situations or to the world of stones, which are alive and called our grandfathers. There is also the stingy and greedy love that white people call romantic love. This love of Christ, this love that chose Agnes and forced her to give up her nature as a woman, forced Father Damien to appear to sacrifice the pleasures of manhood, was impossible to define in Ojibwe.

The boy named Nector ducked into the lodge, sat down next to him, peered at the slight new priest with curiosity. The boy was well dressed, extremely neat, and even wore an expensive-looking, smart, plaid cap. His father finally spoke.

"I am going to send my boy here, this Nector, to your church. He will investigate," said Kashpaw. "He will tell me if this spirit is any good. If there is something to this god, I'll come see for myself."

There was a mutter of protest and consternation from the women in the tent, then, and Mashkiigikwe pounded the earth with her feet.

"Why do the chimookomanag want us?" she growled. "They take all that makes us Anishinaabeg. Everything about us. First our land, then our trees. Now husbands, our wives, our children, our souls. Why do they want to capture every bit?"

Father Damien, whose task it was to steal even the intangible about the woman beside him, had no answer.

KASHPAW'S PASSION

Kashpaw sat on the ground with his sacred pipe before him on a flat pale rock. Gizhe Manito, tell me what to do, he prayed. His heart was so dark and heavy that when he bent over to take up his pipe, it felt like it might tumble from his chest. For all of his power, right now he felt like a frail container. So much conflict was stuffed inside him that his skin seemed too thin to contain it. This young priest's arrival had disturbed everything. Margaret, his one church-married wife, lambasted the others. Pushed past her limit, Mashkiigikwe threatened to brain the older woman. Fishbone drooped quietly and poor Quill, whose mind was sensitive, desperately clung to her older sister and begged Mashkiigikwe not to leave.

"The time for this arrangement is long over," said Mashkiigikwe, "even the other full-blood families are starting to laugh at us. Now that this priest listens to old Nanapush, who as we know is only fishing for a leftover wife from Kashpaw, we'll have no peace."

Kashpaw pressed his knuckles to his eyes. A man's heart was generous, giving, like a skin that could hold more and more water. But there was always a limit, the last drop, a sorrow that could burst it. Thinking of parting with Mashkiigikwe, of not hearing her bold call as she entered the clearing with good news of her hunting, that was unthinkable. Not to laugh at her jokes or wonder at her kindness to her sister, Quill, whom she had begged Kashpaw to marry in order to save her from facing a situation in which her peculiarities of mind were exploited. No, he could not grasp what would happen if Mashkiigikwe were to leave. And yet Fishbone, pregnant, could not be the one to leave either. Vulnerable as she was, and helpless, she must surely stay. She had no family to return to. Kashpaw tried not to allow the vision of her calm grace to sway him, or his wish to curve her against him at night, to feel the heat of her gravid body. He tried not to think of her long fingers or the sadness in her hidden smile. Fishbone, he greatly loved. And he loved Margaret as well. Her acid humor pleased him and the times she allowed him near, unexpectedly, her startling inventiveness and bold behavior overwhelmed him with admiration. Besides, she was the first of his wives, and they had come to each other very young and as virgins. He could not forget those nights and how they had been the teachers of one another. Their children came one after the next, and each was stronger and more intelligent than he had any right to wish. No, Margaret could not leave. Impossible.

The leaves rustled inconclusively. His thoughts turned back and forth in the wind. First one side then the other, quick as popple. This young priest possessed a surprising power, one he seemed unaware of, which made it all the more effective. The young priest had calmed Quill and made her happy. His mere presence had affected the change. After his visit, Quill fell to her knees whenever her mind swelled. By striking her breast and crying out in her own words a message to the priest's god, she emptied her mind of the deadly thing that possessed it. Nothing else, no doctoring, had helped. But the priest, she liked.

So that was the first of several arguments Kashpaw's mind put up. He didn't listen to the self-serving evidence that his covetous friend Nanapush laid out before him. Even thinking of Nanapush's transparent scheming, Kashpaw had to laugh. If Mashkiigikwe ever got her hands on the old dog, she would break him like a twig. And Margaret, he doubted anyone but himself could survive the ravages of Margaret's love. Yet what could he do? It was clear that things must change, only he didn't have the ability to make a decision. Each loss was impossible. Each solution meant destruction. If he did nothing, would his land be seized? Margaret mentioned that, but was she inventing the possibility for her own purposes?

Kashpaw grasped his pipe tenderly and touched the warm red bowl of the stone to his forehead. Why did a man have to love so much? The stone cooled in his fingers while he let his mind wander through all of the sorrows of possible answers.

*

Agnes tried to tell herself, later, that it was not one thing or another that broke up the Kashpaw family and set chaos into motion. Yet she could not ignore the fact that Father Damien started it with his visit. Later, when she was able to reflect upon the fall of events, Agnes pictured a tornado descending, one composed of political gusts and personal fabrics of wind, a twister in the eye of which rose Pauline Puyat, later to become Sister Leopolda, nemesis and savior.

Father Damien knew all that happened through the boy with the plaid cap, for Nector Kashpaw did show up, at first to stand uneasily within the nave, and then later to become an altar boy. The boy served Holy Mass each Sunday with great seriousness and precision, a contrast to his increasingly desperate home life, which he recounted to Father Damien over the post-Mass rolls and meat, tea and dried apples that Damien provided and Nector ate with strict intensity.

The violently independent Mashkiigikwe left her little sister, with Kashpaw's promise that Quill would be the one wife he kept. Mashkiigikwe left at night, knowing that Quill would howl and clutch to her skirts. She took her gun and pack and disappeared onto her trapline. Kashpaw's next youngest son, Eli, was already gone. That left Kashpaw another gun short and in want of hunters to feed the group. Fishbone's baby was stillborn; she fell ill and could not be moved from the cabin. During spring sugaring, her older child crawled into the fire, and for days his screams and whimpers rang the little clearing. Margaret finally struck the child, silencing its cries to bewildered gasps. Kashpaw, sore over Mashkiigikwe, struck Margaret fiercely in return and didn't even care to follow her when she hobbled off in fury to complain to Nanapush.

Who fell in love with her.

Nector didn't tell this last development to Father Damien. The priest found out himself, and the situation provided him with much to consider. So it was Nanapush who threw the Kashpaw household like a pile of sticks into the air, in the night, and waited blindly underneath to catch what fell, or who, and wasn't it a well-deserved and sad piece of luck that the one he caught was Margaret?

During the months that followed, it was apparent that Nanapush wasn't over his first infatuation with Mashkiigikwe. He often thought about her, spoke of her great hunting skills with bashful adoration, spread his hands one way to show the size of her feet to Father Damien, spread his hands differently to show the weight of her breasts, threatened to follow her with gifts of love.

Gradually, though, and with increasing ardor, his attention turned to placating Margaret Kashpaw. She was composed of a shrewd toughness that intrigued him. Her features communicated regal scorn. She was surprisingly light on her feet and could easily run a dog down and whack the rabbit from its teeth. Nanapush had seen it. She could chop wood, haul water, drop a wild goose from the sky by clipping off its head with one shot. Nobody bested her and nothing intimidated Margaret. She was a challenge that Nanapush could not resist.

Quill's Madness

Without her older sister, Quill lost her bearings, for it was Mashki-igikwe who always told her what to do. Mashkiigikwe had soothed her and carefully unwrinkled the pain that crumpled her mind. She had stroked her younger sister's face and sung an old song about the clouds lifting off the surface of the lake. Then she fed her tidbits from her own fingers and lightly pulled on Quill's braids, as though to guide her back to the living. Eventually, Quill would respond slightly, and then Mashkiigikwe would know that once more she'd succeeded in reaching her. And she had wanted desperately to reach her sister, guide her back, for on this side of the spirit world Quill had a daughter who was turning out to be as massive as her father, but very shy, and needed a mother's attention.

Mashkiigikwe had also kept things running smoothly, along with Margaret. There was always food, always wood, always water. Now, all Quill did for hours each day was chop, haul, gather. A frail sapling, her shoulders bowed beneath the weight of the family. Taking care of all the children including her own daughter, and the burnt boy, enduring a lack of food and the nerveless despair of her husband, Quill imagined that she had bent to the ground and been rooted by the ends of her fine, black hair. When she pulled herself upright, earth rained down on her and her thoughts were weak as dust.

Quill sat hunched on pukwe mats while her daughter, whom she'd just named Mary after the female whiteman's god, combed through her hair with her fingers, then the clever brush. Mary divided off the hair strand by strand and removed from the hairs louse or egg of louse or husk or sign of such a creature. Lately, Quill had come to abhor these intimate vermin and to believe that they were biting her to disturb and to disarrange her thoughts. From time to time, her daughter dipped her fingers in a little can of kerosene and pinched off a louse. Quill's thoughts burned. Temptations flared. A harsh volatility depleted her. Quill imagined that if Mary should purse her lips and blow on her head it would burst into flame like a candle. She slapped off her daughter's hands, jumped up, started working.

Quill wove pukwe angrily, not half as well as Margaret. She moved the reeds between her fingers so quickly that they blurred, but the mats were uneven, the edges loose and sloppy. Who cared? One mat, another, appeared. When she stopped, her strength faded and her eyes rolled back, white around the iris. Her breath came short. A strange fear rode in her, and the only way to keep going was to keep working. Faster. Harder. She knit an extra mat and tossed it aside. Another materialized. The mats kept collecting until the reeds were gone. Yet her heart would not be still.

In the center of the day, she abandoned everyone, left them howling for her, crying for n'gah, n'gah, weakly asking for nibi or soup. She stood and walked into the bush, hiked her skirts and peed standing, frowning distractedly at the moving reeds onshore. Mashkiigikwe had always helped her drive away a spirit that annoyed her, a wild old skeletal woman who kept visiting her and putting evil thoughts into her mind. Suddenly, here the old thing came, scratching her way along through the undergrowth until very suddenly she was right next to Quill, invisible, fingering her skirt, lifting her blouse, touching her legs, laughing at Quill's slow tears of fright.

At first Quill resisted. As always, once the old witch operated on her with her words and torture, Quill eventually agreed to accomplish the cruel tricks that the matchimindemoyenh laid out in her mind. When she returned to the lodge, Quill stuffed earth into the mouths of her children. She poured earth into the barrel of her husband's rifle, flung earth into the soup pot, and tamped earth into her vagina. She sat grinning at the world, holding a great makak of dirt. Eat, she said to her husband, offering it when he returned.

DOCTORING QUILL

They tried the sucking bones again and they tried the old remedies but always, halfway through the procedure, Quill rolled over with an alert cry and darted her arms in the air beseeching them to fetch the priest. Perhaps, by then, she had seen too many die too young, too soon, and Quill's nervous mind could not accept this. She'd had only her sister left. Many people went mad to protect themselves from the grief of witnessing the wreckage. Perhaps the old woman with the white hands and black face, hissing in her mind, was the cause of Quill's agitation. The priest, Father Damien, had given her assurance without really knowing how to help her.

Desperate to bring her mind back, Kashpaw brought Quill into Holy Mass. He led her to the front of the church and placed her in the seat beside him, holding her two arms like a large, temporarily docile doll who might at any moment come to life and lash out. Next to them, their great strong daughter gazed impassively upon the altar. When Father Damien raised high the body of Christ, Quill's body went rigid and her eyes crossed in ecstasy. She fell sideways onto Kashpaw's lap and could not be roused until the Blood of the Lamb met her lips. Then she wept, sadly and with copious hunger, for God or for her many precious dead who could say. Father Damien, who sat with her long after Mass was over and who listened to her outpouring with great sympathy but limited comprehension, for it was all in Ojibwe, was shocked when she suddenly changed the cast of her features, laughed low in a harsh unconscious tone, bit down, and ripped the flesh from her own finger.

Rock of the True Church,

I very much wish to know how I am to treat the cases of irregular connection that abound on this reservation. There are some who have remarried in the Church without annulment—can their unions be regarded as a natural bond? Which woman may a man keep who has had several and must be married to one?

My other question is as follows: How far am I permitted to enter into the political picture? At present, I am regarding it from the vantage point of an observer, though I have gathered information. In what ways is a priest allowed to protect the interests of his parish?

The opinion of Your Holiness on these matters is absolutely vital to me.

Modeste

JOHN JAMES MAUSER

One name appears and reappears among the papers that I handle, wrote Agnes in a hand that she had adapted only slightly. She had never written in a particularly feminine hand anyway. Now she stiffened her letters and stacked the words together with a neat solidity that matched, she hoped, the toughness of the priest she was becoming.

"John James Mauser," she wrote in Father Damien's daybook. "I have now begun to conduct a methodical search for information, and found that John James Mauser is a man whose actual person, if not identity, is mysterious. From a news story and engraving, I have determined that he is a tall, curve-lipped, and jut-nosed son of eastern mill barons and shrewd New York socialites. He is a restless man who got his lucky start by correctly guessing where the Northern Pacific railroad would cross the state line.

"John James Mauser bought the land that, in what seemed a matter of weeks, became downtown Fargo. He went from land speculation into lumber, minerals, quarries. He now purchases areas lost to the continual census that shows a dwindling number of Indians. He buys the land tax forfeited. He buys the land by having the Ojibwe owners declared incompetent. He buys this parcel and the next and the next. He takes the trees off. He leaves the stumps.

"New legislation passes. Is reversed. Mauser prospers with every fumble. His hands are always open, ready to receive. He denudes all holdings as they come his way, though sometimes he waits for certain special parcels that produce, as do one series of prime allotments on Little No Horse, oak trees of great density, beauty, and age that will never again be seen in this region."

Agnes threw down the pen and rubbed her face. A desperation

gripped her, an irksome anxiety. She took up the pen, twisted it, bit the end, continued.

"Many people think of the papers that Mauser offers as a treaty. He has taken interpreters and ribboned officials with him to meetings. He himself gives out bolts of cloth, old-time kettles, and twists of tobacco. Though he speaks of and counts the government's agents as his friends, he is careful never to claim them. Up until this time the only agreements that Anishinaabeg have signed have been with the government, and John James Mauser is not government. He is a single man who wants trees, in general, and a particular set of trees also, and to get them he offers what seems a vast sum of money to each head of household, so much money that it seems unthinkable to turn it down.

"A great many sign and take the money. It must seem they can surely buy land somewhere else. But then the winter drags out, children need to be fed, old people buried, and the craving satisfied that never quits. Thanks to Mauser, ishkodewaaboo, the smooth fire that takes their land money, is tidily available just across the reservation line. . . ."

7

THE FEAST OF THE VIRGIN

1912–1913

Seating himself on an overturned cream can at the cooking fire of Alexandrine and Michel Destroismaisons, the latter a well-respected canopy bearer for the Host, Father Damien accepted a cup of strong, black, sugared tea. There was a clash of pots and the rich smell of bannock, pork, oats, more tea, and makade-mashkikiwaaboo. Gratefully, he drained the first cup. Sipped the next. He was just about to ask Alexandrine to press her children into service picking wildflowers for the altar, when, across from where he sat, a strange apocalyptic figure reared.

The Puyat—dressed in her own homemade habit—staggered past, her arms piled with buffalo skulls. Jutting from the veil, raw and planar, her face, like another of those skulls, stared out with deep, unseeing, hollow eyes. Her complexion was bone white and her gaze held a withering power. Gaunt and spectral in her thin height, she stalked through the shallows like a heron, sharp beaked, ravenous. She passed behind Alexandrine and Michel, and was gone. Turning his full attention back to the Destroismaisons, Damien resumed conversation, but with an inner disturbance that he recognized only later not as the effect of the strong hot tea but as an agitation of the heart produced by those great, dead, appalling eyes.

The day continued mild and glorious, and as the sun's light strengthened the Catholics fell in line behind the cart bearing a borrowed statue, for the parish hadn't one of its own yet. As they passed along, men fell to their knees in the dust of the road and women raised a trill—a high-pitched tongue of wild joy, a sound that never failed to tighten Damien's throat. Kashpaw's washed, white horses pulled the wagon with nervous alacrity, rolling their eyes and starting suspiciously at the supplicants. The newly baptized and morose Kashpaw drove it, with Quill sitting just alongside him.

White scarf alight in the sun, Quill sat bolt upright, stiff in her abashed fear. She threw back her head from time to time, eyes rolling, and laughed. Mary Kashpaw, huge in a white dress, crept to her mother and stroked her hand. Quill swiped her daughter's hand like a fish from a stream, madly tore at it with her teeth, continued to laugh. Her daughter winced at the bite, but did not cry, just turned and hunkered low in the back of the wagon with her cousin and the borrowed statue.

The poor, chipped Virgin wore an expression of distaste, but she was decked brightly with wreaths and a crown of wild lilies and arum. At her feet, the two girls sat and threw the petals of prairie roses, pink and blushing, from baskets made of willow withes the red black of old blood. Damien stepped on the petals as he walked behind them, bearing the Sacred Host.

Held visible in an intricate glass lunette, the wafer trembled before his eyes as he prayed. These days, Agnes and Father Damien became one indivisible person in prayer. That poor, divided, human priest enlarged and smoothed into the person of Father Damien. As though the unseen were a magnetic draw upon Father Damien's spirit, his thoughts leaped like iron filings. His requests, sharp black slivers of metal, pierced the sun, and his praises melted in his ears. Now, in that rapt concentration, he moved along the road. Sometimes he held the Sacred Host aloft, feeling a soft power flow through his arms. Sometimes he held the Host before him at a more intimate level. With each step, gentle waves of air brushed around him as though the earth cheerfully flexed underneath each footstep. Each breath was sunlight. Green love surrounded him. Present on the hillside with the body of his Christ, he breathed an easy adoration. One step. The next. Sorrows, confusions, pains of flesh and spirit, all melted into the sweet trance of the moment.

Then, he tripped.

Agnes thought, later, how odd—odd or typical—that she should stumble in the full flow of the gift, in the radiant immediacy of pure grace. What happened next, and next, followed from the first misstep. Father Damien went down holding fast, but, as though an unseen hand yanked, the monstrance bearing the Host bounced upward, turning in the sun. The moment, fluid as he rolled over swamped in flowing vestments, could have been rescued. Had he jumped directly to his feet. Had only the procession halted. . . . But no, it appeared that he was part of something larger. Uncanny, the design. For now it happened. Just as he went to earth, the presence white as flowers and dead as bone, the Puyat woman with buffalo skulls and jackal face, emerged from a hidden spot. Barefoot, dragging the skulls on thongs fastened somewhere within her habit, she raised her arms in horror to see the Host defiled. She bounded forward just before the garlanded wagon bearing the brooding statue, the children, Quill, and Kashpaw. Her oversize habit flapped like a sail. She flung herself into the wagon's path.

The horses panicked and reared in their traces. They pranced, hopped, twisted away from the Puyat, then exploded with a wild energy. They shot down the path until they reached the bottom and could run cross-country. They tore pounding through tangled farmsteads. Through town. Men chased as they wheeled by, shouting, "Cut the lines!" But Kashpaw carried with him only one dull hatchet, and the best he could manage in the wild tumble were awkward scrapes across the reins. Rounding a curve the statue of the Virgin shot out like a torpedo. That, in itself, was an event that caused repercussions deep into the future. For her halo sliced right through an oiled paper window and the rest of the statue followed, straight into the house of seven of the most notorious drunks in Little No Horse, who lay groaning that very moment for whiskey.

THE SEVEN DRUNKS

Instead of a bottle, the Blessed Virgin flew through the window. Skidding across the room, she tipped upright so that, by the time the sodden ones looked blearily up, she stood tall. Her glance of disgusted sweetness shone down upon the four men and three women, including a much too young Sophie Morrissey and a couple of Lazarres. Their sore eyes pinned upon the Virgin, who stood directly in the square of light from the broken window. Of course, the drinkers all knelt, blessed themselves, wept in astonishment and converted—not to Catholicism, but at least to a much less potent form of alcohol: to wine. Henceforward, they were strict in their loyalty to the grape— even though, they claimed, no matter how much they poured down their gullets, they couldn't get satisfyingly shkwebii anymore. And even as a result of their encounter with the Virgin, some were afflicted with a mild friendliness and industry.

THE RUNAWAYS

The children in the back of the wagon jounced along, thrilled at first, then shrieking. The fortunate little girl cousin popped over the edge of the wagon and landed safely in a heap of slough grass. Still, the vehicle flew, banging crazily behind the horses as they galloped toward disaster. It was over in an instant.

The wagon approached a sudden fold in the land with ravenous ease. The violence of the drop broke the back of Quill. A low-branched tree speared Kashpaw. They were mortally wounded, though they lasted in their mutual agony for several hours. Their daughter survived in the overturned wagon box, dragged along until the horses came to the end of their terror. The men who found her deep in the bush had to pry away the crushed and splintered boards from the child. They later told their wives in low voices how she'd wept, as from her arms and her legs they drew the nails.

KASHPAW'S VISION, QUILL'S PEACE

The men laid Quill and Kashpaw out together side by side in the long fine grass underneath a deep-grown oak tree. After her rescue, their child was allowed near to hold their hands and would not be moved from them even in her pain. So the three at least possessed the comfort of one another's presence. In that time, Quill, at peace though her back was severely broken, spoke to her daughter and to Kashpaw, who answered, though the branch that pierced him made his voice pinched and strange. Though the helpers and gapers who approached muttered at the helpless horror of it, they listened. For Quill and Kashpaw were able to talk. In talking, they gave reason for those present to think that in this extremity the eyes of Kashpaw saw into the near future of his people, while the heart of Quill saw far into the past.

The two of them prophesied while they were dying. Quill was rational and spoke in a sincere attempt to right wrongs stubbornly fixed between reservation factions. For his part, Kashpaw first saw a spirit approach, and it was one he knew well, and had spoken with, and feared. Nanapush was called to sit with his old friend and sing him into the next world.

"N'tawnis," whispered Kashpaw, "he approaches. I see him."

"Who, my friend?" Nanapush spoke lightly, though his heart was bursting in his breast. Each breath he took stabbed him with pity and yet he smiled gently so as to ease along his brother-cousin.

"That tall spirit wearing the black hat. My brother, it is he himself, the one who comes to warn me of disease."

"Where is he going, this spirit?" asked Nanapush.

"Coming toward us. Coming here," Kashpaw gasped. "Ah! He will take me first, then he will return for many others."

"This is sad news," said Nanapush, in truth, terrified. "I will give you a smoke." With that, he lighted his sacred pipe and the two shared the fragrant tobacco. A slender curl of it crept out of the hole the stick made in Kashpaw's lower breast and Nanapush nearly cried out, seeing it.

"Give niwiiw a smoke, too," said Kashpaw, jabbing his lip sideways to indicate Quill, and Nanapush brought the pipe to her side—in fact, he then sat between them, passing the pipe to each, hearing as they spoke.

"Our daughter will dig our grave for us and then she will keep on digging," said Kashpaw. "She will dig graves for two hundred Anishinaabeg who will die of this sickness that approaches from the east."

"It comes from the east, you say," said Nanapush.

Father Damien, kneeling beside him in a miserable state of despair, praying with his whole being, looked to the east and then passed a trembling hand over his eyes. Silhouetted against the horizon, a gaunt and precipitous walker wavered toward them. There was a dot at its side, a dog, a companion. Who saw what? This thing was too tall to be human.

It was gone when he blinked.

"If we lighted great bonfires or dug ditches full of water or allowed no visitors—" said Nanapush.

"No use, my friend, it is borne on the wind," Kashpaw answered.

"And you . . ." Quill whispered to Father Damien, who was still kneeling beside them, far gone in stunned confusion at the mystery. "How . . ."

"I stumbled," said the priest wretchedly. "I beg your pardon, I tripped on the beauty of the day."

"And now we must die for it," said Kashpaw, his voice accepting and almost marveling at the strangeness. "Not you, but the Puyat, she is the cause. Life is leaking out of us now, priest. All because of the Puyat."

Pauline Puyat then, with an audacity that spoke both the boundless arrogance and violent compassion of her nature, approached them. With no leave, she knelt beside the sufferers. Freed of the skulls, her back torn, and in a state of pain herself, she stared nakedly into their faces. Her eyes were molten and her face calm with an immense and soothing pity. Wordlessly she dipped a cloth into a bowl of water that she held and allowed a trickle, just the right amount, to pass Quill's lips and then Kashpaw's. She murmured as she bathed their temples, their brows, their chins, their eyelids, and when she was finished with Quill, the madwoman's eyes fixed on the Puyat's face and they exchanged, Father Damien saw it, a look of tenderness and sweetness that would have astounded him then if everything was not already so far beyond acceptance or belief. Quill's face cleared. Her eyes focused. She smiled with pleasure to feel a sudden and poignant sanity, and she squeezed her daughter's hand. The gentle firmness of her touch calmed the big girl's agony. When Quill spoke, it was with the old voice, the soft and compelling tones she had used before the onset of her affliction.

"Hear me," she said. "Come near, for I have something important to say to you all, here on the reservation."

A silence enfolded all, and many knelt to listen.

"Lazarres and Pillagers should eat from the same kettle," Quill said, "join together for strength against the truer threat which is not each other but the damn chimooks robbing every straw from the fields and stealing even the lice from our heads and the tongues from our mouths and the shit from between our butts and the little sense we got left in us after the liquor. Stay together, you families, don't let the land and money divide you!"

Her prophecy was right to the mark, said many, and they went away repeating it—that is, until they saw an enemy Pillager or Morrissey, Kashpaw or Lazarre.

Astounded with joy to hear the sensible quality of his wife's words, Kashpaw gasped, moving the core of wood in his chest a fraction, which completely killed him.

The girl fell senseless, then, still holding her mother's hand. Quill, mercifully, was soon too far gone to notice her husband's absence on the ground beside her, or see the animal anguish of her child. She merely closed her eyes, drifted, came to no shore, drifted farther, until she was somewhere new.

QUILL'S DAUGHTER

Even the nuns were heard to say that Christ took such pity on the girl's suffering, so like his own, that she should never have the cause to weep again. She grew phenomenally, put on weight and bulked up like her father, Kashpaw. And she toughened. During the next, desperate, winnowing winter she avoided every illness, even though she went without mittens or shoes. She would flourish while other girls coughed tubercular blood, increase her strength and quickness until she could wrestle down any boy. The trick of her quiet would help her hide from trouble, too, for after the accident, she seldom spoke.

Quill had a cousin named Bernadette Morrissey, a bony and bleak-spirited woman who took in children to help work the land she kept with her brother, Napoleon. Immediately after Quill's death, Bernadette requested of Sister Hildegarde that the girl live with her. Bernadette took the daughter of Quill home, but soon reported that she regretted her charitable impulse. The big girl apparently turned violent. Unexpected rages shook her like freak storms. Once, she struck Bernadette, and worse, Napoleon seemed to tap some vice in her. If the big man came within arms' reach, she set upon him with claws and teeth. The family soon called the priest to their allotment, where he experienced a fearsome sight.

Mary Kashpaw had left off attempting to destroy her caretakers, and instead took out her frustrations on their land. On the day of Father Damien's visit, she was moving earth with a careening fury. She had already raised mounds of dirt and created a confusion of deep and irregular holes and ditches through the yard and woods. She could not be stopped. Not even a grown man like Napoleon dared step within reach of her shovel, and no word from any woman or girl pierced the intensity of her concentration. She hadn't eaten, hadn't slept. It looked as though she was determined to dig until she dropped to her death.

For a time, Father Damien watched. It was a dry spring day and the crust of the earth was waking and softening. He thought perhaps the girl would hit frost but apparently the dirt was warmed as far down as she cared to dig. A shuddering fear ran through him as he recalled Kashpaw's vision. Was his daughter digging those two hundred Anishinaabeg graves? The holes were the shape not only of graves, but worse, of many interconnected and searching graves.

Since it was useless to remonstrate with her or ask questions, Father Damien took up a shovel. Alongside the huge mad child, where no one would go, he then began to dig. One shovelful after another, careful ones, a heap of dirt to the side. It was not an unpleasant task. In fact, he found, there was much in it immediately that calmed and soothed. Before the girl even recognized or took the slightest notice of the priest, then, Father Damien was digging along in a state of agreeable oneness with his work.

After a while, Mary Kashpaw did notice. She didn't stop, but she did turn to regard the priest as her arms rhythmically swung. A spasm, not a smile, crossed her face, a wave of nerves, and then she more powerfully relaxed into the current of her labor and dug, unceasingly, with renewed strength. Dug to the east for a time, then casually reversed and carved a long pan into the ground heading west. At random moments, she quit her trajectory. Inspired by some other spot, she crossed to the place and sank her shovel. A northerly foray twisted like an eel and then veered counterclockwise until she'd swung directly south. And through the day, through the long afternoon, hands bound with rags on the handle of the shovel, Agnes dug, too.

The desolation of the great child shook Agnes to the core. The girl reminded her of herself. There was no doubt about it. Grief has its own rules and power. Agnes sat with Mary at the table by the stove, where the girl wolfed down huge chunks of bread sopping with gravy-grease. Eyes glazed, Mary Kashpaw gave herself over to eating, chewed with grand solemnity. Her massive jaws crushed and pulverized the food, and she seemed to have no other purpose or interest.

"Your mama and your deydey are not in the ground anymore," said Father Damien in a firm voice, hoping to stop the digging. "They have been taken up into the sky."

Mary Kashpaw frowned, lowered her face like a bull, and walked out the door. It was a fair day. The sky over them was massive and blue with random clouds. Perhaps, thought Agnes, Mary would catch a glimpse of their faces or invent the imprint of their smiles in the vapor. Perhaps she would experience some comfort, but no. Mary Kashpaw raised her eyes and gazed with fixed gravity upward, upward, scanned the brilliance and then turned her gaze onto Father Damien.

"You can't see them," he tried to insist, "but they are up there. They love you."

She looked at him with pity and scorn.

"There is something," Father Damien tried to explain to Hildegarde, "profound about her suffering. And she is most intelligent. I'm afraid she can't be kept at the government school, and an asylum would destroy her."

"Yes, Father," said Hildegarde perfunctorily, as she did when he became, to her mind, either too fanciful or too tender of heart.

"I have an idea about the uncle, as well. Her hatred of the man is abnormally intense."

"She's mad," said Hildegarde flatly.

The nun's stubborn pragmatism annoyed Agnes, but at the same time she could not quite wrestle the proper evidence to life. Why had grief given this particular task to Mary Kashpaw? Perhaps the girl was looking for something buried, maybe the way a dog hides a bone and forgets exactly where. Maybe she'd needed this object, too well hidden. Later, her plan began to take on a cosmic shape. Agnes tried to think of the excavations as a design with some strategy. If birds viewed it from above, what would they see? She took the large view but saw only a tangle of upsettingly random desecrations of the spring undergrowth—it made no sense. And by that lack of law it made no sense, either, to place upon the girl's actions any rational construction. She was digging. The purpose must be poetic, thought Agnes. Perhaps only poetry could explain it, and Father Damien was a priest.

In fact, the answer would come slow and only by degrees over days, until it was entirely explained in a dream: she herself was digging when she uncovered a dream Kashpaw and a dream Quill who rose, brushed off their clothing, and complained of the coldness of the earth. *Fetch my daughter*, Quill said to Agnes, *for the man hurts her.* Agnes woke knowing that Napoleon had done something terrible to the girl. Now Mary Kashpaw was looking for her parents for protection, and to soothe her. Agnes also realized that Kashpaw and Quill held Father Damien responsible.

The next morning, Agnes went to visit. Mary Kashpaw's ravaged stare struck her as more than a look—it was a passageway between this reality and the next. The Kashpaw girl had entered a dark peace from which she would never be disturbed. She sat on a solid mental ledge and frowned passively upon the world, a great brooding child who was too well traveled a visitor in the dream world and the land of the dead. The only place for Mary Kashpaw was the convent itself, or at least the grounds of the church—she didn't like to sleep indoors. The girl must come to live near Father Damien.

At his insistence, Bernadette drove the girl to the convent, where she was to live for the rest of her life. When Mary Kashpaw got down from the wagon seat upon which, curiously, she seemed much at home, untroubled by the frightful events that drove her into silence, Agnes felt a curious twist. Her theory of rescue was upended by an acute intuition. The girl's presence was all of a sudden reassuring. As Agnes approached and took the girl's hand she understood, with a positive prescience, that Mary Kashpaw had come to shield her and heal her—how, there was no saying.

Mary Kashpaw ate more than all of the nuns put together, but when food was scarce she gathered her own, and then some. She was discovered chewing wild tonic of fresh dandelion spears from the borders to the nun's path and munching green apples; sometimes she made herself a stew of gopher and acorns, stolen eggs from the nests of finches and doves, wild currants, cattail root; she gnawed a gum of spruce and occasionally, for the nuns, snared a rabbit or mesmerized a grouse in the weedy graveyard. If all else failed, she brought them a meat she called "ground meat," already skinned and boned, so it was quite some time before they realized it was named for its habitation— it was snake. She could always catch bullheads and frogs. She knew well just how to survive. With her mother's slim height and her father's powerful build, she grew into an arresting presence, though she seemed content to turn her back upon the world.

Summers, she slept in the shack where the sleigh was kept, made a bed on the hard seat and curled up like a babe. In winter, she made a pallet on the convent floor behind the kitchen stove. Her prayers were constant, a mutter just under her breath. Surely, her piety found favor in God's eyes. The sisters envied her simplicity a little and grudged her the loaf of bread she ate each meal. She had no shame—hooked her skirt between her legs, fastened it in her belt like a great wide diaper when she wanted freedom of movement. Her thighs were rock hard and golden. The nuns made trousers for her, underwear, modest bloomers and knit socks, but she just shed them in the joy of her work. Set to the task of planting, she sowed with a matchless fervor and whacked new ground clear in a disturbing contest of joy. Carefully, Father Damien kept from her all sight of shovels. Mary Kashpaw hoed and chopped, whitewashed every wall with a profligate arm, cut weeds, used a scythe with frightful intelligence, polished every pew and wooden surface with beeswax, but her favorite occupation, the work to which she brought the same passion with which she dug, the work that made her so happy that she was heard humming tunelessly and brashly to herself, was chopping wood. It became known all around that she was prodigious, as in the yard great stout piles mounted.

Each stroke was part of her devotion, all seamless, all one. She lent herself to chopping with a prayerful precision and grace, and she smiled modestly and blessed herself when she was done. She slept with her ax, filed it, kept it sharp and clean. As long as she was occupied—they soon hired her out—she attended every Mass, sang with the sisters at every funeral. She made her confession twice weekly, a silent confession that consisted of a tap on the screen and a whisper like the sigh of windblown grass. For her penance, Father Damien rarely gave her more than one Hail Mary to mouth into the clasp of her palms. How could he assign more? She committed no sins. Men were no more to her than the dust in her sleeping robes. Her life was simple. All lies fled past her. She was immaculate of envy. She grew up in no one's shadow and cast her own in solitude. She lived in such exclusive discipline that it seemed to Agnes that the girl was preparing herself, for what, Agnes did not know until it came upon them.

INFLUENZA

1918

Only one road led in and out of the reservation. There was no question. Disease came down the whiteman's road. Some heard it approach with slithering steps, foul and mawkish. Zozed Bizhieu met a man whose appearance arrested her. Great white patches of skin gleamed on his skull and strings of orange hair fell to his shoulders. His face was ravaged, and so thin that his teeth stuck out. He was made of spikes and sticks. Way up high, his skull bobbed, skin white as paper, mouth blood-red. His nose bled, she told Damien. His lips were a blistered purple. His eyes wept black bile and suddenly he fell dead at her feet. When she leaned over to assist him, he laughed as he melted into the earth, and the rank and rangy mutt that shivered at his side ran off, onto reservation ground, howling a deadly breath. Zozed was always seeing things, reporting, but some believed in this uncanny messenger because they'd heard rumors of the illness already.

The Spanish influenza was reported in the papers, which people now bought because six Anishinaabeg men had joined the great war of the chimookomanag. The newspapers reported that the disease was marching all over the world and working hard harvesting the young, old, fragile, and sturdy. Making no distinctions in its eager rush. People hoped that the sickness would be tired by the time it got to the reservation, but, no, when it hit, the illness struck with a young exuberance. Descended, really, on the wings of ducks, in the bones of clouds, on city wagons, and in the pockets of used clothes. It came in meat and on the skin of potatoes. It was waved off the trader's hands, and dusted tongue to tongue with the Communion Hosts served from Father Damien's fingers.

Father Damien's first call was the family Destroismaisons, they of the pride in their handsome boy and intelligent girl child, the devout Destroismaisons who bore the canopy to shade the Host in the procession. This illness, which began with a teeth-rattling chill, slammed into the family and leveled them just before the first snow. Their house was a neat whitewashed cabin, dark inside, but with careful shelves built into the walls next to the stove and a carved wooden bed, store-bought, where now both children labored to breathe. On the floor, their mother lay, far gone, covered only by shawls.

The girl's face burned brighter and brighter. She drenched the quilt with the sweat that poured out of her body, an amazing sweat that pooled in the curve of her collarbone and dripped off her earlobes in glistening beads. She incandesced into her death-flame, fiercer and brighter, until all of a sudden her lungs filled. She coughed out pans of green pus, died as soon as she began to bleed from the nose and ears. Her handsome brother died with her and then the mother. With a surprised squawk the grandmother was struck, shivered violently, and was gone from the room in less than two hours. Father Damien, turning from one to the next, whirling in a vain death dance contained in the small cabin, tried to catch the slippery tail of death before it slashed the lungs of Michel Destroismaisons.

Mary Kashpaw attempted to save the man by tying him into the bed when he raged to throw himself into the lake. Destroismaisons turned the bed over on himself and crawled with it on his back to the door, but the bed stuck and wouldn't let him through. He survived, but only to sit alone in the silent blankness of his cabin, staring at death, staring two weeks, before he lay down and slept.

He slept forever, with the others. Around them, a deep snow fell.

The cold deepened and the illness flourished. At all hours, the desperate came calling. Mary Kashpaw broke the trail, tramped before the priest in her bear-paw snowshoes, twice the circumference of ordinary snowshoes and reinforced with moose gut and the unforgiving sinews of cow. Mary Kashpaw dragged a small barge of supplies tied to her waist and that heavy load further packed the snow so that, traveling in her wake, Agnes had an easier time of it. Still, in those fits of exhaustion she sometimes put one leaden step before the next with deep anger alone to fuel her.

God had brought her there under false pretenses, after all, aiding her with huge compassion in the flood's aftermath, appearing in person as a man with a horn spoon, calm hands. Brought her there to then abandon her in battling uncanny death. Trudging to the homes of the stricken, Agnes wondered, where was the Trinity? Any one of them would do, she thought in exhausted fury, God the Father, God the Son, God the Son of a Bitch, God the Holy Ghost. But her prayers, said with increasing feverish despair, did not turn back the course of the disease.

The parents of six children were lost. Then in another house four children, while the parents were left alive. Father Damien brought the two devastated families together, only to have them reinfect one another. Old women and brand-new babies, new mothers, the meek, the beautiful, the ugly and the useless, all the same. Lost in hours or days. It didn't matter. And still, Father Damien kept on, and Mary Kashpaw broke the way, and together they left only one trail.

One day, wretchedly sinking and sighing, Pauline Puyat tagged along with apples in her pockets. They were rumored to cure influenza just because some child had eaten one and gotten well, but so far their main assistance had been to perfume the dead or provide an illusory taste of sweetness to the bereaved. Father Damien was too exhausted to exclude any help whatsoever now, though it came from a hateful source. Following Mary Kashpaw in a trance, he made it to the cabin of Mashkiigikwe and two of Kashpaw's children by Fishbone. The fire was out, the room cold, the victims hacked in a stinking corner. Dying, their cheeks were smeared with blood from their noses and they gasped, their faces a deep plum black, straining for air.

Although her heart was charred black, Agnes felt a fresh stab of desperation and threw herself against the disease. Pauline Puyat brought wood and fetched a pot of snow, then had a fire going and the water heating in an instant. The Puyat filled rags with hot grain, tied them tightly into cushions that she placed on the breasts of the sufferers. Agnes was too tired to register amazement until much later, when she reflected upon the Puyat's actions. With the sick to attend to, Pauline was transformed. She bathed their fevers down and cleaned their hands and faces, caught their shit when they lost control, their puke of bile and live worms. Pauline quietly reassured the sufferers with low murmurs. The ugliness of death brought out of her an angel. When Mashkiigikwe opened her mouth and gasped, her neck cords straining for a breath, just a breath, Pauline was the one who thought of pounding her chest to loosen the toughened infection. Mashkiigikwe threw up a bloody gruel and then sighed, took a deep breath, slept a healing sleep.

Outside, Mary Kashpaw had cleared snow from the ground and lighted a bonfire to soften the earth, and then she automatically dug. For the first time, though, there was no use for the holes. The following summer, Father Damien would visit the very children for whom the graves were intended and watch them playing in the deep excavations, jumping in and out.

Agnes slept that night, the first time in weeks. Pauline cured Hildegarde next, nursed her back to health, a feat for which Hildegarde Anne then promised a lifetime of sponsorship. But even Pauline could do only so much, and when the sick died, no matter what their wishes, Father Damien suspected that the Puyat baptized their defenseless bodies. The holes that Mary Kashpaw had dug in the beginning were indeed filled. Two hundred and more Anishinaabeg graves. The illness plucked one after another from their grip. They saved the trader. They saved Bernadette Morrissey. They saved the Waboose family and the good Parisiens. They lost a Onesides. From every other cabin someone was taken—these were the lucky cabins. Agnes dreaded reaching a cabin with no smoke, for it would usually be inhabited by a council of the dead.

There was an end to it, as there was an end to everything.

One day, as Mary Kashpaw walked before the priest, thrashing through slough grass, the two of them aching for sleep, Agnes finally saw the one she had hoped for and cursed. They were walking due west, into cloud cover. Far ahead, Mary turned in her tracks and waited for the priest to toil closer. Behind her, the sun swelled in a dull mist. The sky was a glowing blister. Just a ray stabbed forth and pinned her in its glow. In that strange light, Agnes saw beneath the girl's disguise. She saw that the face of her constant companion, Mary Kashpaw, was the face of the man with the horn spoon. Then she knew. Christ had gone before the priest, stamping down snow. Christ had bent low and on that broad, angry back carried Father Damien through sloughs. Covered him when he collapsed at the bedsides of the ill. Christ had fed him hot gruel from a spoon of black iron. Protected him so that he never sickened even when the dying kissed his hands or coughed their last prayers into his face. Christ was before him right now, breaking the trail. An amazed strength flowed into Agnes's legs and she stumbled through the snow, reaching. Crying out, "Wait, wait, I am coming!" she lunged for Mary Kashpaw. But the girl watched impassively and when the priest drew near enough she turned away, continued walking in her ordinary form.

THE HAIR SHIRT

1919

When, for the fourth time that day, the young Pauline came sweeping across the dingy grass and beaten mud of the yard toward Father Damien's cabin, Agnes thought of sneaking out the back window. Pauline was a creature of impossible contradictions. First she meddled, wheedled, pushed herself in where she wasn't wanted, and then she made some peaceful gesture like the one with Quill, or proved herself heroic as during the epidemic, so Father Damien could not entirely condemn her. No matter, she was a continual scapular of annoyance. A hair shirt. Agnes crossed herself, once, and again for good measure, and then twice more to hold her tongue. All day in the drizzle, Pauline Puyat had left her teaching post to stubbornly pray in the birch grove, for she wanted to effect conversions. She believed that she was blocked in her vocation to work among her people. Blocked by Father Damien. Just that morning, he had said to her, "You are unsuited for life in such an active community. You can heal in desperate times, but you have no patience for teaching or for talking to children. My advice is for you to join a contemplative order!"

Pauline seethed with irritated fury. She knocked hard.

Behind the door, Agnes bit the back of her knuckles. Although Pauline was difficult, she also had her allies, for the novice had a persuasive way of speaking in a whining slur. She had, in fact, extracted a surprising amount of money from one particular and quite saintly woman of wealth. Enough to build a proper kitchen, sink a new well, plumb the interior of the convent. There were enough nuns who knew they had the young hopeful to thank for the fact that the outhouse, freezing and miserable in winter, now held rakes and hoes and wasn't needed for low purposes. That was a major piece of work. Such a good raiser of monies was immensely rare. Even Sister Hildegarde hedged with Damien when he attempted to persuade her that Pauline Puyat's place was elsewhere. After all, during the influenza, Pauline had saved her life.

"Father, may I have just one small word with you?"

The girl's false humility was a stale grease Agnes could taste, but she opened the door unhappily and allowed the girl to enter.

"You've visited me four times today, always with exactly the same request."

"Forgive me, but—"

Damien raised a hand.

"Yes, Father." Again the inward gulp of amusement, the visible attempt at pursing her dry lips and rounding her starved eyes.

"Father," said Pauline softly, "I have heard that Nanapush is still living in sin with a baptized Catholic. If you haven't the care to let me lay siege to his soul, at least have a care for hers."

"Aren't you needed to supervise the play yard?" said Father Damien, again, "surely Sister Hildegarde—"

"Oh no, Father, please don't worry!" Now Pauline lighted with an artificial jollity. Her skull's face glowed, and she trembled, racked with zeal. "Sister Hildegarde will now be giving the children special instructions in hygiene. It is her pet project this month. And as she has them occupied, I thought I might attempt once again, to . . . oh, I know how tiresome you find me, but once again I would like to beg your indulgence . . . I need to confess."

"This evening," said Father Damien.

"Now," said the Puyat in a low and stubborn voice that chilled Damien in some interior and fathomless place for which he had no guard or defense.

"All right," he sighed, making the sign of the cross over her, "proceed."

And so she began, avid, eager in desperation to spill. She knelt beside his desk. Although he tried to remain detached, the pitiable trembling of her hands clenched in prayer touched him. Clearly, she was in a state of grave inner agitation. In her confession, some nameless man appeared *a trimmed French mustache and flat, dark lips. It was a hot close afternoon, the day it happened. He pressed on me in a blinding darkness. Crushed me to a powder and spread me across the floor. Snapped me in his beak like a wicket-boned mouse.*

"Stop," said Father Damien, repelled now by her sly excitement, "you are absolved, say no more."

He drew back, not like he was finished with me, Father, but like a dog sensing the presence of a tasteless poison in its food. Then went on, which he should not have done.

"Peace, my child, let yourself be calm, you are not forsaken." Her wildness shook him, her insistence on strange details, her description of her own nakedness and that of her rapist or uncle or even someone she half allowed . . . he could not tell for sure, and then, her face narrowing and her voice hushed, she confessed the child.

I swelled so tight, Father Damien, that I could hardly lift my arms and every breath was forced, fought for against that baby's weight. I

felt my bones give, the bowl of my hips creak wide, and between my
legs there was a soft and steady burning.

"The child was born . . ."

Yes, taken from me, born, however you put it, there was no stop-
ping it, no—

"Where is that child now?"

Silence.

"Where is that child?"

The silence now held, now stubborn.

Again, his blood pounding, Father Damien asked and this time she
answered, hasty and alarmed at the conclusion that her silence was
forcing him to draw.

Dead, Father Damien, I did not touch it. Born dead!

Agnes waved both hands in the air, lapsing, horrified as if swiping
away hordes of stinging flies. Pauline began to weep now, a dry sound
like the scratching of a spent record on a phonograph. Beating her
breast, she begged for forgiveness. Agnes caught herself. Gasped out
Father Damien's standard absolution, but was unprepared to give, or
invent for Pauline, the proper penance.

"The penance, Father, what shall be my punishment?"

A trickle of spit collected at the corner of her mouth, her eyes were
red with the exhaustion of having wrestled many sleepless nights
with the violence of her past. Her gums bled from her continual fast-
ing. Her ingratiating smile was frightful to Father Damien and hoping
to get rid of her he manufactured an attack of sudden kindliness.

"You take on too much for your strength, my dear. You were violated and that could not be helped. Now rise . . . you will say two
thousand Hail Marys—no, four thousand Hail Marys, and, as well,
you will—"

"Thank you, Father, yes!"

With a sudden energy Agnes lurched around the chair and in a
flash she hoped would take the other by surprise, raised the woman
by the elbow. She was propelling Pauline out the door, when, with a
false step the girl lurched and fell against Agnes, twisting as she went,
clutching at the priest's chest. Agnes had the instinctive wit not to
catch Pauline but to step precisely backward so that the girl fell full
length. She landed hard enough to knock the wind out of her body and

she gasped, dry, fought for air. Even after Pauline picked herself up, Agnes could almost feel the thin claws and sense the cold clutch of Pauline's hands as they raked the air, so close, reaching for her bound breasts. . . .

THE VICTIM SOUL

Shortly after that disturbing confession, Pauline Puyat was found in a state of collapse, naked, prostrate before the altar, covered with muck and raving, but as Hildegarde picked her up and hid the extent of her strange condition, it was some time before the full report leaked down from the convent on the hill. It was said that Pauline Puyat took upon herself an extraordinary penance. In her cell, covered in no more than a sheet, no pillow, sleeping on the bare floor, she maintained a rigorous fast and a strange concentration. Father Damien came to sit with her, and supposedly, to hear her confession or deliver the Eucharist. The moment he saw Pauline Puyat, however, he knew that he'd come into the presence of a darkness not to be assuaged by common means.

Light fell pale gray through a set of curtains pinned together at the center of the tall rectangular window. A searching blade of radiance struck through the slight gap between the pins and fell in a strict golden slant across Pauline Puyat, who refused a bed and lay upon the floor. She would not accept a single comfort, kicked off anything but one thin sheet, yet she spoke lucidly in making her wishes known, saying that she was atoning for a desperate sin and pleading to be allowed to continue her restitutional fast. When Father Damien refused her request, she clamped her lips shut. Her jaws had locked and the muscles of her throat knotted into pull cords. She spoke through her teeth with difficulty, but her words were still calm and sensible.

"Forgive me, Father, for this is what I must do."

Her face, as she gazed upward, was womanly and open, her forehead bronzed by the seeking light. She seemed intent within, very still, as though listening for faint but vital instructions. Reaching across to draw her sheet around her shoulders, Father Damien's hand brushed the point of her chin, alabaster white and cold. Her hands, rigid in fisted knots, were stone smooth, alarmingly bloodless and heavy, clenched around thick bandages that hid her unexplained wounds. Impossible to change because of their clawlike rigidity, the gauze had begun to exude the cloying reek of infection. Hildegarde told Father Damien that she had called for iodine and carbolic soap, water, salts to soak her hands and feet. With her gray skin and deep, black, ravaged eyes Pauline was a figure set to rest on a tomb, a grave's image.

"It is a sin," said Father Damien gently, "to chastise yourself too forcefully. You will receive a blanket. You will sleep upon a mat. You will drink water and light broth; later you'll eat food."

"Ah," said Pauline Puyat, her eyes slowly filling with the loss of her ability to suffer, "please, Father, let me have my penance. It is everything and it is all I own." She spoke through clenched teeth and a shut jaw, but her speech was plain enough. Father Damien felt himself soften with pity, knowing the truth of what she said was profound.

"What you confessed to me was not your fault," he assured her.

The girl looked into Damien's face with a grimace of sorrow, or perhaps self-hatred, for her face slowly turned golden red with a strange shame. Then the red flooded back toward her heart, and she drained to a terrific, nearly translucent, dead white.

"There is more," she said wretchedly, and the veins in her temples jumped with the strength of her emotion.

"I will listen once you are healed," said Father Damien. His sympathy enfolded him in spite of himself, but he determined, then and there, if she lived he would send her off the reservation, down to Fargo, down to Argus.

Her face was ratlike, her teeth stood out, her nose was a severe bone centered like a keel. She shook her head, tried to speak, but at last could not and merely closed her eyes. The shut lids sealed like a hatchling's. She was gone into her thoughts, her prayer, whatever sustained her agony.

She was worse, said Sister Hildegarde, the next day, and so much worse the day after that she fetched Father Damien herself, though she had no way of warning him sufficiently, or preparing him for the bizarre sight that he would witness. On entering her room he was immensely struck and confused. Pauline had bent in the middle. Still more strictly rigidified, her legs were stiffened and raised, her torso also, so that she existed in a kind of permanent V shape, which the sisters had propped up with pillows and blankets, although she held it on her own. Slowly, she was bending in two. Sister Hildegarde, in her practical way, had snaked a flexible piece of rolled wet rawhide tubing down Pauline's throat before the depth of stiffness sank into all of her limbs and froze Pauline's voice box and throat. So it was that, although she fasted, the girl was given water and broth through the tube and was fairly well sustained. Except for the terrible rigidity, her vital signs were excellent now. As much as they could, they left her to peaceful silence.

News travels immediately, mysteriously, on the reservation. Soon it was out that Pauline was seized by spirits. She had left her body to visit in the world beyond this everyday life. Her body had turned wooden, they said, her tongue to stone. Slowly, she was lifting herself into the air, straining toward the sky world, arrowing her spirit toward the west. She was doing it for her people though she was of and not of them, though she was a betrayer and yet, too, betrayed by her raging Puyat mother. Though she was the half sister of a medicine man gravely feared and the rumored mother of a child raised by dog Lazarres, she was holy. Anybody can be holy, even a Puyat, that proved.

People drew near. People gathered. They came by car and wagon, they camped by the door to the convent house. They brought their sick ones, the mad, the dishonored. They brought their too quiet, ancient, dreaming children, their screaming new babies. They brought their old ones, farseeing through eyes cataracted over with isinglass scales. They brought their nerveless husbands, their foolish and silly teenagers, their ailments and failures, and they laid them on the steps of Pauline's door.

Zozed Bizhieu asked Sister Hildegarde to place in Pauline's bed a red-painted stick, which represented a request for help of a sort she wouldn't specify. Danton Onesides asked to see her, and when turned away, begged the good Hildegarde for threads from the saint's death blanket. She was not going to die, Sister Hildegarde told him, determined now that she would see to it herself that the girl survived, not

only because that would discharge something of the debt that Hildegarde owed after the great flu, but also so that the Puyat could clean
up the mess her disquieting illness was causing all through the convent. Sister Hildegarde fumed, threw up her hands. Who, did the people
outside think, who took care of these holy martyrs, these self-
indulgent saints? She could tell them, she knew. She struck her chest,
an act for which she was immediately contrite. Still, it was true.

Linens must be bleached, scrubbed, hung on lines to dry, ironed
smooth. They must be folded and set into the closets. Soon, removed
from their shelves, the sheets would return to be stained, discarded,
and go through the same tedious process. Food must be mashed up,
pulverized, fed through the tube—invalid's food. Pillows stuffed and
restuffed. Pastes and poultices manufactured for the soothing of
limbs. These cleanings and boilings required kettles, pots, spoons.
And then there was the grinding of meticulously gathered herbs (and
the grinder was most difficult to wash and clean). Buckets, mops, a
constant correction of the floors, the state of which Hildegarde was
most fierce over. The continual visitors meant someone must tend to
the gate and door at all times. Not only that, but someone must keep
more or less orderly track of the gifts and petitions with which the
girl was now deluged.

Yes, the Puyat would live. She owed Sister Hildegarde a lot of
work!

The Bizhieus brought smoked fish. The second Boy Lazarre asked
something secret, whispered his request into a small, clean, empty
baking powder can, quickly tapped the lid on, and gave it sternly to
Sister Hildegarde to let out beside Pauline's ear. From all corners of
the reservation, now, pilgrims advanced, asking for assistance in
every possible conundrum and affair. As she closed like a jackknife,
more people arrived to camp. More notes and objects were brought,
baskets and tobacco twists began to clutter the hall and entryway. No
matter how forcefully Sister Hildegarde insisted to each visitor that
Pauline could take no requests, no matter that a nurse came, pronounced on the case, and left, no matter that people kept dying or living to suffer their copious duties, onerous lives, no matter. Belief is
belief. Faith is purely faith. Even when a doctor came all the way from
Grand Forks, sounded Pauline's entire body with small wooden

blocks and a metal hammer, then spoke briefly to Father Damien, who nodded, but said nothing, knowing what he said would be meaningless to the people camped outdoors. No, no matter. In desperation, they made a saint. They made a saint because they had to, in those times, in that swale of loss.

8

THE CONFESSION OF MARIE

1996

Father Damien sipped coffee to clarify his mind—the stuff was burned, as always, by Mary Kashpaw. He was used to the metallic taste. Father Jude wasn't, and his jaw dropped in shock at the first sip of what she poured. They sat at the kitchen table of the small book-stuffed house where Damien had lived since the beginning. Mary Kashpaw set out milk, spoons, packets of sugar, and she turned away in a powerful indifference that was almost contempt. Then she turned back, frowning down upon the two men. Her eyes rested appraisingly on Father Damien, assessing his strength. The glare she held softened to exasperated worry. Her cheeks flamed with distress. She pulled her fingers, but the men took no notice. Gradually, she backed away.

"Please go on," said Father Jude, still unnerved by the presence of the great, brooding housekeeper.

Father Jude Miller leaned forward to better concentrate. He was tired, too, but his was the exhaustion of a physically active person forced to the confinement of a passive task. He yawned, shook his head to clear it, and then as Father Damien was obviously not ready to proceed, he decided to make a quick drive down to the local café to buy a cup of coffee that would not lacerate his stomach. So the first time that his downfall, his comeuppance and destiny, showed herself in the yard of Father Damien, he missed her, missed Lulu.

She descended, quite by coincidence, as soon as Jude was out of sight. Old but not old, laughing as always at the world the way she had ever since a child, she pulled Father Damien's hand into hers and spoke teasingly.

"Mekadewikonayewinini majii ayaan'na? Hihn! Niminwendam gegahwabamayaan, in'gozis. You're coming with me to the bingo tonight. I need your luck."

"What luck?" Father Damien was instantly alert, pleased with his visitor. "You have all the luck you need. You have too much luck! Maybe if you lost once in a while you'd stop gambling. Besides, I'm sure you skew the odds in your favor and it's hard for others to lose so often just to keep up with your winnings!"

"My winnings go to a very good cause, as you know."

"I do know that," said Father Damien, holding her hand tighter, lovingly, "and even if you were the stingiest lady in the world I would forgive you. How are your boys? How's Bonita?"

The question, as always, elicited an extremely complex list of their doings, and an analysis of their probable future doings as well as a comprehensive survey of grandchildren and their doings and all of her pride and complicated plans. When she had finished with her report, she made a swift exit. And so it was that she, too, avoided a certain portion of her destiny.

Father Jude emerged from his car bearing a plastic lidded cup in its cup holder and a bag, already showing grease marks, containing three rounds of hot fry bread.

"You missed her, missed Lulu!" said Father Damien, as soon as Jude sat down to eat the fry bread. It was still hot, soft as butter inside. Father Jude had sprinkled a little salt on the golden crust, and he didn't much care whom he'd missed. He just wanted to eat.

"Lulu doesn't let me use salt," sighed Damien, watching the other priest's enjoyment. "She is afraid it will affect my heart."

"She worries about you."

"Ah, yes," sighed Damien. "I worry over her. And our sisters, too. You know that tired old joke about hearing nuns' confessions, like getting stoned to death with popcorn? Not the case, not here. My sisters are robust women. Full of juice."

"There have been scandals?" Father Jude asked.

Father Damien took this question very seriously. "I prefer to call such incidents," he reflected, "profound exchanges of human love. Mary Kashpaw was one, in fact, whom love did call. She acted upon her passion. After all, we live on earth. We are created of the earth. The Ojibwe word for the human vagina is derived from the word for earth. A profound connection, don't you think?"

"Do you condone such irregular behavior, then?" Father Jude leaned forward, wiping his lips, disguising his surprise at the old man's casual use of a term most priests of his era entirely avoided.

"I do not condone," said Damien. "It would be more accurate to say that I"—here he paused to choose the word—"cherish. Yes. I cherish such occurrences, or help my charges to, at least. Unless they keep them safely in their hearts, how else can they give them up? I tenderly cherish such attractions the way I look fondly upon a child's exuberant compulsion to play. There is nothing more important, yet it is insignificant. God will still be there when the child is exhausted, eh?"

"And the attraction? The fall? The sin?"

"Cherish, as I said."

Father Jude shook his head. "I don't understand you."

"You have never loved?" Father Damien asked.

"In the sense I gather you imply? No," said Jude.

"You are only half joking," said Damien. "You find my lack of moral outrage somewhat strange."

"Somewhat appalling," said Father Jude. "To put it another way, I wonder whether living so far away from Fargo hasn't diluted your principles?"

Damien looked at the younger priest as though he were a marvel. "Truly!"

Jude raised his eyebrows and smiled to dismiss his remark, but as he spoke his gaze still rested curiously on Damien.

"I don't mean to imply that Fargo is a stronghold of virtue, it is just that certain norms of behavior are taken for granted. Right. Wrong. These are simply distinguished. Black is black and white is white."

"The mixture is gray."

"There are no gray areas in my philosophy," said Father Jude.

"I have never seen the truth," said Damien, "without crossing my eyes. Life is crazy."

"Our job is to make it less so."

"Our job is to understand it."

"And in understanding"—Father Jude looked severely troubled— "to excuse immoral actions?"

"Never those that hurt people."

"Sex hurts," said Father Jude, simply.

"Have you seen a doctor?" said Damien.

The two paused, their breathing sharpened, surprised that they had so quickly fallen into such a pleasurable dispute.

"I was not speaking from personal experience," Father Jude affected an irritation he did not feel. He hid a slight smile. "I should have put it more directly. Intercourse outside the boundaries of marriage hurts the order of things. Creates disorder. Breaks traditions, vows, families. Creates such . . . problems."

Father Damien shifted in his seat and frowned. "That is true. Anything, though, of a large nature will create problems. The more *outré* forms of religious experience, for instance."

"Mystical experiences?"

"Exactly."

"So we have come around to that." Father Miller leaned forward and looked expectantly, with sudden openness, into Father Damien's face.

"May I suggest," said Father Miller, "that I set up the tape recorder?" He opened a plastic briefcase, displayed the small box hardly bigger than the palm of his hand. Father Damien peered over his glasses at the box, which Jude Miller arranged with a careful flourish. The older priest cleared his throat, shifted in his chair, and then fell silent as Father Jude pressed a button. Listening to the faint dry rasp of tape turning on a wheel, he stared into the intimate puzzle of leafless branches outside the window.

"Let's get right down to it," said Damien suddenly. He rubbed his hands together. Sat up alert in his chair. "What have you got? First give me the source, then the story."

"All right." Father Jude leaned forward, fingers in a thoughtful curl. "There was in your convent a Sister Dympna Evangelica who served with Sister Leopolda and witnessed, as she said in her testimony, a case of stigmata bestowed by Leopolda upon a young protégée or novice."

"What?"

Father Damien started, fell back in his chair, wiped his hands across his face and then, as though to smooth away some inner hysteria, wiped again. Still, he could not contain a wild bark of disbelief.

"This postulant . . . named Marie?"

"Yes."

Damien had trouble forming words around his tongue, which seemed suddenly in rage to have swollen inside his mouth. He could only whisper, "Marie, Marie, Star of the Sea! She will shine when we've burned off the dark corrosion." Damien tried to contain his reaction so that he could properly explain the trauma of the event, which he knew well, having been a confessor to that very Marie. His voice suddenly cracked out, angry.

"She bore wounds all right, appropriate and cruel. But they were not created by the prayerful intercession of Leopolda!"

"What then!" Jude was caught up in the drama.

"Leopolda took a fork and stabbed the girl!"

"Impossible!"

"I have"—looking suddenly chastened, Damien pressed his hand to his lips—"just violated the secrecy of the confessional."

"There may be an extenuating . . ." Father Jude ruffled his notebook, clicked his pen. "Sister Dympna says that she was there—"

"Oh Dympna"—Father Damien waved his hand in despairing disgust—"never had the brains of an egg." His breath caught in his throat and he began to pant, sweating. A watery weakness came over him. "I have seen what I have seen," he declared. "I have heard the truth."

Trying not to prompt him, lest he influence the story, or again call Father Damien's scruples about the confessional's privacy into question, Father Miller maintained silence and kept his eyes downcast. He was rewarded by a charged burst of information, laid out in staccato.

"It was during my early years on the reservation that I heard her confession. Marie. She slammed into the confessional. Had a way of doing that. *Father, forgive me for I have sinned*, she said, *my last confession was such and such ago.* Then hesitated. I said, 'Of course, what is it my child?' thinking it was hard to tell me. But she was just gathering her words. She had a peculiar habit of expression. Overly mature. Maybe even bizarre. *When I went there*, she said, *I knew the dark fish must rise.*

" 'Went where? What fish?' I asked.

"She continued on, putting it in colors and flavors, you know, like a mad person. Making pictures of what she saw as a monumental undertaking. *Plumes of radiance had soldered on me. No reservation girl had ever prayed so hard.*

" 'I'm sure that's true,' I said, 'I know you're very devout.'

"*I was going up the hill with the black-robe women. They were not any lighter than me. I'd make a saint. They never had a girl from this reservation they had to pray to. But they'd have me. And I'd be dressed in pure gold.*

" 'My dear,' I gently said, 'to be a saint is more than wearing pretty clothes.' That set her off.

"*You can't tell me nothing*, she raged. *Now listen. She's a bitch of Jesus Christ*, she said. *You'd better hear about this nun.*

" 'Of whom do you speak?' I asked gently. Her response was loud and brutal.

"*Leopolda*, she yelled at the carved screen between us.

" 'Leopolda!'

"I jumped up, hit my head. I suppose my sudden interest must have shocked her, for she quieted and in a low voice continued her story with an intensity that I remember to this day. *Threw me in the closet with her dead black overboot, where he had taken refuge in the tip of her darkest toe.* She was, you see, speaking of the devil. This girl had understood before anyone, perhaps more deeply than we now can see, the true nature of Leopolda's faith."

"And what was that?"

Jude Miller had asked his question too soon, however, for Father Damien was still in the past, in the close embrace of the confessional.

"Marie Lazarre was cast from Bernadette Morrissey's care into an ill-concocted family of drunks. Still, she'd turned out pious and developed a special bond with the nun in question. As a result, she was asked to come and visit the convent, to stay there as a postulant if she so chose, under the special tutelage of Leopolda. Later, in my confessional, she described the ascent up the hill. Once she entered the convent, there was apparently no special notice given to her by the other sisters. Leopolda put her straight to work, baking bread, and then there was the incident of the cup. The poor girl, all nerves, dropped a cup. When it rolled underneath the stove, she went down on the floor to get it.

Top of the stove. Kettle. Lessons. She was steadying herself with the iron poker. What happened next was this: Leopolda held this girl down on the floor with her foot and poured scalding water on her back, telling her not to make a move or a sound. *I will boil him from your mind if you make a peep, by filling up your ear.*"

Father Miller winced, shifted in his chair uncomfortably, made a slight sound of protest, but Father Damien kept talking.

"Sometime after that so-called lesson, the two were removing loaves of bread from the ovens when some sort of argument occurred in which the girl, who by now had good reason to hate and fear Leopolda, called her down, as they say here."

"Called her down?"

"Challenged her. *Bitch of Jesus Christ! Kneel and beg! Lick the floor!* That was when our candidate for sainthood stabbed the girl's hand with the fork and cracked her head with the poker, knocking her unconscious!"

Father Miller looked aghast, but also skeptical.

"Was this witnessed? Documented?"

"Unfortunately, your witness, Dympna, entered just after the blow, while Marie was unconscious. Dympna was apparently persuaded by Leopolda's story. Our holy woman told the other sisters that she'd prayed for the girl to receive the holy stigmata as a sign of God's love, and that the girl had swooned when that first mark appeared. Marie woke confused, but soon understood the gist of things and went along with it until she could make her way out of the convent. She returned to her home, married not long after, has been known ever since as a solid and even wise member of her community. Marie. Star of the Sea. Marie Kashpaw."

The two men sat quietly together, the tape recorder humming between them. Jude Miller put his hand out to turn it off, but then withdrew his fingers. The windows were halfway open and the storms pulled up already, the screens down. In the gooseberry thicket just outside, a bird's whistle sounded, piercingly sweet. The breeze shifting through the screen was thin and dry. Father Damien now reached forward and punched off the tape recorder. Relieved, exhausted, he slumped in his chair. Closed his eyes. Before Father Miller could comment in any way or question him further, the old priest sank into a sleep so profound it looked like death. Father Miller watched intently until he saw telltale movements—a tiny twitch of Father Damien's eyelid, a slow wheezing intake of breath. He worried about the open window, but apparently the old priest liked fresh air, so he quietly covered Father Damien with a light blanket. Then Jude Miller continued to sit, watching over his elder, wishing for a cigarette, though he had quit twenty years before. He wanted to replay the tape, form queries, ask everything that needed to be asked, for the troubling story raised more questions than it answered.

An early gnat landed on the old man's nose and swatting at it, Damien roused himself enough to quit his sleep. Father Damien frowned, annoyed when he realized he'd fallen asleep in the presence of the other priest. Standing, Father Damien waved assistance aside, and took high, tiny childlike steps into the hallway of the house of his old age. He was heading for his tiny bedroom. Just before entering, he turned to the younger priest in a crack of darkness from the doorway. He waved his fingers, beneficent, as though dispensing drops of holy oil.

Father Jude blinked. In that instant a strange thing happened. He saw, inhabiting the same cassock as the priest, an old woman. She was a sly, pleasant, contradictory-looking female of stark intelligence. He shook his head, craned forward, but no, there was Father Damien again, tottering into the comfort of his room.

The rectory was made of the same whitewashed brick and thickly slabbed on interior plaster as the convent and church. Entering, after a long walk through the grounds of the church and the cemetery, Father Miller paused—the place held the tranquil mouse-nest scent of all rectories in Jude's experience, an odor composed of male sweat and sweet deodorant, cabbage-y cooking, Old Spice, and the faintly sour breath of sexual loneliness. Someone had thought to build the place with tall rectangular windows—these admitted at late dusk a singular golden light that rose, as though emitted by the prairie town beneath the hill, and flooded through the entire house in a wave. The gift of that radiance would quickly be followed by darkness, noise, the rev of slow truck engines circling below, and the throb of sub-woofers on the faintly moving air.

Father Jude's room was rectangular, too, with the window at its end and southern wall. He always liked south light, and the curtain-less sky-filled panes of glass pleased him. He sat on the single mattress, bounced a bit. There was no comfortable reading chair or bed-side lamp in the room. Apparently, no appreciation here of the intimate pleasure of reading in a pool of lamplight. Perhaps it was considered by the resident priest an indulgence, but for Jude the nightly reading was a necessary prelude to sleep. Without an orderly transition from consciousness, he was often subject to the tedium of insomnia. When so afflicted in his own surroundings, he read himself back to sleep, or, occasionally, if he was in an appropriate place, walked out into the night.

His methods of whiling away those dreadful hours were not much different, he thought now, from the apparent routine of Father Damien. That was not surprising. He, Jude, still thought of himself as young although he had never really had a young man's habits or incli-nations. His combination of energy and reserve had originally attracted him to the priesthood. A loner, he had always felt unsuited to the company of his peers. As a priest, to his great relief, his refinement and discipline of behavior made it possible to live within the limita-tions of his profession. He was an excellent priest, practical and intel-ligent, without the restlessness that so often accompanied the vows of those who had chosen to stay with the Church through its most tur-bulent recent years. He wasn't meek, but he was in his person deeply resigned to what he did. It was this immense resignation to the shape of his life that opened him every day to the experience of joy.

The night before, he'd been too tired to organize himself. Now, he carefully unpacked his clothing, hung up and smoothed each sock and hankie, refolded every T-shirt into a drawer. Everything was put away before he noticed how tired he still was, how graven his exhaustion. He climbed into the bed he'd occupy until he completed this report for the diocese. Father Jude turned out the lights and rolled gratefully between the covers. He lay stiffly on his back, relaxing only very gradually, and in the oily dark he mulled over the information he'd received from Father Damien.

If it was true that his subject had struck a young novice and practiced subterfuge in regard to the deliverance of holy wounds, that invalidated her, he would expect. However, suppose these things were true and yet Christ had seen fit to reward and forgive the penitential vows of Leopolda by bestowing upon her the highest of bloody honors? The stigmata, or wounds resembling them, the hands that held the crown of thorns. Did he or any investigatory tribunal have the right to contradict such awesome signs of forgiveness? Obviously, the thing to do next was to interview the postulant. By now, she would be elderly, if she lived at all.

Marie. What was it. Kashpaw? *Star of the sea. She will shine when we've burned off the salt.*

Where did that come from? First thing next morning, he would track down this woman. Meanwhile, yawning, Father Jude shuffled mentally through files bound in pale manila. In what now he considered his hometown another odd occurrence—miracle, coincidence—documented, no less, with photographs taken by the subject herself. The face of Christ in a pane of ice, the cracks forming a gaunt visage with deep spiritual eyeholes in the skull. Shattered spikes, white and grim, a crown of frozen thorns. The photograph, reproduced in a clipping from the local newspaper and in a small pamphlet printed at the convent, had lost definition and smeared, yet the features of the face were marked clearly enough to resemble those bled into the famous Turin shroud. Those knifelike cheekbones, those pinched and painful brows. Sister Leopolda had been nearby when the cracks in the ice appeared. "The Manifestation at Argus"—title of the thin green pamphlet published by the local convent—noted her presence in the school yard. A child was the cause, or perhaps the catalyst that produced the icy features.

Everything was connected, loop upon loop. That child was, in fact, someone known to Jude in his later life. There was no doubt in his mind that some greater power was at work. Already, he'd done an interview with her as well. A bold girl, she'd smashed down face first from a slick play slide. The cracked visage of Christ appeared where she landed. The miraculous portrait had been sawed out of the ice and carefully deep frozen, only to be lost in a summer power outage.

There was, and more recently, a well-witnessed occurrence in which a local contractor had been struck into the earth by a statue of the Virgin Mary, the statue snapping its chains during unloading. Miraculously, some said, he had been spared. Due to a holy card stuck carelessly in his pocket? A portrait of the nun in question? Or due to a bed of sand that drove the man deep, stabilizing his limbs, and stopped the statue from landing upon him full force?

Father Miller tried to disconnect his thoughts, and even proceeded in a mental exercise to stack the materials he'd gathered, pat the files into a neat stack. He composed his mind to deliver his evening prayers. He usually prayed on his knees, beside the bed, or if he was cold or exhausted, tucked underneath the covers. Tonight, he folded himself comfortably and wearily on his side and mumbled, exasperated and pleading. "God," he said, "help me out, here." Falling away from consciousness, he worked out the bones of a plan that would take him between the reservation and Argus. The mark of the smashed face. The marks of the nails. The contractor rammed into the earth but only dizzied. And yet, what good works? What kindnesses had Leopolda performed? The ordinary markers were the stuff he sought now, the shape of his subject's daily existence. Among the parishioners here on the reservation, he decided, he would find those she had helped. He would sit with them as long as it took, get their stories, record every nuance, every word.

MARIE KASHPAW

Though in age her flesh had tightened and roped to her bones, as though to tether itself to earth, Marie Kashpaw was still a formidable mass. Her hair, dove gray and cut into a helmet, had grown down over her eyebrows, but she refused to trim it. She gazed from beneath her bangs as under a visor, and regarded Father Jude with an indifferent acceptance. They sat on fat, mildewed, easy chairs.

"How come you're here? What's this for?" she asked, for she was a suspicious and brutally intelligent woman.

Father Jude told her he was gathering material about Sister Leopolda. "Leopolda!" She nodded and laughed without mirth. She popped a sourball into her mouth and smoothed her powerfully withered hands across the patterned stuff of her dress.

"What do you want?" she said again. Her eyes were round, hooded with wrinkles like a turtle's.

Father Jude explained in more detail the testimony he was collecting. He mentioned Father Damien, and a slow smile creased her face. He left out most of what was told to him by Father Damien, all that was imparted in the intimacy of the confessional.

"Sister Leopolda Puyat?" Father Jude prompted.

"I don't talk about her." Marie Kashpaw gazed down at the hidden swirls and leaflike gestures in the pattern of her dress material. Slowly, heavily, she frowned. She wore nylon anklets, neatly folded down. Her wide tan shoes appeared to be bolted to the floor.

"I see," said Father Jude. He allowed a deeper silence to cloak them. Together, they sat in the shabby sun. He smoked peacefully, wondering whether or not to tell her more. Finally he asked Marie Kashpaw, "Are you a discreet woman? Can you keep a secret?"

"No," she said.

They lapsed once more into the voluptuous morning quiet. At last, he tried again, desperate to approach the subject.

"Why won't you, or can't you, speak of Leopolda?"

Marie Kashpaw looked bewildered, then annoyed, and once again drew into her stubborn shell. She refused to talk, but seemed, too, unwillingly drawn.

"Because she . . ." Marie shook her head, putting it all beyond her. She looked momentarily distressed, trapped. She froze.

"Because she . . ." Father Jude softly echoed.

But Marie Kashpaw did not take the bait. They sat. It was remarkable, he thought, how long and with no comment they could sit in the peaceable lobby. The sun blazed through the windows, now. Captive, his heart rose.

"Was she a good person, as the bishop sees it?"

Marie shrugged. He tried again.

"You are the only person who can tell us the truth about Leopolda."

She bobbed her head, hunched and neckless. Folds of tough skin came down over her eyes, and she rested within herself. Sitting in the lobby, waiting, Father Jude was overtaken by a midmorning lethargy. He wished for a sugared sweet roll, a Danish. Raspberry! he imagined. And strong, hot coffee. He could almost taste the combination, and he could definitely see it before him in his mind's eye, in his dream. The delicious roll began to float, drifting, a vision. He climbed into it. Started the motor. Soon he was steering toward a tiny, rocky island. He went deeper, his breath caught, ragged. He began to snore. As he did so, with reptile slowness, like the visage of an idol, Marie Kashpaw opened her eyes, which had gone a deep and throbbing brown.

AN ARGUMENT

Embarrassed, Father Jude apologized to the quiet woman for dozing off in the sunlight. She nodded, smiled tightly, and appeared to keep thinking about some closed-off and vital subject, so he thanked her and left. A white dust had risen from the ground and floated in a light band across the afternoon landscape. It was a dry spring haze. The grass on the road's margins was still gray with the residue of road plow and drifted particles of topsoil. Father Jude made his way back uphill to his room in the rectory. Quick with frustrated energy, he lifted a set of weights he'd brought in the trunk of his car. He played back a tape made years ago by someone else, an interview with a Sister Dympna, took notes. Then he located several boxes of files and records he intended to examine for clues to the shape of his subject's life.

As the afternoon lengthened, Father Damien met Father Jude in the yard. The older priest's hair was slicked back with water and his eyes puffy from a nap. He regained vigor and made two rounds of the graveyard, walking with a light swiftness that surprised the younger one. And he spoke with intensity as though the movement generated mental electricity.

"A certain concatenation of events upsets me. Fixed causes. Two martyrs. One lifelong victim whose pain I shelter to this very day. And Leopolda!"

"You said that you were up thinking, remembering. There is a report here? A story?"

"Oh, yes! The question is exactly how to tease it out of the events, Father Jude. For you see, it began with the statue's procession, an occasion of joy, and ended in a howling disaster, and I am not prepared to say I understand, even now, the causes of the effects."

"Leopolda . . ."

"Yes, Father Miller, before she was Leopolda. What I mean to say is this: She was still a Puyat during this event."

"Understood."

"Only if you understand the depth of what being a Puyat implies."

"Enlighten me."

"Father Jude, each name you hear on this reservation is an unfinished history. A destiny that opens like a cone pouring out a person's life. It took Leopolda a very long time to profess her perpetual vows, and during that time she was very difficult to control. She wore the habit and considered herself a nun, but she was a Puyat and there were difficulties from the first."

"Saints. Difficulties. Father Damien, I am beginning to agree with you, not that my opinion matters. I am here to gather information. But about saints. When are they ever simple cases?" Jude sighed and pressed his fingers on his forehead. "They seem by nature to foster problems, surprises, at best or worst, envy. As I read"—he consulted his notes—"our Puyat-Leopolda escaped the horrors of the great influenza and even provided some nursing or at least took care of the dead—that was her job in the traditional culture and it became her task in the life of a religious. She was counted as devout in the Catholic sense and the year after her return from Argus her increasing piety and her service to the nuns was noted. In that same year, she asked one of the sisters whether she might be considered a candidate. She was then invited to stay in the convent for a time. Her blood is at least half Polish, and for the most part she was considered a *métis*, Indian to some slight degree, if that, for she had apparently repudiated her own past and was eagerly engrossed in taking on every aspect of the Faith. It was not long after her visit began that she presented what became her usual problem, that of excessive zeal. She was found face-down on the floor of the church on an extremely cold spring night. There was some concern that she was hypothermic. She never quite regained the circulation in her extremities, it says. There is some cross-out here, as though the writer, Sister Hildegarde Anne, was uncertain whether to include some detail."

Waving his hand as though to take away the cross-out marks, Father Damien sighed with impatience.

"Leopolda was found that night naked and bleeding," he said, "and she was covered with mud."

Father Jude waited for more information, and indeed the old priest seemed to struggle in an effort to provide it—he began to speak once or twice and then fell silent, shaking his head. That was when, with a sudden flash, Father Jude intuited that the old priest was hiding information, secreting it away, and he was amazed and disturbed because he'd been certain that his informant was willing and even eager to divulge all he knew.

"You know more about that night," said Father Jude, sternly, but his older colleague firmly shut his lips.

Frowning, irritated, Father Jude sat back in his chair. He stared at the other man and forced himself to behave with a patience he did not feel. As he watched Father Damien closely, that troubling sensation once more came upon him. It was a problem of perception. A distinct uncanny sense he could only name in one way.

"Father Damien, if you don't mind my asking, have you got a twin?"

"I do not."

"Never mind." Jude shook his head to clear his vision. Ran his finger along the pages of his notes. "Our Leopolda spent some time cared for by her sisters, I am told. Apparently, she experienced what we would call a nervous breakdown, fell into the grip of hallucinations."

"Visitations."

"The difference being . . . ?"

"Ah, you have hit upon the very question. The difference being very difficult, almost impossible, to discern in a person unstable and gripped by false visions as she was. She had a remarkable degree of endurance, and tolerated or even welcomed great physical and emotional pain. What she saw, she saw, whether you view her visions as pathological symptoms or as divine gifts is for you to say."

Jude spoke dryly. "I am sure that a number of mystics would have benefited from a regimen of antidepressants. However, we would all be the poorer."

"That is why," continued Damien, "in the end the discussion will be, should be, made on the basis of heroic virtue. Did she exhibit heroic virtue while nursing the ill, or in her teaching, or perhaps with her sisters? Did she suffer bravely or wisely when afflicted with her illnesses? Was she a good example to her sisters, an inspiration?"

Father Damien winced, then answered himself.

"Not unless her task was to be a holy aversion, a trial, a scourge. I used to call her my hair shirt. Her very existence was an itch. Many a time I pitied her, but Father Jude, I was hard pressed not to hate her as well."

Jude nodded, made a few notes. "Can you think of instances in which she exhibited a sacramental kindness?"

"No."

"Come now, even Satan gives alms on occasion."

"When it is to his advantage. That was the nature of Leopolda's kindness. I consider that a spurious kindness."

"Please think," Jude said in a penetrating tone, for he really had to know whether there was something, anything, she'd done. The light fell golden and raw now, through the moving screen of twigs.

Father Damien thought, and then an odd, sad smile crossed his face.

"Quill," he said at last. "Quill. Yes. Leopolda was the one who cured Quill's madness. Sadly, of course, Quill died of the cure."

"Oh, of course," Father Jude muttered, throwing down the pen. "Died of the cure!"

"But she was sane when she died, completely clear minded!"

Father Jude picked up his pen again, tapped it on his cheek. "I wish there were one, just one thing that Leopolda did that was not of an ambiguous nature!"

"But that is just exactly what the Puyats are," said Damien, "not one thing or the other. Contradictory. I told you that you must look at the name and the clan to assess the person, even a mixed blood like Leopolda. For she was shaped by the double nature of her mother, and who knows what else!"

Damien sighed mightily and attempted to gather his energy, puffing slowly until he straightened his chair. "Now that was how Nanapush began their history," he went on, "I should tell you he was not entirely to be trusted where the Puyats were concerned. He had his motive for spinning a tale to his own ends—he loved to torment Pauline. And whether or not you concede how twisted she became, it was clear to me, after hearing the story again and again from Nanapush in different versions, that the Puyats were subject, as any family on the reservation, to the same great press of forces, and that their clan managed to survive at all was certainly commendable and strange. Still, I'm going to acquaint you with the story, the characters, and then you will see the stuff of which our so-called saint is made!"

With that, Father Damien rummaged in a stack of papers beside him. Eventually, with a short crow of triumph, he thrust into his colleague's hands a tattered and stained, unevenly typed article addressed to the North Dakota State Historical Society. He muttered as he tore off and crumpled one or two rejection letters, then fondly patted the main body of the text as he handed it over.

History of the Puyats
By Father Damien Modeste

The exploits of my legendary predecessor Father Hugo LaCombe, who passed his youthful nights in a coffin and was revered by his flock for attracting divine luck to the great and rowdy hunts undertaken for buffalo, are in the main well-known. Relying on some letters of his, which I have unearthed, as well as firsthand accounts by Mr. Nanapush, an elderly Ojibwe thoroughly knowledgeable regarding Anishinaabeg history, I would like to add to the collective picture of this region by examining the Puyat family trials. Although the history of the Puyats begins well before Father LaCombe's time, the central astonishment of their story touches on one event to which he was a witness: a hunt.

From spring to midsummer, the Plains Ojibwe and Michif people killed the buffalo. Hard as was the killing, those deaths were easy compared with the sheer volume of labor it took to skin the beasts and butcher them, dress the meat, and preserve the extra in the form of pemmican. This long-lasting food was their primary winter and travel sustenance. The beast was deboned, cooked, pulverized, mixed with its own rendered tallow and returned to its hairless skin. The huge, fleet, brutal-willed animal was thus concentrated to a form that a woman could carry on her back. Mostly the transformed buffalo were loaded in stacked bales onto wooden Red River oxcarts that screamed and groaned as they moved across the violently flat plains.

Upon the topmost of these bales, in the partial history I now recount, there rode a young girl in whom the bitterness of seven generations of peasant French and an equal seven of enemy-harassed Ojibwe ancestors were concentrated. Her parents, the mother a crane clan girl of fretful, peaceless energy, and her father, small and arrogant with Montreal-based spleen, positively hated each other. At the same time, they could not abide the frustrations of separation. Their child, created of spilled-over complexity and given the French name Pauline according to the father's wish, seethed in the high noon sun and considered the tedium of their slow and inevitable progress so impossible that she was almost glad, when spotting a party of Bwaanag, a source of mortal hatred, to call out her find from the top of the bale of skins.

The band of Ojibwe and French-Indian Michifs halted in alarm. All who could shoot well were armed and arranged behind cover. The Bwaanug did the same and for hours, without a shot being fired, the two enemy camps exchanged volleys of shouted insults increasing in amazed fury and filth, which of course neither side could understand as they had no language in common, but which did vastly increase the knowledge of the children and their accompanying priest. Good Father LaCombe, whose job it was to bless the hunt, found himself in the middle of an enmity so old that even his holy presence wasn't sufficient to cause the women to contain their contempt. All he could do was to break up his candles and knead the beeswax into plugs, which he stuffed into the children's ears and his own. Ever after, the first Pauline's memory of what followed was mainly a soundless vision— although of course, soon as she could, she removed the beeswax plugs.

She saw at one point her enraged mother, pained to madness by the memory of her brothers' loss to the Bwaanag, climb the bales and throw off her skirts. Pointing to her nakedness and flaunting it boldly, she screamed a challenge so foul and instantly understandable that a Bwaan rushed from cover and was nearly killed, one bullet clipping his ear half off and the other bullet shattering a wooden club that flew from his hand so that he sensibly retreated. The two sides again resorted to shouting, but it was clear, by then, that both parties were returning from successful hunting and were not only low on ammunition but more interested in supplying their home camps with meat than in taking revenge. Still, in retaliation for that bold Anishinaabekwe's affront, a Bwaan woman of equal fury lifted her buckskins and cried a challenge in her own language and in so severe and scathing a manner that one of the men from Pauline's camp leaped forward out of cover and was seriously wounded in the thigh. Pauline's mother threw herself high up the bales and now other women did as well, so that the cacophony of insults exchanged became at once an earsplitting din and the men, seeing their half-naked wives frothing wild, began to think they were by contrast the more restrained and rational.

The first Pauline's father in particular was disgusted by his wife's display. In fact, he became at length so crazed with irritation that he raised a white flag, the symbolism of which long had been learned from the protocol of the U.S. Cavalry, and he walked unarmed to the center of the field. Being French, and of French traders, he knew enough of the Bwaan language to make himself understood. When he raised his hands, a curious silence fell. He spoke to both sides.

"We are not war parties! Hear me! We are laden with meat to survive. Both of our caravans would be wise to depart in peace. But since it is our hotheaded women who are looking to shed blood, and as we are French and Ojibwe men who always satisfy our women, let two of the women race to the death. The winner of the race, we all agree, shall have the other's life. After this is accomplished, we will go our separate directions and meet to fight, as men and warriors, another day."

The child heard this speech by her father with an inner sense of glee, as did the others in the camp, for all knew that Pauline's mother was a superb and unbested runner. She had, in fact, challenged the young men who came to court her to footraces, claiming that she would not stoop to marry a man who could not beat her. She vowed she would marry the one who could. Her boast was the reason she eventually wed the unprepossessing, even ugly, deer-legged, *voyageur* who was her much despised husband. He had embarrassed her by winning, a bad way to start a marriage. Her swiftness had only increased since that day, as had his own. Although, at his speech, her pride rose up instantly, she experienced an inner pang that he, the father of her child, could so arrogantly put up her life. What if there were by chance a better runner among the Bwaan women? Anger beat its wing inside of her. As she walked to the race ground to take her place, she decided to lose the race. In pride before his compatriots, her man would have to offer up his life for her own. At last, and how well he deserved it, she would be rid of him!

The enemy camps, having laid down their weapons, ranged to either side of a finish mark. The Bwaan woman who was to race was short of leg but light boned. Both women wore dresses of light calico. At the starting point, they divested themselves of what might hamper them—the Bwaan woman wore a long bone breastplate, a clapperless cowbell, a cradle board into which a fat infant was bound. Both women put down their skinning knives; over the razor-edged slender blades of steel their eyes met briefly in opaque agreement. They turned away. Pauline's mother carefully lifted strand after strand of trader's beads over her head—those beads, from Africa and Venice, Bohemia and Quechee, Vermont, she put into her daughter's hands. She unbuckled a wide belt of bull leather studded with brass, but did not remove from her ears the shining cones dripping small tinklers of German silver, so that, when the women began to run, her mother's swift progress began with light music that silenced in the smooth wind of her movement.

Running, that first Pauline's mother felt a tremendous ease and freedom. The earth purred underneath her makizinan that day. She reached the turn a bit before her desperate opponent, picked up the stick she was to take with one swift movement, and in returning found it very hard to force herself to lose.

When she did, Pauline, though treated by her mother with no kindness, heard as if from outside herself an animal howl that tore her chest. The incredible noise ripped her breath out by the roots. Her lungs shut. She fell upon her mother in a haze of yellow spots and clutched her dress so tightly that her fingers pressed through the soft weave and her knuckles ground against her mother's thighs. It was, then, more the weight of his treasured daughter's horror than love for his merciless wife or even male pride that caused Pauline's father to step forward just as the Bwaan woman raised her skinning knife, and to offer, as his wife had known he would, to substitute his own life for hers.

The Bwaan woman drew back, her eyes roamed over the man with the pelt on his chin and the child, equally ugly, who so obviously belonged to him. She wanted very much to kill this woman of the Ojibwe because of her own losses in the immemorial blood feud between their tribes, and because she had sensed, in running beside her, that the woman held back her power and could easily have beaten her. Such an ignominy scorched her stone roaster's heart. But then, as the child's grief turned with even more violence upon her father, whom, to be quite frank about it, the girl preferred, the Bwaan woman, recalling the pain of losing her own father at the age of this child, in a nighttime raid by Ojibwe, decided instantly that if she could balance this girl's grief with her own, like a stick on her finger, she would be solved of her need for revenge.

"*Washtay,*" she said in her language. She stood aside to let the other woman rise.

A gift for clever thought, a certain talent for talking, a swiftness with the language, became a Puyat trait inherited from this quick Frenchman who then spoke to save his life. He spoke clearly, as though suddenly struck with his idea.

"Of course, if any of you big-bellied Bwaan men can beat me in a running race, then each of you can murder half of me. The woman can have my left side to cut my heart out, and eat it, too, if there's anything left—after all, my wife has sharpened her teeth on it for years. The man can have my right side because wiinag swings there, long and heavy. When I run, I'm forced to tie it up or it will strike my thigh and bruise me. But today, since this may be the last race I'll run, I'll let it gallop free!"

By the time he finished speaking the two sides were laughing and there was no question that the race would occur. The only problem the Bwaanug had was in choosing a runner. There were two, and equally matched. One was a powerful bull-chested hunter with legs that bulged with fabulous muscles, and the other was an ikwe-inini, a woman-man called a *winkte* by the Bwaanag, a graceful sly boy who sighed, poised with grave nuance, combed his hair, and peered into the tortoiseshell hand mirror that hung around his neck by a rawhide thong. The wife of the hunter refused to let her valued husband risk his life in such a ridiculous game, and she yelled, browbeat, pulled her knife on him herself, while the others were lost in a debate. Was the *winkte* a man or a woman for the purposes of this race?

Some of the Ojibwe, who judged his catlike stance too threatening, rejected him as a male runner on account of his female spirit. Others were wary of the scowling hunter and argued that as the *winkte* would run with legs that grew down along either side of a penis as unmistakable as his opponent's, he was enough of a male to suit the terms. The hunter's wife finally won, delivering to her husband such a blow with the butt of his own rifle that he fell senseless and gagging. The *winkte* narrowed eyes rimmed with smoky black, shrugged off a heavy dress of fine-tanned deerhide, and stood, astonishingly pure and lovely, in nothing but a white woman's lace-trimmed pantalets. At the signal, then, both commenced to race.

They tested each other, pulling a step ahead and dropping a step behind, speeding and slowing to throw the other off pace, and found themselves equally matched. It would be a race of wit as well as strength, then. When to spend the ultimate energy and when to conserve? Draw ahead to the last reserve of strength, in order to discourage the other? Or save some for the final kick? The clever Montrealer decided by the time he grasped the stick at halfway that he'd tag a pace behind and wheeze to confuse his opponent and then in his last lengths, sign of the cross, kiss of God, he'd fly past, surprising the Bwaan, and show him the heels of his feet. This would have worked more easily had not his opponent, whose job it was as a woman to study men and whose immediacy of manhood gave him an uncanny understanding, read the mind of the Frenchman and slowed to conserve his own ability to finish. They both knew, then, that their strategies came down to a hot finale and they each determined to blister straight through their lungs and guts to cross the line ahead and live.

When it came right down to the end, though, the Frenchman had the stronger kick and the *winkte*, losing by a toe, swiped his dress neatly from the grass and simply kept running, across the broad plains, into the hills. Those who wished to start after him were detained now by Father LaCombe, who, though slow to understand the outcome of the wager and the sequence of events, launched forth a God-inspired tirade that cowed the Michifs and brought them to their Catholic senses. As a result, they did not chase the fleeing Bwaan but grudgingly agreed with the priest's diplomatic statement that the race had been an exact tie. No blood should be spilled.

Yet the Bwaan woman would have satisfaction for her relatives. Lunging forward with one arrowing blur of movement, she slipped her skinning knife beneath the ribs of the Frenchman, Pauline's father, and drew a sickening arc so that he found, quite suddenly, he was kneeling in prayer, his intestines slowly popping into his hands. And then his daughter was before him trying gently to stuff them back in their exact mysterious intricate folds, but failing even as he crumpled. Leaning sideways, he spilled about himself. Dying, he looked into his daughter's face and said to her in the clarity of last vision that she must kill her mother.

It was imperishable, the command of the father imposed upon the daughter. And no less the will she had to carry it out. Her intention was forged in the heat of grief and tempered in its freezing aftermath. Though young, the girl now harbored a blade of certainty that waited calmly in her for its chance. Pauline's mother knew. That is why, one day, with no warning and no word but a filthy cry, she dragged the girl to the shit pile and forced her snarling child face-down and said in a deadly voice, "This is where you'll be if ever you go against me."

A mistake, on the mother's part, to challenge one so like herself.

Ever after, the stink of waste reminded the girl. Her mother pushed Pauline into the fire, next, and so that, too, became an unforgettable piece of the promise. The burns of hot coals on her skin were markers of her duty. As was the soup her mother would not feed her—a bitter absence in her stomach. And the sticks of wood that broke against her legs and over her back. The air that tore open her chest each time she breathed with the broken rib, and bloody snow. The only thing her mother let her eat one winter when the meat was scarce was the bloody snow beneath the death of the animal or its butchering.

Yet the girl survived on that. She grew fast on the blows that didn't land and even faster on the ones that did. She flourished in twisted energy and grew taller than her father and meaner than her mother until one day, as her mother lay weakened by fever in a brush lean-to, on the trapline, the daughter brought a horn of foul boiling stew of bark and diseased rabbit and a mole that an owl must have dropped. Although her mother clawed at her, she held the woman's mouth open and poured the boiling stuff straight down her gullet so that her throat was seared, her mouth severely blistered, and all she could do was gasp, in her agonized delirium, for three days, the name Pauline.

That girl sat as far as possible from her mother, by the fire, surrounded by warm blankets and skins. With satisfaction, she watched the woman who bore her shake and chatter her teeth like a turtle rattle and weep as the fever alternately scorched and froze her. Recovering, the woman lost one side of her face. The nerves destroyed by inner heat, her flesh sagged in a bizarre leer that made her suddenly frightening to men so that, though she could still run, there was no one to catch her.

At the same time Pauline, who had inherited none of her mother's grace and all of her father's squat, exaggerated pop-eyed vigor, suddenly became irresistible to men. She was courted famously by love flute. She tried her lovers out across the tent, while her mother burned in dark nothingness. Men brought Pauline shells, miigis, a dress of red calico that reflected fire. They offered her trade silver cut and stamped in the shapes of owls, turtles, otters twining, bears, and horned frogs. They brought her meat so that she never went hungry. A necklace of brass beads appeared, hung beside her door by a night visitor. A very good kettle. Cakes of maple sugar. She wanted for nothing. Men sought her, although they were befuddled by their fascination. Was it her slim long waist, tight in the red calico? Maybe it was the way she looked so boldly at a man, then shyly away. It was not her face, or maybe it was, for her childhood ugliness had become something else: a ferocity, a sexual charm partaking of no sweetness, a look that registered and gloated over everything about a man. A hunger.

The young girl's appetite became a famishment and then a ravenous emptiness that she found men, for very short amounts of time, were capable of solving. Still, even though she had her pick of them, she was restless. The terrible fact was this: In creating the emptiness, the mother disallowed her the means to fill her void. Pauline could not love or be loved. She had been robbed of her capacity either to give or receive anything so profoundly good.

Her mother's face sagged until her tongue froze. Her brain locked. She finally died, removing the burden of her doom from Pauline. Freed, the girl married four times. With every marriage she experienced the beginning as a wicked and promising intensity that grew unbearable and then subsided into indifference. She bore her first child, a boy called Shesheeb, very early in life. Upon him, she raggedly doted. Twenty years after that first child, she bore a daughter. Her children were very different: the boy fathered by a full-blood and the girl by a Polish aristocrat visiting the wilds of Canada. The name of the latter was unpronounceable to Pauline, plus he was no more than a strange encounter during one dry northern summer. She forgot him and named the daughter after herself. Pauline Puyat, once again.

That child, born in her mother's age and raised in her purified bitterness, was the Pauline Puyat who became Sister Leopolda and sponsored, we do not know how, such things as miracles. I relate what I know of this history in order to explain the slow formation of certain seductive poisons in the personality that both slow and require severe judgment. This killing hatred between mother and daughter was passed down and did not die when the last Pauline became a nun. As Sister Leopolda she was known for her harsh and fearsome ways. And her father, the Polish man with the title and the golden epaulets, who went back to his lands with marvelous paintings and strange stories, who was he? What unknown capacities, what secret Old World cruelties, were thereby tangled into her simmering blood?

If you know about the buffalo hunts, you perhaps know that the one I describe, now many generations past, was one of the last. Directly after that hunt, in fact, before which Father LaCombe made a great act of contrition and the whirlwind destruction, lasting twenty minutes, left twelve hundred animals dead, the rest of the herd did not bolt away but behaved in a chilling fashion.

As many witnesses told it, the surviving buffalo milled at the outskirts of the carnage, not grazing but watching with an insane intensity, as one by one, swiftly and painstakingly, each carcass was dismantled. Even through the night, the buffalo stayed, and were seen by the uneasy hunters and their families the next dawn to have remained standing quietly as though mourning their young and their dead, all their relatives that lay before them more or less unjointed, detongued, legless, headless, skinned. At noon the flies descended. The buzzing was horrendous. The sky went black. It was then, at the sun's zenith, the light shredded by scarves of moving black insects, that the buffalo began to make a sound.

It was a sound never heard before; no buffalo had ever made this sound. No one knew what the sound meant, except that one old toughened hunter sucked his breath in when he heard it, and as the sound increased he attempted not to cry out. Tears ran over his cheeks and down his throat, anyway, wetting his shoulders, for the sound gathered power until everyone was lost in the immensity. That sound was heard once and never to be heard again, that sound made the body ache, the mind pinch shut. An unmistakable and violent grief, it was as though the earth itself was sobbing. One cow, then a bull, charged the carcasses. Then there was another sight to add to the sound never heard before. Situated on a slight rise, the camp of hunters watched in mystery as the entire herd, which still numbered thousands, began to move. Slightly at first, then more violently, the buffalo proceeded to trample, gore, even bite their dead, to crush their brothers' bones into the ground with their stone hooves, to toss into the air chunks of murdered flesh, and even, soon, to run down their own calves. The whole time they uttered a sound so terrible that the people were struck to the core and could never speak of what they saw for a long time afterward.

"The buffalo were taking leave of the earth and all they loved," said the old chiefs and hunters after years had passed and they could tell what split their hearts. "The buffalo went crazy with grief to see the end of things. Like us, they saw the end of things and like many of us, many today, they did not care to live."

*   *   *

Father Damien sighed and for a while the two priests were lost in a meditative silence, then he spoke softly to Father Jude. "What does that tell you about Pauline? About her mother? About the great pain of the end of things that lives in every family, here on the reservation, in some form or another? What does that tell you about our so-called saint? Pauline was, of course, the warped result of all that twisted her mother. She was what came next, beyond the end of things. She was the residue of what occurred when some of our grief-mad people trampled their children. Yes, Leopolda was the hope and she was the poison. And the history of the Puyats is the history of the end of things. It is bound up in despair and the red beasts' lust for self-slaughter, an act the chimookomanag call suicide, which our people rarely practiced until now."

PART THREE

MEMORY
and
SUSPICION

9

THE ROSARY

1919–1920

Late that summer the body of a man was found in the woods. Father Damien was sent for. Already, it was known that the dead man was the vanished Napoleon Morrissey. With that identity in mind and knowing the length of time he had been missing, Agnes was at least in some measure prepared. She had by then seen life from start to finish and was familiar with death's peculiarities.

Father Damien arrived in the hot, green, earth-smelling woods and approached the circle of men, who parted for him, hands or sleeves held to their faces. There, in a child's play spot, surrounded by tufts of goldenrod and beds of blue asters, the body sprawled. Someone had laid a potato sack over it for modesty, but the poor nakedness was really the least obscene thing about the tableau. A gaping mouth, inhabited by tiny, busy creatures, crow-plucked eyes, hands clutched up about the neck. Father Damien excused himself and threw up, casually and efficiently, behind a tree, then returned with a handkerchief held to his lips. The men waited for him, accustomed by now to the priest's combination of delicacy and shrewd toughness.

Steadier, he bent to the piteous human scraps, brushed a scraping of dirt from the throat, stared at the sight until it lost some of its horror and became a puzzle. Questions occurred, a great many questions. Of course, to begin with, the cause of death. Damien observed the stretched, fixed features, still apparent even after the summer's heat—an effort to speak or, more likely, to gasp, to take air? And the hands to the throat. The man had surely choked, or been choked. If the latter, not by someone in a face-to-face death struggle, hands on windpipe, but something else.

"Was there a rope," Damien asked of the men surrounding the body. "Did you find anything, a noose, twine, leathers, something that might have been used to strangle this man?"

There was no answer. As though thinking as one, they abruptly left the priest and fanned evenly through the woods. The undergrowth was thick and tangled with wild grape and raspberry, springy brambles, a summer's growth of oak seedlings. The men stamped out a carefully widening circle. As they searched, Damien continued to take a meticulous inventory of the features of the body that might provide further information. The eyes—wide open—before they had been plucked? The feet, close together, had the body been dragged? The ankles bound? Alcohol. Any way of telling whether Napoleon was drunk at the time? Had there been a struggle? Was this a fight typical of drunks, and if so, with whom did he drink? Was there anyone missing from the reservation, a companion who'd perhaps run off in horror of what had happened?

"Neshke," said George Aisance. In his hand a long rope of beads, a twine of knots and black prayer markers, a rosary.

Damien accepted the beads and tried to coil them around his fist. That was when he realized that this particular rosary was different from all others—it was strung on something stiffer, which kept an elegant shape. It was wire, some sort of wire, and then the barbs pricked his palm and he realized what kind. The crucifix of the rosary went cold in his hands.

He wasn't of a sufficiently certain mind to say anything yet, but there were marks, yes, there were, a necklace of deep pits decayed in small dents around the dead man's neck. After he bid George and the other men to leave, to find a sledge to transport the body back to town, he measured the rosary beads in his hands. Gently, as though he was fitting to a woman's throat a string of pearls, he compared a decade, ten beads and a larger bead, barbs between, a set of mysteries that exactly fit the wounds.

That night, in the trembling radiance of candles, Agnes laid the rosary out before her on the covers of the bed and then sat next to it, looking at it, imagining just how it had been shaped. A pair of pliers, certainly, to untwist the wire. The beads were about a half inch in diameter as on a rope rosary, and they had accommodated—either naturally or by being enlarged—the wire and the barbs between. For the rosary had been cleverly planned to utilize the spun steel thorns, perhaps to prick a finger between each decade or perhaps . . . Here Agnes picked up the rosary dangling stiff by the crucifix, swept it over her shoulder so it caught in the flap of the overcoat that she still wore. She frowned at herself and disentangled it—a flagellant's whip. It would have left, she thought, gingerly gripping it now, the hands of whomever used it to choke a grown man a bloody mess.

THE TEMPLE WHIPPING

Napoleon's funeral set things going, created divisions that would last for years, during which a complex transfer of power would occur on the reservation. Land would pass from the hands of Napoleon's sister, Bernadette, to the son of Margaret Kashpaw and from there into Kashpaw hands. That's where it started—in the church before a crude pine box. Of course, Father Damien knew by now that the Kashpaws and Pillagers avoided the Morrissey and Lazarre camp. It had been his fruitless work to try to bring together the factions. What happened at the funeral made him give up the notion, forever, and accept that he dealt with a set of clan differences, complicated by loss, land, and money, that would never heal. These differences would go on, in fact, through time and come to define the politics of the place he loved.

Margaret Kashpaw, shrewd and sour, kicked the misery to life.

Some said that Margaret should not have shown her face at the

funeral, given that the man who chased after her was the holdout
Nanapush. She had the nerve to show up in bright clothing, and wore
the garish red hat that made some call her Old Lady Cardinal and others mutter that it was a pointed mark of disrespect. You never wore
that color near the dead, as it confused their spirits, attracted them
back to the living. But apparently that did not bother Margaret. Margaret only said that she came because it was her duty as a member of
the tribe and parish. Her words were met with scorn, right at the
doorway.

"So you came to gloat." Bernadette greeted her with ugly irony.
What she actually said in Ojibwemowin was that Margaret had come
to make herself fat on the sorrows of her enemies. Then she added
that Margaret already was quite fat enough and should go home.

"Go fuck the old longhair in your dead husband's blankets," she
advised, again in Ojibwemowin, a phrase lost on Father Damien,
who was standing near to greet those who'd come to pay their final
respects. He did catch the word blankets, waabooyaanan, and using
his pocked mental lexicon he made the association between blankets and honoring gifts. Thinking Margaret had been uncharacteris-
tically generous, he at once clasped Margaret's hand and began with
a nervous passion to thank her. Caught between the sudden insult
and the copious gratitude, Margaret rocked back. Just for an instant,
though. She quickly discarded the priest's clumsy praise and prepared a barrage of killing wit, which she was unable to deliver. A
crush of sorrowing Morrisseys now swept protectively around
Bernadette, and simultaneously pinned Margaret Kashpaw in the
center of the back pew, so that she had to scramble over the top of
the bench to gain her freedom.

This small woman, though of some age, could move with strength
and economy. Before anyone could knock her down, Margaret Kashpaw wove through the mourners. Quick as a weasel, she popped up
right before Bernadette. As she moved, her mind was working, so that
by the time she confronted the Morrissey she had discarded her crude
witticisms in favor of a bitingly sweet form of address.

"You don't know what you're saying, in your pitiful condition. I
loved your brother as my own brother. You should remember how he
came to chop wood for me when my own husband was out on the

trapline. And don't you recall"—Margaret spoke with brilliant inspiration, lies jumping to her lips—"how your brother so generously gave up his horses and bought my dead husband's team for a good price after he was killed?"

Of course, Bernadette now recalled her brother bragging how he'd cheated the widows and taken advantage of the fact that, as Kashpaw's death was the result of his team's panic, nobody in the family felt right with the beasts. They traded them to Napoleon so cheaply that he couldn't stop talking about his bargain.

"Ishte, Bernadette, your brother was a good man," said Margaret, sopping away fake tears. "He was so good to your niece-girl, the one who dug the dirt. Even, he took in that skinny Puyat who now wears the black gown. Oh yai, he used to bring that virgin to that old shack on Kashpaw land where he—"

Father Damien now freed himself of other hands and again clasped Margaret's, giving her his most profound attention, which worked out perfectly, for all Margaret had wanted to do was lay the foundation of suspicion for Bernadette to stand on, and shade her eyes, and look this way and that. Which she did, thinking surely no one else knew what evil Napoleon did to the Kashpaw girl? And the Puyat? And even if someone knew, at least that Puyat was alone, wasn't she, no family members around to . . . but no, and here Bernadette's mouth gaped open. Perhaps there were people on the reservation who knew about Napoleon's crime. She'd sent Marie to the Lazarres to avoid a repetition. Maybe there were relatives she hadn't considered, vengeful ones. He was dead, wasn't he? Dead by the hand of someone strong and capable. Although she mourned him for the blood he was, Bernadette had no illusions about the character of her dead brother.

He had taken advantage of her too. Recalling this, quite suddenly, Bernadette's face went dark with unshed emotion. She suddenly shook off the maudlin comfort of her family and strode to the front pew, where she brooded with great intensity on what he really was. What he really did. What he left her with. She brooded so hard and cracked her big knuckles so loudly that the other members of her family feared that she was disoriented by grief. But no, her thoughts were properly directed by Margaret's truth. That was the problem.

All through the painful service that Father Damien conducted, her oblivious mutters sounded. Napoleon had tried to cheat her of her own land and left her nothing but a spalted horse and his clothing, the acrid smell of himself in the cloth. She'd burn them now. He'd brought loose women to the house and drank with them. He drank anyway, alone, and sometimes . . . ah, she pushed away the pictures, glad to the bone that he was dead. Maybe she would stand up and kick his coffin. Maybe she would rage at heaven. No longer could she hold it in! She leaped up suddenly, but men were ready. They held her back, from joining her brother in death, they thought, but in reality she wanted to rip his pickled body from the box.

That she went strange in her behavior after talking to Margaret was not lost on her relatives.

"It's her," cried one, totally disrupting Father Damien's attempt to forge ahead with the service. "That damn Margaret Kashpaw put a powder on her!"

The whole church of Lazarres and Morrisseys and those on their side now turned to look upon Margaret, who was perhaps the only woman living anywhere, in all the Anishinaabeg territory now chopped into states and provinces, who could glare back with such authority. More than all of them put together. Her peaked red cap stood up, erect. Her eyes blazed and her bearing was of the old ogitchi-daa-ikwe stance, too powerful to resist. For such a small, sharp woman, her voice carried. It rolled out of her. She put one hand up before she spoke and turned to each direction.

"We will see it coming soon," she cried, her voice echoing in drama, "more deaths out in the woods. The trees strangled the Morrissey because he spoke of selling them all for timber and getting rid of our land!"

In the confused silence that greeted this preposterous statement, she walked out, leaving behind her a massed political war council of those determined not only to cut a deal with the lumber people but also, now, to avenge their martyr, and others scratching their heads and saying, the trees? The trees? Bernadette, pinned to the pew by the excitement of her rage, now sobbed and ground her teeth and begged to be carried out of the church. It was most unlike her, this impulsive weeping, this charging forward. Bony and elbowing, her arms slashed the air. As she was in fact a powerful character by reason of her influence upon the government agent, her agitation acted as a catalyst to further uproar.

Father Damien, now fearing they might burn down his church in their frenzy, patrolled inside nervously, then outside. What else could he do? This was a test. Agnes stopped, put her hands on her hips, rallied her wits and her strength. Was her priest to be driven from his own church? She rocked on her heels. Listened to the mass of would-be mourners argue and shout. She clenched and unclenched her fists, and at last threw her power into the voice and demeanor of Father Damien. Strode back inside.

At first, the muscled backs and shoving arms and jutting chins of the arguers barred him, but he persevered until he gained the altar. Gathering up his courage, he suddenly vaulted up onto the coffin, which sat on a sturdy table. He stood there with fists on his hips, at which point the mourners shut up and gaped at him in mass reproach.

"Bekaayan," he ordered them. "Bizindamoog! You think I am disrespectful to stand full square upon the dead? No different than what you are doing! Be gone! Get out! This is a place of the Lord!"

Father Damien then had the glad luck to spy a strong whip coiled on the front pew. Bounding to the floor, he grabbed it and then commenced wielding it all around, right and left, so that the shamed mourners drew back and scattered. Stumbled through the door, and left. Father Damien emptied the place, and then stood panting near the holy water font, a bowl on a log, and cut the air in the sign of the cross.

Scrawny Mr. Bizhieu crept back in and begged Father Damien to return his whip. His rage leaped high and Father Damien launched it at Bizhieu like a lance.

"Miigwetch," said the whip's owner in admiration.

Soon it would be told all through the reservation and the land how the young priest drove false worshipers straight from God's holy presence with a scourge just like the adventurous Jesus whipped the zhooniya men in the temple. And further, the story embellished, how those touched by the whip itself were saved and could not help creeping back to the church with confessions, while others were cured of goiters, sore eyes, rheumatism. And the whip itself was proudly displayed by the Bizhieus. Only Father Damien felt shame at his loss of temper, and resolved to be pragmatic from then on.

He would conduct two separate Masses for the enemies, so that they would never meet and defile the holy presence with their disputes.

BERNADETTE

After Bernadette came to her wits, she realized that she could do a lot more for her side of things than agreeing with Margaret. Even now, she was the one who made calculations on each parcel of land, the one who figured for the land company and government too, and for the lumbering operation co-owned by John James Mauser. She was the one who accidentally, by virtue only of her skill with small numbers, suddenly acquired an undeserved power over the fates of her neighbors and tribespeople. A half-blood, she called herself French and despised the old ones. She was mirthless and ruthless, and she decided that she would use her brother's death to cast suspicion on the one whose mind no money would affect.

"Nanapush," she told all who would listen. "He and those Pillagers killed my brother because he wanted to sign!" She thrust out her skinny neck. "The backwards ones, the holdouts. They threw his poor body in the bush and went on with their ceremonies!"

Once she said it the first time, her theory was repeated to every listener. Napoleon was killed, horridly and thoroughly, by the full-blood blanket Indians, she called them, who couldn't understand that the money offered for the land and lumber came around once and once only. She asserted that, as a horse trader, Napoleon Morrissey had known a good deal. In no time, she had quite a number convinced that it was useless to do anything but go forward, live forward, take the money in their hands, and find a new place to put their hearts and their feet.

NECTOR KASHPAW

The tension ran so high that Father Damien was relieved he'd had the foresight to conduct two separate Holy Masses for the rancorous families. Their arguments split the reservation, and from then on they would contend for control of everything from jelly recipes and secrets of hide tanning to land and political say-so. The Morrissey and Lazarre camp, aligned with the company owned by Palmer Turcot and John James Mauser, took the early Mass. The Masses were widely spaced apart so that there would be no overlap, no meeting of the enemies in the innocence of the churchyard. Kashpaws, including Nanapush and those in sympathy with Pillagers, came walking to the late Mass. At first, there was complaint from the Morrisseys when Nector Kashpaw returned from government school and served at their Mass, too, but he was still a boy so they forgot about it.

That was a mistake.

For Nector Kashpaw would be the one who would count who was there and who wasn't, the one who would make himself small and very quiet, the one who would eventually hold the power of the pen over Bernadette.

PENMANSHIP

As great towers are by the underpinnings weakened and overthrown, so the seeming insignificance of Nector was the key to the eventual downfall of the Morrisseys. Nobody knew of or saw the quick intelligence at work behind the holy-boy shutter of his face. No one thought to wonder what he learned at the hands of the nuns or from Father Damien. All the time that he was not trapping, hunting, attempting to dig and plant in accordance with the government wishes, and all the time that he was missing from the camps of his elders and the company of the medicine people and their wisdom, Nector was learning to read zhaaganaashimowin and to write the language of the conquering officials and the land companies in the beautifully flowing and elegant script that Sister Hildegarde Anne taught with painstaking love from two books—Merrill's *Modern Penmanship* and the classic *Graphic System of Practical Penmanship* were her bibles.

It was Sister Hildegarde's belief that good penmanship was the defining key to success in life. That and hygiene—but though the hygiene just had to be adequate, the writing had to be exquisite. So she worked with her readiest pupil, Nector, until, using a pencil kept pin-sharp, then graduating to a precious, borrowed pen, he could form letters that rivaled the illustrations in the penmanship books. Soon his writing approached even Sister Hildegarde's own for purity and consistency. His words were in their execution indisputably grander, firmer, and more controlled than the written words of Bernadette Morrissey, who corresponded with the government.

During this time, and while he was getting his growth, other extreme events occurred. The Lazarres and Morrisseys became still more bold and insulting to those who did not agree with their views. Earlier they had gone so far as to kidnap, threaten, and even shave the head of Nector's mother, Margaret. The revenges that followed were distinct to the Pillagers. Fleur killed with fear, Nanapush used piano wire, Margaret flayed her enemies to nothing with the bitter blade of her tongue.

Nector got even by the use of penmanship.

After he returned from government school, he positioned himself carefully by pretending to be neutral. His bland, blinking, new-grown handsomeness caught the eye of Bernadette, who hired him—though that was a fancy word for a job that paid in grease, potatoes, and an occasional dime. He was to assist her in putting into operation an order from the Commissioner of Indian Affairs. That order was this: the administrator at each agency was to mend, classify, and flat-file all of the old files. In this case, the files dated back to well before the birth of Nanapush.

Bernadette thought she could trust young Nector Kashpaw because he'd been exposed to the withering light of the government school. She thought he couldn't hurt a system so snarled that she herself couldn't account for where land or inheritance papers went and what happened to commodities ordered from various crooks. She was tired of the stacks of mail to answer, of the loss of landholdings personal to clans other than her own, tired of trying to account for these losses in words that she couldn't invent fast enough to please the Chief of Methods Division. In Nector, so bright and obedient a boy, she thought she had a malleable, sensible son who understood that the time of the old traditions was accomplished and over, a boy who wished a clean sweep and progressive future, if he wished anything at all yet, for his people. Not that Bernadette Morrissey, cow hips jutting, face long and exhausted, eyes weak from doing money sums, had a vision. She didn't. She only wanted what was most comfortable. What was secure.

Nector could have told her, having drunk down the words of Nanapush, that comfort is not security and money in the hand disappears. He could have told her that only the land matters and never to let go of the papers, the titles, the tracks of the words, all those things that his ancestors never understood held a vital relationship to the dirt and grass under their feet. But he didn't say these things, because they were useless in the first place and would give him away in the next. He said nothing except to lament, with her, the former practice of folding papers and the improper classification of files and the confusing change of names and locations, superintendencies and jurisdictions over various families of Ojibwe Indians.

Nector let Bernadette natter on, directing him to accomplish fair copies of documents. Soon, he learned to use—and here the story was given an unexpected twist—the black typing machine labeled Chicago. He began to love typing and that, plus the way he could sign what he typed, put him over the top. He was now preferred by the commissioner to Bernadette because he could manufacture documents of a more official-looking nature.

He practiced at night.

By frail kerosene light he laboriously struck the grown-up keys, each letter circled by a ring of metal, until his typing was of a consistent quality and speed. Papers moldering in the bottoms of desk drawers, ragged and unfiled or filed by the system that undid those whom Bernadette wished to thwart, Nector typed from her writing and restored. He had done a great many of these old transactions, and he had a great many more to go, when he made the following important decision: he destroyed the originals.

He was now in charge of history, which suited him just fine, and he was only a boy.

NECTOR

In the midst of all that revenge and suspicion—in addition to which, he was fooling with the only thing worth having, land and land ownership—Nector thought he'd best be very careful. Therefore, he never worked past dark and made his way home by alternating routes and unpredictable bushwhacking. And he never went drinking unless with a group of cousins, never alone. In fact, he tried not to be alone if he could help it, which is what got him in trouble after all.

Johnny Onesides was one of his cousins. He was a calm, uncomplicated sort who didn't say much. But the few words he did say made him eloquent compared with his brother, Clay, who didn't speak at all except on very special occasions. These two were staunch friends of Nector's, along with a third cousin, called Rockhead, for reasons that would become apparent, and a friend of that cousin named Makoons. These five stuck together for good times as well as protection.

One still day, when Nector left the agency, they were waiting outside in Makoons's uncle's Model T Ford touring car, which for some reason Makoons was allowed to drive for the afternoon. This exciting privilege moved them all with expectation. They wanted to drive by girls and impress them, and other people as well, with the splendor of their conveyance. So once they crammed Nector in, they started off.

The thing they soon found was that while they'd imagined crowds of people around the trader's and the agency building and the church, it was a very quiet afternoon and nobody at all was out. Therefore, they had to hunt around to find admirers, and they did find one or two people to impress—but Mrs. Bizhieu was impressed with anything, and Father Damien, whom they encountered on a genial afternoon walk, gave no more than a distracted wave of his hand. Finding even those two took some doing and used up gas. So on their fourth time through town they paused the car just outside the door of the trader's. They got out. Nector bought the others each a cold, refrigerated grape pop. There was, in the act of tipping those bottles to their lips and baring their throats and then wiping their mouths manfully on their sleeves, and emitting a sound of relief and pleasure, a great chance for self-display—if only, again, there was someone to appreciate their pop drinking, but there wasn't. The dusty road, the dust on the lower leaves and branches of the trees, a tired bird, the trader himself half asleep, this was all a most unsatisfactory audience.

Rockhead now suggested that they take the car up around Matchi-manito Lake, but Makoons was uneasy with the idea. The road that lumber had carved to one side, in hopes of getting all the way around the lake, was rough and uncertain. Still, there was a certain beach where young people liked to go, and there at least they had a good chance of getting themselves admired. In the end, between vanity and good sense, there was no contest. They started up the car, jumped in, and took off.

Twice on the way there they had to jump out, heave and strain, push the car from potholes. Makoons drove nervously and wanted to turn back, but was unable to find a place wide enough on the narrow track. So he proceeded with ever more trepidation in his uncle's precious car. The road closed over them. And then opened suddenly. Displayed the lake. There, to the boys' glory, sat a knot of people on the shore. These people had heard the auto's tortured approach and now waited and watched expectantly.

It took only a lurch or two forward to ascertain they were Lazarres. And only a lurch backward to get completely stuck.

"What the hell do we do now?" asked Johnny Onesides.

"We can each take two," said Rockhead, who was counting the number of Lazarres now advancing toward them. "Or three."

"Some are girls," said Makoons, straining for a sign of hope.

"They're worse than the men," said Nector. He wished he hadn't come along. All the filing and typing hadn't done much for his strength, not like farm work, and he was the youngest of this bunch. He wondered if he'd be killed, or just beaten until his brain didn't work anymore and he walked around drooling like Paguk, the young fighter who'd gone down to the Cities a god and come back stupid. While he was busy worrying about this and even seeing himself lurching down the reservation roads, and even feeling sorry for this vision that he had of himself, the Lazarres approached and then surrounded the car.

There was Eugene and his brother the Half-twin, there was Mercy Lazarre, grinning with her eyes on fire—she was anything but like her name—there was Fred and there was Virgil, both solid and muscular with mean red eyes, and there was Adik, known as the brains of the group, and several cousins perhaps from the plains or prairie or maybe from hell itself, whom the boys had never seen before but who were sharing a big jug of wine and pretending to fish while they snagged their own relatives.

"This is good," said Adik. "We're glad you're here. We're glad you could make it to the party."

"Miigwetch," Makoons croaked. If the Lazarres beat him up, he was afraid they might then do something really bad to his uncle's car.

"I wanna take that good-looking one in the bush first," said Mercy, nicking her boulder of a chin at Nector, who grinned weakly.

"Show me no Mercy," he said, which made everybody laugh, but the laughter was not reassuring, and Adik soon stopped it.

"We don't find it funny when a Kashpaw mocks our women."

"Well," said Nector with complete sincerity, "I'm sorry then. I didn't mean anything."

"That's good, cousin."

There was a chilled pause, and then—it was like some malevolent force simply reached down and plucked them altogether in a ragged pile from the vehicle and set sheer chaos into motion: beating, growling, punching, kicking, yelling, the enemies fought. Nector and his cousins were tough and labored valiantly to throw off the Lazarres, but there were too many and the conclusion was foregone—soon each was pinned to the ground, held in check by at least two Lazarres as Adik decided what they would do.

His idea came to him in a flash that made the other Lazarres gasp at the genius of it. No wonder people listened to him! Howah! Their agreement was unanimous. It was decided. The Lazarres would stage an accident with the car belonging to Makoons's uncle—the car run deep into the lake and the boys drowned in their seats. That way, they would escape the suspicion of the Indian police and Father Damien, who helped them out.

"Ooh, my cousin, what a wonderful plan!" cooed Mercy. "But how shall we hold them in their seats?"

"We'll tie them with ropes," said Adik.

"We don't have no ropes," she said.

"Then we'll use some goddamn vines," he went on. "You go search them out right now."

So Mercy left and for a while they heard her rummaging and tramping and swearing as she looked for rope substitutes. Finally, she came back, but the vines she found were much too stiff to act rope-like—they would not tie.

"That's okay," Adik said, "forget about the ropes. We'll hit them on the head and knock them out."

"Or you could use the rope underneath the back seat of Makoons's uncle's car," suggested the silent one, Clay.

Nector and the others were so shocked to hear him speak—they'd practically forgotten what his voice sounded like—that they didn't react to the meaning of his words at all. And in fact, Nector was just as glad not to be hit on the head—he pictured poor Paguk—so unlike the others he didn't say a word to admonish his cousin but tried to keep his wits about him. That's what Nanapush said saved his life on tough occasions. Not succumbing to panic. So he tried not to, but his breath tightened in his chest and he saw blurred death lights when the Lazarres pushed him into the car's front seat and then tied his hands to the handle of the door. They tied Makoons to the steering wheel and the ones in the back seat they roped together with elaborate knots and fixed the ends of the ropes to the base of the seats.

"Mi'iw," said Adik, dusting his hands proudly, "do you have any last words?"

Again, it surprised them very much, but it was Clay who spoke. After all, this was a special occasion.

"Every one of you Lazarres will rot in a hell of your own making" was his pronouncement, which Nector would have thought very eloquent were the car not already moving. Laughing at the curse, the Lazarres were pushing the car, rolling it down to the lake. Nector twisted and tugged—his hands were well tied, the knots were good. He admitted that, he would always admit that, he had no reason not to admit that: Lazarres could make tight knots. And he could feel the breeze on his face, the last air he would breathe, and next to him Makoons was saying his prayers as a good Catholic, and Rockhead was crying a little, Johnny Onesides was swearing but Clay was again silent.

They rolled into the water. It made a swishing sound around the tires and for a moment the car was afloat, then it sank and the water came boiling up through the floor around their knees. The Lazarres excitedly pushed it deeper. But as it settled it was suddenly harder to push. They nudged it along. The water crept up Nector's waist, then up his chest, and he gulped air with rockets of fear going off, and then the water surged to just under his chin and the car bucked to a halt, stuck. Nector looked around and saw his friends were all just in about the same position, straining more or less, but mouths safely out of the water. No matter how hard the Lazarres pushed, the wheels wouldn't budge an inch farther.

Adik then said, "We're gonna have to drown the dogs by hand." The rest must have agreed, but either there was some argument about how to do it or who got to drown whom, or maybe they just wanted to take a break, for the Lazarres gathered on shore behind them and now had a smoke and drank from a bottle. Nector could smell the fragrance of their tobacco drifting down over the water. The waves came in underneath his chin but lapped up onto his face. He couldn't help imagining how they would be found. Once they were drowned, their dead faces would bob up once again and stare sightless across the waves. At the same time he imagined this, he couldn't help despising the Lazarres for believing the five boys tied in a car were going to look like an accident. As he was struggling with these thoughts, and wishing he could see his mother once again, and as he also thought how good life would be without this dreadful end coming upon him, he suddenly felt busy fingers working on the knots his hands were still trying vainly to undo. He pulled eagerly—the hands held his still and then skillfully freed him. Clay, he recalled now, was very good with ropes as a result of being tied up often by his big brothers. Clay surfaced on the other side, freed Makoons from the steering wheel. Johnny and Rockhead wiggled their hands at him. They weren't yet swimming so as not to arouse the Lazarres' suspicions, but as soon as Makoons was free they took off their shoes and hell for leather started kicking for the island.

The Lazarres could tie good knots, but they weren't skilled swimmers, except for Adik. He came blasting down the bank when he saw them escaping and he dived in and began swimming right after. The cousins were fast, but Adik came on like a steamboat, and as they passed over the deepest, darkest part of Matchimanito he was only feet away. That's when Rockhead gasped, "You guys keep on. I'll take care of him." And he turned, treading water, as Adik lunged forward.

Rockhead's one fighting skill was renowned, and when they'd attacked, the Lazarres had taken care not to let him exercise it. The biggest Lazarre had grabbed him around the neck and immobilized his head, while two others worked on the rest of him. Now, Rockhead's serene stone-hard skull was all Adik saw, and the last thing he saw, as the two came face-to-face. For when Rockhead cracked him with his one effective weapon, Adik's eyes rolled straight up to heaven. All the air went out of him and he sank straight down to the cold, bottomless, airless, black bottom of the lake, where nothing lived but a horned being and some colorless fish.

So it was another Lazarre who came out of that encounter missing, an outcome that added to the fury of the clan and deepened their thirst for revenge, which they slaked on whiskey for some time.

As for Nector and his cousins, they rested a short time, only on the edge of the island, for it was well-known that spirits lived there. And then they swam on, more slowly, and reached the other side of the shore. From there, it was a long way back to the road and Nector, only, was unafraid of that side of Matchimanito. He couldn't persuade them by any means to go near Fleur's cabin, though they did allow him to lead them and blundered in the dark toward the place where Nanapush kept his shack when he wasn't living with Margaret. That's where they stayed overnight. That's where they told their story first.

Nanapush was a most interested audience. When they had finished, he lighted his pipe and leaned back to smoke and think.

At last he said, "Makoons will suffer when his uncle finds out."

Makoons groaned out loud. Ever since it was clear they would live, he'd been faced with the prospect of telling his uncle that his car was in the lake. More than once, the anticipation of his uncle's wrath and disappointment had caused Makoons such anguish that he almost wished the water had come six inches higher. But then, of course, his friends would have had to die too, which Makoons counted as unfair—especially since they believed the uncle freely allowed his nephew to borrow the precious auto when really Makoons had taken advantage of his uncle's absence at a funeral and sneaked the car out for a spin.

As though reading his mind, Nanapush asked just exactly why his uncle had allowed his nephew the use of such a prize possession, at which point Makoons admitted the truth. Nanapush brightened then, his thoughts clicked into place.

"Ah, my boy, this is good news! And tell me, did anyone witness you boys driving around the reservation to show off this car?"

At this, they well could answer that only Zozed Bizhieu . . .

"Who is unreliable," said Nanapush.

. . . and Father Damien . . .

"Who is oblivious," crowed Nanapush.

. . . had seen them riding in the Model T touring car.

Then Nanapush put both hands out and gestured with his pipe.

"Young ones," he said, "I am supposed to be old and wise. So I can't tell you what I would do. All I can say is nobody saw you take the car, nobody saw you drive the car, and nothing would have happened had you not encountered the Lazarres. And as you lived, I don't see why you boys shouldn't end up heroes instead of punished for a Lazarre crime. Now, once again, who took the car?"

Makoons's mouth dropped open, puzzled, and he was ready to say, "Well I did, you know that!" Nector hushed him.

"No, cousin," he gently said, patting Makoons on the shoulder, "think harder. Wasn't Adik Lazarre at the wheel when you entered your uncle's yard, and didn't you round us all up to go and chase him, and didn't he"—now Nector gestured at Johnny Onesides—"didn't he head for Matchimanito and then, as we came rushing after the Lazarres, looking for revenge and to take back your uncle's car, didn't they overpower us, tie us in the car's seats, and nearly drown us as it plowed into the lake?"

The boys paused only slightly before every one of them agreed that it was so, and then Nanapush sat back, very satisfied, and finished his smoke.

10

THE GHOST MUSIC

1913–1919

Agnes's fingers ached. They moved ceaselessly in patterns that raged up and down the desk and table. The ghostly language that her hands spoke sharpened her longing. Perhaps, she thought, she had been deaf at one time and learned to speak in signs. The utterances of her fingers were complex—whole speeches, whole poems, whole books. She began to think that they knew something she did not. Sometimes she watched her hands, as from far away. Arched, veined with somber blue, the fingers delicate but square tipped, tapping. They tapped wherever they landed, struck the surface of table, desk, basin, paper, with forceful rococo skill. At last, though exhausted, to distract herself and to give her hands a ready focus, Agnes began the task of sorting and organizing the packets of correspondence, the papers and documents, the scrapped plans of Father Hugo.

The other priest had not the thrill for organization that she had developed since her affliction of memory. Before the shooting, as far as she could tell, Agnes was apt to file bills by stuffing them in lard cans. After, and without her shadowy Berndt, Agnes, and then Father Damien, gained a passion for setting small things into a rigid order. Perhaps it was a way of compensating for the loss of events. Perhaps it was a way of gaining back the person she was, or inventing this new one.

At any rate, Agnes tackled Father Hugo's piles with a singular desperation close to happiness. She vowed to finish an incomplete Ojibwe grammar and dictionary. She found church plans of a fascinating nature. She found old bills of lading and a letter from a disappointed woman. She found pitiful mementos of unknown moments—buttons, flags, a dead watch. One day she was pleased to find a crumpled set of sketches and plans for a printed letter, one that Hugo hoped to deliver to a list of subscribers in the Fargo diocese and beyond.

Father Damien called the letter Notes from the Mission at Little No Horse. In it, he described the piteous effects of the most recent illness. The ravages of hunger. The moral effect of land loss and the deep thirst he had already experienced among the people—a thirst for the spiritual drink, curiosity, a hunger for the food of the heart. He did not describe Kashpaw, or the difficulty regarding the question whether to pare down the number of his wives. He did not speak of Agnes's own bitter guilt over trying to enforce such a thing, or the pitiable events after Quill went mad, nor did he repeat the jokes of Nanapush. Father Damien strongly expressed his belief that certain hungers could be assuaged and souls brought to Christ through the consolatory application of money.

Father Hugo had compiled a list of names and addresses. There were four hundred. Father Damien gave to himself the task of copying two letters each night after peace fell, and sending them as a packet at the end of the week. When they were all dispatched, Agnes began each night to direct the letters in her prayers. She asked intercession with each letter, prayed to her personal guardian, whom she believed she remembered as St. Cecilia. She imagined Father Damien's words in the hands of others, begged for a spark touched to a generous fire. Her fingers itched and stung.

Some money arrived, a dollar here and there for which she was profoundly grateful. Then a short deluge of junk. Bales of clothing were unloaded from an army truck—moth-chewed gray blankets. Jackets and pants of drab wool. The entire reservation took on a military air. One thousand cream cans arrived, a windfall. They were used as chairs, storage, canoe floats, anchors when filled with sand, and even by some of the more ambitious farmers, cream. Dozens of yardsticks. Harpoons and lobster traps, though the sea was half a continent away. Finally, a battered green-black upright piano arrived, painted and then scratched down to the white of the wood.

The thing sat before the church. It was floridly carved. Bunches of grapes decorated the sounding board. The feet were claws. Was it a lion or an arbor? Even the metaphor is mixed, thought Agnes with amused interest. The instrument had seen rain, warping humidity, and the sands of a scouring wind. Its keys were black as bad teeth. She touched the keyboard curiously and raised a tone, questing and off key. To Sister Hildegarde, the donation was spectacular.

"The carving, such workmanship!" The nun ran her fingers over the balled grapes, the flowing vines and leaves. Unloaded from a dray cart, the instrument seemed to crouch. Halfway into the church, it rested heavily on the threshold.

"Take it back!" cried Agnes all of a sudden, shocking herself.

A reasonless emotion resembling panic gripped her. She felt too large for her skin, the priest's collar tightened around her throat, and her hands began to move with their own life. She tried severely to check their motion by winding them in Father Damien's cassock.

"Absolutely not!" Sister Hildegarde thought Father Damien was perhaps too diffident to accept such a generous gift. She began to lecture him on having the humility to accept what God sent. As she launched into an attack on his pride, Father Damien regained some measure of control and stopped her, raising his freed hands in surrender.

"All right!" He lowered the curved and recessed keyboard lid and then, with a key that fit within one of the clawed feet, locked the lid. All at once, Agnes felt more secure, although she could not imagine why and shook her head quizzically to clear it as she walked away. It was as though the keyboard itself were a giant set of teeth. As though the instrument were capable of devouring her!

Sister Hildegarde took charge and applied herself to cozening three heavyset parishioners to move the awful wooden creature. She brought them tea and thick chunks of lard on bread. Flattered them into setting the groaning weight *here, no there,* Entschuldigt, *back to the first again.* She agonized over the exact placement and hoped that Father Damien would commission a statue, at last a real statue for the church at Little No Horse. Such a thing would need a place of honor near the piano, where it could be seen and adored.

P R A Y E R

Four times a day—on rising, at noon, late afternoon, and before going to bed—Agnes and Father Damien became that one person who addressed the unknown. The priest stopped what he was doing, cast himself down, made himself transparent, broke himself open. That is, prayed. He prayed that the seething factions merge and dissolve their hatred. He prayed, uneasily, for the conversion of Nanapush, then prayed for his own enlightenment in case converting Nanapush was a mistake. Agnes asked for a cheerful spirit and that her dangerous longings cease. She asked for answers, and for the spirit of the language to enter her heart. Agnes's struggle with the Ojibwe language, the influence of it, had an effect on her prayers. For she preferred the Ojibwe word for praying, anama'ay, with its sense of a great motion upward. She began to address the trinity as four and to include the spirit of each direction—those who sat at the four corners of the earth. Wherever she prayed, she made of herself a temporary center of those directions. There, she allowed herself to fall apart. Disintegrated into pieces of creation, which God might pick up and turn curiously this way and that to catch the light. What a relief it was, for those moments, to be nothing, a smashed thing, and to have no thought or expectation. Whether God picked up the fragments and stuck them back together, or casually swept them aside was of no consequence either to Agnes or Father Damien.

She rose, once she was finished, rubbed her eyes like a child, went on in Father Damien's skin. Her loneliness sometimes seemed a thing not of this world, but a loneliness only that mysterious being, solitary and unique, could understand.

LULU'S BAPTISM

Father Damien baptized a bear and the baby in the woods on the wrong side of Matchimanito, and all because of Margaret Kashpaw. She sent his altar boy, Nector, to fetch him one day. Father Damien went along eagerly, swinging his arms through the bush that seemed to close instantly behind them. Very quickly, Father Damien grew disoriented and then lost. When at last they got near enough to the lake, a slim track that petered out and resumed and buried itself again, Nector pointed where Father Damien should go, then vanished. Agnes stood bereft for a moment, uncertain, then plunged on.

Keeping to the way was exhausting, but soon she could see, as long as she stayed near the shore, the outline of Fleur's cabin. Resting, she took off the pack in order to check the contents and make certain she had included, in haste, all that was needed. She had just removed the vial of holy water when a gunshot sounded from the vicinity of the cabin. Startled, she splashed herself, then crossed herself at the sound of violent crashing, snapping, muttered grunting. In moments, the source of noise was before her, though lightly screened. And then the bear ripped aside the leaves.

Bear and priest gaped at each other in astounded dismay. The bear blinked its weak eyes, its intelligent nostrils rigid and glistening with inquiry. Agnes behaved by perfect instinct. As the holy water was immediately to hand, she dipped her fingers in and made the sign of the cross, giving the bear a tiny splash. Flinching as though shot, the bear jumped away and was gone. The bush closed over. Agnes was left to whack her way forward until she came to the cabin, at last, and stood panting in the clearing.

"Piindigen, Father!"

Margaret Kashpaw rushed out of the cabin and grabbed him so he spun with a jerk and was dragged to the doorway, into which she disappeared, tiptoeing back out with a baby in her arms. Stealthily, she asked Father Damien to baptize the infant.

Perhaps he shouldn't have. It went against his very grain, he later thought, to baptize in secret, but when he saw Fleur's newborn baby something happened to him—or to Agnes, what did it matter? The tender damage was done. Barely one day old, Lulu was the first newly

born child he'd held in all his life. His other baptisms had been
months or more usually years, often many years, old. Calm, deliberate, focused, serene, this new being stared at him with eyes that still
knew the face of unbeing. In the long drinking gaze that grew between
them, Agnes experienced a protective adoration that shook her to the
bone.

"May I hold her?" Father Damien's voice was hoarse.

Margaret gave the baby over, transferring the frail, floppy head and
tight limbs, the exquisite pinch of buttocks and updrawn red knees.
Agnes felt immediately natural holding her, as though her tiny goodness set off a charm in her brain. Father Damien laughed, delighted,
baptized her with a slow enchantment and only reluctantly gave her
back to Margaret. Agnes was still absorbed in the primal sweetness of
the experience when Nanapush decided to walk back with the priest,
and Father Damien was still lost in marveling when he returned to
his own cabin and withdrew, from his desk, the certificate tradition-
ally written out and kept for each new member of the parish. It was
perhaps the imprint of the tiny body against his own, the connection
that still lingered, a dreaminess, that caused him when he signed the
certificate to add his own name, twice, mistakenly and along with
Nanapush, as both priest and father.

Father Damien began to visit more often once the baby was born, for
in the child's presence, Agnes could temporarily forget the burden of
half-realized memory and the load of suspicion that she carried
through her days. Lulu was a touchy, lively charmer, precocious and
fearless, curious and sincere. She was easy to please; anyone could
rock her to sleep in her tikinagan of ash and cedar, the covering intricately beaded with flowers and heavy vines. Watching her drowsy lids
fall, her delicate lip quiver with surrender, Agnes's heart lifted. She
was overcome with strange contentment, not maternal so much as
fully human. During those visits she became a connected being.

Slowly and inevitably, she fell in love with each person in the family, only she didn't know what to call it. She simply found herself
related. Nanapush of course, as teacher and friend, was the first she
knew well intellectually. But Fleur, too, accepted the priest fondly.
The moments when Fleur's rare smile burst out were stunning pock-

ets of light, and Agnes looked for them and courted them with an eagerness she hoped was not too obvious. Margaret, kindhearted and sour-tongued, loved Father Damien in spite of herself—he felt it in her grumpy embrace. He was always surprised when she showed anything at all besides the dour scorn her family inspired. Their love for him, in return, pained him and soothed him. He was thrilled and touched with sadness, he was hungry, and he was practical. He was lonely; he was a priest.

COLLATERAL

John James Mauser appeared, not in person but in the persons of others—in the local commissioner and the tax collector general. Payment-due notices arrived, which nobody understood. In the fine print, it said collateral would gladly be taken. Collateral wasn't birch-bark baskets or buckets of just picked berries. It wasn't a side of venison, a pack of furs, maple sugar, wild rice, dried currants, tanned hide, or anything else that by hook, crook, luck, or grueling work or desperate hoarding anyone was able to get. Collateral was land.

Sister Hildegarde had seen it coming, but she and Father Damien had been battling the spirit of disease, and then, absorbed in raising their church, they'd lost track of land acquisitions and foreclosures. They'd left off filling in the map whose boundaries changed drastically day to day. Father Damien's despair had robbed him of awareness, too, so it was with a tremendous sense of self-castigating helplessness that they both, in stymied dumb surprise, regarded the papers in the hands of Nanapush, papers that transferred the land belonging to Fleur Pillager and to Nanapush himself into the hands of the lumber company.

As he read the notice, a stricken rage boiled up in Damien. It was partly guilt—while paralyzed by an interior misery he had failed to protect his people, his family. The paper crumpled in his hands, he was so furious he imagined the flame of his thoughts might scorch it. His fingers clenched and he said in a small and wretched voice, "I will write to the bishop." It was not entirely too late. By raiding the church account, Father Damien was able to raise enough to keep

Nanapush's family from utter disaster. Still, the best of their land was lost.

Father Damien's letters flowed everywhere. He wrote to the governor of North Dakota, to the Commissioner of Indian Affairs, to John James Mauser, to the Grand Forks, Fargo, and Bismarck newspapers. He wrote the President of the United States and to county officials on every level. He wrote to Bernadette Morrissey and to the sick former land agent, Jewett Parker Tatro. He wrote to the state senators and representatives and to an organization called Friends of the Indians. He was determined to restore that land, but once it was gone, it was gone forever from Anishinaabeg hands. He didn't know that, and as his pen devoured page after page, the Turcot Company and Mauser made roads into the woods. As Damien feverishly plotted, petitioned a tough lawyer, and planned strategies, the crews went in to take the trees and the trees were taken. Some chimookomanag did not come out, it's true, or last much longer than the stealing of Pillager spirits and disruption of their ghosts. Some did not survive, but enough of them lived to ship the great oaks east, to Minneapolis, where they would line the impressive foyer of Mauser's house.

FLEUR

Walking home, after the shock of finding out wore off, she began shaking. She stopped in the center of the road, whirled in a circle, her shawl cutting the air. She was filled with rattles, with clicking bones, with small ticking husks and vibrations of bees. Her vision snuffed out, she whipped along blindly through undergrowth until she came to the end of the lake. She stayed there long into the night.

The waves came in film over film, for the night was very calm and the water barely moved. Her land would be taken and the trees cut down and sold. She had exactly two dollars in an old snuff can, and she needed one hundred and ninety-eight more. She opened her mouth and the night bees burst out, swarmed over the rough surface of the lake, roared in a black cloud toward the spirit island. The anger built up again. She waited. This time she smashed a rock down on another rock until she split the rock in jagged stripes. The rage was deep in her spirit. This man who took everything had put it there. He was faceless and voiceless as a jibay, he was a ghost tormentor, shielded from her sight.

If only I could get to him, she thought, but I am nothing. She pondered her thin old green dress, worn makazinan, her faded red blanket-shawl mended and worn through and mended again. She opened her hands, turned them over, and looked at them—Pillager hands, big and spidery, rough from setting and hauling in nets. Clever hands, fingers she could murder with, or smooth away a knot of pain in old Margaret's shoulders, or swipe a sand of sleep gently from the eye of her little girl. Yes, these hands were clever. Hands like this, she thought, shaking them curiously, would know or imagine everything there was to know about a man. On her face there appeared the glint of a smile—yes, she was nothing. But nothing can go anywhere. Nothing can do things. People don't see nothing, but nothing sees them. She put her hands on her hips, threw her shoulders back, and glared at the sky. It was a wild night, full of black clouds and rolling wind. For a long while she stood on shore, watching the shapes of things. Slowly, in a sky that reflected her mind, directions appeared.

She removed the bones of her parents from the earth, washed them, and wrapped them in red cloth. Then she fed them a dish of manoomin and berries. She laid a pipeful of asemaa in the red cloth for them to smoke. Then she loaded the bundles in a small cart. If things happened as she foresaw, she would need them to come along with her and support her in all that she did. For what she contemplated was a strange thing. It had come to her as the shape of something, not all at once, but by suggestion. She would find the ghost man, the thief, and be nothing around him. She would watch him, learn everything about him, and from the knowledge ascertain just how she could destroy him and restore her land.

He was rich, that she knew. The rich aren't difficult to find, she thought, they live in big wika-iganan.

"Aaniin ezhichigeyan, n'mama?"

Lulu had crept up behind her mother and peeked into the red cloth. Fleur showed her what she was doing. Lulu poked at the bones and her mother took her hands carefully away. A frantic laughter, a

feeling of painful hilarity seized Fleur, and she grabbed Lulu, swung
her around and then put her down and darted off. They raced wildly
up and down the lake shore, pulling at each other's clothes, throwing
weeds. When they fell to the ground, Fleur's heart was beating so fast
it felt like a bird trying to leave her chest. She grabbed Lulu and
crushed the girl close. Although she was quick as an otter and usually
squirmed away from being held and ducked from her mother's
embrace, this time Lulu breathed out one long laugh and then fell
asleep with her fingers gripping the cloth of her mother's blouse. Fleur
sat on the shore for a long time with her daughter's weight heavy
against her and the water rolling in, and rolling in, and without pause
rolling into the shore.

11

THE FIRST VISIT

1920–1922

Agnes slumped at the table in her cabin. Felled with an autumn fever, she had spent a week tossing in bed. To cure her weak dizziness, now, she was drinking a foul, but she hoped nutritious, soup prepared by Mary Kashpaw. There was cabbage in it, she noted, translucent shreds of onions, the neck of a chicken. She closed her eyes to take a sip. The sisters were wary of Mary Kashpaw; except for Hildegarde, they all believed she was dangerous and still advised the priest to be careful lest she attack. Agnes knew that she was endangered only by the girl's cooking, and she usually sent her out while she ate so that her reactions should not trouble Mary Kashpaw. Agnes had done just that and Mary Kashpaw was out in the yard, then, when the dog walked right in through the open window. A rangy thing, coal black and huge, he stood on the small table, front paw in the soup bowl. Agnes untucked the napkin from below her chin, and swatted at the dog.

"Get!" she weakly cried, and then, through the glowing spots of a half-fainting weakness, she heard it answer.

"Get?" The dog twisted the word sarcastically. "Get what, get where?"

Stricken with a sick wonder, Agnes tried to bolt from the room. The soup was terrible, but capable of such an effect?

"You look surprised to see me," said the dog. "As you'll soon find, I serve a greater master than yours. You've seen him at a distance, and you'll soon see him close."

"What do you want?" Agnes gasped the words out and then her mind cleared. Some prank-pulling member of her parish was using ventriloquism. Who? Narrowing her eyes, she spun around, but saw nothing. The dog opened his dog mouth and spoke again.

"I want Lulu! Where does she live?"

The dog explained that he was sent for the girl, Lulu, who was marked for the taking. But he couldn't find her on the reservation. Where was her family hiding her? Agnes jumped up, reeling, so angered that she hardly knew what words passed her lips. The strangeness of the scene palled before the idea of danger to Lulu.

"What could you possibly want with her?" she accused. "She is the only child of a family who has lost everything!"

"All the more valuable to me!" said the dog.

"You cannot have her." Agnes's voice was firm as she could muster, given the fainting languor of her illness. She groped for the crucifix chained around her neck, but her fingers seemed thick as wooden pegs, clumsy, and the dog noticed with a sly glance.

"I hear you're a gambler. I'll strike a bargain with you," he insinuated.

"A bargain . . ." Agnes fell back into her chair, and though sweating and breathless she couldn't help marvel. The joke was clever. Or was this what the mad saw, the fevered? The dog was here and he seemed perfectly real, not only that, but he knew of Agnes's passion. Although she came onto this reservation never having placed a bet, thrown the dice or the bones, she had since found gambling was a compelling way to raise money, for she was unusually lucky, and also she took great pleasure in her small winnings. She knew that she was being tempted by the gambit, tempted to wager even as her lips formed the words.

"Name your offer . . ."

"My offer is this," the dog said. "I will spare Lulu if you come with me instead."

A frozen wind blew through the room and Agnes shivered, couldn't speak. Soon there would be a punch line. Someone would pop around the corner, laughing at the hoax played on the good priest. For the benefit of whomever was listening to the ridiculous transaction, Agnes thought aloud.

"A priest puts the welfare of his flock above all else, for they are entrusted to him by the author of the world, and so even in this lonely and unspeakable moment, my duty is clear!"

Agnes waited for a hoot of laughter, none came.

"I will trade places with the child, with Lulu Nanapush," she declared, "but you must not take me until I am good and ready!"

Now it was time for the applause. Silence. Agnes calmly lifted the dog's paw from the soup bowl. It seemed real enough. She glanced away from the flames of the dog's eyes. Frowning, she regarded the grained wood of the poor log table. When would the instigator of this farce show? And who would play so perverse a joke? Not even Nanapush.

"It is done," the dog conceded just before he loped off, "your lifetime is doubled. But there is more. Your insolence moves me. I have decided to send you a temptation."

It would come by mail, but not until the autumn rains soaked the walls of the cabin and drained the sky of heat.

Agnes put her hands to her cheeks. She was still dangerously fevered. Perhaps, after all, the dog was no prank but a vision produced by the illness. The resinous scent of burnt pitch lingered in the room, and she could not help remember the figure she'd seen on the horizon at the time of Kashpaw's death—the gaunt spirit with the flapping coat, the dog trotting beside, its breath rising, foul steam.

At the thought, Agnes regretted her stubbornness, for what if the creature was real? She got the worst of the bargain. How could she know that she wasn't meant to die that very night? She was young, and in a few more years eternity in hell could well stretch before her. On the other hand, she thought, once she'd calmed her breathing and lay down again, perhaps her natural life span was more like eighty years, in which case there was what seemed a huge amount of time in which to think of a way to win herself back from the black dog's company.

Dwelling on that more cheerful idea, Agnes staggered around the room for exercise, then returned to bed, leaving the full bowl of soup, into which the devil's foot had plunged.

That night, careful as always not to waste a drop or a morsel, Mary Kashpaw dumped the contents of Father Damien's devil's-paw bowl back into the soup pot and brought it over to the convent, where it was reboiled and served up to the nuns. The soup deranged their sleep. What terrible torments the sisters suffered! What a night of temptations! What lurid and arresting dreams! Poor Father Damien, who dragged himself to the church to hear confessions the next morning, was assaulted by a swimming sea of details. The sisters recounted their actions explicitly, and he became such a seething repository of voluptuous nightmares that he found it impossible to accomplish his duties. Weaker than ever, disturbed in mind, he was forced to cancel Holy Mass. As he was hurrying toward the solace of his tiny cabin behind the church, Sister Dympna came toward him from the opposite direction.

"Father," she gasped in a voice of shamed panic, "I have been visited in the flesh!"

"You are absolved!" Damien cried out, and he practically blessed her on the run. Then he shut his door. Alone, he ran to the corner of his room and wrote feverishly, madly, until he had relieved his mind of the burden of an entire convent full of dreams.

Eternal Father,

The people to whom I have carried the faith believe there is a spirit behind or informing all that exists on earth. In dreams, they tell me, these spirits communicate with them. I thought it a harmless and empty fancy until I myself was visited.

Gracious Father, head of the church, the spiritual descendant of the one who has walked on water, what should I do?

I fear I may be losing my mind.

Modeste

As soon as she was well, Agnes went to the postal window at the trader's store and bought the stamps necessary to ship her letter across the sea. As she slowly licked the stamps and pressed them onto the envelope, idly tasting the faintly medicinal glue, the loneliness that so often visited her since the bewildering deaths by influenza sank through her bones. It was a black marrow. Ice. Since those days, prayer had not helped. The intimacy and the special favor shown her in the very beginning, at the river, at the first communion she'd performed, was withdrawn. She endured, instead of that warm broth of rescuing love, a skeletal deadness that surely the dog had sensed. Perhaps, she thought now, smoothing the envelope, Christ was still busy helping admit or reject the dead millions, that harvest fattened by the Great War and by disease. There was probably a lot of paperwork to the admission process. Imagining Christ an overworked bureaucrat amused her. But she wondered whether such thoughts were a marker of her cynicism, and an invitation to the test of her commitment, which was presented in the next moment in the form of a different letter.

"There is something here for you," said the wife of the trader, who handled the mail. She gave Father Damien a letter from the bishop, return address the cathedral in Fargo. Light-headed from the walk, Agnes put the letter in her pocket and forgot about it until, that night, the envelope crinkled in the folds of her cassock.

Dear Father Damien,

I am sending an assistant to work with you, not because you will need his help, though I am certain you will benefit from his presence, but because I would like you to train him.

He will stay with you and learn all that you can teach him.

Yours in Christ,
Bishop DuPre

Agnes dropped the piece of paper and stood mute and numb, staring straight before her at the dark, wet, log walls. For a week, nearly, the skies had opened every day. There was no let-up. Between drenching bursts a slow, cold drizzle descended. And now this letter from the bishop, a stunning threat.

Live with her? Quite impossible.

She wrote back.

I am in no need of assistance, and furthermore, there is no place for a young priest to live. As it is, my quarters are inadequate, not that I mean to complain. But to add another is impossible!

Impossible! Her brain locked on the word and was comforted by the lilt of it. Impossible. She refused in fact to consider or even remember the letter from the bishop, until one day the assistant simply, with no warning and no one to accompany him, arrived.

Father Gregory Wekkle walked up the hill quite alone, apparently having come in much the same way Agnes had originally. As she was striding across the crisp new dusting of snow on the church grounds, she saw him waiting at the door of her cabin, a small rounded suitcase and a wooden toolbox at his feet. Father Wekkle was of medium height and form, but gave the impression of being a bigger man, animated by a complex and slightly awkward energy. He moved eagerly, and had an open and friendly look about him, a disarming lack of polish or priestly grace. His hair was brown as a monk's robe, his eyes a muddy Irish hazel. His smile was a great flash of light. Agnes sighed. There was a sweetness to the man she couldn't have expected, a quality of taking pleasure in his own being. She decided that he had to be harmless. She underestimated, as she often did with men, his intelligence. Already, she imagined his developing into the kindly, rotund sort of priest who dispenses easy penances and excellent reassurances. What did he need from her?

She grasped his hand anyway, and shook it—a hard-palmed warm workman's hand. She looked down at his box of tools and then the heat from his heavy palm flowed up her arm into her heart. Surprised, she took the jolt of his goodness almost painfully and tried to control the sudden flood of happiness that filled her with terror.

"Come in. Let's set things up. Let's make you comfortable, Father . . . ?"

"Wekkle. Gregory Wekkle."

Agnes mustered the stern and kindly formality of Father Damien, and nodded him through the door. His presence startled her into an objective look at her house, and the clutter of it suddenly dismayed her. There were books everywhere. Books she had begged for in her newsletter, intending to set up a library. People from surrounding parishes now gave her books, tried to sell books to her, laid them on the church doorstep. Father Damien had become known for his avidity and was the first one people thought of when a book, any book, became useless. Thus she had a stack of the last century's *Godey's Lady's Books*, as well as Lutheran hymnals, but also treasures. Thomas Aquinas in an endless indestructible leather-bound edition with Italian marbled endpapers and a gold-embossed title on the spine. A complete set of Dickens.

The two proceeded to make way through stacks of books into the tiny cabin. Out of the stacks of books, they made separate rooms. They stacked the books two by two, then crosswise, like bricks, into a wall. Then Father Wekkle was given a bedstead by Sister Hildegarde and the two priests placed it on the other side of the wall. They used blanket dividers, hung them from the beams. As they worked, they spoke, though Agnes tried to remain cool. Father Gregory Wekkle was young, but not as young as Agnes had expected, not that she *had* expected. They were the same age, a peril, as she'd have his questions. Fortunately, Agnes had memorized information from the newsletters sent to Little No Horse by the original Father Damien's seminary. She was able to speak very generally of other priests they might know in common. To her relief, Father Gregory did not pursue their histories except as a polite gesture. He was much more interested in the present, and in learning from Father Damien all that he could before taking up a reservation post—he knew not where, not yet.

He was pleasant, he was congenial, he was both shrewder and more innocent than she saw at first. Already, that night, drifting into sleep behind her woolen blanket curtain, Agnes prayed that something would call Father Wekkle away immediately, that he leave precipitously, anything but risk again that jolt of pleasure in the immediacy of his presence.

The first deep snow isolated the reservation from the rest of the world and sank the cabin in a swirl of white drifts. The roads were blocked until the horse-drawn sledges would pack down the snow, or until the plow tore laboriously through the high snow pack down to the train station in Hoopdance. Still, there were rounds to be made. Communion to bring to the sick and the very old. Children to teach their catechism. Nanapush had taught Father Damien how to make bear paw snowshoe frames and lace them with moose guts and sinew. Now Agnes was teaching Gregory Wekkle.

"Make the fire extremely hot," she said.

He'd brought logs in to feed the stove, and he stuffed its belly with dried birch until the iron glowed pulsing red. She had already split the ash and now she showed him how to heat it and bend it into a circle. In a pail by her foot, she'd covered fresh moose guts with water. Slowly, she smoothed each one clean between her fingers, forming a pile of moose-chewed water lilies on the table.

"Some people eat this," she told Gregory. "It's like salad with a dressing of moose digestive juices."

"Unknown, as yet, in the fine St. Paul restaurants."

Agnes laughed and asked him when was the last time he ate in a fine St. Paul restaurant.

"Before I came here, my parents had a farewell party."

"Do you miss your family?" Agnes strung a loop of intestine between the sides of the hoop, fastening it tight.

"I do," said Gregory. "They're coming up to visit in the spring."

Agnes's heart jumped and sank at the same time. Would he stay here that long? It was too long. It was not long enough. The heat from the overfed stove rose in her cheeks. "No!" she roughly said, grasping the new priest's wrists to help him bend the wood properly. "You do it like this." A mistake. Close, she smelled the wood heat on his skin, the washed soapy scent of his neck, the scorched wool upon which he must have used a too hot iron, and sweat. A faint, low, clean, and intensely sexual workman's sweat. Agnes felt herself leaning into the air around him.

"Damn," said Gregory in a low voice as the heated wood popped from his hands. He laughed in derision at himself and crossed the room to retrieve the piece of half-bent wood. He lingered on the cool side of the cabin, and breathed deeply, disturbed at his own physical reaction to the proximity of Father Damien.

*

They traveled to the deep bush on those snowshoes, brought communion to Zozed Bizhieu and her troublesome daughter, visited Nanapush. When they traveled, they carried blanket rolls tied onto their shoulders, and a pack of bread, dried meat, raisins. Gregory Wekkle brought a flask, always, of his favorite whiskey, for he didn't see anything wrong with a drop now and then. And although Agnes observed there were a good many nows, and a huge number of thens, she nonetheless drank with him a drop, or two, or maybe more than that. It became very pleasant while out on their visits to stop on the way back, build a fire, sit there with the whiskey and the bannock and the raisins, until it was time to go back to the parish cabin.

"Father Damien," said Gregory one night, as they laughed over some clumsiness, "why don't we stay out here?"

"I believe we'd worry Sister Hildegarde" was Damien's answer, and he quickly dumped snow on the fire. As they tramped the miles back, Agnes felt a sting of wishful desire. Nanapush had taught her how to build a brush shelter to conserve the heat of the fire, and the night was warm and starry. The whiskey gave her the temporary illusion of gliding power. She was on the verge of stopping there, making a new camp, and she even paused, turned, and opened her mouth to speak.

There was Father Wekkle, struggling behind her with a hopeful, bearish serenity. After he barged forward, he would stop, breath on his fingers, arrange his scarf, shrug, and surge forward again. He worked his way along in a comical intensity, and Agnes felt her heart squeeze at his endearing earnestness and cheer. Often, even in his snowshoes, he managed to break through the crust of snow. He had a start-stop kind of steadiness about him and kept on lunging forward. She saw the white flash of his teeth when he grinned at her, and she turned back onto the path, mumbling to herself, Be sensible!

So they returned, propped their snowshoes against the sides of the cabin, rekindled the fire that Mary Kashpaw had banked and left, and rolled into their beds. For a while she slept, but then, waking in the dark, a fury of discomfort seized Agnes, as though her skin was being stung with red-hot needles. She prickled all over, and she prayed for help in wrestling with her thoughts. By dawn, most of them were subdued.

Most, not all.

She had to touch him. There was no help for it. There was a faint, sweet, brown to Father Wekkle's skin, a fading suntan, almost golden. His hands were broad, sensitive, well-padded, with wide, spreading, generous thumbs. He was good with a hammer, and one of his most winsome qualities was his sunny energy for carpentry work. He cleaned and oiled and sharpened the contents of his tool chest every few days. Agnes struggled for a while longer, angry and despairing of her need just to touch him by accident, just once! Be sensible, she told herself whenever her thoughts lighted on his hair, brown and wavy, growing out of its cut in swirls.

She was sensible until the night the books fell.

There were times she woke too early, and so as not to wake Father Wekkle, she read the spines of her side of the double wall of books stacked between them. Among others, she had given herself the Russians, all of George Eliot, her beloved Aquinas, Augustine, St. Theresa of Avila's *Interior Castle*, and a two-volume set of the lives of the saints. This last was to atone for the other volumes, only four, of Colette—though, after all, François Mauriac had said that her voluptuousness led the soul to God. She had covered those books in butcher paper and changed the titles to Latin. She also kept the strange assortment of donated books to read through and decide upon—accounts of personal voyages were popular among them, as well as outdated medicinal or fashion advice. Mauriac was on Agnes's side and also Proust, William James, and others she was confident of displaying. Stendhal, Hugo, and all of the Greeks were stacked on Wekkle's side. Plus the histories of states and provinces and the mesmerizing horrors of a collection of Jesuit relations, which had once belonged to Father Hugo.

She knew the wall of books by each title. After the lantern was out, at night, she put out her hand and traced the stamped letters on the spines and the embossed ridges. Some of her newer books were very plainly bound, but she loved to run her fingers over them, too. Their heavily woven cloth covers were of a texture pleasingly dry and soft to her touch. Even when she was exhausted, each night she brushed the books between her bed and Father Wekkle's, and she held her palm upon them until the books warmed to her touch. It seemed to her, listening to the other priest's calm breath, that the books between them were a third, sympathetic, entity. For it was through books that she felt her life to be unjudged. Look at all of the great mix-ups, messes, confinements, and double-dealings in Shakespeare, she thought. Identities disguised continually, in a combative dance of illusion and discovery. Hers was hardly the most sinful, tragic, or bizarre. Hers was merely what it was, and her aches over it as well, but in all of the books that composed the wall between the two priests, and in all of the stories she'd ever read, she never had come across the exact example of what she contemplated doing to Father Wekkle. Nor could she imagine his reacting to her touch with anything but mystery and horror. Therefore, she took her hand away from the wall.

Fortunately, or unfortunately, Father Wekkle was a sleeper who thrashed. He slept in a moleskin robe that his mother had sewn for him and insisted he wear up north in the bitter wild. Every night he put it on with mixed gratitude and embarrassment. As he was sensitive to the cold, its warmth made him thankful. At the same time, as his mother could not bear plain things and had sewn it with a ruffle, he made very certain that no other human ever saw him in it. As he slept, he warmed, and as he got warmer, he flailed in the moleskin gown and kicked away his covers, tossed and muttered. Also, he dreamed, and his dreams were always action masterpieces. All he'd left undone or half done during the day, he'd finish. More than that, he'd start new projects or he'd make parish visits, leaping high in his snowshoes and skating, even flying, to the rescue of those stranded from the presence of the Host. All that he imagined, he acted out and he had, many times, awakened Agnes. He'd also kicked or struck the book wall, making it lean so perilously that it sometimes had to be rebuilt by Father Damien, who could not help remember Agnes's convent days as Cecilia and the careful construction of the birdbath containing only the brickworks word, Fleisch, and now again the wall she made containing thousands, perhaps millions of words, and still in her mind only that one word.

The moleskin robe stuck to Father Wekkle when he sweated,

twisting around his hips so that he sometimes dreamed erotically. He had, in fact, that night, been the victim of a most intense and mysterious veiled female whose lips, only, were revealed by a small, round hole in the cloth. Her lips moved, mouthing the words *Be sensible*, words that require the most seductive motions of the lips. The advice aroused him and he lunged for her impatiently and in his sudden movement toppled the books.

In the stillness of the night, they were a skidding avalanche. One struck Agnes full in the face and she started awake, heart pounding. Groping around herself in panic, she touched him. His hand grasped hers. They didn't move. The collapse of books had also torn down the blanket divider, so the moon-pale light from the window on Gregory's side of the cabin washed across their beds. Raggedly breathing, hearts quickened, blinking, hands touching, they poised. If either had simply withdrawn a hand they would have laughed, rebuilt the wall of books. But they continued, in their staged paralysis, to search each other's dim-lighted faces. Both were desperate for clues—what was to happen? At the same moment, both imperceptibly leaned forward. Brightness from the full moon rested evenly upon their hair, but their faces were in shadow so that, as Gregory tipped his chin questingly forward into that final space, he felt that he ducked into a cave. Once he entered that half sphere of shadow, he was lost. She was lost. They lay down together among the scattered books. Into Gregory's mind, there surged the awful and appalling joy of knowing he was one of those whom the Church darkly warned against, the ones who lay with men as with women. The sin he would commit would be equal to the sin of murder, one of those sins crying out to heaven for vengeance.

In Agnes's mind, a willing despair to be discovered. Her nipples burned against the cloth and her body slipped its boundaries of skin. Darkness sifted through her and she rose toward him, light, powerful, and calm. Gregory touched her breast through the night shift, and in a dreamlike reversal of who he feared he was, he held her like a raft in a torrent. They spoke now, their whispers incoherent. They undressed each other slowly, with formal innocence, shocked into foolishness at the pleasure of each discovery. Gregory had no experience at all of a woman's nakedness, and the final sight of her, strong and unbound, washed in silver, astonished him so that he could merely sit with her for a time and touch her as one might a fabulous animal before suddenly, at her gesture, he spread her thighs open and entered the shadow between.

In surprise, once they began to move, they sighed in relief and smiled, delighted and aghast, to find themselves utterly safe and at peace. That was the strange and unexpected component of their passion—how safe, how ordinary, how blessedly normal it felt. For the next few days they lived in a daze, but nothing changed. In their work they were more zealous, more dutiful. They drove themselves harder than before. Secure in the night, they took no chances in the day and were remote but friendly with each other. Weeks accumulated in which neither spoke of what was happening. Only, in the depth of the night, with the window curtained, they made love with a charged tenderness that left them faint and weeping. Before falling asleep, they set things straight and returned to either side of their wall of books. Each whispered good night to the spines, the massed pages, then lay still underneath the heavy patched wool of the quilts of army blankets.

The snow melted into the earth and they walked now, through mud and swollen mashkiig, to bring communion to the laid-up devout, to instruct for various sacraments. Returning one cold spring day, they paused to rest on the soft old winter-dusty grass. They sat down silently. Gregory tore off a piece of the bannock given to them, and Agnes accepted the bread from his hands and ate. The massed reeds in the slough were a scorched and radiant yellow. The sun shot down from a half-gray sky, picking out the birch with a fierce light.

"I belong to you," said Gregory to Agnes. "I love you."

When she said the same to him, the bread went dry on their tongues and they felt spreading from those words a branching fury of impossible difficulty.

BERNADETTE'S CONFESSION

As Father Damien hustled across the yard to hear confessions, he saw that the nuns had frozen their pump again and were using Mary Kashpaw as their beast of burden. He watched her as he walked, saw her stagger as she rounded the corner to the back door of the convent, a great pole laid across her shoulders, two buckets hanging down from either end. He made a note to stop the sisters from overusing the girl's strength, and passed at once into the church. There were a few parishioners hunched in contemplation near the jerry-built box of boards and blankets in which he heard confessions. He sat in the middle box, on a small cushioned stool, and bent to the muslin shadow. A discreet cough. The sinner spoke.

"What is it when you know of a sin and do nothing?"

"That is a sin of silence."

"So it is a sin."

"Yes."

"Then I must confess it," said the woman unwillingly.

In a few sentences, then, the woman whose voice was familiar to Damien—it was Bernadette's—confirmed the truth of what he had long ago suspected of Napoleon Morrissey. He heard the rest of her confession in a numb, unfused state of tension. He absolved Bernadette, heard the other confessions. Once they were all finished, he continued to sit in the little booth, in his lap the soft, old, battered breviary that had belonged to Father Hugo. At last, he believed he knew the murderer of Napoleon Morrissey, and he pitied and loved the killer—his own Mary Kashpaw. According to Bernadette, Napoleon Morrissey had forced himself on Mary Kashpaw, most probably raping her. It followed in his mind that Mary Kashpaw had the strength to have strangled Napoleon with the cunningly wrought necklace of thorns. As for her hands, they were tough as leather mitts, scarred, and roped with calluses. If the barbed-wire rosary tore her palms, it was impossible to tell anymore. And yet, why would Mary Kashpaw construct such a dark-spirited artifact?

Agnes put her fingertips to her eyes, kneaded her forehead with her knuckles. She thought of Mary Kashpaw digging, digging, and her heart went hollow. Yet she was so tired that she could feel only a pale, exhausted pity for the angry confusion of that violated girl. Perhaps too much feeling had withered her heart and now it was a frail, paper husk. Whirling with frustration, she jumped from the confessional and walked back to the cabin. There, she began to work, cleaning with a mad zeal similar to Mary Kashpaw's. She shoveled ashes out of the stove, then fetched a pot of blacking and painted it, opening the doors to let the spring air carry off the sharp odor of the paint. She worked on her papers until between her hands she snapped a pen. Then she cleaned up the spilled ink, dusted her books. Muttering and on the verge of weeping, she suddenly flung herself onto the bed. In a moment, she fell into a well of thick unconsciousness.

She was still asleep when Father Wekkle and Mary Kashpaw returned from a wood-hauling trip. Mary stamped down the snow for him too, broke the trail. Sometimes he teased her, called her Mary Stamper, and the big girl flushed, although whether she liked it or was embarrassed by the name there was no telling. While Father Wekkle went back to the church to set it all to rights and lock it for the night, Mary Kashpaw quietly drew near to Father Damien. For a long moment, she looked down at him with solemn watchfulness. Then she pulled a rough blanket from the back of a chair, shook out the folds, and secured it around the sleeping priest's body with awkward, firm, tucks. Lastly, she plucked loose the laces of Father Damien's boots and stealthily eased them off and then stripped the socks from the priest's long, narrow, tender white feet. She set the boots beside the bed, hung the socks over each toe. She tucked the end of the blanket over the vulnerable feet, and then blew out the candle before she walked out to sleep upon the broken bales of hay, within the questions of the owls and the tremble of mice, and behind the barred door of the shed.

The Cloud

"How many ways are we damned?" said Agnes into the black air.

Gregory pushed his hands over her face, smoothing her features up into a smile he could feel with his fingers. Then he stretched full length alongside of her and tucked her close to him. His throat pinched shut with raw sadness, and he could not answer. He had started to become a priest when he was only nine years old. He had never questioned or doubted his vocation, and he had never been tempted beyond the usual ways boys are tempted, by thoughts and dreams. But it was as though he'd saved his whole life so far for this one outrageous test. What happened with Agnes was as direct a piece of knowledge as when he knew his calling. There was no way to question its truth, and veracity was for Gregory Wekkle the essence of his soul. One particular volume from the stack between the two priests had fallen into his hands one night and Gregory, though not a violently greedy reader like Agnes, read it again and again. The book was a mystical work called *The Cloud of Unknowing.* In it, the author had said that to know God one must first know oneself. One will know God in oneself. Gregory knew himself and knew his love for Agnes was a good love, filled with tenderness and light. He tortured himself in his prayers to find evil in his actions, but knew only harmony and righteous peace. Nothing, none of this, fit doctrine.

"How many ways are we damned?" asked Agnes, again.

"Every way possible, I imagine," said Gregory lightly, though his heart was squeezing shut. "Have you counted?"

"Let me," said Agnes. After a moment, she put up her hand and gravely ticked off her fingers the types of sins she taught children in catechism. "We have sinned mortally of course, although our sin is so grave there isn't an exact definition for it."

Gregory shook his head. Willfully drowsy with a kind of lazy despair, he mumbled as if by rote, "I've done this with the full consent of my will, and clear knowledge of the act."

"The wages are eternal punishment," said Agnes. They held each other closer and he breathed along the curve of her collarbone.

"We've sinned against the Holy Ghost," he whispered. "I feel deliberate resistance to the known truth because, Agnes, I know the truth. It is in me and it tells me to love."

Agnes silently stroked his hair, smoothed her hands along his temples and down his jaw. This truth was hers, too, the kernel at the center of all she did in the blackest night was an unwilled simplicity. Her desire was one with a kind regard that felt both sinless and irresistible.

"We've sinned by omission," she said, thinking of it. "We've sinned by silence, since we're responsible for giving each other up to the authorities, reporting. We haven't committed the sin of Sodom."

"That's something." Gregory could not help imagining the act, all of a sudden, but the whole catalog now struck him as ridiculous. "We haven't committed murder, buggered each other, or oppressed the poor."

"Sins crying out to heaven for vengeance."

"We've done Actual Sin, Formal Sin, Habitual Sin."

Gregory kissed her forehead and cupped his broad hand around her face. The way the curve of her face fit into his hand took away his breath for a moment, and then he took a painful gulp of air and laughed.

"I hope Dante was right about hell," he said. "I don't think I would mind so much whirling in that dark wind with you forever."

"Cut off from God."

"If we are cut off from God by sinning," he said, low, "why do I feel so close to God when I touch you in this darkness, in this cloud?"

THE LETTER

In the lucid green blush of early summer, Agnes wrote the letter. Not until autumn could Father Damien bear to mail it.

> *Reverend Bishop,*
> *I have instructed the good Father Wekkle to the limits of which I am capable. He is an honorable priest and devoted to his calling. Please make your assignment of his new post known to him as quickly as possible.*

She had to write the letter so that, when he received the one that would arrive in reply, the sight of him reading it wouldn't kill her. It didn't come by return post. Not for many weeks. But when it did, she knew. The envelope had no weight. It was only a paper rectangle set into her hand with such a light touch, nothing. Yet when she bore it to the cabin the paper was so heavy that it drove her to her knees. Her legs went out from under her. Mute, she handed it up to him and then sat like a stunned child on the floor until he raised her up and, very kindly now, said to her, "Agnes, why won't you say it? It is so simple to me. Why can't you say it? We must leave. We have to leave together. We'll go north, go west, be a couple married legally and happily. We'll have children, a life. Why can't you say it? Why won't you?"

Agnes shook her head, dumb with shock. Her tongue stuck to the roof of her mouth and she was nerveless, bereft.

"Say it," he pleaded. But she could only look at him. Already he seemed smaller and farther away. An hour, two hours passed in which he talked himself hoarse to persuade her, and only then, at the last, could she even say the word no. That word inflamed him, set him beside himself and he argued with the two letters. They argued long into the night, not loudly, but with such fervor that Mary Kashpaw knocked on the cabin door and when Agnes opened it, said nothing. Just stood there eyeing Father Wekkle with a look of baleful intelligence.

"Izhah," said Agnes, her tongue finding these words easily, "mino nibaan, n'dawnis."

Only with great reluctance did Mary Kashpaw move away.

Deep in the night Agnes found another way to say it. "I cannot leave who I am."

In wild hopelessness Gregory now blurted the thing they'd said between them with physical eloquence only.

"You are a *woman*."

The word seemed large in the dark cabin, its vowels voluptuous and thick with the burden of secret life. Both were silent but the word hung between them like a great flesh doll. They closed their eyes and the word spread open between them, hot and red. Gregory sank his head into his hands and tasted the word and there was nothing like its exalted spice. He wanted her in his mouth. But then she spoke, and said, "I am a priest."

The four words rang down Gregory's spine, and then, at last, between wanting and despairing of her, anger surged up with a force that weakened him, sent a cold shiver through his gut. Rage shook in his voice.

"Agnes," he grabbed her shoulders, his voice rose and cracked and fell, "a woman cannot be a priest."

"I am a priest," said Agnes calmly, again. She had left the body they shared and for this moment she existed only in a spirit sad with knowledge that could remove his hands. "This is what I do. Without it, if I couldn't say the Mass . . ." She held her hands out, tough with work and empty. Nothing.

"You're sacrilege," said Gregory, his voice beyond all hope. It was the worst word he could summon, and he knew it, but he wanted her so much he'd even shame her into coming with him. "Sacrilege!" he cried again, more hesitantly, almost plaintive.

Agnes stepped backward, as if to let the word fall at her feet.

"No," she said, looking at him with her heart tearing, helpless against the simplest truth. "I am nothing but a priest."

AGNES'S PASSION

Gregory was in the walls, in the crawl space between the board floor of the cabin and the bitter ground. He was gone, but he was everywhere. He was on the small pantry shelf where canning was removed. The air of the cabin still held Gregory. He filled and expanded every dark corner, tight, to exploding. He was jammed between her legs so that no matter how she moved, he was inside of Agnes. She couldn't shake him from her vestments or burn him from the stove. He nested in the books, of course. She couldn't stand to touch their pages. He was in the sweet, fragrant wood Mary Kashpaw chopped, split, and piled. In the cloth of curtains, the clasp of doors, he waited. She turned the handle, let the light in, and he came, too, solid and good and alive.

He sent her letters. She sent them back. He sent them again. She burned them. What else was she to do?

Awful questions appeared in Agnes's mind. Am I right? Can I bear this? Have I invented my God? Is God my yearning? Is my yearning God? She fell asleep with questions thrumming and woke with more blaring. She chewed questions over with her breakfast food, salted her dinner with the day's uncertainties. She prayed over the questions until it hurt to think, until her brain felt too tight in her skull. She then craved silence. Into her lover's absence crept compulsion. She thought obsessively of shedding the priest's clothes and donning a frilly hat, a gown of figured lilac, a flowered wash dress with buttons of mother-of-pearl. Imagined walking to the parish of Gregory

Wekkle, for some reason eating ice cream with him. And then they would leave and find a new place where he could tenderly stroke the hungry expanse of skin that covered the body that housed two beings. Father Damien's thoughts nagged, Agnes's temptations stung. Or maybe it was the other way around. Sometimes at night her body moved as if over the waves of a dark lake and she woke wet with tears and burning heavily between her legs.

Talk to me! Talk to me! She angrily prayed to the Christ who'd saved her from the river, to the God who'd brought her here, to the Holy Ghost who had sustained her through the great influenza and yet betrayed her by allowing the dog to visit her and to set before her Gregory. Since the damage was done, she prayed to see her damage again.

Mary Kashpaw sat stonily through this at the entrance to the cabin, snapping beans, glaring at the white dust rising off the far roads. If only, thought Agnes, she could again see the divine in Mary Kashpaw, maybe that would help. But the girl hardened and retreated. Each Mass that Father Damien said was duller than the next, and he dreaded genuflecting before the crucifix—a stamped piece of brass, two strips of tin, and the suffering Christ, a contorted lie.

Fountain of Hope,

I find to my distress that I suffer from an inner complaint before which all my skills and strategies fail. I cannot name what it is, exactly, I can only say at times it feels like something so wholly other to the ground of my being that I've entertained the fear that I may be possessed.

I tell you this in childish trust. No doubt, were the leaders of my diocese to learn of my condition, I would be yanked from my post straight into a sanatorium. Kept quiet under lock and key. Father, not only am I certain that would do no good, but I also cannot, must not, will not, desert my people here.

Many of the Indians (they call themselves the Anishinaabeg, the Spontaneous or Original People) have come to depend upon me. There is really no one else I feel can take my place, no one so committed to their well-being or engrossed in their faith—I am becoming one with them so as to better lead them into the great Corpus Christi. And the closer I draw, the more of their pain do I feel.

Still, what eats me is something composed of my own weaknesses and sins, I am sure.

Have you any spiritual anodyne or comfort, any small practice that might assist in my travail? Good Father, I cannot sleep . . .

Not quite of the body, yet not entirely of the soul, pain closed like a trap on Agnes and held her tight. Some nights it was a magnetic vest drawing blood to swell tightly just under her skin. Agnes wanted to burst from the cassock in a bloody shower! Other nights a shirt of razors slit and raked her and left no mark. Her womanness crouched dark within her—clawed, rebellious, sharp of tooth.

No amount of calm pleading moved the steady anguish. Some nights, she tried to slide the pain off her body like the husk of a spent and sleeping lover. She tried to breathe calmly and evenly to loosen the pain by degrees, but it stayed clapped on.

A mourning dove called from a tree, a small oak in the graveyard behind the cabin. The vowels of its inquiry floated to Agnes one eternal dusk and she went into herself to strike a hopeful bargain. What do you want of me? she asked. But her pain had no needs, so there was nothing to offer or trade. She attempted with the deepest resolve to ignore it, but its grip on her chest intensified and she felt the iron seizing to her ribs. She wondered if she could scare it out. She sat up, gathered her breath, began screaming. There was no one to hear, the cabin was chinked so tight and the nuns asleep, calm at a safe distance. So night after night, she screamed in the darkness. Huge jagged rips of sound tore out of her but the pain was not impressed.

Only Mary Kashpaw, curled in the rough bench bed of the sleigh, stared into the great dark and listened.

Agnes woke with tiny veins broken in her eyelids. She tried again the next night. Again, the next. Finally after nearly a week of sleeplessness, beyond all weariness, agitated to the death, she rose in the dark, lighted a candle, and walked out of the cabin. She let herself into the school infirmary to search for some remedy. Without acknowledging her mission openly, she knew that she wanted the means either to cure the pain or to put herself to sleep forever.

With the brass key marked from her ring of keys, she opened the door and then lighted a lantern. She unlocked the white wall cupboard that Hildegarde bartered for with the government office, who contracted for these items to be sent every year. They had little use for them without a doctor. There, on the shelves, was an array of possible anodynes and comforts.

Agnes examined the bottles carefully. Tartar emetic in a green paste. Perhaps she could puke it out? Strychnine sulfate, a carefully sealed black jar—there was her last resort. Atropine in an innocent clear flask. Digitalin, tiny pills. Ginger and ergot. Belladonna with its own eyedropper. She shook the bottle and the clear stuff turned cloudy with promise. She tucked it into her pocket. What was this? Glycyrrhiza. Pure carbolic. Boracic powder, which she thought was for the eyes. Cocaine hydrochlorate, $1/6$ grain, twenty-five tubes of etched glass with red rubber stoppers at the ends. She took ten. Benzoic acid. Charcoal in a blue jar. Compound of gentian in a square bottle with a long wax-sealed neck. Myrrh and nux vomica, in identical rusting tins. Clove tincture of opium. Agnes sighed, frowned. Only one bottle and so obvious it would be missed. Still, she took it. Pepsin for the stomach. Oil of Ethereal Male Fern. Quinine. Cod liver oil. Sulphate of morphia set far back in the cabinet and very dusty. Four $1/8$-ounce bottles of clear deep-brown amber glass. She took them also and shut the case.

FATHER DAMIEN'S SLEEP

For one delirious month, the anguish was survivable. It was Sister Hildegarde, of course, who dispatched herself to the priest's cabin when he did not show up for morning Mass. She knocked, she prayed, she knocked again, prayed some more. After a while she went to the window, peered through, and saw that Father Damien was sleeping. Or was he dead? Crossing her breast, she entered the cabin. Drew near to the priest apologetically, put her hand to his lips and was satisfied. Yes, sleeping! But what a deep sleep. Likely, the good priest was ill or exhausted beyond illness, and Hildegarde took pity. She tucked the robe just underneath the chin of the priest and was turning to go when a great moon-black shadow fell across her.

Mary Kashpaw did not acknowledge the presence of the nun, but fixed her attention on her priest. Across her powerful features, as she stepped into the cabin, there stole an unlikely expression of protective gentleness. It was a look that certainly had not been seen before on her person by Hildegarde. The girl bent over her priest, and with huge compassion she brushed her fingers on the old buffalo robe she'd dragged from a trunk to warm Father Damien. Then she sank to the floor beside the bed, composed herself, and refused to leave. Mary Kashpaw stayed day and night with the priest from then on, keeping watch. She lighted his glass kerosene lamp and kept it going.

For although he appeared to be lying inert in one body, heavily sleeping underneath the burly brown robe, Father Damien was, in truth, wandering mightily through heaven and earth. He was exploring worlds inhabited by both Ojibwe and Catholic. And had Mary Kashpaw not kept that beacon going, he might, in his long and rambling journey, have become confused or even got lost. For the countries of the spirit, to which he was now admitted, were accessible only via many dim and tangled trails.

DAMIEN'S INNER TRAVELS

Mary Kashpaw watched how his hands pierced the air, always moving. Fingers rippling on the covers, he smiled, humming endless, complicated, unrepeatable music that went on all night and made Mary Kashpaw sigh with radiant emotion.

All the while that the priest was traveling, she stayed at the side of his bed, first crouched on the floor and then, a great womanly boulder, on a chair that she had made of peeled logs hacked to planks. Motionless, rapt as an ice fisherman, she watched. Gazing into Father Damien's shuttered face, she hummed or rocked slightly on the uneven boards. From time to time, as though she were burning off a bit of surplus energy, she shuddered all over. Then she bit her lip and leaned to peer closer as if gazing into a deep pool ruffled on the surface by a stray breeze. Sometimes she left off staring at his face and frowned heartily at the wall, as if maps of Father Damien's current whereabouts were posted there. Eyes closed, she traced the imaginary paths, the roads of rivers. At last she came to wonder why she saw no whiskers and recorded no beard growth on his chin.

Other white men had them, these whiskers, and in truth she was curious to see them sprout. On Damien, none showed. On the third day of his sleep, Mary Kashpaw put her hand out and, with one finger, lightly stroked his chin. She drew her finger back and continued to sit, thoughtfully, staring like someone who has glimpsed the shade and outline of a larger picture.

Every morning after that she heated a kettle of water, readied the mug of shaving soap, dipped in the brush, stropped the razor, and was seen, ostentatiously, to be putting these things aside just as Sister Hildegarde arrived.

The practical Sister Hildegarde was in fact pleased to see how carefully Mary Kashpaw cared for Damien, and she tried to say so in signs, for she never did quite accept that, although Mary Kashpaw refused to speak, she understood everything around her perfectly. Hildegarde nodded at the carefully damped or blazing fire in the tiny metal drum of the stove. Gestured approvingly at the shine on the windows and the urgent cleanliness of Mary Kashpaw's floor. The big girl scrubbed with an artificial madness of intention. The floor smoothed and the wood settled underneath her punishing hands.

Watching her zeal, one day, Hildegarde was sobered to observe a mechanical strength, as though her body were able to operate without the direct guidance of her mind. Bending before Mary Kashpaw, the nun passed her hand rapidly before the girl's eyes and sure enough, she got no reaction. Hildegarde stood, scratched her nose, an act for which she must later say a penance. So, she thought, scrubbing floors! As well as who knows what! Hildegarde had seen her eat, too, with just this sort of blank fixity. These were actions Mary Kashpaw did in her sleep.

SLEEPERS

The sleepers traveled deep into the country of uncanny truth. Mary Kashpaw scrubbed floors in her sleep while, on the low bed above her, through dense thickets Father Damien plunged onward. He soon became thoroughly and miserably lost. Having strayed off the dream path leading to the house of his friend, Nanapush, he made the mistake of continuing—after all, dusk was nearly on him and he didn't want to spend the night in the woods, even though it was a dream woods. That, however, is exactly what happened. Damien sat against a tree, drunk with exhaustion. After a short period of electrified panic, he felt a dim fuzz stealing over his brain.

Just as he dropped with a jerk into the pit of unconsciousness, he thought how odd it was that he was falling asleep in his sleep. When he entered the dream that he was dreaming, later, it was a dream within the dream he dreamed originally when he lay down in his bed. And so it went from there, a series of dreams, tunnels of brilliance snaking and tangling into the low hill, then out, then farther back—through unknown swamps and broad lake fields high with sweeping reeds and farther yet into the great many islanded lakes with their powerful, secret rock paintings. Impossible to say how many dreams within the dream before he met the one who followed him in to guide him back: Mary Kashpaw.

It was good she found the priest. For if Damien had dreamed himself much farther into that overgrown country how could he ever have returned? Who is to say this isn't exactly how, one morning, people wake up mad? They have simply dreamed themselves down too many paths and at each turn or pause, as they attempt to travel back, they are swept up in the poignancy of being. Except it is another dream that they unknowingly inhabit.

THE SACRAMENT

Father Damien walked through the woods in a state of pleasant resignation, his satchel full of strychnine. For a while he pretended to wander in a meaningless attempt to lose himself, so that he could die with

no bother to anyone else, but he had to admit finally that he was on
his way to Nanapush. Well, why not? Why not say good-bye to the
person who had been most kind to him and most understanding of all
Anishinaabeg. Besides, out of a sense of pride and rightness he had
inherited from his predecessor, he hadn't told Nanapush of what he
suffered. The way Damien understood it, he was to help, assist, comfort and aid, spiritually sustain, and advise the Anishinaabeg. Not the
other way around. Still, when he entered the familiar yard that afternoon, heart full, the pleasure and kindness in Nanapush's face somewhat eased his certainty. In that moment of relaxation, he showed
Nanapush the poison and admitted he had come into the woods to
die.

Nanapush gently took the bottles from Damien's hands. Miserable
with relief at his admission, Damien dragged himself to the side of
the yard, lay down in a patch of grass, on a blanket, and fell into a sudden and childlike sleep that lasted for most of the afternoon. He came
swimming to consciousness and was vaguely aware that there were
several men working in the yard, then he passed out again. When he
came to the second time, the world was dark and Nanapush was sitting next to him with his pipe lighted, blowing the smoke over Father
Damien in a faint and fragrant drift.

Father Damien sat up, embarrassed at himself. As though he'd
upset some inner water level, tears filled his eyes. He looked at the
ground, his hands trembling.

"We put up a sweat lodge for you," said Nanapush. The glow of a
huge, steady fire lighted his features. Nanapush took the priest's
hand, then, and led him to the entrance of a small, domed hut, gestured for him to crawl inside. He did, entering on all fours. Then
Nanapush himself followed and crouched next to Damien. "Give me
your robe," he said, and Father Damien removed his heavy cassock,
but kept on the light black shift he wore beneath. The shadowy presences of men surrounded him and he could see their faces by the light
of the glowing rocks that soon were brought in a pitchfork and lowered into the pit at the very center.

Every so often, someone would make a little joke. Otherwise, they
were calm with expectation.

"This is our church," said Nanapush.

Hunched in the pole hut and sitting upon bare tamped ground, Agnes at first smiled wanly at the irony. But once the flap was closed and the darkness was complete, once the glowing rocks were splashed with water, then sprinkled with sharp medicines that gave off a healing smoke, once Nanapush started to pray, addressing the creator of things and all beings to every direction and every animal, Agnes knew that Nanapush had spoken truthfully and without double wit, and that this was indeed her friend's true church, which held him close upon the earth and intimate with fire, with water, with the heated air that cleaned their lungs, with the earth below them, and with the eagle's nest of the sweat lodge over them.

Straining to make sense of the rapid prayers, her Ojibwemowin at the level of penetration at which words made sense a beat or two beats after she heard them and puzzled out the meaning, Agnes surrendered. According to Church doctrine, it was wrong for a priest to undertake God's worship in so alien a place. Was it more wrong, yet, to feel suddenly at peace? It wasn't as though she made a choice to do it—Agnes simply found herself comforted.

That night, stretched out in blankets beside the fire that had heated the stones, Agnes lay peacefully alert. For the first time since the pain had gripped her, she felt a deliciousness of honest sleep close down. Not weariness or exhaustion, those things Father Damien strove toward in his work to try to outwit the grip of insomnia, but the luxuriant stretching of an utterly relaxed spirit.

After returning from despair, Father Damien loved not only the people but also the very thingness of the world. He became very fond of his stove—a squat little black Reliance with fat, curved legs. The stove reminded Agnes of a cheerful old woman who had given her bread as a child, and raw carrots, when she'd been hungry and there was nothing to eat at home. The old woman had pulled the carrots from the ground and held them under the spout of her pump until the dirt flowed off and they glistened. Then the old woman, whose fat legs ran straight down from her knees into her shoes, sat Agnes on a stump in her yard.

The gold secret tang of sweet marigolds was on the woman's hands. She had put the bread in Agnes's lap, soft and fresh, and the carrots, and a clear glass shaker of salt. Kindly, she'd left her to eat. Agnes could still taste the crisp juice of the carrots, the buttery interior whiteness of the bread, the salt bringing them together on her tongue, when she looked at the stove.

Thus was her salvation composed of the very great and very small. The vast comfort of a God who comforted her in a language other than her own. The bread of life. The gold orange of washed carrots and the taste of salt.

12

THE AUDIENCE

1922

Just behind the log church, a long, flat slab of rock rose abruptly at a steep angle into a craggy cliff. Father Hugo's dream had been to build upon that floor and against that rock. Now Agnes continued to work the idea into reality. The vision absorbed her, it was nothing she'd ever done before. She took measurements, observed the fall of the sun, used a level and compass and pencil to sketch. She lighted a lantern, spread out her papers on the table, and drew long into the night, planning, driven by a sudden and engulfing force of practicality. She fell into it as a way of not thinking about Gregory, and then the idea took on its own life. Soon she could fully imagine the church—it was a most absorbing vision.

A church with the floor of stone and the altar built against the stone. There would be two stoves, both set directly upon the floor of rock. Every morning in winter those fires would be kindled, and then the warmth would flow into the rock and toast the feet of worshipers. The stone behind the altar would be carved and polished bit by bit;

she could see it, a most incredible grotto, an attraction that people would come to see from miles away. And of course, the useless but somewhat decorative piano.

All that Fathers Hugo and then Damien intended came to pass, very slowly, but it was within the working out of that small destiny that Agnes realized how even careful plans cannot accommodate or foresee all the tricks of creation. The church planned in October mud, mulled over during the winter blizzards, plotted in icy April, raised in early May, was enough shelter in mid-June for Sister Hildegarde to move the piano inside. It stood to one side of the altar. As soon as the sides of the new church were framed and the roof on tight, the Superior wanted to test the acoustics. She wanted to hear the notes bounce off the spars, walls, ceiling, stones. Not that she could play. No one played. Sister Hildegarde had sent away to Fargo for instructional books, but Father Damien pretended to have lost the key to the shut keyboard.

A nameless and disturbing energy about the piano haunted Agnes. She felt uncomfortable whenever she chanced to be alone with it and she found, then, that she always kept an eye on the piano, as though it were alive and waiting for her to turn her back. Why? So that it could flip up its keyboard protector? Laugh? Agnes wondered at herself. Did she really believe the instrument would move forward, gnashing its poor, stained, ivory keys?

She stood in the entrance to the new church one afternoon, regarding the placement of the piano with an uneasy, critical eye. Later, she was sure it was the long summer light, the full golden quality of afternoon light that wakened her hands and set them moving about more restlessly than they had for some time. She thought of Gregory's hands, then put the thought away. The key to the keyboard was hidden in the piano's odd claw foot. An aperture behind a toe. Suddenly, Agnes bent and removed the key. She then opened the keyboard. All of a sudden there it was, the notes spread out before her in the slant light of afternoon, the discolored ivories of the sad keys gaping at her, the breath of the thing sighing out like an animal.

There was a small brown bench Sister Hildegarde had found and placed before the creature. Agnes sat, adjusted the distance, and watched the keys carefully. Nothing happened. There was nothing to be afraid of, after all, except that her hands sprang out of her sleeves. Then they jumped off her lap like claws and crashed down in an astonishing chord. She clutched her hands to her chest. The sound reverberated. With a soft and, she feared, insane longing, her hands crept forward again. This time, quite movingly, they brushed the keys in the secret contradictory melody that opens the Pathetique. Her hands moved on and on. She crouched over the keyboard in amazed concentration and played, or allowed herself to be played by, the music that had racked her inside and struggled for release. This was how it was with her gifts. God had taken the music away for a time to bring her closer, then returned it when removing the last sexual love she would ever have. Even in the astonished flood of her discovery, she knew that this sudden solace was presented to help her through her loss. As her hands assembled and disassembled their patterns of old harmony and counterharmony, the mystery of their motions became entirely sensible. She understood the intricate purpose of a language she had guessed in the dark and even practiced on the body of Gregory. Music poured out in a rational waterfall.

Time passed, or no time passed. Absorbed in the rush of knowing, Agnes felt eyes watching. Perhaps children, she thought, unable in her awed greed to quit. Or one of the sisters, or an Ojibwe curious or gripped by longing. She played in the embrace of that special sense of being heard, that expectancy, but when she finally set her hands in her lap and looked up to acknowledge the listener, no one was there. Only the still new leaves faintly twitching between the studs and the haze of gold light through the tremulous scatter of clouds. It wasn't until she saw a twist of movement from the corner of her eye that she looked down and saw the snakes.

The rhapsody woke them, Debussy drew them forth, Chopin made them listen, and Schubert put them back to sleep. It was luck that Agnes was alone that day, for the nuns, except for Hildegarde, screamed for the hoe whenever they saw a serpent and killed it on the spot. The occurrence explained, anyway, the reason that so many snakes did appear in their garden—the rock beneath the church sheltered their ancient nest.

There were at least a hundred. More. Another moved, quick as a lash. Yet another seeped forward and Agnes put her fingers back upon the keys. A third uncoiled in a question mark that she answered with a smooth *bacarolle*, which seemed the right thing to play for snakes. She watched them out of the corner of her eyes. They were motionless now, their ligulate, black bellies flat against the stone. Parallel gold stripes down the center of their backs seemed to vibrate in the fresh June light. The snakes looked polished brand-new. Perhaps they'd shed their skins at the door, she thought, and even as her fingers rippled she imagined a pile of frail husks. Their heads were slightly raised off the floor and if they weren't actually listening to the notes, they were positively fixed on the music. They were suspended, somehow, by whatever means were available to their senses.

Agnes continued to play. Once, during the music, Sister Hildegarde came near, she heard her enter. Though tough, the nun emitted a stifled gagging hiccup and fled. Not long after, Mary Kashpaw came, unafraid, and worshiped as though with her kind. A crowd collected murmuring outside the church door. Growing weary, Agnes at last hit upon the Kinderscenen from Schubert and finally, playing "Sleep" repetitively and with all the kindness of a good parent, she succeeded in driving the snakes, the ginebigoog, back to their beds.

GINEBIGOOG

The news of Father Damien's suddenly revealed musical ability caused an excited curiosity. People came in shy numbers to listen. For one month he played concerts instead of delivering sermons. When they felt the music, the snakes still flickered to the edges of the main floor of the church, even with the full congregation. As for Nanapush, when he heard about the snakes, he became intent with interest and told Father Damien that this was a sign of great positive concern among the old people, for the snake was a deeply intelligent secretive being, and knew all the cold and blessed spirits who lived under stone and deep in the earth. And it was the great snake, wrapped around the center of the earth, who kept things from flying apart. After the snakes, Damien was gratified to find that he was consulted more often and trusted with intimate knowledge. Perhaps he was considered to have acquired a very powerful guardian spirit, or perhaps it was the piano. A grand wave of baptisms followed in the wake of his music, people of all ages, some new.

Agnes loved smelling the milky-sweet and faintly sour new babies. She rocked them in their carefully made cradle boards, their tikina-ganan. She talked to the babies, pitching her voice low and pretending to have no wish for a child of her own. But she could feel them in her arms, their tensile dependence, and sometimes a wish stabbed. After baptisms, she played music with an extra sweet load of yearning, and was consoled by the sounds and challenges that rose beneath her hands. She accepted, now, the great gift of the music as a substitute for all she had lost. Still, one question sometimes nagged. Had the devil in its original tempter's form returned her art, or had God? And furthermore, what did it matter?

THE PIANO

Once the memory of the music unknit in troubled and ecstatic skeins from her hands, Agnes remembered. In recalling, she wept for her drowned Caramacchione, played now only by fish, and the strange cruel river that had utterly changed her life. With the outline of new memories, interior bits of the puzzle emerged. Fortunately, there appeared in these new visions a windfall. As she regained more of the past, she recalled the source of the money she'd wakened long ago to find in the lining of Agnes's jacket. She'd deposited that money in a bank in Fargo, under a false name. Cecilia Fleisch, she remembered it.

She wrote down the sum and the secret number under which it was deposited, and then decided how to use it. Perhaps in this decision Agnes ignored certain moral implications. The money was, in fact, stolen. But hadn't Agnes suffered and hadn't Father Damien? And would the anticipated use of the money constitute a form of justice? For Agnes must have a piano—not just any piano. A real piano.

Perhaps, truly, Father Damien could have bought food or medicines, blankets, pots, necessities of all sorts, seeds and seed grain. Perhaps he could have purchased a bell with a far more pleasing toll than the hollow clang of the one bought by the diocese for Little No Horse. Certainly, he could have purchased comforts and warmth for the sisters, who routinely suffered deep chills, or the old people, who were in great need, but he didn't. Not as Damien. Not as Agnes. Not as priest and not as woman, not as confessor and not as the magnet of souls, consoler, professor of the faith. When it came right down to it, she acted as an artist.

TIME

Once Nanapush began talking, nothing stopped the spill of his words. The day receded and darkness broadened. At dusk, the wind picked up and cold poked mercilessly through the chinking of the cabin. The two wrapped themselves in quilts and continued to talk. The talk broadened, deepened. Went back and forth in time and then stopped time. The talk grew huge, of death and radiance, then shrunk and narrowed to the making of soup. The talk was of madness, the stars, sin, and death. The two spoke of all there was to know. And although it was in English, during the talk itself Nanapush taught language to Father Damien, who took out a small bound notebook and recorded words and sentences.

In common, they now had the love of music, though their definition of what composed music was dissimilar.

"When you hear Chopin," Father Damien asserted, "you find yourself traveling into your childhood, then past that, into a time before you were born, when you were nothing, when the only truths you knew were sounds."

"Ayiih! Tell me, does this Chopin know love songs? I have a few I don't sing unless I mean for sure to capture my woman."

"This Chopin makes songs so beautiful your knees shake. Dogs cry. The trees moan. Your thoughts fly up nowhere. You can't think. You become flooded in the heart."

"Powerful. Powerful. This Chopin," asked Nanapush, "does he have a drum?"

"No," said Damien, "he uses a piano."

"That great box in your church," said Nanapush. "How is this thing made?"

Father Damien opened his mouth to say it was constructed of wood, precious woods, but in his mind there formed the image of

Agnes's Caramacchione settled in the bed of the river, unmoved by the rush of water over its keys, and instead he said, "Time." As soon as he said it, he knew that it was true.

"Time. Chopin's piano was made of time. What is time in Ojibwe-mowin?" asked Damien.

Nanapush misunderstood then, and did not give the word but deeply considered the nature of the thing he was asked to name. When he spoke his thoughts aloud, his voice was slow and contemplative.

"We see the seasons pass, the moons fatten and go dark, infants grow to old men, but this is not time. We see the water strike against the shore and with each wave we say a moment has passed, but this is not time. Inside, we feel our strength go from a baby's weakness to a youth's strength to a man's endurance to the weakness of a baby again, but this is not time, either, nor are your whiteman's clocks and bells, nor the sun rising and the sun going down. These things are not time."

"What is it then?" said Father Damien. "I want to know, myself."

"Time is a fish," said Nanapush slowly, "and all of us are living on the rib of its fin."

Damien stared at him in quizzical fascination and asked what type of fish.

"A moving fish that never stops. Sometimes in swimming through the weeds one or another of us will be shaken off time's fin."

"Into the water?" asked Damien.

"No," said Nanapush, "into something else called not time."

Father Damien waited for Nanapush to explain, but after he'd lighted his pipe and smoked it for a while, he said only, "Let's find something to eat."

Agnes brushed the rich ebony rectangles, the black keys of the extraordinary piano on which she'd spent the bulk of the stolen money. A grand, exquisite and important, not a Caramacchione, but a new Steinway. The piano had taken a year or more to make of woods, she knew, collected and seasoned by the craftsmen, each type destined for a different piece of the sounding board and trim.

Time was in the wood. Time was in the hammers. Time was the existence of the piano. Time was the human who had voiced the piano, who had balanced the keys, shaped, hardened, softened each hammer.

With the stolen money, Agnes also purchased, from an eastern parish, a chalice of fine gold, a ciborium, a platen, an embroidered burse studded with semiprecious stones, and two cruets of fine crystal. They were part of the art of Father Damien's Mass, as were the vestments—an extraordinarily ornate and meticulously worked chasuble in green, for hope, a less ornate one in passion red. A plain silken stole embroidered only with a cross, but in gold, and a maniple to match. His alb and cincture had been Father Hugo's, and he accepted from Sister Hildegarde a rough amice that he donned with great devotion and seriousness at every Mass. It was his symbolic helmet and he wore it to repel the assaults of the devil. Rotten mutt! Better yet, he commissioned Margaret to add beadwork anywhere that it would fit on the vestments. She covered every bit she could—each robe weighed upon him like a shield, like armor.

Agnes bought deep blue paint for the ceiling of the church, as well as metallic gold, a special gilding from Chicago. That was the only paint that would do for the stars she envisioned upon that blue. And last, with the spurt of money left at the bottom of the pile, the money which had nearly fallen from Agnes's fingers clumsy with terror, she bought urtext music, stacks of it from foreign publishers—Masses, choral pieces, sensuous rhapsodies and pieces beyond her capabilities, as well as Easy Pieces for Small Fingers, for she had determined to teach. She also commissioned a statue from a maker of religious artifacts up north, bought it sight unseen.

The Madonna of the Serpents

There lived in Winnipeg an old *mangeur de lard* who had put down his paddle and taken up the tools of a wood-carver and a statue painter. He made cigar store Indians and mannequin shapes, shop signs, and carousel horses, but statues of a religious nature were his specialty. For those, he used a secret recipe of plaster. He had in his workshop special molded blanks for Joseph, the Blessed Mary, Baby Jesus and adult Jesus, for Saints Anne and Theresa, for Saint Francis, and a few others especially popular in the region. These raw white forms spoke to him sometimes, especially when he worked late into the night. The shadows, he claimed, moving in the light of flames, often inspired him. One particular night he began to work on a special blank and found that he couldn't stop. This statue, commissioned by a church just south, he'd determined to finish as soon as possible in order to finance a lengthy drunk he antici- pated commencing, soon, to celebrate the proud fact that, at age seventy- five, he was to be yet again a father. Though he'd bought the woman's favors, she was inexperienced enough to have gotten pregnant. She would have to marry him now!

He thought about her as he worked on the plaster in the flicker of candles. Yes, she was fat and her chin ran into her neck in a way that made him think of a snapping turtle. Her nose was a bulb. Her teeth were all crooked. She was a good person, though, and her eyes were very beautiful, sad and kind. Extremely beautiful! He thought of her eyes. What good were they in a face so cunningly wrought to inspire a man to wince and look away?

Those eyes made him happy. They nearly brought tears to his own eyes.

"A son," he prayed. If the boy inherited her features, he would at least be a man, though just why that should make such a difference he couldn't say. He worked carefully, carving folds into the gown, the robe. He took special care with the snake she crushed, refined the moon, painted the scallops of her toenails a delicate pink. He worked out the proportion of the face and then refined the features and the hands, so complicated that he just curled the fingers up and thought, Be done with it. Yawning, he touched paint to the masterpiece and just before dawn tumbled into his rough rope bed.

The next morning, when he squinted at her in the light, he saw that he had made her ugly. Just the same as his bride-to-be, however, her eyes were both kind and extremely alive. He would have taken up his chisel, he could have removed the paint, he could have changed her. Somehow, all that next day, just when he was about to get started, every time, he dropped his hands to his sides and stared at her, shaking his head.

"Forgive me, Saint Joseph," he said out loud, at last. "I like her this way. There are advantages, see? I've lived, and in my life I have had many women. I would not choose a beautiful wife ever again, oh no, I would choose for myself a pair of kind eyes over the most magnificent breasts. *Difficile!* But Saint Joseph, you poor God-fucked cuckold, if you'd chosen a woman nobody envied you for, you would have had many children of your own. You would have died a happy man sur-rounded by his own children, just as I will."

With that, the old *voyageur* put his tools down, patted the Virgin's rump, and began to whistle as he constructed a shipping case to send her straight down to Little No Horse.

On a pure fall day the statue arrived, packed in golden straw inside a wooden crate built around it, perhaps not so much to protect as to contain the features. The nailed, heavy crate was pulled along in a wagon. Father Damien and the sisters and the wagon driver wrestled the crate off the bed of the wagon, prized open the boards that pro-tected the statue, pulled down the wads and sheaves of golden straw, and at last brushed the dust off the features of her face. They kept brushing, for as soon as her eyes and nose and lips came clear, she startled, she fascinated, she elicited some repugnance, she evoked sor-row in one heart and derision in the next and in still others peace and loving quiet, so that she needed to be touched to be believed and for many hours stood outside the doorway of the church.

"Send her back" was Sister Hildegarde's immediate judgment, but Father Damien disagreed, much as Hildegarde had regarding the piano. The other sisters mainly disagreed, too, saying that the Virgin's eyes were remarkable.

"The carver had a strange talent," Damien pronounced, "and his vision was of this face. Who is to say among all creation God should choose only a beautiful human mother for His son?"

"I suppose there is a lesson in this." Hildegarde's voice was a bit sour. She narrowed her eyes at the statue, suspicious. The snake that writhed beneath the Virgin's feet not only was too realistic, but did not look at all crushed down by her weight.

The Sermon to the Snakes

"What is the whole of our existence," said Father Damien, practicing his sermon from the new pulpit, "but the sound of an appalling love?"

The snakes slid quietly among the feet of the empty pews.

"What is the question we spend our entire lives asking? Our question is this: Are we loved? I don't mean by one another. Are we loved by the one who made us? Constantly, we look for evidence. In the gifts we are given—children, good weather, money, a happy marriage perhaps—we find assurance. In contrast, our pains, illnesses, the deaths of those we love, our poverty, our innocent misfortunes—those we take as signs that God has somehow turned away. But, my friends, what exactly is love here? How to define it? Does God's love have anything at all to do with the lack or plethora of good fortune at work in our lives? Or is God's love, perhaps, something very different from what we think we know?

"Divine love may be so large it cannot see us.

"Or it may be so infinitely tiny that it works on a level where it directs us like an unknown substance buried in our blood.

"Or it may be transparent, an invisible screen, a filter through which we see and hear all that is created.

"Oh my friends . . ."

The snakes lifted their bullet-smooth heads, flickered their tongues to catch the vibrations of the sounds the being made somewhere before them.

"I am like you," said Father Damien to the snakes, "curious and small." He dropped his arms. "Like you, I poise alertly and open my senses to try to read the air, the clouds, the sun's slant, the little movements of the animals, all in the hope I will learn the secret of whether I am loved."

The snakes coiled and recoiled, curved over and underneath themselves.

"If I am loved," Father Damien went on, "it is a merciless and exacting love against which I have no defense. If I am not loved, then I am being pitilessly manipulated by a force I cannot withstand, either, and so it is all the same. I must do what I must do. Go in peace."

He lifted his hand, blessed the snakes, and then lay down full length in a pew and slept there for the rest of the afternoon.

13

THE RECOGNITION

1923

Surely it was delirium, thought Agnes, looking at the peaceful scene of twirling popple leaves and new-growth maple. Beside her sat Nanapush. He wore the huge plaid wool jacket Margaret had brought home from the sisters, and his hair, long and gray, was pulled back and tied with a reed. I was not really visited by the terrible dog, thought Agnes, nor did I nearly poison myself out of love and then despair. Her terrible abyss of mind seemed impossible now.

"Do you believe in the devil?" Agnes abruptly asked her friend.

Before he spoke, Nanapush gazed keenly at Father Damien through his little, round, wire eyeglasses. He tilted his head, considering. Damien lighted a cigarette, put it in his hand. Nanapush thanked the priest, his mouth pursed.

"Not yours," he decided.

Father Damien waited for more.

"We have our own devils," Nanapush said piercingly, all at once.

"And our devils are not all bad. Ours are sometimes capable of showing pity, that is, if you can think of the right thing to say."

"What, then, would be the right thing to say if you met up with a devil?" Damien leaned forward intently, eager.

"You would have to be clever about it," said Nanapush.

"Say, for instance," Damien decided to be specific, "I was sitting down to eat, and a devil in the form of a black dog walked in through the window. Say it stood on the table, one paw in the soup bowl. What would you say to it?"

Nanapush leaned toward him, thoughtful. "You would say this: 'Get your foot out of my soup bowl!'"

Father Damien frowned, doubtfully. "And then?"

"If it took its foot out, you would know it had understood you and was no ordinary dog."

Nanapush settled back into his chair.

"It wasn't ordinary. No, the dog spoke to me."

"Ah," said Nanapush. "In that case, you would open your mouth and bark!"

"I don't understand . . ."

"In order to confuse it."

"I see. I would pretend to be a dog . . ."

"You already have a collar around your neck," Nanapush pointed out.

Father Damien didn't tell his friend about the conversation he'd had with the spirit, or about the sacrifice that he had made for Lulu, or about the painful temptation that followed. Instead, he took out the chessboard, an occupation that currently absorbed the two, and the playing of which they owed to a priest of a past century, Father Jolicoeur.

That young and largely unhistoricized eighteenth-century Jesuit had carried with him, into the unknown, a chessboard. He used it as an excellent means both to convince the natives of the superiority of a Catholic god who could design so perplexing and glorious an entertainment, and as a comfort to himself. Though he was uncertain whether his native guide and companion had the capacity to play such a game, he nevertheless made an attempt to teach the rudiments. Jolicoeur's foundation belief in the innate superiority of himself was shattered when, to his amazement, in the space of just nine-teen minutes the Indian trounced him in a match. Father Jolicoeur played again, hoping to recover his pride, but was the more severely beaten, causing him to put away his arrogance.

The fever for chess shook the Indians with the likeness of another epidemic, and they simply re-created the board and pieces to their own ability and began playing among themselves, often for deathly stakes. Long after Father Jolicoeur's bones were cracked by wolves and cleaned by ravens in some lost corner of the wilderness, another lone adventurer, believing himself the first to gain a path into the uncharted glory of the west, was astounded when he accepted an invitation to a chief's lodge only to be confronted with a chessboard properly laid out on a deerskin and his opponent waiting in eager anticipation of a violent game of wits. Of course, the stakes being, as they usually were, life or death, the trader wisely opted to pretend total ignorance of the game and used his evil queen, potent spirits, to bribe his way out of an encounter. It saved him then, but he was never the same in the estimation of the chess-playing Indians, for they did not count him a true man and took their peltries and tanned deerskins and bales of dried fish elsewhere, to another trader, who had learned the confounding game at his mother's knee.

Father Damien now set the board up carefully on the level stump before Nanapush, the wooden pieces comforting to the touch, the ritual of putting them into order a small pleasure. Nanapush laid down his pipe, his hands careful among the pieces. Choosing white in the toss, he opened with a hopeful gambit that did not fool Damien. The afternoon was golden, the mosquitoes bearable in a light breeze. The sounds of birds accompanied their thoughts. Some time went by with little but the motion of their hands, and then Nanapush suddenly spoke.

"What are you?" he said to Damien, who was deep in a meditation over his bishop's trajectory.

"A priest," said Father Damien.

"A man priest or a woman priest?"

Agnes's hand froze, pinching the knight, and her mental processes collapsed. A hollow roaring noise began around her, swirling, a confusion of sounds. Her mouth opened but no word emerged and slowly, very slowly, she drew back from the table and raised her eyes to

Nanapush, who was simply looking at the priest as though that was not the one question in the world that would most upset Father Damien. The priest's terror and confusion immediately registered on the older man, who leaned forward, frowning with perhaps too calculated a concern. Agnes still couldn't answer, though now some little choking noises emerged. She tried to right herself, pretending she was heartily surprised at such a question but taking it as a joke. Agnes tried to laugh, but a spasm of sorrow cut the laugh in two. She found, maddeningly, that her eyes were spilling over with tears.

"I am a priest," she whispered, hoarsely, fierce.

"Why," said Nanapush kindly, as though Father Damien hadn't answered, to put the question to rest, "are you pretending to be a man priest?"

So then it was out between them, and the fact of it out in the open was tremendous. The tedious balloon, pressing inside of Agnes day after day so tightly, now floated out of her mouth, up into the air. She was instantly lighter, so light that when she took in a breath she felt she would lift from her chair.

"We used to talk of it, Kashpaw and myself," Nanapush went on, "but when we noticed that you never mentioned it, we spoke of this to no one else."

"So it is that obvious?"

Nanapush shrugged. "Nobody else ever said anything. But still, it is a question maybe just in my mind why you would do this, hide yourself in a man's clothes. Are you a female Wishkob? My old friend thought so at first, assumed you went and became a four-legged to please another man, but that's not true. Inside that robe, you are definitely a woman."

Later, she understood it was the simple recognition, that level and practical regard that moved her to weep with relief. Nanapush was sorry, very sorry to make the priest cry, but he said anyway, abruptly, "Your move."

Agnes moved her piece in a blur. Nanapush moved again in short order, and it was up to Agnes, who paused, moved her piece miserably, and answered her friend's question all at once, trying not to cry for the relief of talking, trying to behave with a clarity and goodness that she did not know or feel. Nanapush, of course, waited to make his next observation until Agnes finally returned to the game and was deep in thought over her next move.

"So you're not a woman-acting man, you're a man-acting woman. We don't get so many of those lately. Between us, Margaret and me, we couldn't think of more than a couple."

Something struck Agnes, then, and she realized that this moment, so shattering to her, wasn't of like importance to Nanapush. In fact, she began to suspect, as she surveyed the chessboard between them and saw the balance tipped suddenly in her opponent's favor, that Nanapush had brought it up on purpose to unnerve and distract her. The next move, in which Nanapush made an unexpectedly suave play and removed the bishop she protected for so long, convinced her. She looked sharply at the man to whom her defenses had fallen.

"Ginitum," said Nanapush with relish.

The old man had used the subject in a sly bid to undermine his opponent's concentration. And it had worked. There was at last no way to recover from the lapse and Father Damien let go now of piece after piece under the driving craftiness of Nanapush's strategy.

"I'm losing," Agnes muttered. "You tricked me, old man."

"Me!" said Nanapush. "You've been tricking everybody! Still, that is what your spirits instructed you to do, so you must do it. Your spirits must be powerful to require such a sacrifice."

"Yes," said Agnes, "my spirits are very strong, very demanding, very annoying."

Nanapush nodded in sympathy.

"Check," the old man said.

Infallible Eminence,

My hand is a human hand. My heart a human heart. My feet walk the earth to which our bones return. Directed by His voice, His hand, by the prompting and guidance of His spirit, what else was I to do?

14

LULU

1996

Rain, time, Emeraude, silence, fried onions. Their first meeting was an explosion of the ordinary and the vast unknowable, the pure and the underhanded, all Lulu. Father Jude sat in the cave of an old-fashioned brown recliner and Damien dozed in the deep crevice of a sagging purple couch covered with star quilts and pillows. Their unfinished plates of onion-slathered fried liver cooled on a coffee table set carefully with napkins and shakers of salt and pepper. In the kitchen, Mary Kashpaw alchemized her unspeakable coffee. They were digesting their early suppers, waiting for a new burst of energy to go on in their work, when the crackle of slow tires on gravel announced a visitor.

Later, Father Jude was to recall details that he didn't know he'd noticed. He took in more than he admitted to his conscious mind, like a man under hypnosis. He recalled that the woman, who seemed only six or maybe eight years older than he was, entered the house, and sparked pleasure and lighted affection in Father Damien when she knelt beside the chair. She crouched gracefully, laid her hands upon Damien's arm, and whispered to him in Ojibwe until the old man's eyes opened and he came awake smiling in her laughing hug. It was an enviable hug, Father Jude thought later, a long, loving, unabashed embrace that tipped back the old man's face and closed his eyes like a doll's eyes, stretched his grin as far as it could stretch.

"Father, forgive me," she said with mock penitence, "my last visit was one week ago. Who's this?"

"This is Father Jude, my interlocuter." Damien held her hand in his, unwilling to let go, and nodded at his companion. She released Damien and took Jude in, then, *took him in*. He felt it. Her drenched black eyes rubbed him all over with a curious heat. She absorbed him with her eyes and then, as though waiting for him to say something, fixed her gaze upon his mouth. Her gaze had a physical effect. As though he'd bitten into a hot pepper, his lips tingled and he broke into a light, fresh sweat. Embarrassed, he went remote and greeted her with a cool and abrupt manner, which did not in the least diminish her keen examination of his face.

"So you're Jude, I heard about you. You'd better be giving the old man here lots of rest."

She drew up a chair, sat, gave Damien's hand a squeeze, all without taking her eyes off Jude's face for a second. She stared into his eyes. Unsettling. He looked away, looked back, but she was still staring. He blinked and in that heartbeat, that instant, he was caught. And it was so easy. He was blinded and the sun wasn't in his face. Heard nothing and yet the breeze as she entered the room was level and sweet, stirring the mild faces of the violet pansies that she'd bought to set early into the dirt around the trees by the door. Oblivious to taste, he gulped coffee from the cup set into his hand by Mary Kashpaw.

"Oooh," said Lulu, setting hers down with no other comment. She excused herself and spoke to Father Damien in rapid, floating Ojibwe, which he answered in the same after a thoughtful pause. It was all right with Father Jude to sit there ignored. It gave him a chance, after all, to attend to himself and to try to decide what had happened to him, just now, right here, when he'd taken leave of sense and time. A mild stroke? He put his hands on his chest. Ticker going strong.

Checked his pulse. Not much higher than after running six miles. The light breeze dried the sweat off his throat and he wiped his forehead with a plaid hankie, which suddenly seemed all the wrong plaid. What was happening? It all felt wrong, the scene, the season, how his trousers bit across the small of his back, how his breathing was uneven. It all felt wrong and then, just as suddenly, it all seemed right again.

She spoke, smiling into his face.

"Father Jude, do you know any stories?"

"Not really," he stumbled, "I mean, I know stories but they're all true things that happened."

She was oblivious to his discomfort.

"That doesn't matter. You're drafted."

"For what?"

"You'll visit my little class. It's a culture class. I mostly teach traditional dance, but every so often we study the foreign element—in this case, you."

She smiled at him again, and her face opened like a flower. The wrinkles around her eyes were beautifully aligned; the sweeping uncontainable amusement brimmed up in her and spilled. He had the odd sensation that petals drifted in the air between them, petals of a fragrant and papery citrus velvet. Then the wind whipped them off and she was all business.

"Tomorrow at two o'clock in the fourth-grade classroom at the school. Be there!"

She raised her brows slightly and parted her lips. Distinctly, he heard the sound of her purring. She was wearing a simple white dress.

It took him a week to put the words with the feelings and, then, it came clear to him because of a dream. Inside it—as at the school, where she wore her jingle dress of red and silver—Lulu stood with her lynx eyes and face of a hungry cat and her fan held rigid and upright like a weapon, like a shield. As she turned to him with an imperious and practical grace, he thought, So this is what it's like to fall in love.

There were times, many times Father Jude had admired women, but it had been his fate, his fortune, certainly his luck, never to have fallen in love. He was unprepared. He thought he had tested his commitment, his faith, certainly his vow. He was secure in his relationship with God. If so, why had the Almighty waited until now, until he was at his lowest, out of his element, away from his familiar terrain, to set this enigma before him, this magnet of hope, this slip of intrigue, this woman?

"Because God has a very dark sense of humor," said Father Damien. He was not referring to the frightening disorganization of Father Jude Miller's new and untested emotions, but to the erratic tumble of ants scurrying to rebuild a nest disarranged by their feet. Both men were sitting outside the door of the house. The tough pansies were planted, and nodded at the borders of the walk like the faces of spoiled babies. "Every so often, as though for His awful amusement, we are overturned. The desperate methods we use to right ourselves must seem hilarious."

Father Miller emphatically agreed. He had been awake all night thinking of Lulu's ankle, picturing the curved bone. He said nothing.

"That was my situation with the rosary," said Father Damien. "I knew it had been used to strangle Napoleon and Napoleon was in the ground."

"What about the police?"

Father Damien laughed. "That would have been Edgar Pukwan Junior, reliable only on the rare occasion he wasn't drinking. He was drinking when we found Napoleon."

"So the investigation, or whatever you want to call it, was left to you."

"Such as it was, yes. But although it was important, it wasn't the central locus of my thoughts. It was peripheral to the political situation on that piece of homeland. To tell you the truth, I first believed that the killing of Napoleon was done for the precise reason Bernadette assigned to it—to shut up a prime opponent. I even suspected Nanapush. And then I found out . . . ." As though suddenly disconcerted at having spoken too much, Father Damien gulped down the rest of his words. Throughout his interviews, he'd carefully sidestepped certain facts that would have disqualified Leopolda, for at the same time they would have pointed toward the truth of his identity. Now Damien had trouble keeping it all straight. What he'd told, secrets he couldn't tell.

"Father Miller, have we got to go on? Don't you have enough evidence by now, enough proof that this Pauline Puyat who became Leopolda is not, was not, could not be a saint. Why, she sent the black dog!"

Father Jude breathed in, breathed out. He was exhausted, unbent, he really did not want to hear another word about the ghost dog, the hallucination, delirium tremens, most probably. Before he could reject the argument, Damien proceeded.

"And that was the least of it. . . . In concrete terms, yes, proven and concise, let me list the faults that most assuredly block her beatification. Primarily, Leopolda skewered the young postulant Marie."

"Still open to debate."

"All right then, the horses. Witness the horses! By raising their terror, she got two Kashpaws killed and is also responsible for the consequent madness of their daughter, Mary Kashpaw. You've tasted her coffee!"

Jude didn't capitalize on the reference to the vile stuff in his ceramic mug, but weighed what the old priest proposed very cautiously in his mind before he spoke.

"Does the eventual outcome neutralize the circumstance? The peaceable conversion of Quill? The lifelong devotion of her daughter to the fixtures of the church? The runaway was unplanned, an accident, Father Damien. It wasn't as though she deliberately set out to spook the beasts."

"Of course she did! You're indefensibly naïve," Father Damien observed, sitting back in his chair. "Willfully ignorant. That's dangerous."

"So is sitting back too far. You'll fall," said Father Jude dryly. Damien righted himself with some difficulty.

"I repeat, she spooked the horses with the specific intent to cause a runaway."

The younger priest waved his hands. "All right, fine, suppose I even give you that! Even so, what bearing does it have on her eventual consideration—"

"Why, character, Father Jade. Spooking horses to cause a dangerous runaway is hardly a mark of heroic virtue."

"No, you are right. However, since we have established that her purpose was also to rescue the consecrated Host, and even, perhaps, that was her primary, maybe only purpose, her sin once again is the overzealousness of one who burns with the Holy Spirit."

"Oh, she burned, all right," said Father Damien. "She was a regular spiritual arsonist."

Father Jude couldn't help but smile, and the old priest took advantage of his momentary diversion.

"The whole convent suffered. These are hardworking women and when one of the sisterhood is incapacitated for whatever reason, an extra burden falls upon the community. Even if that reason is, say, a visitation from God—say God is having an intimate and passionate spiritual interaction with someone who must strictly attend to it— the circumstances into which the other women are put . . . to say the least, difficult! The others had to take on her chores and duties, not to mention wait on her hand and foot. Things were hard to hold together, quite as if the greater work of the church was sabotaged by one member's . . . well, I'll say it, *piggish* involvement with God."

"And when did this all take place?"

"She had countless episodes, or bouts, or visitations. Whatever you want to call them, they were sicknesses that confined her to bed. Of course, in her later years she received many petitioners. It was known as her bed of intercession and her suffering was considered a form of physical prayer. She referred to herself as a sacrificial victim."

"A victim soul."

"Exactly. She regarded herself as one chosen to sacrifice her health, her happiness, after the example of Christ crucified, for the advantage of the Church and the general good of her people."

"Whom—and this is important, Father Damien—would you say that she loved? She loved her people?"

Father Damien shook his head. "The love of a mixed blood for what is darkest communion in her nature, both the comfort and the downfall, source of pain and expiation, a complicated love. She loved her people but she had no patience with them. You've heard of Louis Riel, a *métis* who went to the gallows for his convictions on the political rights of his mixed-blood people. She, too, went to the gallows in an effort to free her people from what she saw as spiritual bondage. Their gods had not, in recent times, served the Ojibwe well. Of course, gods are not required to be consistent—in fact, gods aren't required to be anything at all. There are no requirements for gods," said Father Damien a little wistfully.

"And you," Father Jude asked curiously, "do you believe as Sister Leopolda believed?"

"That conversion would bring about redemption?" Father Damien seemed surprised to be asked such a question. "Oh no, I believe we were wrong!"

Father Jude stopped the recorder, folded his arms, gathered himself. Although he had, on some level, expected what he heard, yet to have it out in the open demanded some response from him.

"If you think that, how could you go on?" he asked.

"Well, of course, at first I didn't think we were wrong. Everything seemed clear. It was only after the epidemic that I knew. There was no doubt . . ." He trailed off. "By then I was so knit into the fabric of the damage that to pull myself out would have left a great rift, a hole that would have been filled by . . . well, others perhaps less in sympathy. I'll name no names. And I believe even now that the void left in the passing of sacred traditional knowledge was filled, quite simply, with the quick ease of alcohol. So I was forced by the end to clean up after the effects of what I had helped to destroy, Father Jude. That's why I stayed."

Father Jude took this in with a certain degree of sympathy: to not believe in what one did, but to persevere out of duty to the practical desperation of the situation—in a way it was no less than a quiet heroism. Or idiocy, was his next thought. And then he felt a pang of irritated pity. What a waste to live your life without the assurance of faith. No sooner had he thought this than admiration for the old priest gripped him once again. Whatever his belief, Father Damien had acted on the fundamental dictates of a great love. Sacrifice had been his rule. He'd put others above himself and lived in the abyss of doubt rather than forsake those in need.

Was doubt when coupled with devotion a greater virtue than simple faith? Father Jude had been sent here to gather knowledge, but the more he learned, the more he thought, the less certainty he grasped. And too, his fundamental self-assurance was put in jeopardy by this bewildering attraction to a woman whose presence he ached for.

Idiocy indeed! Lulu. Before her name rang twice in his mind, he was already putting away his notes and preparing to go and find her. By way of simply getting near to her, he would ask her to talk to him. He would question her about the woman, Fleur, who so preoccupied the old priest's memory. He'd sit across from her, inching closer, fiddling with his tape recorder, hoping she could not intuit his yearning fascination and confused hope.

15

LULU'S PASSION

What I never forgot, what I'll always remember, was my mother stroking the soles of my feet. She woke me gently that morning. I hated her for it later. She was tender, yet she knew just exactly what she was doing. The only way I could keep from despair was to hate my mother's rough hand, the sinewy palm, hard as rawhide, the fingers of steel, grace, and lies. A mother's hand should not be like that, Father Jude. A mother's hand should never lie to a child.

We put thick slices of cold bannock in our pockets and started out. "Aaniindi gi-izhamin ina?" I asked. My mother just frowned, and when she did that, I never prodded her for more. She wasn't the kind of mama you could beg things from, Fleur. The trees were deep and just beginning to sigh in the first breath of the day. Oh, I love that, Father Jude, have you ever seen the leaves click together and break up the sun in circles? My mother put tobacco beside the trail, and still said nothing to me. But I had my freedom in that moment and didn't care.

"Maybe she couldn't," Nanapush told me later, "maybe her heart was too full, maybe she hurt too, did you ever think about that?"

"Of course I did," was my answer. "But she was my mother, she could have chosen differently. Grandfather! Fleur had the choice of saving me, her daughter, or having her revenge."

She chose revenge.

I choose to hate her for it.

That was the day it started.

She took me by the hand when the path was broad, I dropped behind when it narrowed. I liked walking behind so I could watch my mother's makazin heels as she stepped down and the hem, so even and careful. I watched the movement of her old majigoode as it flopped ever so lightly against her moving calves. I remember that dress like it was before me now—a print skirt of old greenish purple, deep and muddy with tiny cream-colored flowers that glimmered from the dusk of a slough.

The day was warm. Late summer, Manominike-giizis, when the Anishinaabeg knock the wild rice. Our Pillager's own lake, Matchimanito, was too cold and blue-black to grow rice and nobody even liked to fish it that much. We always offered tobacco for the fish. Once, in a fish stomach, my mother found a person's thumb. She kept it in her medicine bundle along with the heart of that fish. There were all sorts of things in her medicine that I did not approach, but to walk behind her was to forget for a moment who she was from the front—the forbidding woman with the medicine. From behind, she was someone who didn't know what kind of face I was making or how, mockingly, I copied the headlong force of my mother's stride.

Arrogance, she had that. I never did, though some mistook it for my joy.

Now I could hear the sound of other people as we came through the woods, but as we crossed the clearing into town, I was surprised to see so many children. We continued forward, and it looked as though we would join the others. A crowd of so many was strange in the first place, but as we got closer, I was covered with an itchy blanket of feeling. I reached out for my mother's hand and knew—that was it. The children weren't running. They weren't loudly playing, racing, teasing, apart from their parents. The children were clutching their mothers' hands just like I did now. They were silent, close to their parents, bits of their mothers' skirt squeezed tight, standing pressed against their fathers' legs.

Around the front of the crowd, I now saw four big audoomobiig, as Grandpa Nanapush called them, waasamoowidaabaanag, the wagons that moved by themselves. The first one, audoomobii, was the white word. There were four of these big cars and they were drawn up together in a line. Next to each, there was a man with a piece of paper clamped onto a piece of wood. He was writing down the name of each family and each child. As soon as he wrote down the name—as if with his marks he somehow suddenly possessed the spirit of the child—abruptly the child climbed into the auto and was swallowed into the dark as into the body of a fish. I saw the children looking out through the windows, sad, vague, and indistinct as though gazing from underwater.

No! I tried to get my mother's attention. Let's go home, I said, I want to go home. But my mother was staring at the people with the boards and the paper, and at the other Anishinaabeg gathered around them. Her face was neutral and heavy. A sickness of fear seized me. I tugged and pulled my mother's hand as if to bring it to life, but her hand was stiff, and cold, like the paw of a trapped, dead animal. And then she dragged me forward.

I had never cried before that day, not really, unless you counted my bawling as a tiny baby and that one time I froze my feet. My mother had always picked me up, given me what I wanted, rocked me, never let me weep. And why did she teach me all this tenderness, this love, if she then threw me in a pit? For that is what the school would be, and better if she slapped me from the first and taught me to be hard. Now, I cried. For the first time, I cried. In this squeezed mass of children, I was a birch-bark scrap. I was floating downstream in a roiling current, twisting and spinning. Tipping. Dark water rushed up through the center of me and leaked out of my eyes. The motor, like a throbbing strange drum, bore us off the reservation, in the direction that the birds went, zhaawanong. My mother told me to pray to that spirit, talk to that aadizokaan, but my throat was filling, filling. I was going down and a sick blackness overcame my vision, until, all of a sudden, this boy next to me nudged my arm, just a rude little push, the best he could do and still be a boy.

I dared to look, and it was Nector. Neshke, he said. In his fist he held a piece of lint-rubbed hard black licorice from his pocket. Licorice in the shape of a little curved pipe. He said take it and I took it; then he reached into his pocket and pulled out a licorice pipe just like the one he gave me. He turned his over and tapped out the imaginary old tobacco, then filled and pretended to light his little black licorice pipe. His movements were exactly that of a old man, of Nanapush. He gestured. I took my pipe, tapped it out the same way, and as I did so my tears stopped. I swaggered, clenched my pipe between my teeth. Nector pretended to have trouble lighting a match, and I started laughing. By this time I had my pipe going and I was smoking it, like Margaret, with a little squint in my eyes. Me and Nector Kashpaw were looking at each other, both laughing, blowing pretend smoke from our little black pipes.

I would grow to love that boy. I would get into trouble because of that boy. He would get into much worse trouble because of me. On the bus ride down, going south like the wild geese, we sat close, smelling the alien stink of burning gas, and each other, unwashed, washed, in fear. We ate food I would come to know—the strange, delicate, delicious cheese sandwiches on white flour bread and the toad-skin pickles, sweet and crunchy, fished from a huge gray crockery jar, and the fat olives with the pits. I had never eaten these big fleshy green seeds. Tears filled my eyes at the taste of them. I started to cry in earnest, unstoppable, because of the evil taste of this thing they called olive.

Nector turned to another boy and I was alone. Once I was alone it continued, the crying, for which I had no shame or remedy. It was a simple weeping in which the tears came up and flowered over. It wasn't painful and it wasn't unpleasant, this crying, it just was. *It just was and it just was*, I said once I became an adult woman known for never shedding tears. No, I never cried, not in love or in childbirth, not at death and not over any particular want or loss or piece of bad fortune. My tears had simply run out on that ride down to the school. That's when I came to know that to be left, sent off, abandoned, was not of the moment, but a black ditch to the side of the road of your life, a sudden washout, a pothole that went down to China.

That's what the kids did when they saw the globe of the world and put their fingers on either side and the teacher told them theoretically it is possible to dig to China. They started a big hole behind the girls' dorm, in the sandy spot where water flushed down off the tall roof, out of the square metal drainpipe. They used their tin cups to dig. They got the hole down and then said, Let's throw Lulu in! Then the matron came out ringing the big brass handbell and hollering *little kids, little kids*, and they all jumped away like rabbits and I was left in that hole.

It was cool, it was autumn by then, but I was wearing a jacket and the hole was warm. I was out of the wind. After I realized the others were not coming back, I tried once to pull myself out. But the top of the hole was crumbly and the collapse of sand scared me. So I dusted myself and sat, knees drawn to my chest, in the bottom of the hole.

Now I was glad for the ugly, big, brown-plaid wool skirt they gave me. Too long, it covered my ankles when I curled up tight. And the jacket was good, too, with its big raw wood buttons. It was quilted on the inside with a smooth fabric that felt slippery, but warm when I held myself close. I held my arms by the elbows and looked up from the bottom of the hole. Soon it got dark, then it was night. Maybe some of the big girls balled up their coats and put them in my bed so the matron would be fooled, so they would not get in trouble for throwing me down the hole. I was not afraid. I didn't care. That's how I survived, by not caring. I tucked my head into my collar like a bird, and went to sleep.

Then woke because the moon had stopped right above me. It was caught on the peaked corner of the dormitory roof and it was nearly full.

"Aaniin, nokomis," I said and I felt the kindness of the moon shine down on me as I went back to sleep.

That was the first night.

That day was the first day.

I heard them running, yelling, herded off to the dining hall. Then I heard them from farther off calling again. Their sounds faded and the sounds of morning were above me. I had to pee. But I didn't and then I forgot because I heard the buses. My heart thumped with shock. Then regret sliced me. I realized that I was missing a trip that the whole school was taking. It was a trip given to the children by a lady—a very big, doll-haired, red-cheeked lady with red fingernails and pointed red lips who spoke to us in the classroom—a trip to a circus. I knew all about the circus. Nanapush had once seen the circus. Ever after he had loved to describe its wonders. There was an animal called the anamibiigokoosh, the underwater pig. There was a horse with a long neck, genwaabiigigwed, which I had seen on the alphabet. The giraffe. There was a striped horse and little peoplelike creatures who constantly searched one another for lice. Nanapush had seen great brown panthers jump through circles of flame, and watched a woman launch through the air like a flying squirrel. Down in the hole, I went into a low grief. *I had a black dejection*, I would say when grown up, of my worst feelings. And it would mean I was again lost in my spirit, the way I'd felt in the bottom of the hole knowing I'd miss the circus, which was worse, much worse than wondering if I would ever get out.

My feet went numb from their old freezing, and my legs prickled. I danced up and down in the hole until I felt all warm again. That was how I made the time go, when my legs numbed. Or I sang. "Our Country" and other songs that I had just learned in school. Nanapush's love songs and hunting songs. Songs that went with my mother's name. My own songs. Then songs I'd made up for my dolls. Each of my dolls had their own names and songs. I knew every little thing about my dolls and their lives and I felt stricken all over again because I didn't know where my dolls were now. Had my mother kept them? Did Nanapush have them? I missed my dolls more than I could allow myself, ever, to miss my mother. The sun passed over, briefly flinging down a pour of radiance, and then moving on.

The buses returned very late in the evening and the children were sent straight into the dorm. All of a sudden I heard a voice. "Lulu!" A cloud on a stick dropped into my lap. I was so shocked I couldn't move. I touched the thing—pale, raspberry scented, sticky sweet, a balled-up spiderweb. I touched my fingers to my tongue, then I ate the stuff. After I ate every bit of it, a strange buzzing started just behind my eyes, as though my brain were a hive of bees. My thoughts kept flying in and out, impossible to catch. I danced, my feet moving in a quick floating flat-footed skip, and I sang a song to keep myself company and then curled up when I was warm.

I slept, woke. The moon was caught in a mist of secret spiderwebs, of circus floss, cottony and quick to vanish. The moon blazed at me, as though it were thirsty too.

"Ingitizima," I softly said, words I had heard in prayers, I am pitiful.

"You are pitiful," I heard in answer. "I am sorry for you."

There was someone in the hole with me.

That someone turned out to be a spirit who kept me company from then on out. There were those who wondered at me, all through my life, starting when I stayed at the school and refused my mother, who came back rich. People thought Lulu Lamartine was heartless as a cat. And like a cat, too, in my mind's limber strength and survival toughness. People thought I was too bold. Many resented how I had no fear, not enough to cause me any sensible concern for what people thought. I just did what I pleased. Married men and left them. Had my babies and brought them up. Raised my own money through my thrifty profit. Showed my breasts rude and shockingly. Wore my skirts tight and my heels tall. Wore makeup paint. True, I had land. True, I was clever leasing it. True, I was even more clever in the use to which I put my talents with men. But it was that spirit who taught me that to laugh or to cry was all the same, and who gave me the strength to spit pain in the face and love the world in joy. I sat with that spirit, who would never leave me. And the spirit said, Look around you and if you think all there is to see is a rotten hole, look again and see the color and the beauty and the constant life of the earth. I stayed two nights and two days in the hole before a big girl broke free of the line and sneaked out back to pull me out.

That big girl was a Pentecost. Rose Pentecost. Named as a family by a priest in the last century who tired of translating and just added feast days to the roll of names that year.

I got into the line with the other children and walked in to the morning meal. No dirt was on my face and no dirt was in my hair. I was neat and clean. My eyes were clear. I never told on the big girls, for which I was then a hero. None of the matrons ever knew. So even then, I did not get in trouble.

But later. Trouble? I ate trouble. I *was* trouble.

Being trouble started when they told me that I was not going home for the summer. Staying there, with the matrons, at school. At first I tipped sideways, as though the words pushed me over. Not going home was as much a shock as coming there in the first place. Not seeing my mother, my grandpa and grandma, the Yellowboy girls and the Anongs and again my mother—especially my mother, because in the beginning my skin ached for my mother's touch and my ears kept straining. I hadn't decided to hate her yet. And not that my mother exactly said, *I'll be back to get you*, but I knew she would. When they told me I would not be going home, I staggered in a red zigzag and then sat by the bridal wreath bush outside the school office, there on the grass.

It was out-of-bounds to sit there, it was an offense. That's why I did. I sat there for a while and then slowly edged myself into the shadows of the thousands of tiny leaves. Through the shadows, then, and farther back, until I was in the curved space between the bush and the wall of the building. A clean space completely hidden, a place where I could look into the crossed and baffled twigs, the timid green leaves, the sprays of white flowers, the petals, clouds of frail dots.

The idea first came to me when I boarded the school bus to visit the local school where we would do our yearly goodwill performance. I danced shawl and traditional. Rose Pentecost performed "The Lord's Prayer" in sign language. I had got stuck on Rose after Rose came and got me. I learned "The Lord's Prayer" in trade sign language, because Rose Pentecost always got so much applause. I thought I would like to have that, and to stand up there alone and silent, only my hands moving, my hand and arm making the upward spiral, so graceful, to indicate the spirit. I was thinking about that, and at the same time walking up the school bus steps when I dropped the little fan that I carried, on loan from our dance advisor. The fan flicked under the bus, blown by wind, and I lay flat on my stomach to get it. That was when I happened to look sideways and up, under the school bus, and noticed the little shelf.

The thin, black, metal shelf hung down from the body of the

engine to support three exhaust pipes. It was just the right size for a child, an intriguing little place. I scrambled backward with the fan, a beautiful and cunning fan made of a prairie chicken tail. I caught up with the other dancers and I did my dance piece, but all the time that I danced, I was busy thinking something I could not define, something that had to do with the shelf and pipes underneath the bus.

It was easy for me. When they loaded the buses two weeks later for the summer trip home, I slipped around back. I rolled into the shadow of the undercarriage, crawled under the body of the engine, onto the shelf with the pipes, and spread myself out flat on my stomach. I grasped hold of the brackets like handles, as though I were on a sled. Only I couldn't steer, of course. I would go where we were bound to go, flat and straight over the road until we stopped at Little No Horse, home.

Bubbles of excitement welled up in me as all around the motor came to life and as with slow grandeur the bus began to move. The shelf was more perilous than it looked. As the bus gathered speed I found I had to hold tightly to the brackets. Still, using one arm and then the other, I could rest. And the gas-smelling air was flushed out behind the bus so I wasn't breathing it. I had worried about that, my only worry brought on by Rose's declaring that gasoline was squeezed from dead bodies and you'd die if you breathed it. The air was fresh, then, still with a raw spring bite, and cold. My teeth chattered at first but then the pipe under me, the middle pipe, grew warm. It ran straight down the center of me, warming me, burning me, although that would be in the end a complete surprise.

All through my life, to the mystery of my devoutest lovers, I have borne that central scorch mark—a thin stripe of gold lighter than my skin, a line evenly dividing me, running between my breasts and vanishing between my legs. And that surprised me, for although the pipe did indeed grow uncomfortably hot, it did not seem to burn me, certainly not to the point where it would leave a mark. Perhaps the cold air that kept on flowing all around me cooled my awareness, or perhaps it was the fear. One hour, then two hours, passed. When they stopped to fuel up, I wrung my agonized hands and arms. Got the blood moving. With the pavement a sweeping blur just inches beneath me, and the certain knowledge that if I let go or fell asleep I would die, I managed to stay awake. But that was the hardest thing of

all. My brain wanted to go to sleep. The heavy movement was soothing, the vast unintelligible roar, the workings of the metal bowels.

At my birth, a bear had visited. I came from the lake. Nobody
knew who my father was or nobody would tell. I am the last of the
last of the Pillagers, Lulu, so how could I not go home?

At the next stop, I was able to rest. All I did was breathe hard and
stare into myself, rubbing my arms. The other children were eating
their cheese sandwiches. I was so keen with hunger that I could smell
them in a park beside the gravel parking lot, having a picnic. I was in
a blur of pain and sleepiness, and I wanted to be with them—just a
child munching on a sandwich, bound home. To comfort myself I
imagined Margaret and Nanapush. My eyes closed. When I opened
them, I was staring into the startled face of the bus driver, checking
the tires, who thought at first that I was dead.

They sent me back.

I sat in the sheriff's office for hours, wrapped in a blanket, while
Mr. Eaglestaff drove from the school to fetch me. He was the school's
head janitor, and he really didn't care what I did. That was one good
break. They issued me the longest, ugliest worst dress on earth—the
punishment dress—a solid block of green reaching to my ankles,
shapeless and embarrassing. Then I went to work scrubbing the side-
walks that led around the campus. Down on my knees, I washed section after section of concrete. Day after day that summer, I scrubbed
the cement in watery circles. Kneeling above, staring into the swirls, I
sometimes saw the face of my mother in the evaporating water. When
I did, I scrubbed harder, twice as hard, erasing her.

One day as I paused there on my knees, brush in my hands, I
looked up at the sky. I had the sense, though there were no clouds,
that something bigger than a cloud passed over and through me, a
huge thing that trailed a terrible breath-stopping sorrow. There was
no one to disturb me. The campus was entirely still. I didn't cry, of
course, in spite of the pain. It was at that moment that my love for my
mother left me, simply flowed out of me like a heavy cloud. Useless.
Then gone. I stood up. I was so much lighter without this useless
love. And this scrubbing was tiring. I marched back to the matron and
said, *You don't have to punish me anymore because I learnt my lesson and I won't run away again.*

Mrs. Houle was matroning and she herself was partly Indian so she had pity. "Let's burn up that damn green dress," she whispered. Her eyes flashed with pleasure as she rummaged through the school clothes until she found one of black-and-white check so smart it looked like a town girl would wear it. I put it on, brushed out my hair down my back, and started work first on "The Lord's Prayer" in sign language and then the Twenty-third Psalm. I beaded my own makazinan and they gave me a dress of fawnskin as soft as the softest fabric. I wore an eagle feather and an underskirt and I got to go everywhere with Rose for those next few years. Us two perfectly synchronized our movements and really looked good in a spotlight.

One day, my mother arrived wearing eye paint and lipstick, white woman's clothes: a small blue hat, a suit with blue stripes, a square black handbag, leather shoes that matched. She was there to retrieve me, who would not be retrieved. She disappeared into the school building. Walked to the office door. The principal, looking at her and the car she drove, parked right outside his window, sent a little girl to fetch me immediately.

Since I behaved both the best and the worst of anyone else, I didn't know whether I was in for a prize or for punishment when I was called to the office. Nobody told me. But the woman in the office wore those clothes and had that high, white-woman attitude. Maybe my mother was a charitable person, like the lady who sent us to the circus. I had no warning at all of my mother's presence, except the scent of smoked moosehide, just a faint and elusive whiff in the corridor, which made me pause, and then I was in the principal's office. He beamed as he readied himself to witness a tenderhearted reunion.

Which did not take place.

The minute I saw my mother, or rather, absorbed her, took in the hat, the shoes, the tightly fitted beautiful suit, too exquisite to be worn, really, that perfect and that simple, that achingly sharp cut, the minute I took in the scent of smoked moosehide under Paris perfume, the tiny swatch of veiling that hung down off her hat, the immaculate, casual handbag and gloves, and again the shoes, tight calfskin and buttoned to one side, a blue to match the blue in the thinnest stripes of the suit, the minute I saw all of this and saw that the face beneath the hat was indeed my mother's face I took it all in and spat it out.

"She ain't my mother," I said, flat as bannock.

I whirled and ran away down to the spot at the powerhouse where the steam pipes blasted exhausted moist air down into the ground. The grass stayed green all year-round there. I sat tight for about an hour before I thought, What are they going to do about it? If they believed me, and did not send me back with my mother, I'd proved my point, and if they did send me back with her I'd proved my point, too. Either way, I had done what I had to do. So I went back to the dorm and got together with my friends for kitchen duty and I didn't say a word about my mother's visit.

Nor would I, when my mother came again and again, meeting with the principal and meeting with me. Alone in the room together, I could feel my mother's strength pull upon me like a sucking wind. I could feel my clothes flutter. Flaps of yearning prayer cloth. Strings of hair tugged and twined from my braids and snaked into the space between us. I could barely breathe. I took in my mother's air. I couldn't look at her. I had to focus all the hatred inside me upon my mother's feet, slim in their fancy heeled shoes, in order to keep any sense of myself at all. I had to call on my spirit, the one who came from the earth, to strengthen me whenever I had to meet my mother's gaze.

She ain't my mother.

You ain't my mother.

I allowed myself four words, exactly four and those only. As long as I stuck with them, I was safe enough. Six visits into the year, the principal took the paperwork and shoved it at Fleur.

"I'm satisfied," he said. "Whatever the reason for her denying it, she is indeed your daughter. You may withdraw her."

Now he was talking about me like a library book.

I closed myself tight as a book then.

"No." My mother's voice. "I won't take her unless she wants to go. I won't force her, she's too much like me. Daga," she said for the thousandth time, in a voice of great longing, "daga, n'dawnis, ombe. Gizhawenimin. Izhadaa."

I felt the pull very strong then, it almost pulled me over, and I knew if she had just taken my hand I would have gone with her then.

But she couldn't, and I righted myself, walked out of the room. Outside, alone in the hallway, I fell on my knees as if shot. Then I picked myself up.

So it was, always, with me after that. You can go up to a certain point with me and I with you, giving, giving, but then the line might snap. My loving goes very deep unless you cross that boundary, do to me what I will not tolerate. I am not an all-forgiving person, not Lulu. Even when Nanapush and then Father Damien went to work on me shortly after, in regard to my mother, they had no success. The line had snapped. I had no interest. Even if I love you, the way I am, Father Jude, if you hurt me, I'll turn cold on you. Turn away like a cat.

PART FOUR

The
PASSIONS

16

FATHER DAMIEN

1921–1933

Word by word, I trudge closer, stumbling through the underbrush of sound and meaning. Agnes bit the end of her scarred fountain pen, switched back to English, *As I understand the place of the noun in the Ojibwe mind, it is unprejudiced by gender distinctions. That is some relief. Yet there occurs something more mysterious. Alive or dead. Each thing is either animate or inanimate, which would at first seem remarkably simple and sensible, for in the western mind the quality of aliveness or deadness seems easy to discern. Not so. For the Anishinaabeg, the quality of animation from within, or harboring spirit, is not limited to animals and plants. Stones, asiniig, are animate, and kettles, akikoog, alive as well.* In the sweat lodge, red-hot stones glowed with a power upon which she'd once gazed full on and scorched her eyeballs. For a day or two, everything she saw was surrounded by a halo of warm frost. *Amid the protocols of language, there is room for individual preference, too. Some old men believe their pants are animate.* Nanapush had sometimes chastised his baggy trousers.

Perhaps it is fortunate after all, she wrote, *that Ojibwemowin is a language lean in objects. That leaves its bewildering wealth to reside in the storm of verbs and verb forms, which, heaven help us, require the literal extension of divine assistance for the novice speaker to comprehend.*

Agnes set aside her carefully kept pen. Most often she cleaned it with a toothpick and alcohol before retiring it, but tonight she was agitated with thoughts and sensations. The little cabin was too small a container. Outside, the strong cold air of Gashkadino-giizis, the freezing moon, lay still as iron on the ground. The reservation was suspended in its grip, snowless and icily tranquil. The moonless sky was a rich wild blackness of stars. She took up her pen once more and composed, instead of the rest of her article, a letter.

My Lord Bishop,

I am writing to inquire, on rather a long shot, whether you have any knowledge of a woman in your diocese who is widely rumored to have moved to Minneapolis. Although she is a woman yet adhering to the non-Catholic ways of her people, she has been in close contact with members of our mission here at Little No Horse. Fleur Pillager is her name. Perhaps one of your mission priests, someone running a charitable clothing dispensary for the indigent or perhaps providing free bread and soup, has knowledge of her whereabouts.

If so, we would be most glad for the information, as I am anxious to tell her news of her daughter.

Father Damien Modeste

Soon there arrived an answer.

Dear Father Damien Modeste,

It was with great interest I received your letter, and I am happy to report to you that I do have knowledge of a woman by the (former) name of Fleur Pillager. She is, however,

*anything but in want of either bread or soup. I myself
performed a marriage ceremony between this woman of our
soil's natal blood, and a prominent member of our community
(whose marriage was annulled on grounds of the wife's
insanity resulting in lack of consummation). Having entered
the Mount Curve Avenue household as a domestic, Mrs. John
James Mauser is currently presiding over household affairs at
that same address and she is received, not without some
ironic curiosity, in the highest society here. She is known for
her good works among the people of her background in
Minneapolis, who roam the streets.*

*I hope this information serves your purpose and helps you
in your quest.*

Every month or so, after his first letter, Father Damien wrote to
Fleur, or, it would be more accurate to say, he cast a letter to the
winds in her direction. She could not read the letters but must finally
have got someone to translate them for her. At long length, a package
of red cloth arrived with her Mount Curve return address embossed
on the box. Gorgeous red cloth. Brocade. Obviously meant for a
priestly robe. No writing to accompany it, and only, as the years went
on, that one package. Similarly, Margaret and Nanapush received
goods Fleur shipped: blankets, a great cast-iron stove with blue
enamel doors, crates of oranges, a fat doll with golden hair and eyes
that shut, bags of hard candy, more cloth, tobacco. And money. She
certainly had money. Still, they heard nothing from her, no word, not
even when Nector borrowed Father Damien's fountain pen and paper
and wrote her to say that Lulu was home.

All they heard of Fleur was from newspaper clippings sent by city
relatives. Fleur ate with so-and-so. Visited so-and-so. Motored to
Wayzata. Motored to the banks of the St. Croix River. Picnicked.
Vacationed. Bore a child. All they saw of her were three or four
printed photographs, her figure slim and unrecognizably dressed, a
round hat shading her face. Her hair was long again, held up in a
chignon in one photograph. In another, she wore a slender, white,
scandalous, gravity-defying gown. Next to her, and everyone puzzled
about him, her husband stood. He was dressed to match her—formal,

complete—every detail of his getup observable and described in print too, right down to the cuff links. Gold nuggets. John James Mauser had invested in the Black Hills gold that Custer coveted and died in an attempt to secure. His face was taut, strained, soulful. Even in that grainy society-page photograph, it was quite clear that Fleur's husband was different from the jowled and coarse-whiskered bankers in whose company he smoked. Of course, he had to be in order to fall in love with such a dangerous woman. The photograph had caught him midglance. He looked sideways at her. She was poised in the white gown, standing before a dance floor as though she'd alighted and folded her feathers. She gazed upon the array of St. Paul society with an eagle's unconscious ferocity. Her husband's look held something any man anywhere could understand, or any woman, or for that matter any priest.

He would kill for her, thought Agnes, the poor man suffers a wrenching passion. When she witnessed the insanity of love, Agnes made upon her breast the sign of the cross, the emblem to her of protection and pity. Thoughts of Gregory or Berndt were usually acceptable features of her history now, yet there were other times, in her dreams, when old feelings assailed her with a sudden and crippling sickness of emotion.

The moon vanished and retrieved itself. Vanished again. In those years, a great want descended upon the nation, and the Ojibwe were no longer the only vagrant and hollow-eyed beggars on the plains. There were others. Farmers. Those who had stolen and plowed the earth were upended by the earth, buried in dust. Yet in the scrap of reservation, the lake remained, the woods, the poor cabins with no more than a streak of grease to wipe across the bread. Winter did in the old people and the young died of rotted lungs. Most people forgot about Fleur, or gave her up to the city. But of course there came a day, it was inevitable, when Fleur finished with the man in the beautiful tuxedo, and returned.

Spring brought her to the reservation in a tumult of wild birdsong. Agnes sensed it the way an animal knows low pressure in its bones. There was a spring storm approaching. A dark cloud. Behind it, a full and aching, female, swollen, hungry moon. Sure enough, it was Fleur.

Not only that, but as though to present an opposing force, Pauline Puyat was sent back as well from Argus and the exhausted community where she had finally professed her permanent vows and become Sister Leopolda.

Father Damien kept to his breviary, tried to attend to his daily office and his predictable rounds. But he could feel the wary energy of people at Mass. Fleur's return, and the Puyat's, were the subject of tense whispers. In the watery weight of air and the burgeoning light, people talked.

FLEUR'S CHILDREN

At first, no one thought that the boy Fleur brought back to the reservation could possibly be her son. He was so white, so soft, so strange. But then, said the old women, in the land of the chimookomanag she'd probably forgotten all the things that a pregnant Anishinaabekwe must do—for instance, never to roll over in her sleep. Had she twisted the boy up inside of her somehow? And when it was born, did the men of the father's chimookoman dodem make loud noises to frighten off evil and give the boy courage? It did not appear so, nor did the women think Fleur had kept him long enough in the tikinagan—not that there was anything visibly crooked about him. Yet he did not look straight, either, so perhaps the crookedness came from the inside. Had she remembered to rub him with bear grease? with goose oil? to bathe him in strong cedar tea? Had she sung the old songs to him before and after he was born and had she done the right thing and introduced him to the drum? They doubted it. Some even came and whispered to Father Damien. It was the flesh of the boy—too pale and soft, like risen dough, that upset them. And the eyes. Sometimes blue, sometimes black. As if his whole being could not make up its mind, which gave them the answer, at last, to what was wrong.

They had seen it before in a child whose indis was lost, or even worse, thrown away. Maybe by a nurse in the chimookoman hospital. Maybe the father, who did not keep Anishinaabe ways. For the boy seemed both clever and foolish, huge and weak. Had Fleur dried the boy's birth cord in tobacco, then wrapped it in sage, and sewn it into a bag made of fine skin? If not, the boy would be hunting for it ever after. And he did appear to be looking too hard at everything, the people thought, maybe searching, but with such a quiet oddness that it truly seemed to them he must have lost the center of himself. Anyway, who knew if she was ever a good mother, seeing her own daughter would not speak to her anymore? Fleur didn't treat her son with affection, never set her hand upon his hair, never even told his name to anyone. Perhaps he didn't have one. Nameless, then, the boy trundled after her, begging, always, for sweets. More sweets. They called him Sweets for a time, and then someone looked into his eyes. That name was dropped.

Of course, from the newspaper record, his origin was known. Here was the son she had borne with John James Mauser. This was the son of the ravenous man in the tuxedo suit, the one who had stolen her land. The truth came clear. Upon that Mauser, it appeared she had taken her revenge, an idea. This son she brought home was the visible form of that revenge. So was he, or was he not, human? Was he then not something concocted of a bad form of medicine, or at the least, her purpose gone wrong?

The mother and son went back to their land and camped there, even though it was a place nobody liked to go. She put on men's overalls and tied her hair back, bought an ax and a few other tools, then the two started building out by the ruined shores of Matchimanito. Some said she returned her parents' bones to the ground. Dodem markers soon appeared, thrust upside down into softened earth. If so, there were still more reasons to avoid the place. More ghosts. A reunion of the dead.

As for the great trees, over which Fleur's force was narrowed, then stilled, they were gone forever. But although the son and mother could not bring back the trees which, quarter sawn and polished with beeswax, composed the stylish foyer of the grand house Mauser built on a tranquil ridge in Minneapolis, the peace of which Fleur destroyed, there were other trees. Fresh green saplings had grown in Fleur's absence. Kind trees, popple trees, flourished on her land, enough for her to construct a neat cabin of poles and mud. Once she was living in her new popple-pole house, she sought out her daughter Lulu once again. But in her adamant refusal of her mother, the girl would not change.

As soon as he knew Fleur was there and settled in her cabin, Father Damien walked out to Matchimanito. The old ladies constructed invisible webs of signs of crosses when they saw Fleur passing near, but Father Damien felt simple eagerness to see her, friend of his first years, and he walked the grown-over paths eagerly. That first visit, as though she'd taken on some city ways, Fleur was surprisingly talkative. It was only once he'd gone that Father Damien realized she'd told him nothing. City ways again. After that, she grew increasingly quiet and the boy, tanned and suddenly fond of daily fishing and hunting, stomped in and out of the house in silent concentration. Father Damien found the quietness of Fleur reassuring, not threatening or even mysterious. Often, they sat in silence and considered that period of absence of talk a good visit.

Fleur was usually waiting when Father Damien arrived, for he had never learned to walk with any degree of discretion. Sticks snapped beneath his heels and he cheerfully blundered this way and that, making a zigzag harvest of berries or mushrooms along the way. He always showed up with something: once a tremendous fluted oyster bracket, tender and fluttering, pulled off a tree; another time a dead bird of a brilliant and iridescent blue so intense the color caused tears to start into his eyes.

As he gave the bird to Fleur, he was surprised to experience the sudden sensation that he was traveling swiftly through the air. The blue of its feathers seemed to span the spectrum of emotion. Fleur regarded the bird with her usual calm, though her eyes grew uncommonly gentle. He brought her hazelnuts, ears of fresh corn, old army blankets and heavy coats to piece into quilts. He brought her strings of cut-glass beads, sewing needles, tins of good tobacco. Fleur accepted these offerings with an artless pleasure. They were little enough, thought Father Damien, considering that he couldn't help her to obtain Lulu. The girl, now a young woman, was stubborn as a rock.

That day, Fleur took her beading out and worked in the sun while Father Damien worried the concept of a word, jotting notes on a tiny pad of paper, asking her for confirmation. Suddenly, he stopped what he was doing and looked at her, watched her as though from far away, thought about her life and their connection. She had a fierce intelligence and nothing slipped by her, so he accepted that she'd known his secret from the beginning, and it hadn't mattered. Not because she was so tolerant, but because certain details of other people's personhood were not worth her notice. She simply didn't care. Nor did she care about other things people usually found essential. The good opinion of friends and family were useless—she had none and lived with a son whose character would not have relieved loneliness. Or loneliness itself—if she ever did experience such a thing, and Damien was quite sure that she did not—she made no mention of it, even where Lulu was concerned. She never said she missed her daughter, she never asked where Lulu was, she did not even say Lulu's name. And yet, there was no doubt she loved Lulu and yearned after her, for he knew that many times Fleur had tried to see her.

Before Father Damien left, she set a pair of beadworked makazinan into his hands. They were lined with the softest rabbit fur, the uppers were of a beautiful smoked hide. The flowers were worked of the finest grade of beads and flawlessly put together—except for the tiny black bead on the edge, the spirit mistake done on purpose so as to allow any bad spirits that may have been trapped in the foolishly arrogant perfection of the work itself a chance to escape. There was no question for whom these makazinan were intended, and Damien took them with a heavyhearted smile.

The gift was evidence of the bewilderment in Fleur's mind, the confusion. She did not understand the reflected substance of her own revenge in her daughter. It was up to Father Damien to try to explain. But what can be explained when the stone meets the stone, when the earth mixes, when water flows into water? You are alike, he wanted to say, alike in your stubbornness. One will not ask forgiveness and the other will not forgive. What use is that? You sent Lulu to the government school and Lulu will never forget.

"The best thing to do is ask Nanapush to talk to your daughter, ask him to lay it out plainly. That is the only way."

Fleur raised her eyes to Damien in a moment of unusual openness, and he gazed into their reflecting depth with an ease that he'd never known. Her sharply cut eyelids, so fine and enigmatic, were only enhanced by the dark upward sweep of two lines that had appeared in her age. Her skin was still perfect, taut, of a gold so deep it seemed the tawny cover of a fabulous metal. And her straight nose, the nostrils so artfully flared, and the charged symmetry of her mouth, all were unchanged. If anything, deepened. Her beauty had ceased to intimidate Father Damien, though some had forgotten and were awed by it all over. When she'd first appeared on reservation ground, wearing her immaculate and tailored white suit, she'd been taken for a film star or singer strangely dropped from the new movie screen in Hoopdance. Now, clearly, the suit, hat, and heels stored carefully away, the makeup washed off, the fancy car she'd arrived in sold, here was Fleur again—her fate to chase one thing to lose another. She had regained her land, but lost her daughter.

And the son, what of the son, Damien wondered.

"He will stay with me," Fleur said.

But Damien could tell already that the boy would not.

LULU'S CANARY YELLOW

It was Agnes's practice to try to control her irritations, to monitor her horror of certain dishes made by Mary Kashpaw—the strangely acidic pea soup, the leather venison, the weird maltish cake and soapy oatmeal. But sometimes she couldn't help exclaiming over the strangeness of the food, or recooking it herself. At those times, Mary Kashpaw glowered and stomped off, yet she herself did not partake of the loving and sometimes nearly lethal feasts that she prepared for Father Damien. Sister Hildegarde's picayune frugalities also upset Agnes. Why must she remember to collect old scraps of soap in a sock? As for socks, would the priest ever have a new pair, smooth, without the bumps and ridges of impatient darning? And then, there were more serious, heart-sinking times she believed that the black dog's bargain was real. At those times, she could not help her pettiness from surfacing. Not only was Lulu's practiced avoidance of her mother tiresome, but Agnes couldn't help wishing that, as long as she had sacrificed her soul and was facing eternity in hell, Lulu would behave with a modicum of thoughtful decency.

It's not that I'm a prude, thought Agnes, *I can't have changed that much, it's just that Lulu is so careless with her charm, so bold. Can any good come of it?* True enough, Lulu became a noticeably sensual young woman. She curled her hair with a permanent wave. She laughed with an irresistible intensity of mirth, shot jokes at people, tempted, and rejected. Returning from an off-reservation town, where she had paid a white woman to *poison her hair*, as the old ladies said, she was the talk in the church vestibule. People hushed when she entered, her curls tightly wound, glossy, rippling along the side of her head. After Mass, she was the centerpiece of a crowd of women who poked at the spirals, wondered, pinched their noses at the chemical smell. She wore face paint, too, and carried a little brown pocketbook. Her shoes were shocking. Toeless, heels like railroad spikes. Her shoes caused men to lick their lips and women to marvel at the odd, sharp tracks she left.

Her transformation presented Agnes with a small clutch of embarrassing resentments. Seeing the young woman's tight-skirted sashay, she brooded on the distinct possibility of her soul's entrapment all in order to save the very thing Lulu seemed intent on tarnishing. At last, she vowed to have a talk with Lulu.

"Bring her to the back of the church right after Mass tomorrow," Father Damien directed Margaret one day.

The next morning, having fortified himself with Saint Augustine, who in his youth had stolen pears, who had gone to fleshpots of Carthage, Father Damien sat in back of the church, waiting. These last few pews, empty and quiet in the morning, were where Father Damien had many a long discussion with troubled members of the church. *Saint Augustine, Nanabozho, whoever can hear me, give me a little help now*, he prayed. The saint would have condemned the young girl's self-display, and the notorious Nanabozho would have taken advantage of it. Such were Damien's sources. His bedrock now was aggregate. The voices that spoke to him arose sometimes out of wind and at other times from the pages of religious books. Still, he was determined to help guide Lulu Nanapush. It was his duty to her mother, not to mention his old friend.

Just as he composed his purpose, Lulu entered and disarranged it. She wore a blouse of canary yellow that dazzled the eye. Her shoes had pieces cut from the sides and heels, and her skirt, though an appropriate length, was immodestly snug. She jingled a little memento bracelet on her wrist as she sat down beside Father Damien in the pew. Excitedly, she greeted him. He could feel immediately such a mild and innocent warmth that he was tempted to hug her as though she were a child. But she was most emphatically a woman, and lovely, so smiling and fresh that Father Damien's irritations melted. Even with her lips stained the glossy purple of wild plums, she looked completely without guile. Father Damien took her hand and held her painted fingertips in his own.

"You have dipped your nails in the blood of the damned," he sighed, hoping she could not tell that he admired the color.

"It's called Happiness."

From time to time, little things of this sort still pricked through the long years of Damien's subterfuge. Even in his age, he was charmed by pure harmless feminine vanity. He knew immediately that she spoke of the color of the polish. He took hold of himself.

"Lulu, my child, that is only a label on a pot of lacquer. Happiness is more complex, as you know."

Lulu nodded. The smile dropped abruptly off her face, and Father Damien now learned that this young woman he had known mainly as a child had inherited her mother's lack of compromise, Margaret's sharp sight, Nanapush's unbiased curiosity, and perhaps his own natural sympathy.

"You are happy, I think," Lulu said simply. "Without someone else."

Her earnestness demanded that he truly consider an answer, not give her some pat ecclesiastic's line. He put her fingers down gently and held his folded hands to his lips, as though praying.

"I have loved," he said softly, "and yet the happiness of love is not the only thing. It is not even the most important thing. It is momentary, ungraspable, impermanent as the paint on your fingers, though I suppose the stuff is advertised as long-lasting."

"Oh yes," said Lulu, smiling sunnily again. "I think that I already know something about myself . . . it's very sad." She made an unconsciously flirtatious mockery of sorrow. "I am very bored with men. I get tired of them quickly. For a short time, I am insane, I can't stop thinking about one or the other. And then, all of a sudden, I don't want them around me. Just when I decide that I wish to do without him, any him, that one becomes most attached, Father Damien, and won't leave!"

The color of her blouse, Father Damien thought, that blithe yellow, was the outward manifestation of the careless cheer and stubborn sensuousness of Lulu's character. He immediately foresaw, indeed, exactly what came to pass in Lulu's life. A series of passionate but inconclusive liaisons. Fatherless pregnancies. Children without support. He did not envision the number—eight sons, one daughter. Had he done so, he might have collapsed right there before her. Alarmed at what she told him, he turned practical. He had learned one truth in his work—there was no changing the true arrangement of a human heart. One dealt with the earthly exigencies.

"You need a profession," he decided. "One that will support you here, for it appears you do not want to move to the Cities. And if you are as bored with men as you say, you will not marry one for long, no matter what the Church advises. You need an honorable profession," he repeated. "What will it be?"

Partly as a consequence of Damien's pragmatic approach, Lulu became a self-sufficient woman. Father Damien helped her from the beginning, so she didn't falter. She survived the fires in her heart by using all of the skills she had developed—sewing, which she'd learned at the government boarding school, as well as knitting and beading, the making of gauntlets and makazinan, and feather bustles. She created quilts, dolls, vests, shirts. Sold eggs, bartered chickens, even horse-traded on occasion. As she could add and subtract quickly in her head, she left her children with a friend and worked for the trader's market. A few pennies here, a dollar there. She leased out some land. Kept a cow and shot her own deer, dressed it efficiently just like her mother. Taught her boys to hunt, work in the fields, pick rags, bead and sew as well as she could. It was in fact a surprise she had any time for men at all. Where did she fit them in? people wondered. The old hens and dried-up roosters gossiped in the sun.

A short time with men went a long way with Lulu. She liked the thrill of not-having, became impatient with their daily presence, as she'd confessed. One hour here on the way to work, another well after dark in her private room, the boys arranged in the rest of the house on roll-aways and sound asleep. She collected and she discarded, she used and she tossed. So Father Damien's weak attempt at counseling her succeeded only insofar as he was able to help her support the one real true romance of her life—her children, to whom she was devoted.

Father Damien's talk with Lulu did yield one other good, perhaps, for Lulu was never herself scourged by the evils of drink. It was a subject they discussed, though Father Damien was not sure at the time how he had come out of their small debate.

He asked her, point-blank, if she imbibed. He spoke suddenly, and rather forcefully, hoping to catch her by surprise. She did look startled by his penetrating tone.

"Why, yes." Half-ashamed, she glanced down at the wood grain of the pew.

"You mustn't."

"Why not?" She raised her graceful head, looked Father Damien in the eye with her bold and gleaming gaze. "Christ changed water into wine in Cana, at the wedding. He could have changed it into water or milk, something else. Is a taste of wine so bad, Father? You drink it every day . . ."

Father Damien opened his mouth to answer, but she went on.

"I'm not like some, if that's what you're thinking. I don't drink any more wine than you yourself at the Eucharist. No more than a swallow, now and then a glass."

Father Damien looked at her chastisingly. Still, she had a point.

"You cause talk," the priest said softly to her. "You would sadden my friend, old Nanapush."

"That's what you think."

She laughed, her voice a rushing sound of snow-melted water, of summer leaves in high wind. Her eyes sparked with a sweetly wicked glance.

"Nanapush hardly ever touches the bottle, it is true, but he gave me the money to buy these shoes. Remember when I was little, how I almost froze my feet off in a blizzard? He saved my feet with old-time medicine, and he likes me to show off the good work he did."

She lifted her foot a little, rotated her ankle, wiggled her toes, in light stockings, through the open wedge.

"I suppose that I can't argue," said the priest grumpily. "I'm only thinking of your soul."

Father Damien was thinking of his own soul, that was the truth of it. He resented anew the indifference she showed to her salvation, manufactured though it might be behind the scenes.

Lulu cast her eyes down. Her lashes were long and feathery. Realizing that she probably had no intention of taking his advice, Damien turned away from Lulu. Frustrated, intrigued, helpless with love for this young woman, he gazed steadfastly at Our Lady of the Serpents, whose hands were outstretched even as she balanced on a writhing snake and a slivered moon.

"Pray to her." He pointed to the statue, but his voice was hoarse and a little desperate with the sympathy he felt for Lulu.

Those who clucked over Lulu were also fond of sighting the actual devil. One visit spawned others; there were periodic rashes of hysterical reports, each more creative than the next. The devil entered and possessed the body of a cow, which gave pitch-black milk. A hairball was found in that same barn. It contained a jagged tooth. The cow was heard, later, mumbling a curse. Every so often, the black dog made his rounds, barring the path of Mrs. Pentecost and her daughter as they walked to Holy Mass. A man in elegant dress sauntered through the woods, seducing women on the paths to church.

These eager visions broke Agnes's patience. Ridiculous! Was she mad? Fevered? Overwrought? She examined the memory of the conversation with the dog who'd interrupted her meal, and wished she knew. Each night Agnes looked into the sky, for it comforted her to see the dancing of the northern lights, the spirits of the departed. *Our souls are tethered by the love of things that cannot last*, Agnes wrote, a note in her pocket. But she had sometimes to think the opposite. Our souls are freed—the only problem was that freedom was an open and a lonely space.

Agnes also continued, every so often, to wake feverish and panicked. Where was God in all of this? Where was justice? Why did the devil reportedly put on flesh and walk among the people, while God remained silent, producing only the false miracles of Sister Leopolda, never deigning to speak again to Agnes personally, no matter how deep the darkness in which she waited?

One picture salvaged the dubious bargain. One scene from Lulu's life.

1945

Lulu's house was small, an old-fashioned pole and mud cabin with a tamped dirt floor. It had been Nanapush's once, and Lulu had taken it over once she left the Morrissey whose child she was large with now. She lived on the money from the wild, mean chickens she raised. They scratched and complained in the yard, flew toward Agnes with menacing cries. She shooed them off, laughing, as she once had her own dominickers. Lulu's older son hauled water up from the tiny lake behind the house. Then, though he could hardly lift an ax, he began to split wood.

"Go on in," he pointed to the cabin. "My little brother's in there."

Agnes pushed open the door and there, before her, spinning in the dark air, the baby hovered. She stood motionless, astonished, gazing into the child's brown eyes as the pecking chickens rushed in around his feet. The baby laughed at Agnes and held out his small, padded hands. His pale robe glowed, his face was all excited pleasure. Gently, Agnes touched him, found the harness that fit cunningly around his chest, fashioned from scraps of old leather. The child was attached by the harness to a rope that in turn was threaded through an iron ring set into the roof. The rope ran through the hook and down to a knothole in the door. When the door was opened, the child rose into the air, out of reach of the fierce, sharp-beaked chickens. When the chickens were thrown out and the door was closed, he played safely on the ground, tethered away from the hot stove.

Agnes swung the child. He laughed, kicked the air, touched his hands. She felt a rush of lightness. Peace. Her heart trembled and beat low. The glowing robe, the way the child hovered—an angel. She believed in the essential angelic nature of that tiny boy, even though the baby grew up and went to prison, even though Lulu saw so many sorrows, and even though Agnes continued to wake in the night overpowered by spiritual dryness. Often, when she suffered from an aridity of faith, one of her comforts was to hold fast to the picture of that laughing, swooping child.

LEOPOLDA'S LAST CONFESSION

Abruptly, without knocking, Sister Leopolda entered Father Damien's cabin. "Sister Hildegarde Anne says that I must have your permission to wear a potato sack."

Father Damien glared at her, disturbed, and consented with a flap of his hand. He did what he could to avoid the nun, and still she continued to creep up on him in his refuge. Her presence disturbed his equilibrium, forced a wary and combative stance he disliked maintaining. Even now, he suspected her visit contained some challenge and he went back to his work hoping to discourage her. But Sister Leopolda did not leave. Instead, she knelt with a creaking flourish and abruptly stated that she required absolution.

"Visit me in the confessional, as your sisters do."

"Father, I cannot," she said impatiently.

"Sister, you must."

Father Damien stared at his desktop, toyed with his pen. Had she finally gotten around to it? Was she, at last, ready for this confession he had long avoided? He knew that Sister Leopolda waited to explain the meaning of the scars in her palms. He had seen those long ago. He didn't want to hear their cause, any detail of it. What earthly good was it, now, and why thrust her ancient guilt his way? Because she could not bear it? Unlikely, after all these years. More probably, she wanted to force some knowledge upon him. To plague him with a morbid responsibility. For he did know. He stole a glance at those palms, and the spurs of the tinkered rosary raked into his mind. It had not been Mary Kashpaw, after all, who killed Napoleon. Beyond that, Father Damien wanted to hear nothing. Desperate not to receive her story, he turned away. He wanted to bless her and be done with it. But he had vowed that he would carry out his priestly duties to the very letter, so he set his forehead in the cup of his hands and gestured for her to speak, at which point, after an audibly muttered inner struggle, Leopolda began, with a bitter and oily enthusiasm.

I am told in my dreams I must atone for what I did and what you know I did, though at first I didn't know it was him, for when I seized him and forced myself upon him, grew around him like the earth around a root, held him still, I believed he was the devil!

"Go on," muttered Damien.

I strung the noose around his neck and counted each bead in my fingers as I tightened the link. The joyful and the sorrowful myster-ies, Father Damien, and him pounding and thrashing under me and taking his good time choking so I went dizzy with the effort of hold-ing him. God held those beads along with me, his strength the grip of lions. My fingers closed like hasps of iron, locked on the rosary, and wrenched and twisted the beads close about his neck until his face darkened and he lunged away. I hung on while he bucked and gagged and finally fell, his long tongue dragging down my thigh.

Father Damien squeezed out a low croak, waited, gathered all of his wits, and finally spoke to her softly. "You confess to the murder of Napoleon Morrissey."

"I confess to strangling the devil in the shape of the man!"

Father Damien set his face harder in his hands, felt a fuzz of sleep overtaking his brain, a protective shield of drowsiness. He tried, though his thoughts were listless, to imagine what he should do with the nun kneeling to one side of him. His first duty was quite clear.

"You must offer yourself to the authorities. Your penance is to appear before the law."

"Ah," said Leopolda quite readily. "That I cannot do."

"Explain please?" Damien's head was heavy and his hands felt thick and cold. He spoke gently, buying time, wearily perturbed that he and not the sheriff should have this question set so baldly before him.

"If I am locked up for my crime, I will not be able to pursue my work among my people. I cannot serve God as well in jail."

"You must go there anyway," said Damien.

"That I cannot do," the nun replied with sly regret.

Father Damien's head began to pound with a loud pain.

"Do you sincerely repent of what you did?"

Sister Leopolda did not answer. Instead, she began to rock in agita-tion, and she laughed that low secret and uncanny jeer he'd first heard the day he said his first Mass on Little No Horse.

"I know," she hissed. "You are considering how you can turn me in yourself. I wish to be absolved, and you will take my sin away! I know what you are. And if you banish me or write to the bishop, *Sis-ter* Damien, I will write to him too."

Slowly, with nightmarish calm, the priest turned toward the nun and regarded the starved and shrunken lips, caved cheeks, the monkeylike bared teeth. There was a ready poison in her deep-set eyes. She seemed very far away, to exist almost in another dimension from his own. How had she become this frightful creature? By what means? Had the murder, no matter how justified, worked on her over all these years like an inner caustic, burning away all human joy? The nun was such an awful spectacle of fascination that what she said, though threatening enough, failed to excite any degree of concern in the priest. He listened in a frozen trance.

"You love writing to the Pope," she spat. "Well, I can write too. I have beautiful handwriting. I can write to the bishop."

The nun pointed to her eyes, set a sharp bony finger on each cheekbone.

"You have the voice of a priest, true, but these eyes are not fooled! You are mannish, unwomanly, yet your poor neck is scrawny. Too chicken skinny for a man's neck. It is obvious to me you wrap your chest. Apparent that you haven't a man's equipment, though that is useless anyway upon a priest. I am not as stupid as the others. I have waited outside your window after the ox, Mary Kashpaw, is snoring in the ironing shack. I've seen you undress."

Momentarily, the words struck deep and Agnes went a furious red, embarrassed at the thought of Sister Leopolda peeping in. Her face bloomed hot, and she had to keep herself from patting her cheeks. But she rallied her dignity and decided that her only hope was to remain firmly within the boundaries of the deception.

"You flatter yourself." With an actor's skill, Agnes pretended to struggle with a manly ego. Craftily, she assumed an air of tragic dignity. "You are not as perceptive as you might imagine. True, I am not Herculean, but I am all the same a man. If you do not believe I was ordained and sealed as a priest and bound by the duties of my calling, why have you come to ask me for a priest's absolution? What good would it do your soul to obtain the empty blessing of an impostor?"

The nun shrank back, narrowing her eyes until they were two dashes of black rage in her mask-pale face. Father Damien's voice strengthened. He stood up in a sudden outrage manufactured to hide the shaking of his knees.

"Leave me! You'll get no absolution here, murderess. Not until you turn yourself in to the tribal police!"

She crept away. As soon as she was able to bolt the door behind Sister Leopolda, Agnes collapsed into her chair. She made her mind up immediately to purchase a thicker gauge of material for her curtains and never to let the moonlight fall through.

Eternal Father,

The bond sin creates between the absolver and the confessing sinner—I have no guidance as to its nature or its quality. Having recently learned that the perpetrator of a pardonless crime is a member of my sisterly flock, I am left with the responsibility to contain the strangeness—this knowledge is a form of violence. I exist with this forlorn sense of horror. Forlorn because it is my solo cup. None may drink it for me, none may spill it from my grasp.

Except you.

Modeste

The next day, Damien unhooked from its nail deep in his closet the rosary found by George Aisance. He carried the rosary over to the convent. Knowing that Leopolda had responsibility for cooking that day, he went to the kitchen. He held out the rosary, hoping to drop it into her hands, to get rid of the dirt of the confession and the tired old killing. It felt as though he were carrying drops of bad blood—acid, lethal, black. He was chagrined not to find Leopolda. Disappointed to the bone, Damien took the rosary back into his cabin and replaced it on the nail. He knew he would not have the impetus to get rid of it again.

So Agnes could not jettison the poisonous ring of stones. And the threat of exposure nagged her. She could not bear the prospect of Damien's uncovering. The word happiness, a nail color, poked at her now. For Agnes realized that her happiness was composed of a thousand ordinary satisfactions built up over a life lived according to what might seem to others modest and monotonous routines. As a priest, as a man, after the long penitential years and the challenges of her own temperament, she was at ease. As Father Damien, she had blessed unions, baptized, anointed, and absolved friends in the parish. In turn, Father Damien had been converted by the good Nanapush. He now practiced a mixture of faiths, kept the pipe, translated hymns or brought in the drum, and had placed in the nave of his church a statue of the Virgin—solid, dark, kind eyed, hideous, and gentle. He was welcome where no other white man was allowed. It was apparent, to the people, that the priest was in the service of the spirit of goodness, wherever that might evidence itself. Were he exposed, were he known to have fooled, deceived, and hidden his most fundamental nature, all would be lost. Married couples Father Damien had joined would be sundered. Babies unbaptized and exposed to the dark powers. Deaths unblessed and sins again weighing on the poor sinners. And, if in spite of her own fears, Sister Leopolda should expose him and cause him to leave, there would surely be no one who would listen to the sins of the Anishinaabeg and forgive them—at least not as a mirthless trained puppet of the dogma, but in the spirit of the ridiculous and wise Nanabozho. Anxious, unnerved, Father Damien played his music, begging for the mercy of sleep. Or he wrote, late into the night, feverish, cramped letters and reports.

Your Holiness, etc.

According to your faithless servant Voltaire, Louis XIV and de Brinvilliers went to confession as soon as they had committed a great crime. They confessed frequently, he said, "as a gourmand takes medicine to increase his appetite." I ask you, in light of such cynicism, would it be improper to suggest that a murderer's confession sometimes serves as a salt to the food of evil? And I have also read that Pope Gregory XV, in his papal bull of 30 August 1622, ordered confessions to be revealed in certain cases. Would the situation I have described in my most recent reports qualify as a "certain" case? I await, as always in the darkness, your answer.

Modeste

17

MIST AND MARY KASHPAW

1940

No one stays long on the reservation without somehow coming by a name. Since Fleur would not say it and nobody dared ask the boy with the dead eyes himself, he was named by invisible consensus. Awun, he was called, the Mist, for he was silent as mist and set apart from others, always, by his impenetrable Pillager ways. He hired out on farms surrounding the reservation. When he bulked out and thickened, Awun lost his nimble touch, but retained a fixity of unknown purpose. Awun was either very simple or so deep and devious that his mask could not be penetrated. What was he? From a childhood in a stone-floored mansion to a youth in a poor, pole cabin by a lake, and his mother would tell him nothing. Did she love him? Was he more than the child of Fleur's revenge and restoration? He was a Pillager, he was Awun, so of course he became something other than a function of her will. He became will itself, unpurposed, set loose on the world, and looking as all great weak things do for a stronger counterpart.

Brooding on the trick of his identity, Awun worked his way

through farm after farm, splitting wood, cords and cords of it, toward the first woman who could match him stroke for stroke. Still, Mary Kashpaw might never have come within his range, his span, but for the sisters. And so perhaps blame for all that happened should be placed where proper: at the nuns' square toes. For it was Sister Dympna who raised the request for Awun to haul wood from the Kashpaw family's lot for Mary Kashpaw to cut. In her restlessness the woman had already chopped too many birch trees near the convent and the sisters now feared for their apple orchard.

One morning in slow July, the son of the wealthiest man in Minneapolis threw on his shirt of a worn blue so vaporous it embodied his name, ate his kettle of oatmeal, and hauled a wagon load of wood into the churchyard. When he had finished unloading the wood, he then stood behind the church in lilac shadow. The thin shade reached only to his waist. No trees near the wood lot were tall enough to conceal him. His hair was the brown of winter grass, turned back in wind, his shirt's whitened threads were the blue of his washed-pale eyes. His face bore the complex gloom of his German father leaded over with the Pillagers' old, frightful calm. He stared at Father Damien, his hands buckled around the chains, and one after another he began to drag the logs across the road into the bare yard just planted with young trifling oaks. Across that piece of ungrassed dirt, Mary Kashpaw waited, eager to reduce them to stove lengths.

Awun did not notice her at first, busy as he was with the hauling. He fitted the great leather glove of his hand around the chains and pulled as Father Damien supervised and joked and speculated about why the nuns wanted all the wood so deep into summer. Even as he set the logs to ground, Mary Kashpaw took up her eager ax. Once she began to work, the regular strokes fell with such a precise rhythm that the sounds did not at first intrude upon the men's conversation. Only when she stopped to sharpen the edge of her blade with slow strokes of a file did Awun notice the ring of silence. His glance searched, and stuck.

Mary Kashpaw wore a man's shirt with the sleeves ripped out. Her arms were bare—hard and roped as the turned legs on a table. Her long skirt hung crooked and her great, solid feet were planted with monumental firmness below the hem. She had used a grapevine to tie her heavy black hair away from her face. From beneath a notched leaf, she regarded the two men with the indifference of all powerful creatures. Then, the blade honed to her satisfaction, she turned with a light motion, rose on the balls of her feet, brought down the ax, and split the length with a natural blow.

Agnes noticed, with some suspicion, that the great draft-horse Pillager, this Awun, took a jagged breath when the blow landed. Next, his eyes lost focus and drifted like the mist of his name. But the young man was no more than a giant boy and Mary Kashpaw, though innocent, a fully grown and mature woman. It took more—a strangled cry from Awun, a hot breath, obvious panic—to inform Agnes. She turned a close eye on the situation, now suspicious. Awun's eyes followed the inflection of muscles in Mary Kashpaw's arms and shoulders as she continued her work, and now, to Agnes there was no doubt. She sighed, knocked her chin lightly with a fist, and tried to divert Awun in conversation. But the young man's verbs exploded like the caps off bottles. Go! Stay! His voice was hoarse with bewildered agitation. He wouldn't leave and would not be argued by the priest into a cup of coffee, or shamed into leaving. Awun preferred to stand in the fragrance of wood chips, waiting for Mary Kashpaw to finish her work.

When at last she paused to lean for a moment on her ax, Awun walked over to her, mumbling, stood before her with his great hands revolving a crumpled hat against his chest. Although she gave no sign of awareness, she did not drive him off. Perhaps, as he was so much younger, he seemed harmless, beneath her notice. Awun was all the more taken with her unconcern. Being so large and grim, he had never found a woman at ease with him before. The fact that Mary Kashpaw did not notice him with surprise or suspicion charmed his heart. When she left him there, alone, he still did not move and stood waiting as the light went out of the day.

She walked straight past Awun on her way to the convent kitchen, but paused at the door and shrugged hugely, in distress. Some sense of his interest at last pierced the armor of her self-concentration. As though she'd passed a source of intense heat, the marks where the wagon nails were drawn from her flesh burned.

She entered the dim cooking space. Carefully, she washed her great face in water already darkened from the cleaning of potatoes. The silky brown water gave back a face so calm it seemed at once dead and ecstatic. She kneaded bread with rounded thumps, her arms dusted with flour, and then she set out plates for the nun's table. At her own place, in the kitchen, Mary Kashpaw ate quickly, surreptitiously, as much as she could manage, and then she poured boiling water over the big kettles and began to scrub. It was dark by the time she left the pots drying on six meat hooks, and darker in the shack where she slept, sitting up in the sleigh. Most nights, she would have paced in the mosquito-haunted yard before settling, breathing cooler, fresher air and whittling twigs to whistles. Tonight she laid her ax beneath the seat and barred the double doors.

THE MIST

Mary Kashpaw did not pray aloud, but every night gazed upward into the dark of the lathe-and-tar-paper roof with a fixity that slowly became sleep. As always, once she dropped off she slept heavily, profoundly, and very loudly. Sinking immediately into her dreams, she groaned and spoke aloud as if, drugged unconscious, all the unspoken words of the day suddenly flew from her relaxed mind. Awun's name was not among them, not that he could distinguish anyway, though he listened hard from his place, in the corner of the shack, where he'd crawled, crouched, and covered himself with bales of scorched ironing.

THE RIVER OF GRASS

The grass was long that year and slippery from rain. That is why it was possible for the Pillager boy, once he'd carefully unbarred the double door from inside, to harness himself to the sleigh that carried the sleeping Mary Kashpaw, and to tow it across the yard and along the margin of the road. This was before reservation lands were entirely fenced. He found it a simple matter to continue along the grass paths that led through the woods from slough to slough.

In a clearing where he paused, sword grass tall and iron black, Mary Kashpaw finally woke.

Awun jolted forward down an incline and his bounds gathered. Mary Kashpaw found herself traveling over grass, as in a dream, in a sleigh pulled along by a man with hair white in the moonlight. She looked to either side at the ghost arch of pale birch and the press of adamantine oak beyond. She breathed the slough's low reek, the sweet grass, gulped again the summer rose air, and saw the laboring back of the man who pulled her, powerful as a draft horse, over ground, through the bending reeds, deeper into the tangle of the world.

And all of a sudden her amazed cry, her thoughts, the cast of her mind, her heart, as she lifted the ax.

AWUN AND MARY

When she carelessly regarded him from under the picture-puzzle leaf of a bloodroot plant, then turned, lifted on the balled muscles of her monumental feet, and split a stove length down the center with one dropping swift blow, Awun was lost to Mary Kashpaw. She seemed, to him, to connect the heaven of her leafy-haloed head to the earth in which her blade buried to the top of the shank. He didn't know, of course, her history or how she had been stolen many years before, as a girl with a basket of roses, by horses muscled like himself. So when he took her from the shed in the sleigh, it was with an oaken innocence in which he could not hear the screams of panic or the branch surging through Kashpaw's breast. Mary Kashpaw, of course, felt the thunder of fear and heard the shouting from all sides, just as she had as a child, only this time, unlike her father, she managed to cut the lines.

So it happened, many years later in the green of summer once more, Mary Kashpaw managed to sever the lines that her father's hatchet had only scraped across. And once she did and Awun kept moving, walking, out into the sloughs and woods and farms that would gather to towns and disperse, like a spill of child's marbles here and there across the plains, she too was set free.

An hour passed, during which she brooded on the sleigh bench. A world of consideration passed through her mind. She pictured Father Damien, though she had no words for an attachment so complete it was like breathing in and breathing out. Her heart stabbed and her brain hurt at the prospect of leaving the priest. She felt a great dullness, an iron heaviness settle into her limbs, and she decided she would remain still forever. So she sat in the sigh of slough grass, the resonance of searching owls. And then there was a curious pull. Was it the moon, or were the lines not really cut, but invisible? Was she still attached? Tugged behind as the Pillager walked? A thrill of anxiety gripped her, an anger to be with him, suddenly, coupled with despair at leaving the priest. Fear leaped in her and then a sensation of painful joy.

Mary Kashpaw jumped out of her cradling sleigh, took her bearings, and loped after Awun. She chased him down, came at him from behind in the dim moon's surcease. He turned around in a weak wonder and she pushed at him like a boy in play. He pushed her back. She pushed him again, but this time the push was in quality slightly different, a leading give to her arms, perhaps on the far edge of barely coy. Awun took her broad shoulders under his broad hands, and then the two peered into each other's steady eyes. Found there a mutual wariness, a nervous calm.

The ease of two equally matched beings came over them and they walked together into the night groaning, frog-quick dark. There, they began work on a tiny baby boy who would one day in their future drop from Mary's body like a plum, and she hold him, hardly knowing what he was, so infinitesimal and severe and demanding. She would care for him until he was taken from her and she went mad, or perhaps she went mad and he was taken from her because of it. Who knows, who can set this straight? The weaving of this great woman was so crooked to begin with that no one would wonder when, ten years later, brain shocked and bearing the nerve deadness of confinement, she came walking back from the disastrous marriage with empty arms to care, as she always had, for Father Damien.

18

Le Mooz

or

The Last Year of Nanapush

1941–1942

By the time Nanapush and Margaret shacked up for good in the deep bush, they had lived so hard and long it seemed they must be ready for quiet. Over the years, they'd starved and grieved, seen prodigious loss, endured theft by the agents of the government and chimookomanag farmers as well as betrayal by their own people. They were tired for sure. At last, they should have courted simple comfort. A harmless mate. Companionship and sleep. But times did not go smoothly. Peace eluded them. For Nanapush and Margaret found a surprising heat in their hearts. Fierce and sudden, it sometimes eclipsed both age and anger with tenderness. Then, they made love with an amazed greed and purity that astounded them. At the same time, it was apt to burn out of control.

When this happened, they fought. Stinging flames of words blistered their tongues. Silence was worse. Beneath its slow-burning weight, their black looks singed. After a few days their minds shriveled into dead coals. Some speechless nights, they lay together like logs turned completely to ash. They were almost afraid to move, lest they sift into flakes and disintegrate. It was a young love set blazing in bodies aged and overused, and sometimes it cracked them like too much fire in an old tin stove.

To survive their marriage, they developed many strategies. For instance, they rarely collaborated on any task. Each hunted, trapped, and fished alone. They could not agree even on so little a thing as how and where to set a net. The gun, which belonged to Nanapush, was never clean when it was needed. Traps rusted. It was up to Margaret to scour the rifle barrel, smoke the steel jaws. Setting snares together was impossible, for in truth they snared themselves time and again in rude opinions and mockery over where a rabbit might jump or how to set the loop. Their avoidance hardened them in their individual ways, and so when Margaret beached the tough old boat and jumped ashore desperate for help, there was no chance of agreement.

Margaret sometimes added little Frenchisms to her Ojibwemowin just the way the fancy sounding wives of the French *voyageurs* added, like a dash of spice, random *le*'s and *la*'s. So when she jumped ashore screaming of *le mooz*, Nanapush woke, irritated, quick reproof on his lips, as he was always pleased to find some tiny fault with his beloved.

"*Le mooz! Le mooz!*" she shouted into his face. She grabbed him by the shirt so violently that he could hear the flimsy threads part.

"Boonishin!" He tried to struggle from her grip, but Margaret rapidly explained to him that she had seen a moose start off, swimming across the lake and here were their winter's provisions, easy! With this moose meat dried and stored, they would survive the clutch of starving windigoog in fine style. "Think of the stew! Get up, old man!" She screamed in fretful incoherence now, grabbed the gun, and dragged Nanapush to the boat, forcing him in before he even properly prepared himself mentally to hunt moose.

Nanapush pushed off with his paddle, sulking. Besides their natural inclination to disagree, it was always the case that if one of them was particularly intrigued and eager about some idea, the other was sure to feel the opposite way just to polarize the situation. Contradictions abounded between them. If Nanapush asked his wiiw for maple syrup with his meat, she gave him wild onion. If Margaret relished a certain color of cloth, Nanapush declared that he could not look upon that blue, or red—it made him mean and dizzy. When it came to sleeping on the fancy spring bed that Margaret had bought with this year's bark money, Nanapush adored the bounce and she was stingy with it so as not to use it up. Sometimes he sat on the bed and joggled up and down when she was gone, just to spite her. For her part, once her husband began craftily to ask for wild onion, she figured he'd developed a taste for it and so bargained for a small jar of maple syrup, thus beginning the obvious next stage of their contradictoriness, which was that each asked the opposite of what they really wanted and so got what they wanted. It was confusing to Father Damien, but to the two of them it brought serene harmony. So when Margaret displayed such extreme determination in the matter of the moose that morning, Nanapush was feeling particularly lazy, but he also decided to believe she really meant the opposite of what she cried out, and so he dawdled with his paddle and tried to tell her a joke or two. She was, however, in dead earnest.

"Paddle! Paddle for all you're worth!" she yelled.

"Break your backs, boys, or break wind!" Nanapush mocked her. Over the summer, as it wasn't the proper time for telling Ojibwe aadizokaanag, Father Damien and Nector had taken turns telling the tale of the vast infernal white fish and the maddened chief who gave chase all through the upper and lower regions of the earth.

"Gitimishk!" Margaret nearly choked in frustration, for the moose had changed direction and they were not closing in quickly enough for her liking.

"Aye, aye, Ahabikwe," shouted Nanapush, lighting his pipe as she vented her fury at him in deep strokes of her paddle. If the truth be told, he was delighted with her anger, for when she lost control like this during the day she often, also, lost control once the sun went down, and he was already anticipating their pleasure.

"Use that paddle or my legs are shut to you, lazy fool!" she growled.

At that, he went to work, and they quickly drew alongside the moose. Margaret steadied herself, threw a loop of strong rope around its wide, spreading antlers, and then secured the rope fast to the front of the boat, which was something of an odd canoe, having a flat, tough, wood bottom, a good ricing boat but not all that easy to steer.

"Now," she ordered Nanapush, "now, take up the gun and shoot! Shoot!"

But Nanapush did not. He had killed a moose that way once before in his life, and he had nothing to prove. On the other hand, his namesake, Nanabozho, had failed in the old moose-killing story, which began much in the same way as the event Nanapush found himself living out. He decided to tempt fate by tempting the story, for such was his arrogance that he was certain he could manage better than his namesake. He would not kill the moose quite yet. He hefted the gun and made certain it was loaded, and then enjoyed the free ride they were receiving from the hardworking moose.

"Let's turn him around, my adorable pigeon," he cried to his lady. "Let him tow us back home. I'll shoot him once he reaches the shallow water just before our cabin."

Margaret could not help but agree that this particular plan arrived at by her lazy husband was a good one, and so, by using more rope and hauling on first one antler and then another with all of their strength, they proceeded to turn their beast and head him in the right direction. Nanapush sat back smoking his pipe and relaxed once they were pointed homeward. The sun was out and the air was cool, fresh. All seemed right between the two of them now. Margaret admonished him about the tangle of fishing tackle all around his seat, and there was affection in her voice.

"You'll poke yourself," she said lovingly, "you fool." At that moment, the meat pulling them right up to their doorstep, she did not really even care to pursue her husband's idiocy. "I'll fry the rump steaks tonight with a little maple syrup over them," she said, her mouth watering. "Old man, you're gonna eat good! Oooh"—she almost cried with appreciation—"our moose is so fat!"

"He's a fine moose," Nanapush agreed passionately. "You've got an eye, Mindimooyenh. He's a juicy one, our moose!"

"I'll roast his ribs, cook the fat with our beans, and keep his brains in a bucket to tan that big hide! Oooh, ishte, my husband, the old men are going to envy the makazinan that I will sew for you."

"Beautiful wife!" Nanapush was overcome. "Precious sweetheart!"

They looked at each other with a kindling ardor.

As they were so gazing upon one another, holding the rare moment of mutual agreeableness, the hooves of the moose struck the first sandbar near shore, and Margaret cried out for her husband to lift the gun and shoot.

"Not quite yet, my beloved," said Nanapush confidently, "he can drag us nearer yet!"

"Watch out! Shoot now!"

The moose indeed approached the shallows, but Nanapush planned in his pride to shoot the animal just as he began to pull them from the water, thereby making their task of dressing and hauling mere child's play. He got the moose in his sights and then waited as the animal gained purchase. The old man's feet, annoyingly, tangled in the fishing tackle he had been too lazy to put away, and he jigged attempting to kick it aside.

"Margaret, duck!" he cried. Just as the moose lunged onto land he let blast, completely missing and totally terrifying the moose, which gave a hopping skip that seemed impossible for a thing so huge and veered straight up the bank. Margaret, reaching back to tear the gun from her husband's hands, was bucked completely out of the boat and said later that if only her stubborn no-good man hadn't insisted on holding on to the gun she could have landed, aimed, and killed them both, as she then wished to do most intensely. Instead, as the moose tore off with the boat still securely tied by three ropes to his antlers, she was left behind screaming for the fool to jump. But he did not and within moments, the rampaging moose, with the boat bounding behind, disappeared into the woods.

"My man is stubborn, anyway," she said, dusting off her skirt, checking to make sure that she was still together in a piece, nothing broken or cut. "He will surely kill that moose!" She spoke in wishful confidence, but inside she felt stuffed with a combination of such anxiety and rage that she did not know what to do—to try to rescue Nanapush or to chop him into pieces with the hatchet that she found herself sharpening as she listened for the second report of his gun.

Bloof!

Yes. There it was. Good thing he didn't jump out, she muttered. She began to tramp, with her carrying straps and an extra sharp knife, in the direction of the noise.

In fact, that Nanapush did not jump out was not due to his great stubbornness or bravery. When the moose jolted the boat up the lake shore, the tackle that already wound around his leg flew beneath his seat as he bounced upward and three of his finest fishing hooks stuck deep into his buttocks as he landed, fastening him tight. He screeched in pain, further horrifying the animal, and struggled, driving the hooks in still deeper, until he could only hold on to the edge of the boat with one hand, gasping in agony, as with the other he attempted to raise the gun to his shoulder and kill the moose.

All the time, of course, the moose was wildly running. Pursued by this strange, heavy, screeching, banging, booming thing, it fled in dull terror through bush and slough. It ran and continued to run. Those who saw Nanapush, as he passed all up and down the reservation, stood a moment in fascinated shock and rubbed their eyes, then went to fetch others, so that soon the predicament of Nanapush was known and reported everywhere. By then, the moose had attained a smooth loping trot, however, and passed with swift ease through farmsteads and pastures, the boat flying up and then disappearing down behind. Many stopped what they were doing to gape and yell.

Mr. Onesides saw it and said that his attention was attracted by a blast from the gun of Nanapush and that he saw the moose stop still in its tracks a moment, as though struck by a sudden thought. As there was nothing to aim at for Nanapush but the rump of the huge animal, he had indeed stung its hindquarters. But other than providing it an unpleasant sensation, all Nanapush succeeded in doing was further convincing the moose that he'd best flee, which he did suddenly, so that the boat jumped high in the air and cracked down as the moose sped forward, again, raising a groan from Nanapush that Onesides would always remember for the flat depth of its despair. Still, although he ran for his rifle, he was too late to shoot the moose and free poor Nanapush.

One day passed. In his moose-drawn fishing boat, Nanapush toured every part of the reservation that he'd ever hunted, and saw everyone he'd ever known, and then went to places he hadn't visited since childhood. At one point, a family digging cattail roots were stunned to see the boat, the moose towing it across a smaller slough, and a man slumped over inside, for by now poor Nanapush had given up and surrendered to the pain which, at least, he said later, he shared with his beast of the shot rump. He'd already tried to leave the best part of his butt on the canoe bench, but no matter how he tried he couldn't tear himself free, so he had given up and went to sleep as he always did in times of stress, hoping that he'd wake up with an idea of how to end his tortured ride.

He did have a notion. He lifted the gun and this time tried to shoot the rope, which, being a target nowhere near the size of the moose's great hairy, heaving cheeks, he missed, again stinging the moose who, as he told it later, soon commenced shooting back at him, the moose pellets zinging to the right and left as the moose began again to run, heading now for the very most remote parts of the reservation, where poor Nanapush was convinced he surely would die. He began to talk to the moose as they strode along—the words jounced out of him.

"Niiji!" he cried, "my brother, slow down!"

The animal flicked back an ear to catch the sound of the thing's voice, but kept on covering ground.

"I will kill no more!" declared Nanapush. "I now throw away my gun!" And he cast it aside after kissing the barrel and noting well his surroundings. As though it sensed and felt only contempt for the man's hypocrisy, the moose snorted and kept moving.

"I apologize to you," cried Nanapush, "and to all of the moose I ever killed and to the spirit of the moose and the boss of the moose and to every moose that has lived or will ever live in the future."

As though slightly placated, now, the moose slowed to a walk and Nanapush was able, finally, to snatch a few berries from the bushes they passed, to scoop up a mouthful of water from the slough, and to sleep, though by moonlight the moose still browsed and walked, toward some goal, thought Nanapush, delirious with exhaustion and pain, perhaps the next world. Perhaps this moose was sent by the all-clever creator to fetch Nanapush along to the spirit life in this novel way. Just as he was imagining such a thing, the first light showed and by that ever strengthening radiance he saw that his moose indeed had a direction and intention and that object was a female moose of an uncommonly robust size, just ahead, peering over her shoulder in a way apparently bewitching to male moose, for Nanapush's animal uttered a squeal of bullish intensity that was recognizable to Nanapush as pure lust.

Nanapush now wished he had aimed for the huge swinging balls of the moose and he wept with exasperation.

"Should I be subjected to this? This too? In addition to all that I have suffered?" And Nanapush cursed the moose, cursed himself, cursed the fishhooks, cursed the person who so carefully and sturdily constructed the boat that would not fall apart, and as he cursed he spoke in English, as there are no true swear words in Ojibwemowin, and so it was Nanapush and not the devil whom Zozed Bizhieu heard passing by her remote cabin at first light, shouting all manner of unspeakable and innovative imprecations, and it was Nanapush, furthermore, who was heard howling in the deep slough grass, howling though more dead at this point than alive, at the outrageous acts he was forced to witness there, before his nose, as the boat tipped up and his bull moose in the extremity of his passion loved the female moose with ponderous mountings and thrilling thrusts that swung Nanapush from side to side but did not succeed in dislodging him from the terrible grip of the fishhooks. No, that was not to happen. Nanapush was bound to suffer for one more day before the satisfied moose toppled over to snore and members of the rescue party Margaret had raised crept up and shot the animal stone dead in its sleep.

The moose, Margaret found, for she had followed with her meat hatchet, had lost a distressing amount of fat and its meat was now stringy from the long flight and sour with a combination of fear and spent sex, so that in butchering it she winced and moaned, traveled far in her raging thoughts, imagined sore revenges she would exact upon her husband.

In the meantime, Father Damien, who had followed his friend as best he could in the parish touring car, was able to assist those who emerged from the bush. He drove Nanapush, raving, to Sister Hildegarde who was adept at extracting fishhooks. At the school infirmary, Sister Hildegarde was not upset to see the bare buttocks of Nanapush sticking straight up in the air. She swabbed the area with iodine and tested the strength of her pliers. With great relief for his friend and a certain amount of pity, Father Damien tried to make him smile. "Don't be ashamed of your display. Even the Virgin Mary had two asses, one to sit upon and the other ass that bore her to Egypt."

Nanapush only nodded gloomily and gritted his teeth as Sister Hildegarde pushed the hook with the pliers until the barbed tip broke through his tough skin, then clipped the barb off and pulled out the rest of the hook.

"Is there any chance," he weakly croaked once the operation was accomplished, "that this will affect my manhood?"

"Unfortunately not," said Hildegarde.

The lovemaking skills of Nanapush, whole or damaged, were to remain untested until after his death. For Margaret took a long time punishing her husband. She ignored him, she browbeat him, but worst of all, she cooked for him.

It was the winter of instructional beans, for every time Margaret boiled up a pot of rock-hard pellets drawn from the fifty-pound sack of beans that were their only sustenance beside the sour strings of meat, she reminded Nanapush of each brainless turning point last fall at which he should have killed the moose but did not.

"And my," she sneered then, "wasn't its meat both tender and sweet before you ran it to rags?"

She never boiled the beans quite soft enough, either, for she could will her own body to process the toughest sinew with no trouble. Nanapush, however, suffered digestive torments of a nature that soon became destructive to his health and ruined their nightly rest entirely, for that was when the great explosive winds would gather in his body. His boogidiwinan, which had always been manly, but yet meek enough to remain under his control, overwhelmed the power of his ojiid, and there was nothing he could do but surrender to their whims and force. At least it was a form of revenge on Margaret, he thought, exhausted, near dawn. But at the same time, he worried that she would leave him. Already, she made him sleep on a pile of skins near the door so as not to pollute her flowered mattress.

"My precious one," he sometimes begged, "can you not spare me? Boil the beans a while longer, and the moose, as well. Have pity!"

She only raised her brow and her glare was a slice of knifelike light. Maybe she was angriest because she'd softened toward him during that moose ride across the lake, and now she was determined to punish him for her uncharacteristic lapse into tenderness. At any rate, one night she boiled the beans only long enough to soften their skins and threw in a chunk of moose that was coated with a green mold she claimed was medicinal, but which tied poor Nanapush's guts in knots.

"Eat up, old man." She banged the plate down before him. He saw she was implacable, and then he thought back to the way he had got around the impasse of the maple syrup before, and resolved to do exactly the opposite of what he felt. And so, resigned to sacrifice this night to pain, desperate, he proceeded to loudly enjoy the beans.

"They are excellent, niwiiw, crunchy and fine! Minopogwud!" He wolfed them down, eager as a boy, and tore at the moldy moose as though presented with the finest morsels. "Howah! I've never eaten such a fine dish!" He rubbed his belly and smiled in false satisfaction. "Nindebisinii, my pretty fawn, oh, how well I'll sleep." He rolled up in his blankets by the door, then, and waited for the gas pains to tear him apart.

They did come. That night was phenomenal. Margaret was sure that the cans of grease rattled on the windowsill, and she saw a glowing stench rise around her husband but chose to plug her ears with wax and turn to the wall, poking an airhole for herself in the mud between the logs, and so she fell asleep not knowing that the symphony of sounds that disarranged papers and blew out the door by morning were her husband's last utterances.

Yes, he was dead. She found when she went to shake him awake the next morning that he was utterly lifeless. She gave a shriek then, of abysmal loss, and began to weep with sudden horror at the depth of her unforgiving nature. She kissed his face all over, patted his hands and hair. He did not look as though death had taken him, no, he looked oddly well. Although it would seem that a death of this sort would shrivel him like a spent sack and leave him wrinkled and limp, he was shut tight and swollen, his mouth a firm line and his eyes squeezed shut as though holding something in. And he was stiff as a horn where she used to love him. There was some mistake! Perhaps, thought Margaret, wild in her grief, he was only deeply asleep and she could love him back awake.

She climbed aboard and commenced to ride him until she herself collapsed, exhausted and weeping, on his still breast. It was no use. His manliness still stood straight up and although she could swear the grim smile had deepened on his face, there were no other signs of life—no breath, not the faintest heartbeat could be detected. Margaret fell beside him, senseless, and was found there disheveled and out cold, so that at first Father Damien thought the two had committed a double suicide, as some old people did those hard winters. But Margaret was soon roused. The cabin was aired out. Father Damien, ravaged with the loss, held his old friend Nanapush's hand all day and allowed his own tears to flow, soaking his black gown.

And so it was. The wake and the funeral were conducted in the old way. Margaret prepared his body. She cleaned him, wrapped him in her best quilt. As there was no disguising his bone-tough shkendeban, she let it stand there proudly and she decided not to be ashamed of her old man's prowess. She laid him on the bed that was her pride, and bitterly regretted how she'd forced him to sleep on the floor in the cold wind by the door.

Everyone showed up that night, bringing food and even a bit of wine, but Margaret wanted nothing of their comfort. Sorrow bit deep into her lungs and the pain radiated out like the shooting rays of a star. She lost her breath. A dizzy veil fell over her. She wanted most of all to express to her husband the terrible depth of the love she felt but had been too stubborn, too stingy, or, she now saw, afraid to show him while he lived. She had deprived him of such pleasure: that great horn in his pants, she knew guiltily, was there because she had denied him physical satisfaction ever since the boat ride behind the moose.

"Nimanendam. If only he'd come back to me, I'd make him a happy man." She blew her nose on a big white dishcloth and bowed her head. Whom would she scold? Whom would she punish? Whom deny? Who would suffer for Margaret Kashpaw now? What was she to do? She dropped her face into her hands and wept with uncharacteristic abandon. The whole crowd of Nanapush's friends and loved ones, packed into the house, lifted a toast to the old man and made a salute. At last, Father Damien spoke, and his speech was so eloquent and funny that in moments the whole room was bathed in tears and sobs.

It was at that moment, in the depth of their sorrow, just at the hour when they felt the loss of Nanapush most keenly, that a great explosion occurred, a rip of sound. A vicious cloud of stink sent mourners gasping for air. As soon as the fresh winter cold rolled into the house, however, everyone returned. Nanapush sat straight up, still wrapped in Margaret's best quilt.

"I just couldn't hold it in anymore," he said, embarrassed to find such an assembly of people around him. He proceeded, then, to drink a cup of the mourner's wine. He was unwrapped. He stretched his arms. The wine made him voluble.

"Friends," he said, "how it fills my heart to see you here. I did, indeed, visit the spirit world and there I greeted my old companion, Kashpaw. I saw my former wives, now married to other men. Quill was there, and is now beading me a pair of makazinan to wear when I travel there for good. Friends, do not fear. On the other side of life there is plenty of food and no government agents."

Nanapush then rose from the bed and walked among the people, tendering greetings and messages from their dead loved ones. At last, however, he came to Margaret, who sat in the corner frozen in shock at her husband's resurrection. "Oh, how I missed my old lady!" he cried and opened his arms to her. But just as she started forward, eager at his forgiveness and acceptance, he remembered the beans, dropped his arms, and stepped back.

"No matter how I love you," he then said, "I would rather go to the spirit world than stay here and eat your cooking!"

With that, he sank to the floor quite cold and lifeless again. He was carried to the bed and wrapped in the quilt once more, and his body was closely watched for signs of revival. Nobody yet quite believed that he was gone and it took some time—in fact, they feasted far into the night—before everyone, including poor Margaret, addled now with additional rage and shame, felt certain he was gone. Of course, just as everyone accepted the reality of his demise, Nanapush again jerked upright and his eyes flipped open.

"Oh yai!" exclaimed one of the old ladies, "he lives yet!"

And although the mourners well hid their irritation, it was inevitable that there were some who were impatient. "If you're dead, stay dead," someone muttered. Nobody was so heartless as to express this feeling straight out. There was just a slow but certain drifting away of people from the house and it wasn't long, indeed, before even Father Damien left. He was thrilled to have his old friend back, but in his tactful way intuited that Margaret and Nanapush had much to mend between them and needed to be alone to do it.

Once everyone was gone, Nanapush went over to the door and put the bar down. Then he turned to his wife and spoke before she could say a word.

"I returned for one reason only, my wife. When I was gone and far away, I felt how you tried to revive me with the heat of your body. I was happy you tried to do that, my heart was full. This time when I left with harsh words on my lips about your cooking, I got a ways down the road leading to the spirit world, and I just couldn't go any farther, my dear woman, because I wronged you. I wanted to make things smooth between us. I came back to love you good."

And with that, between the confusion and grief, the exhaustion and bewilderment, Margaret hadn't the wit to do anything but go to her husband and allow all of the hidden sweetness of her nature to join the fire he kindled, so that they spent, together, in her spring bed, the finest and most elegantly accomplished hours that perhaps lovers ever spent on earth. And when it was over they both fell asleep, and although only Margaret woke up, her heart was at peace.

Margaret would not have Nanapush buried in the ground, but high in a tree, the old way, as Anishinaabeg did before the priests came. A year later, his bones and the tattered quilt were put into a box and set under a grave house just at the edge of her yard. The grave house was well built, carefully painted a spanking white, and had a small window with a shelf where Margaret always left food. Sometimes, she left Nanapush a plate of ill-cooked beans because she missed his complaints, but more often she cooked his favorites, seasoned his meat with maple syrup, pampered and pitied him the way she hadn't dared when he was alive, for fear he'd get the better of her, though she wondered why that ever mattered, now, without him, in the simple quiet of her endless life.

19

THE WATER JAR

1962

Mid-July and a windless morning. After the day began, dust would lift and hang solid in flat ribbons along the reservation boundaries, but for now the dew held down the surface of the roads. For the ladies, who had risen early, who now stood behind the long plate-glass windows of the Senior Citizens' lounge, the air was clear enough for them to see that, for the third morning in a row, the man had come through the night and was still sitting in his car.

It was a dull green two-door Chevrolet, the kind of car that escaped most attention, but the man inside it, usually obscured by blowing dirt, could be seen clearly at this hour. Even from the shoulders up, his good looks were obvious. His face was bold and strong featured. His thick gray hair was trained to sweep back over the ears. He looked well dressed, but not until some hours later would the full effect of his dark and well-cut suit be shown. He sweltered and sweat in it all that time. The heat descended and the air was thick and punishing by noon. Breezes too faint to stir the heavy brown drapes hung by the government's contractor occasionally filtered through the screens below the glass. Men with bad knees or weak lungs joined the ladies who might, in their privacy, have worn nothing but their baggy nylon slips. By now, the dozen or so who sat and watched had little left to say that was original. The man was simply there.

In two days no one had seen him leave the car, take a drink of anything, or eat a bite of food. He never dozed or relieved himself, by daylight anyhow. He was so silent that a bird flew in the window, hopped around and flew back out. He was so handsome that Mrs. Bluelegs looked his picture up in her collection of star magazines. He wasn't anyone. The good looks were a distant impression, too. Up close, the tribal police said, he was surprisingly old. They stopped twice on their rounds to make sure he wasn't dead and examine his license.

Father Gregory Wekkle. Eyes brn. Hair brn. Height 6'3". Indianapolis address. There was nothing out of order. Everything was up to date. He was not possessed of liquor or narcotics. He wasn't wanted for any crime. When they asked what he was doing, he asked if there was any law against a guy sitting in his car. He kept his eyes on the convent, the church, but did not seem interested in those who came and went.

Someone thought it might be best to tell the sisters up the hill. However, when it came right down to it, no one wanted to interfere.

He wasn't blocking any traffic. He wasn't in people's way. He wasn't anybody's business, and so they let him be. As the day went on and he sat without moving, he drew escalating interest from the young who roared past, raising dust, then stopped just to watch it settle on his windshield. Thicker by the hour, that dust coated the fenders and hood, his hair and the one arm crooked half out the window, thicker, heavier, until he was obscured, almost part of the landscape, and it was a shock that caused the men to crane forward and the women, finally, to open the door and file onto the sidewalk and shield their eyes against the sun when upon that third day the car's engine roared into gear.

It was as if the road itself had moved. The ladies behind the window, deaf to the engine's catch, pointed to the car bucking into first gear and chugging up the remainder of the hill.

From there the story came down.

Sister Mary Martin was the one who told what happened after he had parked at the convent, got out, and walked up to the door.

When he disappeared into the entry, the women outside the Senior Citizens dropped their hands from their eyes and retreated. There was nothing to see from all that distance. According to Sister Mary Martin, the man knocked on the door and she opened it wide. By then, his hair was the tan of the air and his face and clothes were drifted with the road's same powder. He would not come in, but he would be very much obliged for some water. His voice was hoarse, his look was patient. Sister Mary Martin left him standing, went back into her kitchen, found a clean mayonnaise container, and filled it from the tap. She brought this back down the hall. The man was standing just inside the door. In exchange for the jar of water, he gave Mary Martin the contents of his pockets. Then he removed the cover of the jar, allowed himself one careful swallow, and sealed it again.

"You don't look well," said Mary Martin. "Please come, sit down."

His skin was dead-white, gray around the deep-set eyes, his lips were baked and cracked. His hands shook so badly that the water in the jar rippled.

"No, thank you," he said, backing to the door.

He pushed out into the yard with his shoulder and Mary Martin grasped his elbow and helped him to balance. The wind had risen. His hair, caked with a clay of sweat, dust, and oil, remained secure and stationary, but his dark suit flapped.

The man pointed at the low rebuilt cabin where Father Damien lived, and asked if he lived there still. When Mary Martin said yes, but that just at present he was hearing confessions, the man started off eagerly, striding in a rapid uncontrolled stagger. She stared after him in amazed concern and didn't think to look into her hand until he had passed beneath her gaze. Not until she turned to enter the convent did she open her fingers. Then she found that she held a piece of paper money folded into a tiny square, a quarter, a penny, a sodality club button, and two car keys on a small aluminum ring.

FORGIVENESS

Even though a younger priest lived in a brand-new rectory and said the Mass every day and shared the confessional, most who practiced faithfully preferred to visit Father Damien. Something in the quality of his forgiveness really made people feel better—his human sympathy, or his divinely chosen penances. He was in demand. Therefore, Father Damien studiously kept confessional hours.

Father Damien rubbed his stiff knees until they loosened, slid to the side of the bed, climbed out, then with a careful bow entered the cassock he'd hung as always on his bedroom door. Clothed, Father Damien peered around the door, looked to both sides. He'd been ill lately and the nuns were infinitely solicitous, loving, a nuisance. He stepped out and then sped straight to the back of the church and sidled through the entry, from there to the cabinet, where he kissed his stole as he donned it. He sneaked along the wall. Panting, he fell into the priest's box of the confessional. His head spun a bit. He took deep breaths and counted them waiting for his first customer.

A slight rustle, and Father Damien opened the screened shutter. The voice, a low rasp, was familiar. Yet this was not one of his regulars or even, as far as he could ascertain, a parishioner. He strained to understand the heavy clunk of words. Low distress in the breathing. There was a long, then longer pause after the preliminaries.

"Are you still there?" said Damien at last. His voice was gentle, for it seemed very possible that this was a sinner who had borne his guilt for years, until it ate away his resolve, at which point the poor sinner finally, belatedly, had come in to be forgiven. Damien took pity on such people. Their sins weren't usually even terrible—just the worst in their own minds. Infidelities, usually, or shameful little thefts.

"Go ahead," urged Damien, compassion flooding him, "you will be forgiven."

"I . . ." said the petitioner, "I . . ." The man could not continue.

"Do not be afraid," said Damien, but the sinner lapsed again into a miserable quiet.

"I will wait with you," said Damien, tenderly. "I will sit with you here until you have the courage to speak."

"I am . . ." Again, the sinner could not complete the sentence, but then he didn't have to because Agnes knew. Sudden ice. Frozen, breathless, Agnes sat motionless and then she panicked. Threw her trembling hands up to her face.

"Oh God, forgive me," she prayed silently, her heart in her throat. "This man I cannot absolve!"

GREGORY

As they regarded each other across the uncertain band of dim space just outside the confessional, a thrill of self-consciousness washed over Agnes. Father Damien was not beautiful. Agnes wanted to touch back her hair and bite her lips. The mere thought of such gestures made her cheeks flame red. Then she wanted Father Wekkle to leave, immediately, to leave her to the simple contentment she'd nurtured to replace the great drama of human love. Get out of here! Get thee behind me! she wanted to yell at him. The urge passed and she only blinked hard at the apparition. Her vision cleared and she saw that he was ill.

Not just poorly, but seriously ill. His racked, dry body told her this as soon as she was a foot away from him. As she walked him to the cabin, she noticed the dazed and careful way he stepped, like one uncertain of his tenure on the earth. She ducked her head and let him into her house. When she closed the door, and they were inches apart, pausing before they crushed together and there was no space between them, she was positive that he was dying.

Father Gregory Wekkle had continued, by slow means and over many years, to outrage his liver with hard drink, and now the cancer accomplished what he had begun. He was in a silent period of remission, he knew it, and while he had the strength he had driven straight from Indiana intending to throw himself at Agnes's feet, but he had stopped midway up the final hill and sat there on the side of the road, sat there not quite knowing why. Afraid of many things—perhaps Father Damien was dead, or if he lived, perhaps his side of the cabin was occupied, perhaps books had filled the space, perhaps a dozen or two dozen outcomes were possible, but only one was capable of causing that dusty paralysis. Driving onto the reservation, Gregory Wekkle was struck by the recognizable ordinariness of all he saw, which caused him suddenly to fear that all he'd felt in his youth for Agnes, and all that he had suffered since, was an illusion.

For two days, he took stock of his memories and questioned the reality of each touch, each act, each recognition on his part and on hers. Finally knowing that there was no way for certain to understand what she felt, but positive he had felt what he did, and moreover, sick with thirst, he moved.

"So here I am."

He sat in the ruins of a chair he remembered, and he allowed a sudden weakness to drain him and to ice his blood. He shivered in the awful heat and Agnes brought a blanket. Practice had perfected her masculine ease, and age had thickened her neck and waist so that the ambiguity which had once eroticized her now was a single and purposeful power that, heaven help him, he found more thrilling. She sat before him and held his hand, just as both of them had done with so many of their own ill, and merely waited.

"Is it too much to ask?" he drank in the new version of her face the way he'd drunk to forget it, with a voracious calm.

It was too much, truly, but she couldn't say it. Agnes put her hands out and bent slowly until her forehead touched his knee. She sighed and rested it there. Holding on to his knee like a rock, she breathed in the dust he brought while he stroked her short, man's hair. In the dark beneath his hands, in the dark of her mind, while she simply breathed and existed, she absently put out her tongue. She tasted the cloth of his pants. Tasted grit in the weave. Tasted his medicinal sweat. Tasted soap and the burnt, tarry odor of his death, and her own death, and at last the cavernous sweetness of their old lust.

Over the years, the log walls of Father Damien's cabin had been plastered over, then Sheetrocked and Sheetrocked again, wallpapered, rewallpapered, painted and painted over, then bookshelved, so that the little house was now thickly insulated as a bear's den. It was painted white on the inside, but contained a sweeping array of intensely colored beadwork and Ojibwe paintings. A gorgeous dress of white buckskin, fringed and set with blue-and-gold designs, hung off a hook in the wall, next to a cradle board decorated with tiny miigis shells, dreamcatchers, cutouts made of birch bark. The low tables were covered with quilled baskets and rattles, and set around with stacks of books. The shelved walls were darkened with lettered book covers and spines. The books were neatly shelved by category and then alphabetized all through the house, even in the kitchen.

From the first, Father Wekkle was comforted by the order. He weakened quickly—the trip seemed to have exhausted his temporary gift of strength, and it was clear that his remission was only a short touch of grace. For weeks, to begin with, they talked long into the night and there were even—tremendously secret, shrouded, final—nights they entered the exquisite and boundless quietude of the body. And then those nights stopped. He relapsed into the illness, and spent his days on the fold-out couch, watching birds at a feeder through a large plate-glass window cut into a small addition. From the window, he could see a bright wedge of sky and several branches of the tall pines and thicker oaks that had been striplings when he first knew Agnes.

He prayed, as he gazed into the soft wash of needles, to Saint Joseph, the keeper of the happy death. More than anything now, Father Wekkle hoped for a serene deliverance. He prayed to die before the window, in the night, peacefully and with no trouble to Agnes. But of course that did not happen.

In she came, striding big, with a tray of food. She set it down beside the couch on a little table and uncovered the simple dinner—mashed potatoes, beans, chicken, an oatmeal cookie. He regarded it dubiously, but when he ate some of it he felt better. The sky was darkening, the sun was a deep gold haze in the pines. The diffused radiance lighted the sides of trees and when the small birds popped from the bird feeders the undersides of their wings flashed red. Fire tipped the needles and then slowly bled to purple.

"Gregory," she shook him slightly, "do you want to sleep here or walk to the bed?"

Agnes's face glowed a deep sere on one side, and Gregory reached out to touch it. She put her hand over his hand, and held it there without smiling, looking into his eyes.

"I think I'll stay right here," he gently said. "For now."

Until the air was entirely pitch-black, she sat next to the couch, on a chair. Later on, in the music of cicadas and crickets, she took a short walk around the grounds of the church, to calm herself and to release the strange collection of feelings—some noble, she supposed, some unworthy—that his presence engendered. It made her uneasy to have him here, an embarrassing outcome after all she'd wished and felt! And the difficulty wasn't even the disease or his dying, or the years they had not been together, and how much of each other's lives they'd missed. The difficulty was that Father Wekkle subtly condescended to her. He was unaware of it, but in all worldly situations, where they stood side by side, he treated her as somehow less. She couldn't enunciate the facts of it, but of what she experienced she had no doubt. She wondered, Had he patronized her way back then? Had she noticed? Or had he learned this? Did she patronize women too, now that she'd made herself so thoroughly into a priest? It was never anything that others might note, but when they were together, he spoke first, took charge even when he felt most ill, took information from doctors regarding his disease and translated it for her into terms, simpler, he thought she would understand.

And there was another thing: that tone in his voice when they were alone. An indulgent tone, frankly anticipating some lesser capacity in her—whether intellectual, moral, or spiritual, she could not say. The most difficult thing was, however, something that was really not his fault. Again, when they were alone, he called her Agnes. But for so long now she had been the only one who called herself Agnes, that for him to say it made her anxious, as though he'd stripped out and revealed something much more private than that part of her anatomy but having to do with some irreducible part of herself that only she was meant to possess. That Agnes. Agate. That stone made translucent by pressure. That was absolutely hers.

Out of the mystery of one dark pine tree, an owl called as she walked along. Nimishoomis, she said, grandfather. Sometimes owls came near to warn of death. Sometimes they just asked people to be careful. Sometimes they were just owls. Agnes hooted back, giving a sleepy, hollow call. There was a pause, and then with some interest the owl answered, and again Agnes asked the question, and the owl did too, and for a while they asked together into the black night. That was what it was, she thought now, to love someone else's body in the darkness. It was to ask that same question, while knowing that the answer would not be given. The owl flew down to look at her, launching on wings feathered so softly that its flight was soundless, ghostly. It came so close she felt the wind of its movement along her neck.

There was a park near the hospital in Fargo, and after Gregory died, Agnes went there. The grass was studded with acorns and fat squirrels busied themselves in the wealth. Mothers walked by with strollers and carriages, dressed in pink, aqua, lime. There was a wading pool at some short distance, and from the bench where Agnes sat, she could hear the faint splashes and cries of children and the hysterical notes of gathered crows. The air moved over her quietly, with a city exhaustion, like a half-spent breath. Agnes really didn't know how to feel at all—she wasn't devastated or even terribly sad. Those feelings were for when Gregory had wrestled with pain, struggled to get free from it, to throw it off. Now that he had, there was a lightness, a numb pleasantness, a newness, to everything she did. It was while she examined this curious state of mind that a figure, approaching from across the coarse green blanket of grass, caught her eye.

A huddled shape, it lurched forward then slowly tottered back, then threw itself forward again just a pittance, as though it were fighting a great wind. As it got closer, she could see that the person was dressed fantastically in a church-basement assortment of sagging clothing, a vibrant dress over men's plaid pants, a filmy blouse of fairy-pale floating polyester, a green man's hat, and thick unmatched shoes. An old Indian woman. Hunched, drunk, half collapsed. The woman stumbled closer and peered at Father Damien, then put her hand out and asked for change. Her voice was ragged and her cheeks sunken. She had lost all of her visible teeth but the two sharp incisors, and her eyes were covered with a dull, scratched film, but Agnes recognized her and rose, now taller than the stooped old lady, and took the gnarled claws of her hands in hers.

"Mashkiigikwe!"

The woman reeled back a bit, suspicious, at the sound of her own name, and snatched away her arthritic paws.

"It's me. Father Damien."

"Could you help me out with some pocket money?"

"Mashkiigikwe," Damien tried again.

"What are you calling me by the old name for?" said the old woman in English. "Left that one years ago. Do you have money?"

"I am the priest from Little No Horse. Father Damien. Don't you remember me?"

Shaking her head, ruffling her fantastic costume, Mashkiigikwe started away from the priest, mumbling half under her breath, throwing her arms out in erratic little gestures.

"How did you get here? Where are your children? What's your name now?" Damien tried again, following her along just a few steps. The woman laughed, suddenly lucid.

"Winos don't have names, priest. Go back and save the others like you saved me."

Then she let her lip drop and shambled off with surprising speed. Agnes sat back down on the park bench and looked at the shined black tops of her shoes. When she closed her eyes, the color of emptiness assailed her. She gazed deeper into the color of that absence and slowly, for the first time in many years, remembering those first years and Kashpaw, the round children and that woman's strength and skill, Agnes felt tears gather behind her eyelids. Soon they would spill over, drag slowly down her cheeks. These tears horrified her, suddenly. They were tears of self-pity for the seeming waste of her own life, her own efforts.

With that thought her eyes dried and she jumped up, heart pounding, wrenched into a sudden fury. She spotted the bright dot of Mashkiigikwe, now far off, opportuning someone else, and with a swift jog Agnes powered herself down the sidewalk until she drew up behind Mashkiigikwe. She grasped the old woman's shoulder and swiveled her roughly so they stood face-to-face.

"Here," Father Damien said angrily, pulling what dollars and quarters he had from inside pockets, smashing them into the old, brown hands. "Here and here. Take this! Ando miniquen! I didn't put the bottle in your mouth! I didn't make you suck the sauce!"

The old woman's mouth had dropped wide open in astonishment, but now she closed it to a firm line and her eyes flickered. Her face unblurred and just for a moment her features composed into the real face of Mashkiigikwe, aware, intelligent, bewildered to find herself in hell.

"Who did it then?" she asked the priest. "How did it happen? For I don't like to be this way, and yet, Father Damien, I am."

20

A NIGHT VISITATION

1996

Now she was old, truly old, of an age she'd never imagined. Her skin was waxen and her brain flickered, dropped things, seized others. Still, she possessed a startling vigor. There were days she did her stretches and arm whirls and went out walking and nothing hurt— not the hip gouged by the bullet so long ago, not even her toughened beanbag of a heart. And she listened to confessions with more attention and stamina than she'd ever possessed.

One such evening, walking out of the church, in the half darkness, Agnes was suddenly afflicted by an unbearable thirst. Instinctively, she bent to the font at the entrance and steadily as a parched horse pulled water from the surface into her dry throat. The blessed water was mineral stale and soothing, and she stood after a few moments, wiped her face, and went on, refreshed. Straight back to her dinner of ham and pickled beets, then an immediate swoon of profound, dreamless sleep.

Having drunk so deeply of the holy water, Agnes woke in the middle of the night. Two things were happening. She was in the throes of a sense of overwhelming blessedness—from within. And also, she needed to relieve herself. She rolled over and swung her legs out over the cold floor. Gingerly, she touched down. Stood. She walked through the dark hallway to the bathroom, and then, returning to her bed where she planned to lie still and enjoy the interesting inner effect of the blessed water, she was suddenly directed elsewhere. When, many years past, the church had acquired the loud organ with pipes running to the ceiling, the door of her cabin had been enlarged and the Steinway moved inside. She found herself standing before the instrument, serenely lustrous in the dark.

Sometimes, now, at this brittle age, she buried her hands in a cast-iron pot of wet, hot sand for ten or fifteen minutes before she played. Tonight, she had no chance to set up the hot sand, so her fingers twitched on the keys. Still, as Chopin had been kind to aging musicians and written some particularly easy preludes of great beauty, she played. The piece she loved best was meditative and slow, aching of the world's sorrows and fugitive joys. As she played, she gradually awakened. Her fingers loosened and forgot their age. She played on. Wondered. Had she the promise, could she exact one from the black dog's muzzle, if the thing should appear to her again, dare she ask: Was there a good piano in hell? The music soared, her hands curved around an intricate series of trills. If there were a good piano in hell, would she play this well once she got there? Her music, inaudible to all the sleeping reservation, spilled through the little house, uncurled beneath her hands like smoke. For an hour, two hours, almost three of her waning life, Agnes lived fully and intimately in a state of communion.

THE MIGHTY TEMPTER

Agnes felt it in her bones when the wind came up—a freedom in which she imagined, sleepless, springing from the narrow bed. She was sleeping very soundly, so heavily, in fact, that she lost track of the current of her life. Waking in the dark, she surprised herself. Old again! A priest! She did not move. She could not move. She wondered what had awakened her. Then she smelled under the fugitive breeze the low and maggot-quick, rich, warm, fish-gut breath of dog.

"Where are you? Show yourself!"

She tried to struggle up on one elbow, but a weight of air pinned her in the sheets. There was a panting and a lolling. A dogness surrounded her. The dog itself walked heavily up her legs and stood there in the dark, one paw on her heart and the other on the green scapular she wore under her nightshirt. Faintly, Agnes hoped. Might the scapular offer some protection? But her voice box rusted shut and bitter anxiety zipped down her windpipe.

"Get off!" She tried to say it, willed it. The visitor slouched massive on her chest, and then it spoke in a cloud of foul whispers.

"*Wie geht's?* How's my little priestette?"

Dug scraggly claws into Agnes's frail skin and settled full length. Stretched its legs along hers. She sensed fleas shooting off her nemesis like popcorn. Felt the soft plop of the dog's heavy balls between her knees.

"Open that black door in your chest," rasped the dog, "I'm hungry."

"Never!" Agnes's brain squeaked.

"Oh," the dog whined, "for a taste of nice fresh heart!"

A racking dryness. A hacking, lung-wrenching cough sent needle-fine pains shooting through her lungs, warning her not to move a muscle, a hair. The pinching pains radiated from each breath, from her center, like pulses of the sharp light depicted in paintings of the sacred heart. Now, at last, Agnes was horridly awake; her mouth went sandpaper dry and her esophagus shut.

"Talk to me," said the dog, and its voice was insufferably gentle.

Agnes gritted her teeth against the longing, sharp and sudden, for she knew that her only refuge lay in categorically not giving in to the false compassion in the dog's tone.

"Get thee behind me," she managed to croak. "I'm not ready to go."

"Still, I will take good care of you." The dog settled its lanky, bony haunches. "I am very loyal."

"You want me to die."

"You are tired, and you want to die, too."

"I don't know anymore," said Agnes, wearily. "Is there a good piano in hell?"

"The devil owns all of the finest makers of musical instruments," the dog said. "That darkness, that blood of sorrow in the most expressive woods, where do you think that comes from?"

"Suffering," said Agnes.

"Causing it," said the dog.

"I want an angel, a real dog, a good dog! I'd like to have a dog to protect me," Agnes blurted out.

"I will not let her, it, whatever, live," said the black dog. "Just as I can kill every person you love, I will kill whatever dog you love."

Agnes's heart thudded to the very end of her gut and she pleaded.

"Leave me."

"I can't," said the dog, wheezing with a sly and malevolent sympathy. "I am yours, and don't think I enjoy my work! Watching over you has been infuriating, though it had its moments. I did enjoy tickling Berndt with those bullets, and Gregory with the black knives of cancer. Recall when you made love how dutifully their hearts beat under your hand—how steady and warm? I stopped them. I shut their dear eyes . . ."

Agnes started to tremble.

". . . just as I shut the black eyes of Napoleon via the rosary in the hands, the very hands of the nun . . . how could you forgive those two, and others, the worst of sinners? Your forgiveness has opened many a door to me, old friend."

It was then that Agnes was assured that her Father Damien had done the right thing in absolving all who asked forgiveness, and the realization filled her with a sudden and bouyant strength. Here it was—the reason she'd been called here in the first place. The reason she'd endured and the reason she'd been searching for. This was why she continued to live. She shut the dog out and drew strength from the massive amounts of forgiveness her priest had dispensed in his life. She saw that forgiveness as a long, slow, soaking rain he had caused to fall on the dry hearts of sinners. Father Damien had forgiven everyone, right and left, of all mistakes and shameful sins. All except for Nanapush, who had never really confessed to any sin, but had instead forgiven Damien with great kindness for wronging him and

all of the people he had wanted to help, forgiven him for stealing so
many souls. Nanapush!

"You were not able to silence Nanapush!" laughed Agnes. "He
sneaked past your two-way road onto the road of life. He's probably
gambling day and night, eating berries without getting the shits,
telling stories with old friends and enjoying his many wives. You had
no power over Nanapush!"

There was a pause before the dog responded.

"Who could silence that talker?" But then a slinking insinuation.
"So you did love him. Yes, I knew it. Oh, you little priestette, you
loved him, you lusted after him, you kept this secret from me, didn't
you? Yes, but now I have it. I have your memory."

"No, you do not!" Though weakening, Agnes was indignant. "You
will never have my memory. Even I don't have it all, you rotten
hound. You stole it in the form of the Actor and in the person of the
gun. You took my memory, and I have spent my whole life gathering
it back."

Agnes shut down, closed her eyes, imagined herself a bulwark, a
wall. "Of course I loved Nanapush," she went on, impatient. "The old
man was my teacher, my confidant, my priest's priest, my confessor,
my friend. Plus, he was funny and you don't get funny much in this
life. God, how we used to laugh! Even his funeral was hilarious—I
miss him. There is no one I want to visit except in the Ojibwe heaven,
and so at this late age I'm going to convert, stupid dog, and become at
long last the pagan that I always was at heart before I was Cecilia,
when I was just Agnes, until I was seduced and diverted by the music
of Chopin."

"That neurasthenic pierogi snarfer?"

The dog ranted—it had never liked the composer, it turned out it
was jealous—but Agnes didn't notice anymore. She fought. She gathered every memory and prayed starting from her center and radiating
outward. Called every ancestor, blood and adopted. The aadizokaanag, spirits. Bent her thoughts on Nanapush. Asked for the old
man's help. Filled herself with every good that had been done to her
and every caring act she'd known. Cried out for the young, strong
spirit of Mashkiigikwe. For Chopin. Sucked with thin threads of air
the ravishing stillness of the ghost note that lingers after each chord

of Chopin's three repudiated posthumous nocturnes. Went further, back into the folds of brain that hid and held in their recesses such memories as she had of her childhood, girlhood, lost messages. Gathered in her strongest molecules the urge to live and the strength to snap shut her knees, suddenly, clasp with viselike ardor and squeeze with Catholic ferocity the testicles of the black dog.

Death. That was its name. That's what she dealt with and she knew it, dreaded it, hated death's intimacy and the strange greed with which it pursued every living thing. Agnes screamed, bent her fingers into wire hangers around the mange-bald throat, locked her knees, squeezed harder, harder, harder, until the dog yelped, gave up, and disappeared.

THE WINES OF PORTRARTUS

Most High Eminence,
I remind you, we both exist in the compassionate dream of an unseen God. Please send me an answer . . .

"Are you that answer?"

Father Damien peered hard at Jude. Morning. Or maybe early afternoon. Father Damien spread his hands resignedly upon the tray and tilted his chin back to accept a solicitous towel pat from his visitor, the one who'd brought him his breakfast. Damien had wakened groggy, and was annoyed to have been restricted to his room by Sister Mauvis.

"I'm not entirely feeble." Damien suddenly clawed the napkin from the younger priest's hands.

"I know you're not," said Jude, "it's just that you had a bit of oatmeal stuck to your chin."

"There. Satisfied?"

With one sharp movement, Father Damien swiped at his chin once more and sat back in bed.

"They insist upon this, periodically."

"Bed rest," said Father Jude, sympathetic.

"Confinement!"

Father Jude tried to soothe the outraged and frail man before him. "I'm sure it is rather demeaning, in a way. But you see, they weren't able to rouse you this morning." His voice took on the chiding parental quality that vigorous, impatient people sometimes use with the elderly. "It seems that, last night, you were just a little . . . tipsy." The younger priest's voice was suddenly prim.

A cunning, soft, puzzled expression crept over Damien's face. "Tipsy!" he mocked, his voice lilting. "Do you mean to say, drunk?"

"More or less."

"Loaded, shkwebii, pinned to the leather, purpled, pumped, schnockered?"

Father Jude didn't smile. He found no humor in these words, none whatsoever. Oh yes, he had seen the misery of alcohol's effect and believed such words were not just words! His reply was stiff. "They found no sign of a bottle, but yes, you were sloshed."

"No sign of the bottle, you say?"

"None," said Father Jude, leaning close. "And you didn't particularly smell like wine, or what have you. Yet last night you were distinctly intoxicated."

"And no bottle?" Father Damien's voice grew in intensity. He fixed Jude with a deep stare.

"None!"

"My house was searched?"

"Completely."

"No explanation? No clue? No cause?"

"Not that your good Sister Mauvis could discover, or any of them for that matter. But you can trust me with the knowledge." Father Jude leaned very close to Damien, smiled in conspiratorial sympathy. "Tell me, where on earth are you hiding your stash? We took the cupboards apart, the closet, the woodpile. What's your explanation?"

"Explanation? Obvious!"

Father Jude waited.

"It is a miracle."

Father Jude laughed at the joke, but the old priest maintained a dignified calm and lightly stabbed a leather bone of a finger at him.

"I have only to refer you to the early saint Portrartus."

Father Jude looked indulgently blank, and Father Damien persisted stubbornly. "While tending sheep in the mountains, our Portrartus manifested a profound drunkenness in spite of the isolation of his flock. There was no tangible source of intoxicants. Like Portrartus's, my drunkenness is not of this world."

"Ohhhh?" Father Jude reacted with exasperated amusement.

"I do not"—here Father Damien grew intense—"require the fruit of this earth in order to experience an exaltation of the spirit. I have only to think back and consider my life. Soon, I find myself in a state of delirium, which, I understand, resembles the less rarefied behavior exhibited by—"

"Habituated winos," Father Jude cut in, his patience lapsing.

"Last night I was also visited both by musical manifestations of the Holy Ghost and, I am sorry to say, of the devil himself."

"These manifestations, they consisted of . . . ?"

Father Damien put a trembling hand in the air now, and appeared much troubled.

"A stinking mutt," he whispered, "a dangerous intelligence."

"What are you talking about?"

"Recall, when the dog plunged its foot into my bowl of soup and that soup was tasted by the sisters across this lawn. I kept the dreams of the nuns in a locked tin box. I should not like them to fall into the wrong hands, though I must admit some were novel to the point where I read them again and again—"

"You read demonic torments for your own pleasure? Should I be scandalized?" Father Jude was diverted by Damien's ploy and, Damien could tell, his curiosity was piqued. The older priest resumed with sly ease, "I found the dreams instructive. I did not avert my eyes. To others it may seem odd that a curious and passionate being, for I do consider myself such, should have chosen a life of denial. To me, it was not at all strange, for the choice itself was made with lust. Passion over passion. Hungrier for God, I came here . . ."

Controlling his interest with some effort, Father Jude attempted to double back.

"And so the black dog, it was a delirious vision? Or was it possible," said Father Jude in the most respectful and nonthreatening tone he could manage, "that for a time, you went mad?"

With an outraged jerk of his head, the older priest quashed Jude's gesture. He folded his hands, composed himself, and shot the younger priest a shrewd glance.

"When our senses are weakened by hunger or illness, we see things and hear things that are not of this world. The question is this: Do we invent these things in the cabins of our sorry brains, or are they there always and we too comfortable to reach them or to care? At any rate, whether the answer is the former or the latter, I have no doubt, none at all. Last night's visit has persuaded me. I saw the black dog."

The old priest sank against the pillows, limp, folding like a window blind, but he was thinking very deeply and the thinking visibly exhausted him. His head dropped to his chest and he began to breathe deeply. Jude felt a pang of quick guilt, although not enough for him to let the old man sleep.

"Can I fetch you some water? A blanket?"

Damien shrugged off the false solicitousness. "These old bones. This old flesh. The devil will have me soon enough, cold or hot." Damien then laughed, a dry, papery sound. "At least I know his shapes, the ones he manifests here on reservation land."

Father Jude finished his adjustments to the tape recorder, moved it closer to Damien. He turned it on and clipped the microphone closer to the old priest's lips, for he had lapsed into the near whisper that he used when he was exhausted or wandering.

"You believe I mean the devil . . . metaphorically . . . of course . . ." Father Damien nicked his head, weary, but as he spoke his voice gathered passion. "Metaphors have very little influence in this world and the devil a great deal. The black dog! What is the devil but the lack, the crying hole in the skein of thought, Father Jude, that reasoning that says, *All is plain to see and yet you are deceived.* I am a priest. All that I am is based upon belief. And to begin, now, after all that has passed, to think perhaps he did not speak to me as a dog and from the dog's mouth is, quite frankly, to cast doubt upon all else . . ."

Father Jude switched off the tape recorder and leaned back, frustrated and shaking his head. He'd had a truly inadequate breakfast and thought now of driving to the café he'd found, the next town over, where the food was edible.

"You don't believe me," said Damien, after a long silence fell between them. "That's only because he's never paid you a visit. If he had, the question you would be forced to ask is this: If the devil can take the time to make an appearance, where's God? Why can't God make more of an effort?"

"God is not a politician," said Father Jude, his voice neutral. He kept his thoughts to himself, his expression blank, and took his mind off the hot roast beef sandwich he craved. He reminded himself that his task was to record, not judge, what he heard. Still, the idea that the devil should appear in person was disappointing, an unworthy piece of superstition, a marker of Father Damien's unreliability. He saw that Father Damien was ready to start his morning, so he left him in peace and gladly sought a meal.

After the younger priest left, Father Damien gathered his wits, his strength, and then sat up and waited for the fog in his brain to clear. He got out of bed. Teetering stiffly with hands on the back of his chair, and then taking minute steps, the old priest shuffled off through his small residence. The exchange had actually rejuvenated him a little, and he sat down at his desk and began to write with enthusiasm. "Consider the word spirit, manidoo," he wrote, "and all of the forms in which it resides. That which we consider vermin, insects, the lowest form of life, are manidooens, little spirits, and in their designation it is possible at once to see the penetration of the great philosophy that so unites the smallest to the largest, for the great, kind intelligence, the Gizhe Manito, shares its name with the humblest creature."

Returning later from the café where he'd eaten, thoughtfully, alone in a scarred brown booth, Father Jude frowned into the blond sky. He was well thought of in his parish, calm and good. Things had been going smoothly down in Argus. He'd had a comfortable routine figured out. And now, what an unwelcome complication, in spite of the huge honor, to be afflicted with so many new problems, uncertainties, even doubts. And how terrifying, this feeling of loving someone. Thrilling. Awful. With an explosive shake of his head, Father Jude put the thought of Lulu from his mind. Not only had he fallen desperately in love, and at this age, but he was failing at the task entrusted to him by the highest levels of Church authority.

These interviews with Damien Modeste were not going as he'd hoped. Father Damien was an extremely difficult subject. Impossible to penetrate one day, and all too transparent the next. There were gaps in the old priest's story, missed connections, all too many loops of obfuscation. It was clear, too, that the old man regarded Jude's presence as a disappointment. Father Damien had been hoping for an envoy directly from the Pope, and was irritated by the younger priest's humble, local origin. Now, exhausted with their sparring, Father Jude decided that he would once again visit the person Damien had pointed out as Leopolda's first young victim. Marie Kashpaw.

THE INTERVIEW

Marie Kashpaw liked to bake in the outdoor heat, and could sit for long hours in a lawn chair in her courtyard garden, motionless, head tipped to catch the most intense angle of the sun. She seemed lethargic, but when threatened, she could vanish with surprising swiftness. Catching the shadow of movement from Father Jude, who approached across the courtyard, she disappeared into the safe gloom of her Senior Citizens apartment, from which he was unable to rouse her by knocking.

It was clear she didn't want to talk to him, but that didn't matter to Jude. He had to talk to Marie Kashpaw. He had to persuade her to share her story with him. Still, he had no idea how to accomplish his mission. Sitting in the lobby, thwarted, he planned. She took the Eucharist every week, but that was from Father Damien. He could bring the sacrament to her himself, since Father Damien actually was indisposed, but, he wondered, did that put him in the highly uncomfortable position of using the Sacred Host as the lure for an ulterior purpose?

It felt wrong, but half an hour later he returned with the black leather traveling Eucharist kit, 100 percent calfskin, as official-looking as a spy toy. He knocked at the door to her apartment. Seeing who it was, she frowned, but nevertheless she allowed him to enter and stand next to her kitchen table.

"Would you like to take communion?" he asked her.

She shrugged at a chair. He sat, the case in his lap. Again, she just looked at him with those opaque eyes, and waited.

"Are you in a state of grace?" he asked.

Here, she smiled.

"Are you?" She threw her question back at him, and touched her gray forelock absently. "You shouldn't," she went on, "use the holy body of God as bait."

Father Jude actually flushed.

"I know what you want." Her voice was flat.

Now it was Father Jude's turn to go silent. In what he now thought of longingly as his "regular life," he was routinely in charge of every human exchange. He led and directed conversations. He did not resort to subterfuge, certainly of this nature. And yet, even if he had, not one of the Catholic Daughters, nuns, or Theresians, would have challenged him. This elderly Ojibwe woman did so with a perfect ease. He sighed, caught, and as he had some humility even as spoiled as he was by his authority, he set the case carefully aside on a metal tea tray, folded his hands in his lap, and said to Marie, "Yes, you read my intentions. I am sorry."

And so she nodded. And so again the silence.

"I will tell you a few things," she said to him at last.

So, of course it was fortunate that he happened to have carried along the tape recorder, which he now removed from within the soul-saving kit he'd brought. He set the recorder carefully between them, tested it by counting into the microphone, played it back. Now she was a little nervous. At first, as she began to speak, she stared at the tape recorder as though it were a separate consciousness. But then, as her memories collected, the picture shaped itself between them.

RED MOTHER

Marie Kashpaw

When you don't have a mother, as I never did, you have to make one. Get yourself a piece of clay and shape in your fingers and the shape you always make will be a mother. Or press her together of mud and sticks. Sometimes a tree would do, gnarled around me. Bundles of reeds. I used a blanket rolled and bunched in the shape of her. Rags.

Sometimes there was a little extra stew in the pot and I stole it and said to myself she gave it to me. Sometimes just grass, grass was all I needed. The warmth of it in the sun was her golden green smell and the soft brush of it her fingers, stroking my face.

You don't have a mother, you make one up. That's how I made mine and still she is standing where I made her, dark and red in the heavy woods.

What happened to me when I went up on the hill with the black-robe women is between me and my confessor, Father Damien. I came down with a broken head and a bloody palm wrapped in a pillowcase, with a raging spirit and a man who would be my husband. But that is not the story here. For I came down with an inkling inside me of what I knew. I later found that my instinct was true. There was something about that nun that drew me to hate her with a deep longing. How, you say, can that be? To long for that black scarecrow flapping for crows. She had a face like a starved rat and a taste for cruel games. But the worst thing of all was that Sister Leopolda loved me—I felt that like a blow.

It is hard to hate a person if they love you. No matter what they do. What you feel in return twists between the two feelings. Not one. Not the other. But painful.

At the time, I was kept by the Lazarres. But I was a dog to the Lazarres. So instead of going back to the Lazarres, or claiming my new husband right after the convent, I went to the woods. I aimed to live by myself in the old shack Agongos had died in the winter before. The place was deep in the birch, other side of a little pothole. Slough ducks came to land in there, turtles haunted it, muskrats made their twig-pile houses, and there was plenty to eat. I had decided just how I would support myself. Before I'd left the Lazarres, I stole two dollars, my life's wages. I used it to buy two bottles of nameless brown-red whiskey. I knew where there was a heap of old bottles in the woods, and I polished up two empty ones. Then I added some slough water to the good stuff and made four bottles in all, plugged neatly with white strips from my nun's pillowcase.

Those four bottles, I sold for twice the profit. I bought more whiskey. I kept on moving up. I was just a child, just a girl, but I was a bootlegger now. And I sold to the best and I sold to the worst. I bought a long steel hunting knife for when my customers got ugly. I bought a rib-skinny paint horse named Brownie, and fattened her on good sweet grass and boughten grain. I traded a stove off an old white farmer, and nails and boards to fix some shelves on my walls. Blankets. At last my winter store, a fifty-pound sack of flour, potatoes, onions, apples. I dried a load of berries for some winter sweetness, and I dug a deep pit behind my little house and lined it with slough grass. Into that pit, I set a cache of whiskey, precious bottles. Each wrapped in reeds like an offering. Then I covered it up and let the snow fall where it might. I was ready for whatever came to me, I thought. But I was not ready for the truth of my beginnings.

One day, I returned to find Sister Leopolda had come for me. She was a pillar of stark blackness praying in the yard.

"Come back," she said. She put out her hands and they were pierced in the palms, like mine.

I let her stand there, and I stood to watch her in a dull trance. Sun turned through the yellow leaves, rippled across her one way, then rippled back. I thought lazily of all that black hate that boiled up in me back at the convent, but I could not catch hold of it. I guess it had steamed away with the water from the kettle. Nothing was left, not shame, not indifference, not even a numbness or a heaviness—although, for the first time in my whole life, I thought with interest of my whiskey. I never drank my profits before, but maybe I would start.

I left the nun standing where she was, her arms held out stiff. Maybe she would stand there all night. I went on my rounds. She was gone when I returned. I staked Brownie in the clearing, where he could stuff himself, and I fried myself a potato with deer meat, boiled up a pot of tea. Then I went outside and sat on the little stump I had put right beside my door. There was something so deep of a pain in me, Father, like the end of all things was drawing near. I didn't think it over, I just picked up the bottle. As I drank my first whiskey, I watched the darkness collect.

It came peacefully out of the hearts of things. Bled from the leaves. The clouds sifted darkness out of them and it swirled into the air. I put my head back against the log wall, still warm, and I felt comfortable. I drank again, deeply. The stuff burned, then spread through me with a radiator comfort. Before me, as the dark was all of a piece, then, I saw my real mother rearing up. Even booze has a spirit. Yes, I said, it is the liquor who cares for me now. Alcohol is my red mother. She was fire, she was stupidity, she was light. She was all I needed. Her heart was a golden catchall of sorrows and pains. She told me that if I chose her, she'd stay by me and she used the word forever, which with her I could believe.

As I said, I was a dog to the Lazarres. I ate the scraps when there were scraps. The old dress I wore sagged off my shoulders. My shoes were hides I tied onto my feet and my coat was the blanket I slept with. Besides my own so-called family, my best customers back in those days were Morrisseys. If someone was on a long dirty bender and coming down slow, I'd bring the bottle to them on Brownie. We'd make special delivery of the booze to certain drunks like Sophie Morrissey, who was long ago, as a girl, in that house hit by the Virgin's statue and found it almost impossible after that to manifest a drunk state, though she tried. Anyway, this Sophie returned the favor by telling me the answer to the origin of Marie Lazarre.

We were sitting on broke chairs in her stomped-over yard. Sophie, she used to be a pretty woman in her time. When she told me these things she knew, her face still showed it, even though her body was strange—big bellied and spidery soft. Her features, blurred over with drink, were mild and stupid. She had brown skin and big wild green eyes, a straight little delicate nose, a darker sprinkle of tiny freckles. Her lips were slack and puffy, but when she smiled at the cork as she pulled it out, there was still a ghost of that girl I'd heard about. Frowzy hair caught up in a bun, wrinkled hands tough from the farmwork she did when not in ruin, she slugged back a good one, then carefully corked the bottle again and looked at me, eyes watering.

"You're a good little niece to me."

"Miigwetch." I thought she was grateful to me for getting her wasted, and I didn't take that serious. I sat with her for some time in the pleasant sunlight of her blasted yard—nothing grew there. It was peopled with dogs, fur sticking every which way, dogs nursing pups and biting fleas and sleeping belly up.

"This here's my last bottle. I got to taper down so I can go cut hay." She grinned at me, friendlier even than before. "Geget igo, you are a good little niece."

Once again, I nodded. I took that in, but she wouldn't let go of it yet.

"Eyeh, your deydey, he was my uncle."

That was like a lightning wand went down my back.

"Take a hit and tell me more," I said, all merry like I was a drinker too. I smiled with pleasant expectation at her, as though my heart weren't beating in my throat, as though I didn't have that sick way-down empty craving feeling that even at that moment I understood why she turned to the liquor to fill.

"She showed early. I was just a girl at the time and these things weren't anything to me, but her belly popped right out!"

Sophie laughed, a cackling screechy sound, not unpleasant—unless she is laughing at your mother's little tub of a stomach that once contained a baby who was you. I just wanted to slap her face, and it was even harder to stay in control of my tongue. All my life I have fought my quick anger and I did so, then, looking at my feet in their heavy, black, men's boots. Listening. She knew about my mom. The Puyat. All I knew about my mom was her last name and the fact that not even the Lazarres would talk about her—she was that bad, I guessed, or that dead.

"My Puyat mama," I commented, letting it hang in the air.

She took another long drink, extending her wrist to my mom's memory, and then she began to talk, like all drinkers seem to do, about all the wrongs accomplished against them. In this case, the wrongs were specific to my mother, so I listened closely to try and gather more information.

"She witched me! She stole my virginity!"

Sophie started laughing until she choked.

"To be a Puyat is to be a thing not of this earth. Down below it"— she spat—"down where they put together dead bones and skin and hair and raise things up—witch creatures."

"What are you talking about?"

"I never left my hair around her. I burned it, my fingernail clips neither. I threw them on the fire. I never let her get a part of me. At night, she witched me. I know what she was doing."

"What?"

"Working me! She tried to work me like a puppet on a string!"

Some people, they go so deep. They are like a being made of tunnels. Passageways that twist and double back and disappear. You have a foot on one path and you follow for a while, but then there is a sinkhole, bad footing, a wall. My mother, she was this kind of person, so deep and so intricate of design. Now, when I think about her, I feel my head go heavy. My brain hauls freight—all that I will never know. For it seems to me that in my life I have thought everything there was to think about my mother, the Puyat. Only then, I didn't know her fate.

And wouldn't have, except for Sophie.

Of course, she told me. It didn't come out in so many words, but little by little. First I heard more about the way Sophie was enforced by the Puyat to witless behavior. As she told it, the witch drew a certain pattern in the spongy ground just beside the outhouse. Buried in Sophie's path a rag of monthly blood. Cursed her with owl's feathers laid underneath the mattress. My mother bit like a wolf into her dreams. She, poor Sophie, was subjected to the advances of handsome men and, although she didn't want to, the witch forced her to give in. Sweets tempted her. Again, she could not resist, and it wasn't her own faulty determination but the Puyat's bad medicine that weakened her so much. Drinking, likewise. She was still being influenced.

"I don't want to drink you!" She held the bottle out at arm's length and spoke to the ishkodewaaboo itself. "Geget igo, you contain an awful spirit! I don't like to take the spirit of this evil water into my person. I resist. But the Puyat has done me lasting harm. She overcomes my poor arguments, splashes the first drops on my brain!"

Obvious, I thought, false blame was getting thrown here! Yet the smoke means fire. My mother was in Sophie's life a source of corruption, that was clear enough to me whether or not she was in herself a weak person to begin with. There was a long—a very long—silence. In that quiet of Sophie's brooding, I remember the air. Sour reek of gone slough mud. A blue sound of birds. Berries crushed underfoot and a resinous, sweet pine scent from deeper in the woods past her house. Dry, hot, dog fur. Cheap white-lady powder from the folds of Sophie's last clean dress.

"Yet no matter how much I drink," Sophie said, "I never really get drunk anymore. Once I get down to this last dress, though, I know I gotta quit."

So even Sophie had some kind of limit—her vanity did not permit her to go on into the filth of habit more than four dresses deep, which is exactly what she owned. Four dresses. In the quiet, I felt a curtain open, and then the air swept through, a breeze, a fresh stirring of low wind from the east.

"My mother . . ." I prompted.

"Now she acts like she's so holy!"

That's all she said, but from those few words I got so much. The *now* meant my mother was alive. The *holy* meant she was showing herself in some hypocritical way, going to church perhaps. First the *now* acted on me like the clap of a bell. While I was still letting the ringing die down the *holy* came in and kicked me from behind. I whirled in my thoughts. And one thing more. From the unsaid ground of the sentence there could be no doubt Sophie saw her or knew of her, which meant she must be living near. Which seemed impossible.

"Tell me who she is!"

I jumped on this immediately.

But now that she imagined herself slightly juiced, Sophie wasn't so eager to speak to me, and she wanted something else.

"Gimme your horse."

"No."

"Borrow me your horse!"

"No."

She stomped toward Brownie, so I grabbed her skirt from behind, whirled her around, and threw her in the gooseberries. I knew her mind. She wanted to ride into town or to some drinker's house, where she could continue on until this last dress was too filthy for even her to wear. As she fell, arms outflung, I neatly plucked away the half-gone bottle from her clutch.

"Hihn! Daga, miishishin!"

"Who is she?"

"Who what?"

"My mother!"

"Why, don't you know?" Sophie was stark sober, anyway. Perhaps she realized, for a moment, how much her answer meant in my life.

Perhaps she understood and cared with some nondrunk's understanding, but the drinker's crafty power overcame her and she bargained for all she could get.

"That will cost the other bottle you got stuffed in your carry sack, plus a ride to Call the Day."

We bargained back and forth. Call the Day himself was waiting for the bottle in my pack, so in the end I hoisted her up, held Brownie's halter, and started to walk, as we'd agreed, her nursing her hope of drunkenness along now slow and easy from the back of my horse, until we reached Call the Day's corner, where, after I had helped her down, she told me as we had agreed. She said my mother's name:

"Leopolda, the so-called nun."

I still remember the complete and upright stumped nature of my surprise. Sophie bawled at the house and Call the Day scurried out, a wizened young fellow afflicted with great picklish lumps on his face and neck. He gave me the money he'd raised, and I gave him the bottle. It was the last I was to sell. As he took it from me, the hand that gave it up burned, the center, the palm where I'd been stabbed by this very nun, this Leopolda, my teacher and my sponsor in the holy convent. My mother. From my hand the burning spread, flowed up my arm like a streak of blazing grease. Ringed my throat. Bloomed in my face. Spread until the whole of me flared. Then the lick of flame tweaked my brain and struck me as so funny that I laughed. I laughed until I screamed.

So that was who she was, Father Miller, this Leopolda was the Puyat who bore me in secret shame somewhere on Bernadette's farm. It was the Morrisseys who passed me on to the Lazarres, whose dog I was until I got the power and they had to come to me begging for a drink. As I say, I quit that soon enough because I found, I got, I wanted to keep, and I did keep a man, Nector Kashpaw. I held on to him in spite of his own charms to himself and in spite of his mother. I stayed with him all his life. I married him, I buried him. I bore his children in between. And never did he know the name of my mother. And never did he know the name of my father. All he knew of me was that I was raised by Lazarres and escaped them. All he knew of me was what I let him know, and all he understood of me was that I was salt, not sugar. Salt, you've got to have to survive. Sugar, you can take or leave.

Oh, he had sugar too, Father Miller. Sugar by the name of Lulu. Lulu Lamartine. I see from your face that you understand about Lulu. Don't blame yourself, don't worry—a handsome man like you, wasted on the priesthood—you had no chance here, no chance at all.

21

THE BODY OF
THE CONUNDRUM

1996

Father Damien looked even more frail the next morning than he had the day before. The smooth planes and knobs of his bones pressed out against his skin and his cheeks were sunburnt and his temples throbbing and drawn. During the night, the blood had surged to Father Damien's heart. He sat up, dizzily, and he made the instantaneous and rough decision at last to tell everything, though it meant he was implicated in the cover-up, everything. Risk all, even the ultimate. No matter were he stripped naked and found out, yes, he must at last quash for good and ever any question of Leopolda's consideration. He must lay out the plain and simple truth to Father Jude, who was too obtuse after all to grasp it any other way.

Haunted, strained, his eyes searched Jude's face for questions.

"Father Jude, what if your candidate for sainthood was a murderer? Let us imagine it. I think you have."

"No," said Jude, shocked and then despairing at the abrupt statement. It had been quite enough to learn, the day before, that his saint was an abandoning mother. He had brought his own coffee and tried to hide his agitation now, carefully pouring out his first cup from a thermos he'd found in the rectory. Father Damien's statement shouldn't have rattled him. He should have understood by now that he understood nothing. Even so, he stammered. "I hadn't, of course. Up until this moment . . . even now I have no idea what you're talking about—and still, what evidence, what proof?"

"Incontrovertible," said Damien, delivering to the younger priest a piercing glare.

"What now?" said Jude, faltering. The other priest was sly, extremely intelligent, and possessed of a hidden stamina that had foiled Father Jude's imagination. He was truly taken off guard. Whenever he thought he knew the truth it merged into another truth. "What now?" he croaked again.

"We enter into the body of the conundrum," Damien answered with some pleasure, gaining strength from the younger priest's confusion. "We have established that there are miracles, real ones, solid evidence of good. Moral as well as physical miracles. Suppose, suppose. Suppose that in addition to her miracle working, however, your Leopolda killed a man with her bare hands? What weighs more, the death or the wonder?"

"The death," said Jude. "Certainly. But again, where is your proof?"

Damien laughed, without mirth, without lightness. "It is part of the miracle."

He sank into a silence so profound it seemed like death, stared at the toes of his shoes, closed his eyes. Jude Miller let the tape run on, scraping down the batteries, and was rewarded when, with a wild sleepwalking vigor, Father Damien Modeste sat up and spoke emphatically.

"I kept the barbed-wire rosary in a drawer all by itself, fittingly, and from time to time I looked at it and speculated on its use. One day, in frustration, I gripped it in my own hands and doubled it, then swung it around the post to my bed until the barbs nearly pierced my hands, went deep enough anyway to leave blue marks of bruises.

Quickly, I drew diagrams of where those marks fit. Again, again, I practiced the murderer's art, and each time I stopped I added a detail to the picture until I had a very good idea where the rips, the wounds, the marks, the damage would have occurred in the hands of the killer. The barbs were long. I believe they would have torn short seams, at least two, upwards into the curve of the palm like so . . ."

Here Father Damien brushed three marks up the inside of his curved old hands.

"I began to look, Father Jude, I began to observe. To my unsurprise, although many of my parishioners wore scars and marks, none were striped with the regularity of my killer. I proposed excuses and theories, became a reader of palms, made a continual nuisance of myself, let it be known that I had some peculiar medical reason for examining the inner landscape of people's hands. Nobody matched, Father Jude, nobody matched until I took off my blinders and began to look where I had rather not—close in, right next to me, inside the shape of Christ's body."

The old one drew a troubled breath, disturbed even now to recall the scene. "Father Jude, I can see it clearly, the moment out of time when she opened her hands. In the beams of afternoon radiance, she implored me to allow her some penance or other. That's when I saw that her palms bore the jagged white streaks, the raised scars, the triangular healed gashes where the barbs had cut into the flesh."

The two men fell silent in contemplation, and then Jude remembered.

"The miracle," he said to Father Damien, "you said that the proof was part of the miracle. What did you mean?"

A slow smile cracked Father Damien's face, squeezed the fine wrinkles to careful sheaves. "Oh, I thought it would be apparent to you early on, my friend. I thought it was clear—the stigmata—the marks she insisted she wore as the result of the vision in which she was given Christ's crown of thorns. Those marks were not made by thorns, but by wire barbs, of course. As for the sign and the wonder, hear this. The metal bore a bloody rust. The true miracle was this: the fast that our so-called saint soon endured, the amazing rigidity, the miraculous possession that gripped the imagination of the parish, was not the visionary trance her sisters supposed, but tetanus."

THE MOUSE

An irritatingly persistent mouse woke Father Jude, scrabbling lightly behind the studs and plaster, gnawing with businesslike devotion on something—electrical or phone wiring—inside the thick rectory wall. At night, against the hills, the powerful yard lamps doused, the dark was so heavy that he labored in the blackness to breathe. The chore of inhaling and exhaling became so tiresome that he switched on the dim reading lamp to divert himself. In its feeble show, he sat up dizzily and banged the wall to frighten the mouse. It stopped chewing for a moment, then recommenced, which was when the thought formed.

Startled, Father Jude spoke the thought aloud.

"He knew all along!"

Scrambling out of bed to scrape through his notes, he tried to reconstruct the chain of dates and confessions, realizations and facts, that culminated in this absolute conclusion and conviction. Father Damien had known, from the first perhaps, that Pauline Puyat, later Sister Leopolda, had, with a cruelly modified rosary, strangled the farmer Napoleon Morrissey. Father Damien had known and yet kept the knowing secret to himself. He had made no move to contact the diocese hierarchy. There was no letter written to the bishop hinting obliquely of a grave crime. Father Damien had made absolutely no move either to contain or to punish Sister Leopolda. And any priest would have done as much, no matter how dear he held his vows regarding the secret nature of the confessions he heard. Something else was at work, then. Father Jude Miller cogitated. The mouse began munching another wire and a white moth fluttered into the pool of lamplight.

Cogito ergo sum. Turn it around. My heart is clear, therefore I act. I am, therefore I think. I am, therefore I speak. Guilty, therefore I'm silent. Some premise known and understood by Damien and Leopolda, basic to the argument and essential to the agreement between them. Some premise powerful enough to cause a collusion between two enemies. Some secret endgame in which both of their triumphs were thwarted, a checkmate, a stalemate, and the result was the covered-up truth of a man's ugly death.

The conclusion was inescapable: Father Damien had also done something that he wished to hide.

And Sister Leopolda had known what that something was.

Father Jude Miller banged on the wall again. The dry, scattering scuttle of the mouse was like the random disarray of his thoughts. What, what did Father Damien do? He wanted to ask Leopolda herself, but of course the only way to do that was to appeal to her supernatural attention. Abruptly, Jude laughed, for the answer was to treat her as a saint and say his prayers, address her in the afterlife, the world beyond, only whether he should aim for heaven or hell there was no telling.

Between heaven and hell, he thought now, wearily, here I am in North Dakota. I am in love. My life as a priest is over. My vows are stripped of sweetness. They become a desert in the face of human love. All I will know from now on will be a purgatory of the senses and a suspension of possibilities. Still, he must finish his work. He would try to pray. And what if Leopolda should answer?

The next day, paging carefully through the stacks of papers, the marriage certificates, the records of death and birth, he came across a piece of paper that told him everything. Among the carefully organized papers of Father Damien's first years—he had been a meticulous file keeper—the birth record surfaced. Jude read the hand-printed certificate over, once, twice, again and again, absorbing its claim. Then carefully he culled it from the official records and slipped it into a manila file folder all its own. Once he found the informing document, he was too disturbed to do anything else but try to absorb its implications. He went outside to walk the dusty road that led to the high school running track, where he would circle and circle in his springy shoes. It was perhaps on the third mile, though he'd lost count of laps, that startled, he again spoke a thought:

"By God, she did answer!"

FATHER JUDE'S CONFESSION

When Damien moved aside the panel of wood and bent to the screen, he knew at once that he spoke to his fellow priest—it was the keen citrus aftershave. That gave him away, though he would have known from his voice as well. He naturally chose, as he did always, to allow Father Jude his privacy, and Damien spoke as though to a stranger. The younger priest went along with this and confessed anonymously, though he, too, knew that the screen was practically transparent and his voice was familiar to his colleague. Of course, once he spoke of Lulu, all pretense was abandoned. And anyway, Father Jude could not keep the emotion from filling his talk. He had not slept more than a few hours at a time for days.

"It is actually"—his voice was low—"a form of madness. A special aspect of which is the inability of the afflicted one to see beyond the thorns of the flesh and loving spirit. I feel ludicrous, pained, hurt, drained, exalted, and sick all at once. Ludicrous because, quite obviously, at my age I should have dispensed with and put these feelings in their places. Pained because I cannot tell her. Hurt because the hurt of unattainable intimacy lies before me constantly. Drained . . . well, obviously all of this emotion takes its toll on the body. Yet, thrilled! I have never felt so supremely right in my emotions, not since I took my vows. To love another human in all of her splendor and imperfect perfection, it is a magnificent task, dear Father Damien, tremendous and foolish and human. I'm sick because I can't eat for the beauty of it, and the anguish is beautiful too. Can I have her? No, I can't! Can she ever be with me? Just once? Of course not, unless I leave the priesthood. I'll do it. Nothing like this has ever happened to me. Ever."

"My dear son," said Damien, and his heart twisted in flat-out pity.

"If I was more perfectly committed, more noble, more secure, more Christ-like, I'm sure I would be immune to her, Father."

"No one is immune to her," said Father Damien, quite kindly.

"There is no vaccine? No cure for the malady? I'd like a little something to ease the pain."

"What would help?"

"Music."

"Of course."

"Would you play for me tomorrow?"

"I will."

"And Father . . ." now there was in the sound of the younger priest's pause something that put Damien on alert, some shift of attention and focus. It occurred to him that Jude, having admitted what he considered a great weakness, needed to extract a similar weakness from him, to put them on a more equal level. He considered tuning out and giving a huge, fake snore, but didn't want the other man to feel he was wanting in attention to his first problem, so he quietly asked Jude to go on.

"I know your secret," said Father Jude.

It was a wallop. Agnes's wind left her. For a moment, she was panicked to nerveless buzzing. Then, suddenly, the air flooded into her body.

"Oh!"

"Yes, I do."

Another pause. A yellow sheet of stars descended and Agnes thought, faintly, that she must not babble if she went unconscious. But the stars resolved to dusk air once more as Father Jude went on talking.

"I've already decided not to speak of it. I can't, I won't, though I might have before I experienced the confounding process of falling in love with Lulu Lamartine. I understand now, I actually identify to some degree with what you must have experienced. I cannot cast the first stone. Or any stone."

"Thank you," said Agnes, confused and unnerved.

"Don't you want to know how I found out?"

"Yes." Agnes's voice was very faint.

"I found the papers," said Jude, "while doing research on our subject. Of course, I looked up the birth certificate of Lulu, as I looked up everything about her in the church files. You didn't bother to hide it very well."

"Hide?"

"The birth certificate, of course. Father Damien, I *know* about it. You are, or would be, but of course you *won't* . . ."

"What?"

"My father-in-law. If only . . . I mean, if only I could have her."

"My dear son . . ."

"Yes! I saw your name on Lulu's birth certificate. *You are Lulu's father.* I know now, should have grasped before, from your words, how deeply you loved her mother, Fleur. I understand. To my great sorrow, no, joy, I truly and fervently know what it is to become undone by a woman. I shall keep your secret, as I know you'll keep mine."

And then, to Agnes's astonishment, the stolid and nerveless man on the other side of the screen began to weep into his hands.

BINGO NIGHT

Father Jude was engaged in what was perhaps the greatest moral struggle over a bingo game conducted in the history of the Church. But of course, it wasn't that alone, at all. Most things on the reservation, he was beginning to find, either connected with or came down to Lulu. Bingo was no different, especially when it concerned an invitation to accompany her to the Sweetheart Bingo Bash, with games commencing at midday and running through the night. Special prizes. Honeymoon trips. Weekend getaways in Grand Forks. Champagne suppers up in Winnipeg. A year's worth of chocolates.

How was he supposed to define himself free of wishing now that he had a wish? How ignore the sleepless reality of the struggle in his thoughts? How configure his embarrassment? How not say a word? And accept that he was human, therefore ridiculous?

Playing bingo, she said, raising her eyebrows and sliding her eyes obliquely away, was just one of her many failings. She was sorry, but what was the harm in it after all? She never lost more than she could afford to lose or won so much that it made her act better than her friends, and if she did happen to win a lot, she spread it around with a generous hand. What was the problem, then, and did Father Jude think it was simply in the nature of gambling? If so, shouldn't he try playing for himself and seeing how childish the game really was—just a diversion, really, like playing Monopoly, only in a vast roomful of people?

"No, I cannot go with you," said the priest, for perhaps the tenth time.

As always, she smiled a particular smile he had come to think of as her neutral gear. She smiled that way when she was buying time. When her brain was clicking forward with a new argument.

"It's probably better that you not go." She said this easily, which caused his heart to catch in a stabbing and painful stitch he breathed deeply to loosen. He wanted to reach forward and tuck a strand of hair behind her ear, though her hair was perfect. He wanted to lay his face against her neck, brush the curve of her throat. Instead, he pressed his fingers to his lips to contain the words that would expose his longing. Women her age were not supposed to have slim waists and smiles so joyous. And her radiant laugh! She was laughing at him, mocking his last ditch attempt at self-control.

"You want to," she held a finger up to him. "I know. I can tell."

Wanting was not the problem. Not going with her was the problem. In desperation, Father Jude went to ask Father Damien what he should do, and to try to elicit counsel that would shore up his resolve not to venture to the Bingo Palace, or anywhere, with Lulu.

"I'm no help," said Father Damien, "I won't tell you what to do. You wouldn't listen if I did."

"I'm not asking you to dissuade me," said Father Jude, gathering his pride. "I suppose, anyway, it's not a place a priest should likely venture."

"I venture."

"Do you go with her too?"

"Of course," said Father Damien. "The years between us have shrunk away. Since I retired from my active role in the Church to write my reports, Lulu has been kind enough to relieve my solitude with occasional trips to the Bingo Palace. There, we sit among friends, enjoying the workings of chance as we sip on cold drinks. We listen to the gossip, the bragging over grandchildren and lamenting of the actions of grown sons and daughters. She listens and I smile. She does not judge and I need not absolve, for after all these years my forgiveness is taken for granted."

Father Jude nodded, flexed his hands, sighed wearily. "I should just go to bed and forget about this. But I know I won't. I'll end up going with her and going to the devil."

He said the last extravagantly and earned a disapproving frown from Damien. "She is good," said the old priest, "one day you will understand this. She is goodness itself."

Three hours passed in which he thought she'd forgotten all about him. Then she came back and asked him again, just to make sure, and she brushed against him when she did this and he said, in that instant, yes he would. He got into her car. As soon as he did so, he realized that he'd never let a woman drive him anywhere before. He should have seen it coming, then, as he rode along in the sun-struck, dark, red seat in unaccustomed passivity. He'd never been so alone with a woman, except in the anonymity of the confessional. And now that it was just the two of them in so small a space, he wanted to drive forever. And then they were at the Bingo Palace.

"I'll stake you," she said, purchasing a bingo package. They sat down together at a long table with ashtrays in front of a big-screen TV on a stage. Not long, and the numbers rolled off the announcer's lips. On B-10, Father Jude's mouth went dry. His glasses fogged on G-40, and by the time they'd cleared and he saw the possibilities his lips were buzzing, numb, and he dabbed delicately on the square O-63.

"Someone else bingoed." She tore off the flimsy sheet of numbers and tossed it away. Then she asked him what she'd got him here to ask him, solo and in her power: "What are you doing with Father Damien?"

The implication being, What are you doing *to* him.

"Interviewing him," said Father Jude.

"He looks tired." Lulu dabbed smoothly, marking a number he'd missed. "But he also looks"—and here she stamped his paper just a bit harder—"stronger. He actually looks stronger and healthier than I've seen him in quite a while. So whatever you're interviewing him about . . ."

"Church business."

"Seems he likes to talk about Church business then. What kind of business?"

Somehow, the way she asked, conversationally and distractedly, as though she had a perfect right to ask and know, left him undefended. He told her. Horrified later, he couldn't remember the exact words and all that went with them, but he did know he'd treated her like a confidante and colleague. Not just telling but discussing the implications of what was to become of whatever findings he made, and even worrying about the difficulty of establishing a literal or factual truth when there were opposing versions of Leopolda's life and story, when the life—as opposed to the evidence of miraculous interventions—did not add up.

"Should I be telling you all of this?" he asked at one point.

"Why not?" she asked calmly.

He couldn't think of a reason, and then he couldn't think of anything. He was looking at her helplessly. He couldn't look away.

"You've got it bad," she said, diagnosing his fever like a compassionate doctor.

He mumbled agreement and the great burden of his feeling pressed up all around him in a buzz of noise. Saying it lifted away the burden of strangeness. Relieved, he smiled at her, and then she was staring straight into his eyes, with an easy, knowing sympathy that made his blood hum in his ears.

LEOPOLDA'S PASSION

Father Jude Miller had always loved to read about saints—the first and oldest of course somewhat apocryphal, the stories structured to end with ingenious tortures, the saints even in agony making clever retorts to butchers and emperors. As well, he loved the more contemporary saints whose lives obtained of more possibility of emulation— he marveled at their sense of sacrifice and fervor. He found himself dwelling on the symmetry of the saints' passions, or stories, on their simplicity of line. He was having trouble with passion, from the Latin *pati*, to suffer, defined in the Catholic Dictionary as *a written account of the sufferings and death of one who laid down his life for the faith*. He was persuaded that the God he knew, at least, wanted him to write a passion, a recognition for this very complex person, Leopolda.

Besides that, he wanted to get the whole thing over with, this mission. As soon as possible, he would then leave the priesthood, immediately marry Lulu, get old with her. Wait, they were old already.

They would die in each other's arms, then. He must concentrate. He turned back to the task of describing Leopolda.

With some dismay, in the welter of files and note cards in fans and toppling stacks, Father Jude understood that to tell the story as a story was to pull a single thread, only, from the pattern of this woman's life, leaving the rest—the beautiful and brutal tapestry of contradictions—to persist in the form of a lie.

Still, he tried.

Sister Leopolda of Little No Horse was born in extremely humble circumstances and during a time when accurate birth and death records were not kept, especially for families of wanderers among the Ojibwe, Cree, and métis families of the plains frontier. Although only sporadically exposed to the teachings of the Church, her piety was marked from a very young age.

Here, he stopped, shuffling through his papers for examples noted during the brief period, especially, when she had lived in Argus with relatives. She was spared during a tornado that had ripped the town apart. Though she attributed her survival to prayer and to the rigid defense of her virginity, an elderly man who, as a child in that family, had been lifted with her into the roil of air that same day, said otherwise: *She used to cuff me around, slap me, scream, if that's what you call praying.* Yet there had also been stories of her fervid attendance at Holy Mass. She was unflaggingly pious. Though Father Damien remembered their first encounter in the church as disturbing, others reported a dull metallic glow surrounded her when she was lost in prayer, and the strong, resinous scent of burning pine pitch, not unpleasant, filled the air when she spoke out loud the sincere act of contrition.

She had a great deal to be contrite about, Father Jude thought, so why was she then rewarded with spiritual favors? Not his place to figure out, he told himself, and continued writing.

Many conversions took place as a result of her example of continual prayer. During what others have called her "marathon adorations," in which she knelt for hours, sometimes whole days, eventually consecutive days, before the Blessed Host, she was in a state of ecstasy almost tangible to those who

approached to touch her. Many reported that they were over-
whelmed with a poignant sense of peacefulness, or that, hold-
ing a hand lightly on her shoulder, they were able to close their
eyes and clearly visualize the answers to their problems and
follow the progress of their prayers out the stovepipe and over
the roof of the church, off the tips of the leaves, dodging the
clouds and away into the sky.

Father Jude Miller put down his pen and dropped his head into his
hands. True, but others had said she left a black stain like oil where
her knees pressed for all of those days. During the time of her longest
confinement or trance, the rigid fast that Father Damien had revealed
as no visionary journey of the spirit but a dangerous case of lockjaw,
he had been told, this from Dympna, that voices were heard behind
the closed door of her cell. Voices arguing, low demonic growls,
hideous moans. And yet when the door was opened there would be
only Leopolda, bones and skin underneath the coverlet, eyes staring
through the roof.

She was accepted as a novice at the Convent of the Sacred
Heart at Little No Horse, and there she proceeded to raise great
sums of money for the improved comfort of her sisters by giv-
ing missionary talks throughout the region. During these
speeches, she would often become inspired to such a degree
that others were moved to extreme acts of generosity. When
she did return to the convent, she was physically and mentally
exhausted, but tried her best to continue her studies in Church
history and catechism, and to work toward the improvement
of her soul.

He had to note, somewhere, what a trial she was to others and
where her piety became terrific and strange. And, too, what to say
about the deadly conversion she had effected with Quill, the useless
baptisms she'd wrought on the defenseless dead, not to mention her
amalgam of ancient practice with Catholic tradition and the skulls
she dragged for years behind the Virgin of the Serpents, dragged by
way of pierced back and arms, until they pulled free, shredding her. . . .

In an attempt to reconcile the two worlds from which Leopolda drew spiritual sustenance, the young novice mistakenly, but with a fervent heart and pure intentions, attempted to graft new branches onto the tree of Catholic tradition.

Father Jude hummed with approval for his metaphor, imagined the great rooted base of an oak spreading wide and the branches reaching hungrily toward light, one among them boldly colored, beaded entirely, and ribboned. He leaned back into the supports of his wooden chair and closed his eyes. Suddenly, he saw that he was mistaken. The picture shifted. The tree was beaded all the way down to the center of the earth and the branch of his own beliefs, the dogma and history of the Catholic Church not even a branch but a twig not strong enough for a bird to perch on, just a weak and slender shoot. He rubbed his eyes and resumed his place in Leopolda's story.

When her efforts to meld the two cultures failed, she chose decisively for the one true church and diverted the fever in her soul to the zeal of conversion. She was assiduous in her attempts to lead her people to the knowledge of the Holy Trinity, and used whatever means were at hand to effect enlightenment. Sometimes, it is true, she overstepped the bounds that may be termed proper. These were crimes of passion for the faith, however, and as she continued in her growth she began to understand just how to channel the great zeal she felt into more effective ploys. While in Argus, North Dakota, she took her perpetual vows and then returned to Little No Horse to continue her missionary work among her own people, one of whom she had murdered—

Father Jude paused, blinked at the word, then shook himself, stared fixedly at his pen, and continued writing fiercely.

Granted, she killed out of revenge for his unwanted sexual attentions, but she actually used a sacred rosary to strangle him. Plus she bore his child and then repudiated the girl—no— lived near and tortured her! Leopolda poured boiling water

*from a kettle onto the girl's back and then, in an act of shock-
ing viciousness she brained the child with an iron poker and
stabbed a hole—*

He jumped out of his chair in extreme agitation and began to pace
back and forth behind his desk. All this even without Lulu's testimony,
without the children Leopolda had bruised and, maybe worse, grievously
humiliated in her classroom, the barbarous use she made of shame,
anger, sarcasm—all poisons of the spirit, which she possessed every bit
as much as the spirit's gifts. Because of Sister Leopolda, and Lulu had
laughed saying this about her teacher, she'd bathed for six weeks in
Hilex water to see if her skin would bleach. Because of Leopolda, children endured memories of ear-ringing slaps, of uglier blows, of the jeering fun she made of their poverty and innocence.

So many know God who never would have! Jude argued with himself, hearing the counterargument. So many turned away from God,
because the messenger was frightful. He could not write other than
the truth, of course, what had he been thinking? Why this deep thirst
to make a saint of this appalling woman? Perhaps the miracles were
false concoctions, as many are, or they were simply phenomena unex-
plainable by what we know of physical science. Then again, perhaps
they were true miracles. A tremor of frustration shook him. He closed
his eyes and into his mind there fell again the image of the intricately
beaded oak tree. He must remember to tell Damien, he thought, and
allowed his thoughts to relax in a welcome diversion.

Father Damien. The old priest had fixed himself in Jude's bland
emotional landscape as the first interesting, though irritating, feature
in a long while, and then of course Lulu had followed. But he wouldn't
think of her. He set his thoughts on the series of conversations he'd
taped over the past few weeks. Placing Father Damien in the context
of the writing he was embarked on, he realized that Damien's story
was not only fascinating in itself, but also probably revealed now for
the first time to him, Father Jude.

There was Father Damien's incredible beginning, the years of starvation and disease, the tireless love he had shown in pushing through
slough and bush to give solace where he could. Damien had not
shirked from physical labor, either, or the tedium of raising money for

the Church or for the poor. He had learned the language of the Ojibwe and continued to translate hymns and prayers, even before Vatican II. There was a special sweetness in Father Damien's relationships with his people. When he spoke, especially of Nanapush and Lulu, the warm humor of his love radiated out. His stories were intriguing—the salvation via Eucharistic corporealization—what to make of that? Then there were the visitation by the snakes, the voices, the continual devilish botherment and baiting of Father Damien.

For the first time, now, stirring himself to frown out the window, Jude considered that Father Damien might actually be telling the truth about the devil. Was Father Damien often in some mystical state of ecstasy? And was he telling the truth about the black dog's temptation? If so, what more deeply generous act of the spirit than to give up his eternal reward for the life of a child? It was an act of Christ-like goodness—no, more. Jesus had suffered for three hours and then gone to his eternal reward, whereas Damien would suffer for eternity—no comparison!

Of course, and here Jude nodded as though to another person's obvious question, Lulu was his daughter. What father would not do as much? And the fact that she was his daughter, well, that was a sin and a breaking of his vows, a scandal. But then again, Saint Augustine himself had a mistress and a son, and certainly—here Jude caught himself making an odd comparison—an act of generation should be considered with far more indulgence than an act of murder.

It occurred to him that he was, in his mind, setting the life of Damien out in a scheme next to the life of Sister Leopolda, and he wondered why until he thought, *The life of sacrifice, the life of ordinary acts of daily kindness, the life of devotion, humility, and purpose.* The life of Father Damien also included miracles and direct shows of God's love, gifts of the spirit, humorous incidents as well as tragic encounters and examples of heroic virtue. Saintly, thought Jude almost idly, then caught himself in wonder.

Saintly? Father Damien? Am I writing the wrong Saint's Passion?

He rose, the papers sliding from his desk in a sighing mass, the note cards fanning from the rubber band binders, books and notebooks toppling.

22

FATHER DAMIEN'S PASSION

1996

Time at last to end the long siege of deception that has become so intensely ordinary and is, now, almost as incredible to me as it will be to those who find me, providing I let that happen. Agnes scratched a red-tipped kitchen match on the rough side of its box. Carefully, shredding the paper, she then burned what she had written over a shallow abalone shell. The fine flakes of ash collected. She was getting rid of evidence. Even as she wrote, she burned what she wrote. That was how she knew her time was coming.

We are ever betrayed by our bodies and animal nature, she went on. *There is no way around the fact that beneath these clothes I am a shocking creature, to be prodded, poked, and marveled at when dead. Defenseless, that's how I picture it, and the prospect is so truly dreadful that I prefer to disappear. That is the word I use. To disappear means that I will be elsewhere, not just dead, although of course that is the outcome I have accepted.*

The decision calmed her fears and allowed her to prepare.

In the cool days of early June, Agnes decided to put her plan into action. Now was the time. She felt abnormally fit, too strong for her age, impossibly vigorous. Now, in this false summer of existence, she would have the strength. She would go to Spirit Island on Matchimanito. The plan was simple. She would invent a travel itinerary, even purchase tickets, pretend to go someplace warm from whence she would not return. Prepare documents to support the fiction of some tragic disappearance. In the meantime, she would steal a rowboat, take aboard a decent vintage of wine, and row herself out to Spirit Island under cover of night. There, she would burn the boat in a merry bonfire, at which she would drink the wine. At some point, when she was very drunk and deliriously pleased with the whole of her existence, she'd decide, No more! She'd drown herself. Cleverly, by the use of heavy stones, she would make sure that her body was anchored to the lake bottom.

Every time she grew faint of heart, she had only to remind herself of the singular horror of posthumous discovery. The thought of being gaped at, examined, the thought of this body that had sheltered and harbored her spirit all this life, poor thing, in the hands of the curious. Agnes could not bear to imagine the silly furor.

Much better to seek the island.

Besides, maybe once she was there Fleur would talk to her. She'd gone there to be with the last of the Pillagers, her cousin Moses. Nanapush might join them with new and outrageous stories of his life after death. She imagined their bones all mixed up together, spirits arguing and laughing as in the old days. As Agnes proceeded to make preparations and to gather supplies for her successful vanishing, she was oddly cheered at the prospect, however slight, of once again meeting up with her friend. She laid the groundwork. Faked letters from a host, shipped boxes, withdrew all of her money—a surprising amount of money—from the bank. She intended to pin it against her body, under her shirt, in a Ziploc bag. A note would accompany the bills instructing any accidental finder of Damien to resink the body or bury it on the spot and consider the bag of money fair payment for the service. She thought of everything and then mailed one last, irate, good-bye-good-riddance letter.

Pope!

Perhaps we are no more than spores on the breath of God,
perhaps our life is just one exhalation. One breath. If God
pauses just a moment to ruminate before taking in a new
breath, we see. In that calm cessation, we see. All I've ever
wanted to do is see.

Don't bother with a reply.

Modeste

After she wrote and sent off the letter, she found herself procrastinating, clinging to life. Small things brought tears to her eyes—the jar of wild clover honey Mary Kashpaw bought to sweeten the ever charred toast, the blue jay stamp put out by the U.S. Postal Service, the tremulous sifting of dark into the room where her piano gleamed. Her piano! Notes of the *bacarolle* she had played to greet the snakes. Leave these things, leave them lovingly and easily, she told herself, touching the angry bedpost where so often she had prayed. But it was not easy to leave.

The job of becoming Father Damien had allowed the budding eccentricities of Agnes to attain full flower. Thus the church that drew tourists, and her friends the snakes. Her rock-floored church, and the statue that Sister Leopolda had claimed wept quartz tears that melted in her pockets, and the slow-growing stunted oaks, the golden light, the lilacs. All these things would remain while she did not. How strange that her absence would have no effect whatsoever on the things of this world. Proving that they were not just things, she thought, proving that they were spirit surrounded by a shell of substance, just like her.

There were drums that refused to sound for any but the one who made them, and drums that got up and walked away in the night if they were neglected or felt lonely or cheated of attention. There were violins that wept for their original owners, cellos that groaned for a woman's touch, guitars that responded only to men. Agnes thought now, with comfort, of her drowned piano. Their fates would match. She sorted her music and took her favorite pieces, thinking, *I have never played the planted* allées *of Haydn or Brahms or even Schubert with the real devotion I gave the thick forests of Beethoven. I always went deeper into the crevasses, complicated the treatment of each note, brought up the minor and scoured the truth out of Bach.*

Why could I not have lived more simply?

It would be suspicious for Father Damien not to take his music, so Agnes planned to burn it at her private good-bye party. These soft leaves of yellowed Chopin bearing her painstaking, hopeful self-notations, at least, should go with her! As for her refreshments, they were in the trunk of the car—an entire case.

On the dawn that Agnes prepared to leave, Mary Kashpaw appeared. She entered the yard so promptly that it was apparent she had been up for some time, waiting for her priest to make his move. As Agnes walked out to the car, Mary Kashpaw stood on the path in the swimming energy of the sunrise, its colors behind her. Her face was half shrouded in the blue pre-dawn light. She barred the way. Watching with a solid and hidden gravity, she extended her hand. In her palm, a book of matches.

"So you know, you understand," said Agnes simply.

Mary Kashpaw's face, illuminated by a sudden streak of new light, was cloudy and exhausted, her eyelids translucent, puffy, her lips bitten almost bloody. She stared blindly. Within her, like water set to boil on a stove, an emotion pressed for escape. It found her fingers, and her hands flapped abruptly as though they were two dishrags. Then her knees shook. A look of distress twisted across her features and she sank to a kneel. Slowly, she opened her embrace. With an intimate and grieving tenderness, she clasped her arms around Agnes's knees and bent so that her broad sweep of forehead rested against her thighs. They were still for a long while, just breathing together. Agnes put her hand upon Mary Kashpaw's great, gray head and stroked the whirlwind of hair at her crown. In its swirl, she saw the flourish of the ax, heard the runners of the sleigh traveling along the grass, saw, as she closed her eyes, how well Mary Kashpaw knew her and had kept her secret.

She took a coat from the mission store, a thing no one would recognize, a hatchet, the Ziploc bag of money, and another waterproof container of matches. Mary Kashpaw hadn't trimmed Father Damien's hair lately and it curled around her pate, a halo of white floss, so she brought a hairbrush. She threw in a heavy blanket, which she'd sink, and a nondescript pillow. She assembled all of these things and prepared for her trip as though for an adventure, which of course it was: death, the ultimate wilderness.

Rowing out to Spirit Island with cheese and crackers, candy bars, a bag of apples, and a case of wine, she stopped often to rest and to contemplate the easy chasing waves that rippled beside her. The wind was with her, so she corrected her drift and breathed the fire from her chest and the stinging emptiness from her muscles. The air was so pure and watery that it tasted like a tonic food. Her mind was phenomenally clear. Memories came back in waves, thoughts, passages of music, old songs Nanapush had taught her. They'd sing together once she reached the island. The trip took her most of the day, and it was dusk by the time she arrived, pulled up, and tied the boat to a tree.

The first night, all she did was start a tiny fire, curl up in the blanket, and eat crackers. Too tired even to uncork the wine, she gazed at the meek velvet tarp of the sky, the stars poking through, and she was visited in her drowsiness with a quiet intensity of happiness. Having unburdened herself of all that regarded her nemesis, she was right with the world. She had even forgiven Leopolda. The spirits of her friends, all those whom she'd loved, surrounded her. Gregory tumbling through the wall of books. His last, liquid golden stare, his hands cooling in her hands, his mouth set in an enigmatic half smile. She had parted lovingly with Mary Kashpaw and left off adequately with Father Jude. There was nothing left to torture herself over except, and this was inevitable, she didn't want to die. And Lulu, she hated leaving her, especially in the middle of one of her flirtatious intrigues. And yet, she thought, with some hope, perhaps here on this island she would be protected from the black dog. Her soul might slip past the cur's slimy teeth and sneak by the hell gates and pearly gates into that sweeter pasture, the heaven of the Ojibwe.

Next morning, she washed her face carefully in bits of broken sun. She took the hatchet to the boat and began to hack it apart, her arms so weak from the previous day's exertions that she diminished it only by splinters. Bit by bit, however laboriously, she fed it to her new fire. The blaze gave off a warm friendliness that drew her to sit near. The day was cool and fresh. She ate an apple. A candy bar. At noon, she opened the first bottle of wine, toasted her surroundings, upended it, and drank to the dead.

"Make room," she said cheerfully to the spirits in the sighing trees.

Dreamily comfortable, she planned. Her death would be simply another piece of the process, she would hardly notice it once the moment came. She'd be drunk, of course, but more than that, she'd be spiritually resigned and prepared. She would accomplish her own end as smoothly as all else. She would simply keep drinking until she got down to the last bottle and then, once she drained it, she'd put stones in her pockets and walk out where the water dropped suddenly to an unknown depth. She would open herself to the water, she would let creation fill her.

Not yet, though. Above her two eagles, a hunting pair, circled. Aloof, lethal, beautiful, they were like two gods who invented and now occasionally plucked their sustenance from the body of the world. She watched them intently, blinking into the whiteness of day. The fire sent shoots of sparks into the afternoon. She reviewed with hope the promise of slipping past the black dog into heaven, and drank, first keenly and then with numb greed, the pleasant blandness of the white Australian wine.

The end of the first bottle undid her. Complications arose. She was surprised how quickly her resolve shrank and how distinctly unpacified her thoughts and her feelings were. No matter what she'd done, no matter how many souls saved or neglected, no matter if she'd betrayed her nature as a woman or violated the vows of the long dead original Father Damien, her life was vapor, a thing of no substance, one note in the endless music, one note that faded out before the listener could catch its shape. Who was this Agnes, or this Damien, this overlay of leaves and earth? Her brain filled with a sound like the terrible jeering of sparrows in the eaves of the church. Her life was vast in its purposelessness, and yet confined to the narrow spectrum of her senses. She rocked beside the fire, her head in her hands.

The long night of the body came flooding back, her losses and stuffed desire. At her age, she was supposed to be at peace with the world, not filled with this darkling rage. The forgiveness she'd bestowed on the author of Berndt's murder twisted in her brain like a weasel and she couldn't subdue it. The forgiveness got out and turned its sharp teeth on her, sank to the quick in her heart a bitter thrill as she imagined the unborn children of Agnes and Berndt wrestling in the clean, straw-raising clouds of sun-glittering dust in the vast and windy barn. Agnes threw her head back, a headache spiked her temples. The pain probed open a door, a last new memory of the robbery came to her out of the dark.

Words. She heard herself as she gazed at the barrel of the Actor's pistol. She told him that it was an old belief of her mother's people that the soul of a murderer's victim passes into the killer at the instant of death. "Are you prepared to bear the weight of my soul?" She had asked just this question before the gun went off, either causing the Actor to pull the trigger or ruining his aim by the hair that saved her life.

It was my soul that pressed him into the deep mud, she thought—I've never realized the weight of myself until now! Can I put it down? She asked this of the black sky, the stars. She no longer saw the constellations as she had before knowing them in Ojibwe, but saw the heavens as her friends defined them. Saw the otter. Saw the hole in the sky through which the creator had shot down at a blistering speed.

"Nanapush, Fleur, all of you!" She cried out to the ghosts of her friends, drunk and marveling with sorrow. "Come and sit with me." When she poured just a bit of wine onto the ground, she felt Fleur approach, knew she sat just beyond the circle of firelight, in the rustling melt of shadows.

Reassured, she now sipped lightly, rested in a trance of increasing ease. Yes, it was time to put the weight down, the burden. The constant murmur of the pines, her beloved music, now became comprehensible to her in the same way that flows of Ojibwe language first began to make sense—a word here, a word there, a few connections, then the shape of ideas. Instead of growing duller, shutting down her senses, turning away from life, she found to her joy and consternation that she was growing keener. Her understanding was more intense, her vision wary and her hearing razor sharp. The roar and whisper of the pine needles intensified and she fell into a reverie of nostalgia.

"Just think," she toasted history, speaking aloud to all of the invisible, assembled spirits. "Think all the way back to Agnes. If only she'd banked an hour earlier or later. If only she'd managed to fall off the moving car. If only Berndt hadn't been going to Upsala to fix that harrow. How different my life. A farm woman with a beautiful piano." Agnes held the bottle high and drank, deeply, to her lost Caramacchione and to her lost life as Agnes Vogel. Then she drank again to the huge life she had known at Little No Horse.

"Forgive me for drinking wine." She asked pardon of the spirits. "I'm too weak and I'm alone. I have too many thoughts. If only the priest, the first Damien, hadn't visited me with his doubts and stories. If only, if only. If only I'd thought to get out of the way when the river came for me. How easy my life would have been. How tedious! Thank god, I met your visionary, strange servant Nanapush!"

Agnes started to remember, and in remembering she couldn't help laughing. In great joy at the foolishness of all design, she allowed herself to think openly and deeply of the incredible events of the last year of her old friend's life. The even wash of black sky, clouded over and starless, fell about Agnes to muffle her closely. Whole sequences involving Nanapush bubbled up and she laughed at the awful absurdity, at the picture of her old friend dodging moose pellets, and the alert look on his face when he sat up at his own wake. Nanapush! The laughter grabbed in Agnes's belly and she doubled over until she painfully gasped. Nanapush. The laughter cut her breath short and she took a huge wheezing gulp of air that made her snort. Aaah, it was all too unbearable. Tears squeezed out of her eyes shut tight in mirth. She'd taper off, but then the laughter spurted out and began, stronger, with a sweet, free vengeance that racked her ribs. Laughter traveled up through her feet, down her arms when she lifted her arms. It burst from her gut, unexpectedly. The laughter made her dizzy.

To clear her head, Agnes tried to lurch to her feet, thinking mirthfully, *I'm going to laugh myself to death!* It was then that she felt the stifled warm report of a blood vessel bursting just above her left ear. One side of the world went dark. She sank to her knees and with an amused wonder watched as slowly, with an infinite kindness, darkness covered up the other side as well. Sightless, now, she sank to earth and felt the heat of the leaping fire on her face. *I am going, I am going*, she thought. Underneath her and before her, a wide plain of utter emptiness opened. Trusting, yearning, she put her arms out into that emptiness. She reached as far as she could, farther than she was capable, held her hands out until at last a bigger, work-toughened hand grasped hold of hers.

With a yank, she was pulled across.

MARY KASHPAW

She paddled out to the island in a beat-up and awkward old aluminum canoe. She got out in shallow water, laced together her big rough shoes and slung them over her neck, tied the boat to a tough tree root, and waded ashore. She sat down on a powerful twist of exposed root. Methodically, very carefully, Mary Kashpaw tied the shoes back on her feet. Creaking monumentally, she stood. The island could be traversed side to side in ten minutes. Walking the rough shore might take half an hour to negotiate. The center was rock, piled rock rising in a solid cliff. Everyone knew the cave that Moses Pillager used and where his drum still lived. His cats had long ago died of boredom or devoured one another. Birds sang thick in the scuttering bushes, and a red squirrel chattered high in the lyre spread of an old white pine. Mary Kashpaw crossed a bed of soft duff, made her way over to the side of the island where the camping was easiest. There, she saw him right away and she stopped. He was no more than a fold of black cloth crumpled near the white ash circle of his fire. One arm was stretched alongside his hip and the other was bent, a pillow under his head. She knew before she understood that the stillness of his body was the immobility of earth.

She relighted his campfire, rolled him into a blanket, and laid out his limbs straight and true. She handled him gently, as though his bones were flower stalks, his skull fragile as a blown egg. She folded his arms across his waist, and then Mary Kashpaw sat beside him. Her eyes were clouded, her body stunned, her thoughts far away and tiny as a view through the wrong end of the telescope. Her heart was numb with a kind of odd embarrassment.

She felt shy now, entrusted with far too much power. Left with the choice whether to bring him back across the lake in the canoe or to bury him here on the island, she froze. She listened to the pines, paced, even considered opening a bottle of the wine at his feet although she never drank. She watched the waves, shut her eyes, fell into a drowsy suspension wherein she received what felt like an answer. She found the Ziploc bag of money and the note. It took a while to read the note, letter by letter she made it out. Of course she understood exactly what he'd expected.

She buried him in the lake.

Pulled him to the hacked rowboat and hoisted him in. Chose rocks to weigh him down, lashed them tightly into his clothes with strips of plastic taken from his stash of goods. Brought her canoe around and lined it up with the funeral boat. Towing her priest in his damaged rowboat, holes hacked in the bottom, she paddled out into the lake. She stopped where the water was of an anaerobic cleanliness, cold, black, and of an endless depth. As the sky filled with light, she watched the old heavy rowboat slowly fill and then sink. Father Damien's slight figure, serene in its halo of white hair, lay just under the waves. As the dark water claimed him, his features blurred. His body wavered for a time between the surface and the feminine depth below.

A FAX FROM THE BEYOND

1997

At the convent of the mission of the Sacred Heart at Little No Horse, it was uncommon to receive donations too large to be set upon the revolving lazy Susan, which conducted boxes of macaroni, surplus apples and eggs, sweet corn in season, and canned corn in winter from the world outside to the world behind the walls. But this afternoon, having rung the buzzer and disappeared, a person or persons left within its original cardboard box an item of the latest office equipment.

Sister Adelphine had followed Father Jude Miller on his permanent move to Little No Horse. He had succeeded in persuading the bishop to allow him to conduct continued research on the question of his new project, the proposed blessedness and possible sainthood of Father Damien Modeste, recently perished. Now, Sister Adelphine answered the ring of the bells. She entered the room in a state of disturbance, for she had been canning passionately, attempting to set by a load of turnips that had appeared just that morning in many bread bags saved and reused by a thrifty farm family. So many turnips, all at once, indigestible. But if preserved, a welcome addition to many a forthcoming winter stew.

She'd dried her hands, given instructions to the sturdy novice who was helping her, and made her way to the anteroom, but was too late to thank the visitor or ask instructions for the use of the instrument, which she carried, with help from Father Jude when he arrived, into the room used for settling the account books, keeping track of donations, sending letters to the diocese, and paying bills.

The room was neat, and upon a wooden desk salvaged from the renovation of the local high school, there was sufficient room for the contraption. Father Jude lifted it from its carton and set it down gently. The fax machine was a small thing, rather pleasant and neat, made of off-white plastic, bearing lettered buttons and a small blank screen for a digital readout.

Jude, who was never good with such things, waved his hands at it humorously and then, in a slight fit of jovial zaniness, blessed it.

"Father Jude!" said Sister Adelphine.

The other sisters, many much older, some here since the beginning of time, crowded to the door after Jude Miller left and watched as Sister Adelphine, upon whose shoulders it now fell to deal with anything modern or mysterious, set the box aside and unreeled an attached telephone cord. The line reached just far enough, to the room's only telephone jack. Sister Adelphine, with a small mischievous smile at the others, unplugged the instrument. She then inserted the clear plastic hinge to the fax machine. She connected the electrical cord to an outlet, too, and stood back with her arms folded. The machine hummed. A roll of slippery paper was already loaded into the drum. A tiny bit inched forward. The sisters voiced low approval among themselves. With an air of discovery, Sister Adelphine bent to retrieve something from the box, and then flourished a thin paper instruction booklet in their direction. It bore a black-and-white image of the fax machine on its cover, and numbered within the buttons to push, operations that could be performed, places that could be reached instantly, in print, from anywhere on earth.

Sister Adelphine paged through the booklet, moving her lips to aid comprehension. Her sisters glanced over her shoulder from time to time. Suddenly, a loud ring sounded. One sister moved to answer it, to lift the machine's receiver, but Sister Adelphine raised her hand against the action. She had just been instructed within the booklet not to answer the phone, but to wait and allow the mechanism to translate for itself the incoming message. Craning forward to decipher the sudden letters that formed on the tiny screen below the buttons, Sister Adelphine read the words Incoming Message. She raised her brows in satisfaction, breathed out.

From somewhere within, the paper burped and skipped forward. The movement was so abrupt that one or two of the older nuns drew back, startled, but the others crowded forward to see what emerged. The message was typed on an old-fashioned ribbon typewriter and the ink was fuzzy in places, the strokes uneven, light and dark, but always legible. The seal in the left corner seemed both foreign and familiar. The women frowned, squinted, murmured among themselves. Then one of them in recognition gripped another's arm, the next, the next, until they were all holding on to one another, trembling. With each line that groaned forward they sighed in consternation, fear, astonishment, for the letterhead gave it all away. Finally they came to the signature at the end of the implacable linked pages. It was written in a trembling, sweet, rounded hand that slanted cheerfully to the right. Some kind of hoax. As he entered the office, Father Jude's eyes narrowed. The sisters cried out:

"The Holy Father! The Pope!"

My dear Father Damien,

In attempting to respond to a fragment of your letter, dated last year, delivered in tatters by the Italian Postal Service, and captioned Most Estimable Pontiff, I asked an assistant to bring me the body of correspondence to which you referred. To my distress, I am informed that the file of your letters and reports, which I am sure was so thoroughly enjoyed and appreciated over the years by my predecessors, has been inadvertently destroyed in an update and purge of the Vatican's filing system.

All is not lost. Copies were sent back to your diocese, as I'll explain.

*I was sufficiently intrigued by the content of your one
surviving letter that I feel compelled to write this personal
note requesting your assistance in reassembling your life's
work. I am certain it would be of use to your colleagues. If you
would be so kind as to consult your notes and produce copies,
the Vatican Library would welcome your papers.*

*Father Damien, your love for the people in your care is a
joyful statement of your faith. May you abide happily in their
return of your affection, and pass your days now in pleasant
contemplation of all the good you have accomplished.*

The signature was distinct as could be, and the small community
marveled over it. Carefully, the document was slipped into a clear
plastic sleeve. Later on, the letter was framed and set within the
entrance of the little cabin where Father Damien Modeste had once
lived, a place the bishop directed, and Jude recommended, be kept as
it was and even restored. The little historical shrine was cared for
now by Mary Kashpaw, whose attention to detail included a careful
stropping of the razor and shining of the copper shaving mug used by
Father Damien.

Every day, she carefully dusted and arranged the papers on his
desk, including words from a long ago sermon she'd saved, scrawled
lightly and fading, *What is the whole of our existence but the sound
of an appalling love?* She polished the wood, washed and changed his
sheets and towels. Dusted his piano. Burnished the pedals. She spent
as much time as she possibly could at these tasks, where she still felt
the comfort of his presence. When her duties on the grounds and in
the convent were finished, she often took refuge in his house and sat
beside his bed. Her body rocked, though the chair was solid. Her lips
moved but she made no sound. Sometimes she dozed off and followed
Father Damien through the underbrush. Sometimes she dug her way
down with a teaspoon toward her priest, her love, through the layers
of the earth.

END NOTES

Ozhibi'iganan: the reservation depicted in this and in all of my novels is an imagined place consisting of landscapes and features similar to many Ojibwe reservations. It is an emotional collection of places dear to me, as is the town called Argus. It is not the Turtle Mountain Reservation, of course, although that is where I am proud to be enrolled.

I would like to thank my daughters for their patience with my work. Kenneth L. Woodward's book *Making Saints* was of great help to me. The Minnesota Historical Society was a great source of material regarding early church work. Those who question the possibility of lifelong gender disguise might read *Suits Me: The Double Life of Billy Tipton,* by Diane Wood Middlebrook, a copy of which was sent to me by Honor Moore. I would like to thank my editor, Diane Reverand, for her meticulous work with endless drafts of this manuscript, and, as always, Trent Duffy, for copy-editing a daunting series and making sense of the tangle of family relationships. Gail Caldwell, thank you for recognizing when the fire was in the room.

*

I feel that I should also include the following passage, sent to (the deceased) Father Damien by fax from the Vatican, and bearing upon my responsibility as the author of this and my previous books:

> *Father Damien,*
>
> *As for the problem of revealing the confessions tendered to you by your parishioners, the problem is more severe than you know. At present, according to an assistant who has managed your correspondence, your letters were copied and returned to the bishop of your diocese. Can it be, however, that these letters went astray and somehow ended up in the hands of a layperson in your same area? My assistant is shocked to discover that a certain writer local to your region (but published even in languages and places as distant as our own) has included a quantity of first-person confessions in the body of her otherwise phantasmagoric and fictional works.*
>
> *Could this writer have possibly come by those letters? In particular, the private confession Marie Kashpaw is quoted verbatim, as are other monologues included in books published lately as two years ago.*
>
> *If so, we are most distressed, beg your apology, and have cer-tain plans to take up the matter with the writer, Louise Erdrich.*

The source of these early narratives is mysterious to me also. Voices spoke to me in dreams, while I drove long distances, nursed my babies, and so on. Sometimes in sleepwalking I would find I'd written book sections. There they would be the next morning, on my desk. I feel sure they originated in my own mind, those stories, how-ever they appeared. Yet sometimes, as I scrutinize the handwriting in those early drafts, I wonder. Who is the writer? Who is the voice? Sometimes the script is unfamiliar—the careful spidery flourish of a hand trained early in the last century. At other times—I am sure, I am positive—it is my own.

*

I also include in these end notes a possible explanation for the name given to the reservation where so many of the events in my books have taken place.

The Story of Little No Horse
(Told by Nanapush to Father Damien)

White people usually name places for men—presidents and generals and entrepreneurs. Ojibwe name places for what grows there or what is found. There was no person named Little No Horse, no battle on that ground, no memory of just what happened, and yet the name goes back in time. It goes back to strange bones that were found there. People put these bones into their medicine bags during the beginning days, before the people had seen a living horse. There were rumors before a sighting ever occurred. From the south came a Shawnee who claimed that he witnessed a man leading on a vine a great dog whose paws, at the end of each leg, were gathered in one glistening nail.

Bebezhigongazhii, it was called, the one-nailed being.

That doesn't sound possible, the people said, but the Shawnee put down his life on the truth of it. When those strange bones were found, bigger than a dog and heavier than a deer, with long strands of silver hair and those one-nailed ends to the paws, some argued that this was the creature the Shawnee saw. Others deducted from the remains an old, old, four-legged woman with a deer's face and long, tossing ancient hair.

Not long, and that mystery was solved.

From afar, there was reported something else very new. It was seen in shadow, glimpsed by a girl and then her family. A spirit with the torso of a human and a strange wild head beneath, running, running, four legs pounding in a terror of swift music. The family hid themselves and waited quietly as it approached. The noise it made, stopping by the river, was strange as a ghost whistle in the mashkiig, or when people died very suddenly and mysteriously, felled by bad medicine. They stayed very still, and next their eyes nearly fell out of their heads. For the top of the being had detached from the bottom. They felt a little foolish, then, for soon it was obvious that the thing was two creatures, two manidoog, a man and a great dog with the paws gathered into one horned nail. The family finally understood and felt a little cheated by the truth: what they saw was human, just a Bwaaninini, hateful.

How their enemy had come to possess this spirit creature was now the whispered question among them. The natural progression of thought was this: how to kill the Bwaan and take the bebezhigon-gazhii. For all day, as they secretly observed, they could see how it loved him, how it cleared its throat when it saw the Bwaan, and nod-ded wisely in agreement with the Bwaan's thoughts, and flicked its rabbit ears to catch his words. They did not pity the Bwaan. Drying on his hoops were two scalps, most surely Anishinaabeg. Those scalps determined them to kill the Bwaan immediately once they captured him, in order to quiet the spirits of their relatives. They never got around to it. A strange thing happened. Right before their eyes, the Bwaan clutched his groin, howled, and fell. He began to writhe upon the ground in the throes of some disgusting sickness.

"Leave him," said the mother, when they saw by morning light what afflicted him. From knees to stomach he was bolting with black sores. They touched nothing, but grabbed the vine, which turned out to be cunningly woven. They led the spirit animal away and it quickly began to love them, too, the same way it loved the Bwaan. With the horse, though, came the sickness, selective but deadly, and it raged among them for two winters before it finally disappeared.

The horse and the illness it brought were the source of the name, which was translated by a Jesuit mapmaker and laid into a thick vel-lum that went under the rapids during his return to Montreal. Little Lost and No Name Lakes were partially erased and the word Horse was tagged onto them to describe the whole region.

We never had a name for the whole place, said Nanapush, except the word ishkonigan. The leftovers. Our words for the place are many and describe every corner and hole. We are called Little No Horse now because of a dead Bwaan and a drenched map. Think of it, nindi-nawemagonidok, my relatives.

If we call ourselves and all we see around us by the original names, will we not continue to be Anishinaabeg? Instead of reconstituted white men, instead of Indian ghosts? Do the rocks here know us, do the trees, do the waters of the lakes? Not unless they are addressed by the names they themselves told us to call them in our dreams. Every feature of the land around us spoke its name to an ancestor. Perhaps, in the end, that is all that we are. We Anishinaabeg are the keepers of the names of the earth. And unless the earth is called by the names it gave us humans, won't it cease to love us? And isn't it true that if the earth stops loving us, everyone, not just the Anishinaabeg, will cease to exist? That is why we all must speak our language, nindinawemagonidok, and call everything we see by the name of its spirit. Even the chimookomanag, who are trying to destroy us, are depending upon us to remember. Mi'sago'i.

*   *   *

And at last:

Nimiigwetchiweyndan gikinoamadayininiwag gaye ikwewag, Tobassonakwut (Peter Kinew), Nawigiizis (Jim Clark), Pagawetakamigok (Lorraine Jones), and Paybomibiness (Dennis Jones). All mistakes are mine.

Nanapush's · · · · · Mirage · · · · · Kashpaw's
mother   mother

{3 wives===Nanapush (4) === = (2) Margaret (1) ===(1) Kashpaw ==
in the   Kashpaw
spirit world,
and children
also}

John James =.=.= Fleur
Mauser   Pillager

                              Lulu
                              Nanapush

Awun
(The Mist)
Mauser
{m. Mary   {8 sons}   Bonita   {Other
Kashpaw}   Lamartine   children}

LEGEND

==== Traditional Ojibwe marriage

· · · · · Sexual affair or liaison

=·=·= Catholic marriage

| Children born from any of the
| above unions

: Adopted children
:

Marriages and liaisons are numbered
    in order of any issue.